W9-CHX-589

Dell

US $7.50 / $10.99 CAN

ISBN 0-440-23739-4

9 780440 237396

50750

S

MISSION FLATS

In the shadows of every cop's life, there are secrets that kill.

"LANDAY WRITES WITH ELOQUENT INTENSITY."
—*New York Times Book Review*

WILLIAM LANDAY

Praise for
MISSION FLATS

A *Deadly Pleasures*
Best Crime Novel of 2003
Winner of the CWA John Creasey
Memorial Dagger Award for Best First
Crime Novel

"A CRACKLING DEBUT THAT ANSWERS THE QUESTION: WHO WILL BE THE NEW GRISHAM? Stylish writing, wickedly convoluted plotting, and an insider's view of big-city jurisprudence and police accommodation. You'll barely finish this many-tentacled tale before you start clamoring for former ADA Landay's next."
—*Kirkus Reviews* (starred review)

"Tough but true: a first-time novelist has to bring something new to the table—something like the trumps that William Landay throws down. . . . With many twists on the familiar tale, **LANDAY WRITES WITH ELOQUENT INTENSITY, EVEN A SENSE OF DESPAIR, ABOUT THE NO-WIN ETHICAL CHOICES THAT CAN CORRUPT OR OTHERWISE CRUSH A GOOD COP."**
—*New York Times Book Review*

"AN EXCRUCIATING SUSPENSEFUL THRILLER. Landay gives us an original detective creation in humorous, self-deprecating Truman, and he also delivers an action-packed plot with a skillfully detonated final surprise." —*Booklist* (starred review)

"Landay takes chances at every opportunity—and gets away with it." —*Chicago Tribune*

MISSION FLATS

Bill Landay

A Dell Book

MISSION FLATS
A Dell Book

PUBLISHING HISTORY
Delacorte hardcover edition published September 2003
Dell mass market edition / November 2004

Published by
Bantam Dell
A Division of Random House, Inc.
New York, New York

Library of Congress Catalog Card Number: 2002034963

ISBN 0-440-23739-4

Manufactured in the United States of America
Published simultaneously in Canada

OPM 10 9 8 7 6 5 4 3 2 1

For Susan

ACKNOWLEDGMENTS

Grateful acknowledgment is made to the following for permission to quote from copyrighted material:

Bracton: On the Laws and Customs of England, Volume II, translated and with revisions and notes by Samuel E. Thorne. Cambridge, Mass.: Harvard University Press. Copyright © 1968, 1977 by the President and Fellows of Harvard College. Reprinted by permission of the publisher.

"I'm Looking Over a Four Leaf Clover" by Harry Woods and Mort Dixon. Copyright © 1927, renewed. Published by Callicoon Music, Olde Clover Leaf Music, and Warner-Chappell Music. All rights reserved. Used by permission.

"Shattered," words and music by Mick Jagger and Keith Richards. Copyright © 1978 EMI Music Publishing Ltd. All rights for the U.S. and Canada controlled and administered by Colgems-EMI Music Inc. All rights reserved. International copyrights secured. Used by permission.

MISSION
FLATS

Prologue

On screen, a woman lounges on a rubber float, her face toward the sun, fingertips trailing in the water. The float is shaped like a doughnut. It turns in lazy circles. The beach is in frame, on the left. The woman is pregnant; the madras shirt over her bathing suit does not disguise her distended belly. She lifts her head and faces the camera, and her mouth forms the words "Stop it! Turn that thing off! Look at me!" The camera shakes, apparently with laughter. The woman rolls her eyes and shakes her fist, the silent-movie gesture for frustration. Soundlessly she says to the camera, "Hi, Ben," then she joins in the laughter before laying her head down again to drift some more.

The woman is my mother, and the baby in her belly is me. It is early summer, 1971. I will be born a month later.

This little eight-millimeter film (it ran two or three minutes, tops) was among my mother's prized possessions. She kept it in a yellow Kodak box tucked under the brassieres and stockings in the top drawer of her bureau where, she thought, thieves were not likely to look. There were not many thieves in our town, and the few we had were not interested in grainy old movies of pregnant women. But Mum was convinced of its value, and every now and then she could not resist burying her hand in that drawer to feel for the box, just to be sure. When it rained, she would lug out a twenty-pound Bell & Howell movie projector and show the movie on the living-room wall. She'd stand by the wall, point to her belly, and announce, with vestiges of a Boston accent, "There you ah, Ben! There you ah!" Sometimes she got wistful and teary. Over the years, I guess we watched that clip a hundred times. It still runs in my head, familiar, my own Zapruder film. I don't know exactly why my mother loved it so much. I suppose that to her it documented a transition, the moment of equipoise between girlhood and motherhood.

I've never liked the film, though. There is something unsettling about it. It shows the world before me, the world without me, and it is a world complete. There is as yet nothing necessary or inevitable about my creation. Nobody has met me, nobody knows me. I don't exist. A woman—not my mother, but the woman who will become my mother—waves and calls me by name, but what is it she is calling to? She is expecting me, in every sense of the word. But it is a fragile expectation. Events branch and divide and multiply, and she and I may never meet. And what of her? Who is this extinct woman to me? Not my mother certainly, nothing as real as that. She is just an idea, a pictogram on the living-room wall. She is my conception.

It has been thirteen months since my mother died, and I have not bothered to check on that little reel in its yellow reliquary. Maybe someday I'll find it and the movie projector, too, and I'll watch the film again. And there she will be. Young and laughing, alive and whole.

I suppose that is as good a place as any to begin this story—with that pregnant, pretty young woman at the lake on a hot summer day. There is no absolute beginning to any story, after all. There is only the moment you begin watching.

Another moment, five and a half years later. 1:29 A.M., March 11, 1977.

A Boston police cruiser inches along Washington Avenue in a neighborhood called Mission Flats. Grit crunches under the tires: sand, ice. An elevated railway straddles the road. Phosphorous light. The cruiser stops in front of a bar called the Kilmarnock Pub, a shadow-hunching structure with neon signs in the windows.

Inside the cruiser, a policeman—his name is not important—uses the butt of his fist to clear condensation from the driver's side window, then he studies the neon signs. GUINNESS, BASS, a generic one with the promise GOOD TIMES. Last call at the Kilmarnock was twenty-nine minutes ago. Those signs are usually turned off by this time.

Now, consider this policeman. If he does not chance upon the bar or if he does not notice those neon signs, none of what follows would ever take place. At this moment, any number of different courses—an alternate history, a hundred alternate histories—remain open to him. He can simply ignore the signs and continue his prowl along Washington Avenue. After all, is there really anything suspicious here? Is it all that unusual for a bartender to forget to switch off a few lights at closing time? Alternatively, the officer can call in a request for backup. A bar at closing time is a tempting target for stickup men. It is a cash business, all that money still in the register, the doors still unlocked. No guards, just bartenders and drunks. Yes, maybe he should do that, maybe he should wait for backup. This is Mission Flats, remember; around here it pays to be cautious. But then again, a cop working the midnight-to-eight shift could check on fifty businesses before he clocks out. He can't very well call for backup every time. No, in this case there is no reason for our policeman to do any of those things. He will make the right decision and yet—how to explain what follows? Bad luck. Coincidence. Innumerable random branchings and sequences have brought him to this place at this time. It is the end of one story, or several, and the beginning of another story, or several.

Consider this, too. As the officer idles outside the Kilmarnock Pub—fidgeting with his radio, deciding what to do, deciding whether to bother—I am five years old, asleep in bed in western Maine, some three hundred miles away.

Back to our policeman. He decides he'll go in, tell the bartender to close up, maybe even make some noise about writing him up to the ABC, the Alcoholic Beverages Commission. No big deal. He calls in his position to the turret: "Bravo-four-seven-three, take me off at the Kilmarnock on Mission Ave. Bravo-four-seven-three, charlie-robert." No concern in his voice. Routine.

Then the policeman walks into an armed robbery.

Inside the Kilmarnock, a wiry man, an addict named Darryl Sikes, puts a nine-millimeter Beretta to the policeman's head. Sikes is coked up, and he has stoked the high with amphetamines, mellowed it with Jack Daniel's.

The policeman raises his hands in submission.

The gesture sends Sikes reeling with laughter. *Hahahahahahaha.* His mind is literally buzzing; there is a purr in his ears that, to Sikes, sounds like the electric hum of a guitar amplifier. *Turn it up! Turn that motherfucker up! Hahahahaha!*

Sikes's partner is a man named Frank Fasulo. Fasulo is not as high as Sikes. Not nearly. Frank Fasulo is in control. He carries a sawed-off pump-action shotgun. He points the shotgun at the cop and orders him to strip. Fasulo cuffs the officer's hands behind his back and orders him to his knees.

Naked, the cop shivers.

The two celebrate, Frank Fasulo and Darryl Sikes.

Sikes plucks the police uniform shirt from the floor and puts it on over his sweatshirt. *Hahahahaha!* They do a little victory dance around the bar. They kick at the policeman's clothes, sending them flying—tube socks, urine-dappled briefs, black shoes. Fasulo fires the shotgun into the ceiling, racks and fires, racks and fires.

The policeman is forced to perform fellatio on Fasulo. At the moment of orgasm, Fasulo fires the gun into the policeman's head.

Now it is nine days after the Kilmarnock murder, four A.M., a bitterly cold winter night. The wind is whipping across the lower deck of the Tobin Bridge, where the temperature is five degrees with the windchill.

Frank Fasulo steps off the side of the bridge and turns slow cartwheels in the air, arms and legs extended. It will take three long seconds before he reaches the surface of the Mystic River about one hundred fifty feet below. He will hit the water at around seventy miles an hour. At that speed, there isn't much difference between hitting water and hitting concrete.

What passes through Fasulo's mind as he tumbles through the air? Does he glimpse the black wall of water rushing up at him? Does he think about his partner, Darryl Sikes, or the murdered cop? Does he think his suicide will end the story of the Kilmarnock case?

Frank Fasulo doesn't know it, but in the last nine days he has learned the original meaning of the word *outlaw*. Today the word has come to refer to any criminal. In the ancient English law, it had a more specific definition. If a court declared you an outlaw, you were literally outside the law—that is, the law no longer protected you. An outlaw could be robbed or even killed without penalty. There was no sanctuary for him in all England. So it is for Frank Fasulo. The Boston Police Department has no interest in arresting and trying him. They want him dead. No sanctuary.

They caught up to Darryl Sikes just two days after the murder. Found him holed up in the old Madison Hotel, near the Boston Garden. Four BPD cops burst into the room and fired forty-one rounds into his body. To a man, the entire entry team swore Sikes was reaching for a gun; none was ever found.

Now it's Fasulo's turn. The police want him even worse than Sikes. It was Fasulo who had . . . well, most of them can't even say it.

And where can Fasulo run? Every law-enforcement agency in the world will return him to the Boston police on a murder warrant.

So it has to end this way. That is all Frank Fasulo knows for sure. As he plummets, in those three seconds as he feels his body accelerate and the wind tugs his jacket off his shoulders like a helpful host, it is his only thought: There was no other ending—some cop was going to find him sooner or later.

Ten years later. August 17, 1987, 2:25 A.M.

Again we are in Mission Flats, in the sort of three-family wood-frame structure Bostonians call a triple decker. On the third-floor landing, eight policemen crouch. They stare at a door, listening intently as if the door might speak.

The door is lacquered in China red. There are two small holes in the door frame, just above eye level, where a mezuzah was once attached with little gold brads. Fifty years ago, this neighborhood was predominantly Jewish. The mezuzah is long gone now. Today the apartment is a stashpad for a crew called the Mission Posse.

No doubt the door has been reinforced somehow. Most likely, it is wedged shut with a makeshift police lock, a board jammed at a forty-five-degree angle between the door and the floor, anchored in place by wood blocks bolted to the floorboards. To get into the apartment, the police will have to reduce the door to splinters. That could take fifteen seconds or it could take several minutes—an eternity, long enough to flush cocaine, burn cuff lists, toss scales and baggies through holes in the walls. Too long. Now, a sheet-metal door you could judge, you could predict how it would hold up. The thin ones bend, become distorted, and quickly twist out of their frames. The thick ones just dent, and your only choice is to try to rupture the hinges, the lock, or the entire door frame. But these old wood doors? Hard to say. This one looks solid.

Julio Vega certainly doesn't like the look of it. Vega glances at his partner, an Area A-3 Narcotics detective named Artie Trudell, and shakes his head. Vega's message: *They don't make doors like this anymore.*

Trudell, an enormous man with an orange-red beard, smiles back at Vega and flexes his biceps.

Vega and Trudell are excited, nervous. This is a first, a raid that is all theirs. The target is a major player: The Mission Posse moves more rock in this neighborhood than anyone else by far. The no-knock warrant is all theirs too, based on their own investigation—two weeks of surveillance, and a stream of information from a CI endorsed by Martin Gittens himself. The warrant is bulletproof.

Detective Julio Vega could be bulletproof, too, with a few more scores like this one. Vega has a plan. He'll take the sergeant's exam in the fall, work drug cases a couple more years, then try for an assignment in Special Investigations or even Homicide. Of course, Vega keeps his careerism to himself because his partner, the big redhead Artie Trudell, doesn't get it.

Trudell does not dream of going to Homicide or anyplace else. He is happy just to work narcotics cases. Some guys are like that. They prefer cases that are victimless, with suspects as professional as their police adversaries. It's neater that way. Vega has tried to instill a little ambition in Trudell. Told him he won't climb the ladder without working victim crimes. He even hinted once that Trudell should take the sergeant's exam, but Artie just laughed it off. "What?" Artie said. "And give up all this?" At the time, they were sitting in a battered Crown Vic looking at the moonscape of Mission Avenue in the Flats—block after block of ashy, broken tenements. How do you deal with a guy like that?

The hell with him, Vega figures. Let Artie chase crackheads around the Flats forever. Let him rot here. But not Julio Vega. Vega is a player. He's moving up. Up and out. If, if . . . See, Detective Vega can dream about Homicide or SIU all day, but first he needs to make a little noise. He needs a few skins to show the Commissioner's office. He needs this score.

Vega and Trudell stand beside the apartment door like sentinels.

The other men avoid the area directly in front of the door as best they can, but the landing is small, and they wind up arrayed along the stairs leading up to the next floor. There are four uniforms among them. The rest—the Narcotics guys—wear jeans, sneakers, and Kevlar vests. Casual. None of the commando-style gear other units use. This is the Flats; these guys have gone through doors before.

For several seconds the men listen for noise in the apartment and, hearing none, they turn to Vega for the signal.

Vega kneels against the wall, then nods toward Trudell.

The burly detective steps in front of the door. The temperature in the hallway is pushing ninety degrees. Trudell is sweating in his vest. His T-shirt is stained. His beard is damp; curly orange tendrils glisten under his chin. The big policeman smiles, maybe out of nervousness. He hoists a five-foot steel pipe into the crook of his right elbow. Later, the newspapers will describe the pipe as a *battering ram,* but in truth it is just a segment of water pipe filled with concrete and fitted with two L-shaped handles.

Vega holds up five fingers, then four, three, two—on one he points at Trudell.

Trudell smashes the door with the pipe. The stairwell echoes with a sound like a bass drum.

The door does not budge.

Trudell steps back, drives the pipe into the door again.

The door shakes but it holds.

The other cops watch, increasingly uneasy. "Come on, big man," Vega encourages.

A third strike. The bass-drum sound.

A fourth—this time with a different sound, a *boom-crack*.

One of the upper door panels bursts out from the inside—

blasted out—a shot fired from inside the apartment—

a spray of blood sneezes out of Trudell's forehead—

red mist—

a scrap of scalp—

and Trudell is on his back, the crown of his head butterflied open.

The pipe falls to the floor with a thump.

Cops jump back, throw themselves flat against the stairs, against one another. "Artie!" one yells. Another: "GunGunGunGunGun!"

Vega stares at Trudell's body. Blood is everywhere. Red droplets spattered on the wall, a pool of it spreading thick under Trudell's head. The pipe lies right in front of the door. Vega wants to pick it up but his legs won't move.

PART ONE

"The quality of a nation's civilization can be largely measured by the methods it uses in the enforcement of its criminal law."

Miranda v. Arizona, 1966

1

Maurice Oulette tried to kill himself once but succeeded only in blowing off the right side of his jawbone. A doctor down in Boston was able to construct a prosthetic jaw, with imperfect results. The surgery left Maurice's face with a melted appearance, and he went to great lengths to hide it. When he was younger (the accident happened when Maurice was nineteen), he wore a bandanna around his face like a bank robber in an old western. This gave Maurice, who was otherwise a mousy and unromantic sort of guy, a dashing appearance he seemed to enjoy for a while. Eventually he got tired of the bank-robber mask, though. He was always lifting it up to catch a breath of fresh air or to take a drink. So he simply discarded the thing one day, and since then Maurice has been about as unself-conscious as a jawless man can be.

Most people in town accept Maurice's deformity as if it were no more unusual to be jawless than to be nearsighted or left-handed. They are even a little protective of him, taking care to look him in the eye, call him by name. If the summer people stare, as even the adults invariably do, you can bet they'll catch an icy stare right back, from Red Caffrey or Ginny Thurler or anyone else who happens to be around, a look that says, *Eyes front, mister.* Versailles is a nice town that way. I used to think of this place as an enormous Venus's-flytrap with glue-sticky streets and snapping wings that snared young people like me and held us here until it was too late to ever live anywhere else. But these people have stuck by Maurice Oulette and they've stuck by me too.

They appointed me chief of police when I was twenty-four. For a few months I, Benjamin Wilmot Truman, was the youngest police chief in the United States, or so it was assumed around here. My reign was brief; later that same year, there was a story in *USA Today* about a twenty-two-year-old who was elected sheriff in Oregon somewhere. Not that I ever enjoyed the distinction anyway. Truth be told, I never wanted to be a cop at all, let alone police chief in Versailles.

In any event, Maurice lived in his late father's white clapboard house, subsisting on SSI checks and occasional free meals from the town's two competing diners. He'd won a settlement from the Maine Department of Social Services for negligent monitoring of his case while he shot the jawbone off his head, so he was comfortable enough. But, for reasons no one understood, the last few years Maurice had ventured out of the house less and less. The consensus in town was that he was becoming a little reclusive and maybe even a little crazy. But he had never hurt anyone (except himself), so the general view was that whatever Maurice Oulette did out here was nobody's business but his own.

I tended to agree with that position too, though I drew one exception. Every few months, with no warning, Maurice decided to use the streetlights on Route 2 for target practice, to the great distress of motorists traveling between Millers Falls, Mattaquisett township, and Versailles. (The name is pronounced Ver-*sales,* not Ver-*sigh.*) Maurice was usually lit on Wild Turkey on these occasions, which may account for his poor decision-making and poorer aim. On this night—it was October 10,

1997—the call came in around ten, Peggy Butler complaining that "Mr. Oulette is shooting at cars again." I assured her Maurice wasn't shooting at cars, he was shooting at streetlights, and the odds of him hitting a car were actually very slim. "Ha ha, Mr. Comedian," Peggy said.

Off I went. I began to hear the shots when I got within a mile or two of the house. These were sharp rifle cracks at irregular intervals, once every fifteen seconds or so. Unfortunately it was necessary for me to go up Route 2 to reach the house, which meant passing through Maurice's crosshairs. I lit up the wigwags, the light bar, the alley lights, every bulb that truck had—it must have looked like a Mardi Gras float—with the hope that Maurice would hold his fire a minute. I wanted him to know it was only the police.

I parked the Bronco with two wheels on the lawn, lights flashing. At the rear corner of the house, I shouted, "Maurice, it's Ben Truman." No response. "Hey, Rambo, would you stop shooting for a second?" Again there was no response, but then, there was no shooting either, which I took to be a positive sign. "Alright, I'm coming out," I announced. "Now, Maurice, don't shoot."

The backyard was a small rectangle of scrub grass, sand, and pine needles. It was scattered with detritus of various kinds: a skeletal clothes-drying rack, a street-hockey goal, a milk crate. In the far corner an old Chevy Nova lay flat on its belly, the wheels having been transplanted to some other shitbox Chevy Nova years before. The car still had its Maine license plate, with the picture of a lobster and the motto VACATIONLAND.

Maurice stood at the edge of the yard with a rifle in the crook of his arm. The pose suggested a gentleman hunter on a break from shooting quail. He wore boots, oil-stained work pants, a red flannel jacket, and a baseball cap pulled low over the brow. His head was down, which was not unusual. You got used to addressing the button on his cap.

I shined my flashlight over him. "Evening, Maurice."

"Evenin', Chief," the cap said.

"What's going on out here?"

"Just shootin' is all."

"I see that. You about scared Peggy Butler half to death. You want to tell me what the hell you're shooting at?"

"Them lights there." Maurice nodded toward Route 2 without looking up.

The two of us stood there for a moment nodding at each other.

"You hit any?"

"Nos'r."

"Something wrong with the gun?"

He shrugged.

"Well let's have a look at it, Maurice."

He handed me the rifle, an old Remington I'd confiscated at least a dozen times. I checked that there was a round in the chamber, then pinged one off a metal fence-pole at the edge of the field. "Gun's okay," I informed him. "Must be you that's off."

Maurice gave a little murmuring laugh.

I patted down the outside of his coat, felt the box of shells in his pocket. Reaching inside, my fingers got snarled in the Kleenex balls Maurice collected there like chestnuts. "Jesus, Maurice, do you ever clean out these pockets?" I pulled out the box of ammunition and stuck it in my own pocket. A box of Marlboro reds I opened and slipped back in Maurice's coat. "Okay if I take a look around and see how you're doing out here?"

He looked up at last. The skin grafts along his concave jawline shone silvery in the flashlight. " 'M I under arrest?"

"No, sir."

"Okay then."

I went in the back door, leaving Maurice where I'd found him. He kept his arms by his sides like a scolded child.

The kitchen stank of boiled vegetables and body

odor. A fifth of Jim Beam stood on the table, half empty. The refrigerator was empty save for an ancient box of baking soda. In the cabinets were a few cans (Spaghetti-O's, Green Giant corn), a few packets of powdered soup, and a tiny hole through which carpenter ants were entering and exiting.

"Maurice," I called to him, "has your caseworker been out to see you?"

"Don't 'member."

With the barrel of Maurice's rifle, I nudged open the bathroom door and shined the flashlight about. The tub and toilet were stained yellow. Two cigarette butts floated in the toilet. Beneath the sink, a section of the wall had rotted, and a piece of particle board had been nailed there to patch the hole. At the edges of the board, the ground outside was visible.

I switched off the lights and closed up the house.

"Maurice, you remember what protective custody is?"

"Yes'r."

"What is it?"

"It's when you put me in the jail but I'm not under arrest."

"That's right. And do you remember why I have to do that, put you in protective custody?"

"To protect me, I guess. That's why they call it that."

"Well, yeah. Exactly. So that's what we're going to do, Maurice, we're going to put you in protective custody before you kill someone while you're taking potshots at streetlights."

"I didn't hit none."

"Well, Maurice, that doesn't exactly make me feel better about it. See, if you hit what you were aiming at . . ."

He gave me a blank expression.

"Look, the point is, you can't shoot at them. They're town property. Besides, what if you hit a car?"

"I never shot no cars."

These conversations with Maurice only go so far, and this one had about run its course. It wasn't completely clear whether Maurice was just slow or a little crazy. Either way, he'd earned some leeway. He'd survived a maelstrom of emotions no outsider could fathom, and he had the scars to prove it.

He looked up at me. In the moonlight, with his right side in darkness, his face was restored nearly to normal. It was the sort of lean, dark-eyed face common around here. The face of a voyageur or a timberman in an old sepia photo.

"You hungry, Maurice?"

"Little."

"Did you eat?"

"Et yesterd'y."

"Want to go to the Owl?"

"Thought you were PC'ing me."

"I am."

"Do I get my gun back?"

"Nope. I'm going to have it forfeited before you shoot somebody. Like me."

"Chief Truman, I ain't gonna shoot you."

"Well, I appreciate that. But I'm going to keep it just the same because—and this is no disrespect, Maurice—you're not the greatest shot that ever was."

"The judge'll make you give it back. I got my F.I.D."

"What, are you a lawyer now?"

Maurice made his little laugh, like a moan. "Ayuh, guess so."

There were a few people at the Owl, all sitting at the bar, all drinking Bud long-necks, staring up at a hockey game on the TV. Phil Lamphier, who owned the place and in the off-season was the only bartender, was leaning on his elbows at the end of the bar, reading a newspaper. The little countertop was L-shaped, and Maurice and I slid onto stools on the short side, facing the others.

A murmur of "Hey, Ben" came from the group, though Diane Harned waited a moment before greeting me as "Chief Truman." She shot me a little smirk, then returned her attention to the TV. Diane had been good-looking once, but the color had drained out of her. Her blond hair had faded from yellow to straw. Raccoon shadows had formed under her eyes. Still, she carried herself with a pretty girl's arrogance, and there's something to be said for that. Anyway, we'd had a few dates, Diane and I, and a few reunions after that. We had an understanding.

Maurice ordered a Jim Beam, which I immediately canceled. "We'll have two Cokes," I told Phil, who made a face.

Jimmy Lownes asked, "You got Al Capone here under arrest?"

"Nope. Heat's out at Maurice's house so he's going to stay over at the station tonight till we get it turned on again. We just figured we'd get something to eat first."

Diane gave me a skeptical look but said nothing.

"My taxes paying for that dinner?" Jimmy teased.

"No, I'm treating."

Bob Burke said, "Well, that's taxes, Ben. Taxes is what pays your salary, technically."

"Yours too," Diane shot back. "Technically."

Burke, who worked for the town doing maintenance in the public buildings, was sheepish. Still, I did not need Diane to defend me.

"It doesn't take a lot of taxes to pay my salary," I said. "Besides, as soon as they find a new chief, I'll be off the dole. Get my ass out of this jerkwater place finally."

Diane snorted. "And go where?"

"I've been thinking maybe I'll go do some traveling."

"Well, listen to you. Just where do you think you're gonna go?"

"Prague."

"Prague." She said the word as if she were trying it out for the first time. "I don't even know what that is."

"It's in Czechoslovakia."

Diane sniffed again, disdainful.

Bobby Burke cut in, "It's the Czech Republic now. That's what they called it on the Olympics, the Czech Republic." Burke was a master of this kind of trivia. The man eked out a living mopping floors at the grade school, but he could tell you the names of every first lady, all the presidential assassins, and the eight states that border Missouri. A man like that can throw off the rhythm of a conversation.

"Ben," Diane persisted, "why in hell would you want to go to Prague?" There was an edge in her voice. Jimmy Lownes gave her a little nudge and said, "Uh-oh," like Diane was jealous. But it wasn't that.

"Why would I want to go to Prague? Because it's beautiful."

"And what are you going to do once you get there?"

"Just look around, I guess. See the sights."

"You're just going to . . . *look around*?"

"That was my plan, yes."

It wasn't much of a plan, I admit. But it seemed to me I'd been planning too long already, waiting for The Opportunity. I have always been one of those long-thinking, slow-acting men, the type that smothers every idea with doubt and worry. It was time to shake free of all that. I figured I could at least get as far as Prague before my second-guessing caught up to me. I sure as hell wasn't going to rot in Versailles, Maine.

Jimmy asked, "You taking Maurice here with you?"

"You bet. Whattaya say, Maurice? Want to come to Prague?"

Maurice looked up and grinned his shy, closemouthed smile.

"Maybe I'll go too," Jimmy announced.

Diane snorted again. "Right."

"Jeezum Crow," Jimmy said, "why not?"

"Why not? Look at yourselves!"

We looked but none of us saw anything.

"It's just, you guys aren't exactly Prague people."

"What the hell does that mean, 'Prague people'?"

Jimmy Lownes could not have found Prague on a map if you gave him a week to look. But his indignation was genuine enough. "We're people, aren't we? All's we have to do is go to Prague and we'll be Prague people."

"Jimmy, really, what the hell are *you* going to do in Prague?" Diane persisted.

"Same as Ben: have a look around. I might even like it. Who knows, maybe I'll stay over there. Show you what Prague people I am."

"They have good beer," Bob Burke chimed in. "Pilsner beer."

"See, I like it already." Jimmy raised his Bud bottle in salute, though it was not clear whether he was saluting Prague or Bobby Burke or just beer.

"Diane, you could come along," I offered. "You might like it there too."

"I've got a better idea, Ben. Why don't I just go home and set my money on fire."

"Alright," I said, "well I guess that's it, then. Me, Maurice, and Jimmy. Prague or bust."

Maurice and I clinked glasses, sealing the plan.

But Diane just could not let it go. Talk of getting out always hit a nerve with her. "Oh, Ben," she said, "you're so totally full of shit. Always have been. You're not going anywhere and you know it. One day it's California, the next day it's New York, now it's Prague. Where's it gonna be next? Timbuktu? Tell you what, I'll make you a bet: In ten years you'll still be sitting on that same stool spouting your same bullshit about Prague or who knows where."

"Let him alone, Diane," Phil Lamphier said. "If Ben wants to go to Prague or wherever, no reason he can't."

There must have been something in my expression, too, that told Diane she'd crossed the line because she looked away, preferring to fuss with a pack of cigarettes rather than look at my face. "Oh, come on, Ben," she said, "I'm just having fun." She lit her cigarette, trying to look like Barbara Stanwyck. The effect was more Mae West. "We still friends?"

"No," I said.

"Maybe I should come over to the station tonight. Heat's out at my house too."

This prompted a chorus of howls from Lownes and Burke. Even Maurice hooted along from beneath the bill of his cap.

"Diane, assaulting a police officer is a crime."

"Good. Arrest me." She held out her wrists to be handcuffed, and again the men whooped it up.

Maurice and I stuck around at the Owl for an hour or so. Phil heated up a couple of frozen potpies for us, and Maurice devoured his so fast I thought he might swallow the fork along with it. I offered him half of mine but he would not take it, so we brought the leftover pie back to the station and Maurice ate it there. He stayed in the lockup that night. There's a mattress in there, and it couldn't have been too much worse than his drafty house. I left the cell door open so he could go to the toilet in the hall, but I dragged a chair to the doorway and slept with my feet across it so Maurice could not walk out without waking me. The danger was not that Maurice would hurt anyone, of course; the danger was that he would hurt himself while he was drunk and nominally in protective custody. Shit happens.

I sat awake in that chair until well after three, listening to Maurice. The man made more noise asleep than most people do awake, murmuring, snoring, farting. But it wasn't Maurice that kept me up so much as all the other things. I had to get out of Versailles, I had to shake off that big Venus's-flytrap already clamped around my ankle. I had to get out, especially now.

2

At the Rufus King Elementary School the next morning, I watched the kids cross Route 2. I greeted them all by name, a point of pride with me. One by one they squeaked, "Hi, Chief Truman." One boy asked, "What happened to your hair?" He dragged out the word, *hey-yer*. What happened to my hair, of course, was that I'd slept at the station with my head against the wall. I gave the kid a look and threatened to arrest him, at which he snorted and giggled.

On to the Acadia County District Court to check on arrests in the neighboring towns. The courthouse is in Millers Falls, a twenty-minute drive. I had no arrests of my own to report but I went anyway. There was the usual chatter among the clerks and the police prosecutors. A rumor had gotten around about some kid at the regional high school who was selling marijuana out of his locker. The chief in Mattaquisett, Gary Finbow, had even prepared a search warrant for the locker. Gary wanted to know, Would I read over the warrant application, make sure it looked alright? I skimmed it, circled a few misspellings, told him he ought to just talk with the kid's parents and forget about it. "Why would you screw up a kid's college application over a couple of joints?" He gave me a look, and I let it drop. There's no sense explaining with guys like Gary. It would be like trying to explain *Hamlet* to a Great Dane.

So, back to the station. The sense of ennui and fatigue—of unraveling—was a palpable thing by now. Dick Ginoux, my senior officer, was at the front desk reading a day-old copy of *USA Today*. He held the paper at arm's length and peered at it over his eyeglasses. His eyes flickered away from the paper for only a moment when I came in. "Morning, Chief."

"What's going on, Dick?"

"Hmm? Demi Moore shaved her head. Must be for a picture."

"No, I mean here."

"Ah." Dick lowered the paper and looked around the empty office. "Nothing."

Dick Ginoux was fifty-something, with a long, horsey face. His sole contribution to local law enforcement was to occupy the dispatcher's desk with his newspaper. This made him about as useful as a potted plant.

He took off his glasses and stared at me in a creepy, paternal way. "Are you alright, Ben?"

"A little tired, that's all."

"You sure?"

"Yeah." I scanned the office. Same three desks. Same file cabinet. Same dirty six-over-six windows. Suddenly but quite desperately I dreaded the prospect of spending the rest of the morning here. "You know what, Dick, I'm going out for a while."

"Out where?"

"I'm not sure."

Dick pouted his lower lip in a concerned expression but he said nothing.

"Hey, Dick, can I ask you something? You ever thought about maybe being chief someday?"

"Now why would I do that?"

"Because you'd be a good chief."

"Well we've already got a chief, Ben. You're the chief."

"Right, but if I wasn't around."

"I don't follow you. Why wouldn't you be around? Where you going off to?"

"Nowhere. I'm just saying. If."

"If what?"

"If—Never mind."

"Alrighty, Chief." Dick slipped his glasses back on and returned to the paper. "*Awwwl*righty."

I'd made up my mind to check the cabins by the lake, a job I'd been putting off for weeks, but I decided to stop at home first and clean up. I knew my father would be there. Maybe that was the true point of the visit, to let my father know what I was up to. Looking back, it's hard to remember what I was thinking. Dad and I had been uneasy roommates lately. My mother had died eight weeks before, and in the chaos that followed her death we'd spoken very little. Mum had always been the link between us, the interpreter, explainer and clarifier. The broker of grudges. Now we needed her more than ever.

I found him in the kitchen, at the stove. Claude Truman had always been a husky, shouldery guy, and even at his age—he was sixty-seven—there was a sense of physicality about him. He stood with his feet spread, as if the stove might rush at him and he would be called upon to muscle the thing back into its place against the wall. He turned to see me come into the room but he did not say anything.

"What are you making?"

No response.

I looked over his shoulder. "Eggs. Those are called eggs."

Dad was a mess. He wore a filthy flannel work shirt, untucked. He hadn't shaved for days.

He said, "What happened to you last night?"

"Stayed at the station. I had to PC Maurice or he would have froze in that house of his."

"Station's not a hotel," he grumbled. He pawed through the clutter in the sink for a relatively clean plate and slid his eggs onto it. "You should've called."

Dad cleared a space for himself at the table, moving, among other things, a forty-ounce bottle of Miller.

I picked up the empty bottle. "What the hell is this?"

He shot me a baleful look.

"Maybe I should've PC'ed you," I said.

"Try it sometime."

"Where'd you get it?"

"What's the difference? Free country. No law against me having a beer."

I shook my head at him, just as my mother used to, and tossed the bottle in the trash. "No. No law against it."

He gave me a dark look to seal his little victory, then turned his attention to the eggs, splitting and smearing the yolks.

"Dad, I'm going out to the lake to check the cabins."

"So go."

" 'So go'? That's it? You don't want to talk about anything before I leave?"

"Like what?"

"Like that bottle, maybe. Maybe today's not a good day."

"Just go do what you have to do, Ben. I can take care of myself."

He sat fiddling with the eggs, his complexion nearly as gray as his hair. He was, finally, just another old man trying to figure out what to do with himself, how to fill the rest of his days. The thought occurred to me, as it does to all sons contemplating their fathers: Was he me? Was this the man I was becoming? I had always considered myself a descendant of my mother's line, not my father's; a Wilmot, not a Truman. But I was his son too. I had his big hands if not his bullying temperament. What exactly did I owe this old man?

I went upstairs to wash up. The house—the same one I grew up in—was small, with just two little bedrooms and a bathroom on the second floor. The air was a little funky; Dad had not been washing his clothes regularly. I splashed icy water on my face and slipped on a fresh uniform shirt. The fabric puckered around the VER-SAILLES POLICE shoulder patch, which was impossible to flatten under an iron even after paralyzing the thing with spray starch. I stood in my parents' bedroom, where there was a mirror, smoothing this imperfection.

Tucked in the lower right-hand corner of the mirror frame was an old photo of my father wearing this same uniform and a grim expression. This was the real Claude Truman. The Chief. Fists balled on his hips, barrel torso, flattop haircut, smile like a grimace. "A man and a half," that was how he used to describe himself. The snapshot must have been taken in the early eighties, around the time my mother banned alcohol from the house once and for all. I was nine the night it happened, and at the time I thought it was my fault, at least in part. I was the one who cost Dad his drinking privileges.

That night, he came home in one of his glowering moods and fell into his chair by the TV. For my father, drunkenness was a bad attitude. He got very quiet, radiating menace like the hum emitted by electric power lines. I knew enough to keep my distance. But I could not resist the gun he dropped on the table with his wallet and keys. A big .38 usually glimpsed on top of his dresser or hidden under his coat. Here it was, in plain view. I inched toward it, mesmerized—my intention was just to touch it, to satisfy a craving for its oily steel surface, its textured grip—and I reached out one finger. My ear exploded. Excruciating pain burst inward from my eardrum: He'd smacked the earhole with the flat of his palm because he knew it would cause the most agony yet leave no visible mark. I heard myself screaming in the distance. Over the roar in my ear, there was his voice: "Quit the boohooing!" and "You want to kill yourself?" and "Let that be a lesson to you!"—for there was always an exalted purpose to Dad's violence.

Mum was livid. She poured out every bottle, warned him never to bring alcohol into "her house" again, and never to come home with it on his breath. There was shouting, but he did not resist her. Instead, he vented his rage on the kitchen walls, punching holes right through the plaster and Sheetrock to the rough planks behind. Lying in bed upstairs, I could feel the tremors.

But Dad must have sensed it was time to quit too. His drinking and temper were no secret around here. To some extent, I'm sure, the exaggerated respect people paid him—the displays of esteem and friendship for the law-and-order police chief—were the false tributes paid to bullies.

For the next eighteen years—until my mother died— he stayed sober. His reputation for violence persisted, but gradually Versellians came to view his rages as Dad himself did: Most of the people he pounded on or bellowed at or otherwise abused probably had it coming to them.

I tucked the old snapshot of Dad back in the mirror frame. It was all ancient history now.

On my way out, I brought down a clean shirt for him and hung it in the kitchen. I left him there pushing scraps of egg around his plate.

Lake Mattaquisett is roughly the shape of an hourglass. It stretches about a mile from end to end along a north–south axis. The southern side is the smaller of the two, though it is what most people are referring to when they mention the lake by name. At the southern tip is the former "fishing lodge" of the Whitney family of New York. It is a camp lodge in the rustic style preferred by nature-minded Manhattanites of a certain class before the Depression. Now owned by a family trust, the big house dominates this end of the lake. There is a sloping trail that leads from the house through the verdant gloom of the pine woods and emerges, a quarter mile later, into the bright reflecting light at the water's edge. The place is generally occupied only in August, when the plague of mosquitoes has eased somewhat. Other, more modest homes dot the banks of the lake, but they do not compare to the Whitney lodge and so, as if conscious of their inferiority, they hide from the road and can only really be seen from the water. The northern side of the lake is far less developed and less fashionable. Here there are only box-frame cabins built on short concrete piles. They rent by the week from Memorial Day to Labor Day, to working folks from Portland or Boston. To people *from away. Sports,* we call them, *flatlanders*—tourists, the lifeblood of this place.

I made an effort to pay equal attention to the dwellings at both ends of the lake, not so much out of sympathy for the working stiffs, but because the little cabins were more likely to be broken into than the grander homes. The cabins attracted local kids looking for a place to party. A kid could get in with no more effort than it took to pop the hasp that held a padlock. A tire iron usually did the trick. So I checked them every few weeks, called the owner when there was a break-in, saw to it that broken hinges and window frames were repaired. I even picked up the beer bottles and marijuana roaches and condoms from cabin floors.

The cabin where I found the body was the fourth I checked that morning.

I might have driven right past it without getting out of the Bronco since it was plain from a distance that there was no damage to the exterior. The windows were covered with padlocked wooden shutters, the door was undamaged. But there was a smell, faint at first but overpowering as I got nearer—an acrid, ammoniac stench, the distinctive smell of decay. I'd smelled it before, usually on deer hit by cars on Route 2 or the Post Road. This might have been a large animal too, a deer or even a moose lying dead in the woods nearby. But this smell was unmistakably coming from the cabin, and I'd never known a moose to die in bed.

I got a pry bar from the truck and popped open the door.

Flies buzzed.

The smell was overwhelming. The muscles in the wall of my throat clenched at the odor. I didn't have a hand-kerchief to cover my nose as detectives do in movies, so I settled for burying my face in the crook of my elbow. Wheezing, I shined my flashlight about in the darkness.

A pile of clothing on the floor resolved itself into a body. A man curled on his side. He wore only khaki shorts and a T-shirt. The bare legs were eggshell white with rose-marble highlights where the skin met the floor. Above the swollen legs, the T-shirt was rucked up to re-veal a bloated white belly. A frizz of red hair ran up to the navel. The left eye looked toward me; the right was obliterated, in its place a cake of dried blood. Above that, tissue blossomed out of a trench in his scalp. The wood floor was stained with dried blood in a wide cres-cent radiating out from the shattered head. The stain ap-peared black in the flashlight beam. Near the head lay the left half of a pair of eyeglasses.

The room began to turn. I breathed hard in the folds of my coat sleeve. The cabin was empty. Dresser drawers were ajar, the mattresses rolled up and tied with twine.

I stepped forward. Near the body, a wallet. A crum-pled wad of bills, maybe fifty dollars total, lay on the floor. I knelt and, using a ballpoint pen, teased open the wallet. It contained a five-point gold star impressed with the words ROBERT M. DANZIGER•ASSISTANT DISTRICT ATTORNEY•SUSSEX COUNTY.

3

The usual cant is that we are blasé about violence, that movies and TV inure us to it. Real violence and injury are not supposed to shock us because we have seen the hyperreality of movie violence. The truth is precisely the opposite. Filmic violence—all those bursting blood bags and death poses, all those actors holding their breath, all that artful realism—only increases the shock value of an actual corpse. The primal weirdness of a dead body, it turns out, is in its very reality—in its lumpish, implausible *nearness.*

I was horrified by the body of Robert Danziger. It assaulted the senses. That glistening cleft in the scalp, the distended and discolored torso. The skin rubbery and taut over the swollen calves. The overpowering stink that hung like smoke in the sinuses. I made it to the woods a good ways off from the cabin before vomiting. Even that did not still the vertigo. I lay down on the pine needles and closed my eyes.

That afternoon was filled with state troopers, assistant AGs from Portland and even Augusta. The prosecutor in charge of the state's investigation was a larval politician named Gregg Cravish (it rhymed with *crayfish*). He had the waxy, artificial look of a TV Game-Show Host. Even the crow's-feet sprouting on his temples looked like they had been placed there intentionally to add a little gravitas to his too-handsome face. Cravish explained that the staties would handle the investigation. Under Maine law, the AG's office has jurisdiction over all murders. "Standard procedure," the Game-Show Host assured me with a little squeeze on my shoulder. "We'll sure be needing your help, though."

So I stood aside and watched.

A team of state-police techs pored over the cabin and grounds like archaeologists on a dig. The Game-Show Host peered in the cabin door now and then but spent most of his time leaning against a car, looking bored.

After some time, I was asked to block the roads leading to the cabin. Beyond that, it was clear, my job was just to stay the hell out of the way. I put an officer about a mile up the access road to the north, and I covered the road from the opposite direction myself. Occasionally cars would pass—troopers, more Game-Show Hosts, the ME to collect the body. They waved as they drove by. I waved back, then returned to scrubbing little spatters of vomit off my shoes with spit and Kleenex. The nausea receded, replaced by a headache. And I realized that I could not simply wait. I had to *act*. For there were two choices at this point: either allow the investigation to proceed without me, as it had already begun to do, or inject myself into it somehow. The first—taking a pass on the whole thing—was not really an option. I was already involved, however unwillingly. I could not walk away from this case, a homicide in my own town.

It was past noon by the time I returned to the cabin, determined to take my rightful place in the investigation. Cravish and his team were already packing their gear into trunks and loading the trunks into the vans. They had gathered enough fibers, photos, and dead bodies to keep them busy for a while. The cabin was trussed up in yellow crime-scene tape like a big Christmas present, and a second cordon of tape had been strung along wooden stakes around the building to deter anyone from venturing near. I was able to walk through this scene unnoticed. To the Game-Show Hosts, I was invisible.

The corpse lay curled on a steel-top gurney, forgotten. In the open air the smell of it had dissipated a little, enough at least that the odor no longer made my head swim. I found myself wandering toward it, fascinated. There was a lurid appeal to the thing. The bare limbs, swollen and pallid and hairless. The face distorted by the fatal wound. It seemed inhuman, this creature. A snail shucked from its shell, left to wriggle about unprotected, to burn in the sun.

I was staring down at the corpse when Cravish and another man came up to the opposite side of the gurney. The new man was small but he had a stiff, combative look, like a rooster. Cravish introduced him as Edmund Kurth from Boston Homicide.

"Boston?" I asked.

The Bostonian Kurth stared at me. He seemed to be scrutinizing me for signs of rural stupidity. I should say right up front that there was something disconcerting about Ed Kurth, even on this first meeting. He was the sort of man one is anxious to get away from. He had a severe, angular face dominated by a narrow nose and two dark eyes. His skin was pitted with acne scars. Thick eyebrows imparted to his face a permanent scowl, as if he had just been shoved in the back.

"The victim was a DA in Boston," Cravish explained to me. He gave Kurth a look: *Do you see what I have to deal with?*

"Boston," I repeated, to no one in particular.

Kurth bent over the body, examining it with the same unblinking focus he had directed at me. The detective snapped on rubber surgical gloves and prodded the thing with his finger as if he were trying to wake it up. I watched his face as he came nose to nose with Bob Danziger's remains. I expected a reaction, a flinch. But Kurth's face remained impassive. To judge by his expression, it would be hard to tell if he was looking into a dead man's ruptured eye socket or just poking through his glove compartment for a map.

"Well, maybe that's why he was killed," I ventured, eager to show my instinct for sleuthing. "Because he was a DA."

Kurth did not respond.

I babbled on. "*If* he was killed. I mean, it could be a suicide." Now, here was an insight. In crime-scene training, I vaguely recalled, we learned that gunshot suicides invariably shoot themselves in one of three places: the temple, the roof of the mouth, or between the eyes. That this man might have killed himself struck me as a profound observation, though I imparted it with calculated cool—in a tone that suggested, *Yes, sir, I'm an old hand at the homicide game.* "Maybe he went to kill himself and he flinched, wound up shooting himself in the eye."

Kurth said, without looking up, "He didn't kill himself, Officer."

"It's *Chief,* actually. *Chief* Truman."

"*Chief* Truman. There's no gun here."

"Ah, no gun, well." My ears went hot.

A little smile puckered the lips of the Game-Show Host.

"Maybe he inserted the bullet manually."

"That would be unusual," Kurth informed me.

"It was a joke."

He glared another moment as if I were the backwardest country clod imaginable, then returned to the creature on the gurney, which he seemed to find less repulsive.

The Game-Show Host asked me, gesturing toward the body, "Did he have any connection to this place?"

"Not that I know of. I spoke to him a little bit while he was up here—"

"You knew him?"

"No, I didn't know him. I just spoke to him. He seemed like a nice guy. Kind of . . . gentle. I certainly didn't expect—"

"What did you talk about?"

"Nothing really," I said. "We just kind of talked for a while. We get a lot of tourists come through here. I don't bother with them, most of the time." I nodded toward the hills around the lake. The trees were daubed with yellow and red. "They come to look at the leaves."

"So he was just here on vacation?"

"I guess so. Some vacation . . ."

We stood shaking our heads over Danziger's body. I did remember meeting this Bob Danziger. He had a shy little wave, a smile nearly hidden under the eaves of his mustache. We'd met on the sidewalk in front of the station. *Hi,* he'd said, *you must be Chief Truman. . . .*

I began to say to the Game-Show Host, "I'd like to be involved—"

But a cell phone chirped on his belt. He held up one finger to silence me while he answered it. "Gregg Cravish." He kept that finger up as he uttered monosyllables into the phone. "Yes. Don't know yet. Fine. Good."

When he was done, I said again, "I'd like to be involved in the investigation."

"Of course. You found the body. You're an important witness."

"Right, a witness, sure. I meant, I'd like to do more than just guard the road."

"Securing the scene is important, Chief. The last thing I need is to get OJ'ed in front of a jury. If the crime scene is contaminated . . ." Cravish looked at me portentously, preassigning the blame for a contaminated crime scene.

"Look, the guy died in my town," I told him. "And like I said, I met him once. I'm just saying, I'd like to be in the loop, that's all. I'm supposed to be the chief here."

The Game-Show Host nodded to signal he understood. "Okay, sure, we'll keep you in the loop." But his expression said, *I understand. You're supposed to be the chief*

*and it wouldn't look good if all these flatlanders swooped in
and chased you off your own case. So I'll humor you, I'll let you
hang around awhile.*

Kurth straightened up from examining the corpse.
"Officer, does the press have the story?"

"The press?"

"Yes, the press—newspapers, TV."

"No, I know what the press is. It's just, we don't really
have a press here. There's a newspaper, but it's more of
a community thing. David Cornwell puts it out by himself. It's the schools and the weather mostly. The rest he
just makes up."

"Don't give him any information," Kurth ordered.

"Well, I have to tell him something. In a town
like this—"

"Then withhold the details. Or get him to. Will he
do that?"

"I guess so. I've never asked."

"Ask."

And that was as much conversation as Edmund Kurth
cared to lavish on me. He snapped off the gloves, dropped
them on the gurney, and stalked off without a word.

"Mr. Kurth," I called to him.

Kurth paused.

I stood there blinking at him. A sentence made its
way to the back of my throat but no farther: *It's Chief
Truman, not Officer.* "Never mind," I said.

Kurth hesitated. I imagine he was weighing whether
to ignore me completely or tear out my heart and show
it to me still beating. In the end, he just gave a little nod
and moved on.

"Have a nice day," I murmured, once he was out of
earshot.

In a few minutes the caravan of official vehicles—
cruisers, late-model Tauruses, a modified camper
marked CRIME SCENE SERVICES, a black van from the
Medical Examiner's office—started their engines and

pulled away. The clearing around the cabin was quiet again. The loons were *rhonking* over the lake.

Dick Ginoux appeared out of the gloomy woods. It occurred to me he'd been hiding there until the strangers left. He came over and stood beside me as the parade rumbled away down the access road. He shuffled the pine needles with his feet. "What do we do now, Chief?"

"I don't know, Dick."

4

Kurth was wrong about one thing: You could not keep the case quiet, not in a place like this. There are no secrets in Versailles, Maine. Information shoots around the town like tremors over a spider's web. Details of the murder began to emerge the same day, and within twenty-four hours most Versellians had a pretty good idea what we'd found in that cabin. Thankfully, people around here don't scare easily, and the case excited more curiosity than fear. It was the hot topic at the Owl and McCarron's. The morning after the body was discovered, Jimmy Lownes sidled up to me at the Owl and confided that he "knew a little about guns," if I was interested. Bobby Burke pleaded for a look-see inside the cabin. No one was immune.

"Tell me what it looked like," Diane prodded.

This was at our poker game, a quarter-ante affair that met at the station to help me pass the Sunday-night shift. Diane was usually the most serious player at the table. She chain-smoked Merits, played conservatively, and rarely lost when she did go after a big pot. But tonight even Diane was distracted, even she had the bug.

"Tell you what *what* looked like?"

"The body."

"It musta been the gormiest thing," Jimmy Lownes snorted. He took off his ball cap to scratch his head in wonder.

"I can't talk about it."

"What do you mean, you can't talk about it?" Diane was offended. "The whole town is talking about it! You're the only one who isn't."

"I can't. They told me to keep my mouth shut."

"Oh, Ben, you are such a wuss."

"Hey, are we playing poker or not?" I scolded.

Of course, they did not give a rat's ass about poker, but it would have been unseemly to abandon the game altogether, so they acquiesced, albeit with murmurs of reluctance.

"Alright, that's better. Seven-card stud, roll your own—"

"I bet it was stiff as a board."

"Jesus, Jimmy, I just got through saying. We're not talking about this."

"I'm not asking you anything, Ben. I'm just saying: I bet it was stiff as a board."

"Ai-yi-yi, how should I know if it was stiff? I didn't feel the thing!" I dealt the cards, sensing their eyes on me. "Jimmy, it's your bet."

"Did it smell?"

"Your bet."

Jimmy checked, and the rest of the table promptly did the same. They barely glanced at their cards.

"Alright, dealer bets two bucks." I tossed in two blue chips.

"What, you can't even tell us if it smelled?"

"Alright, yes, Diane, it smelled."

"No, but what did it smell *like*?"

"You really want to know what it smelled like?"

She put her cards down, exasperated. "Yes. I really do."

"I tell you what," Dick said, apropos of nothing, "The Chief never had a murder case."

My father had retired, reluctantly, in 1995, but even two years later when people referred to The Chief, they meant him, not me.

"Dick," I explained, "The Chief never worked a murder because nobody ever got murdered. It doesn't make me anything special."

"Well now, I didn't say you were anything special, Ben. I just said The Chief never had a case like this one."

"Jimmy, it's two bucks to stay in."

"What are you gonna do now?" Diane pressed.

"We're waiting for the AG to sort out what they found in the cabin."

"You're just gonna wait? That's crazy."

"Most murders are solved in the first twenty-four hours, you know, Ben." This was Bobby Burke with one of his signature factoids.

"Look, this isn't the Hardy Boys. You can't just run out and investigate a murder on your own, just because you want to. There's laws. The AG has jurisdiction. It's not my case."

"Well it happened here," Bobby retorted.

"And you found the body, Ben."

"Doesn't matter. Not my case."

"The Chief would have grabbed it," Dick tossed in. "You could ask him to help you out, like a—whaddaya call it?—a consultant."

I rolled my eyes. "I don't need help that bad. Besides, he wouldn't work for me."

"Did you ever ask him?"

I answered with a non sequitur. "Hey, do any of you guys know where he might have got a beer?"

"Claude had a beer?"

"One of those big bottles. Where did he get it?"

"Could have got it anywhere. It's just beer."

"It's not just beer. If you hear who sold it to him, you let me know."

"What are you going to do? Arrest somebody for selling your old man a beer?"

"I'm going to have a talk with him is all."

"Well," Dick sighed, steering us back to an older, hardier image of my father, "The Chief wouldn't have listened to some smartass yuppie lawyer. No, sir. I'd like to see that kid tell your old man, 'It's not your case.' The Chief would have given him what-for."

"Dick, he'd have listened because he had to listen, same as I am."

"Well," Diane retorted, "your mother wouldn't have listened." She exhaled cigarette smoke. "Why would she listen to some lawyer? She never listened to anyone else."

There was a pregnant moment while the four of them waited to see how I would react to that. There was some risk in mentioning my mother. In the ten weeks since she'd died, I had wrapped myself up in righteous Yankee stoicism. Never mind that my grief carried something extra, a tinge of guilt and shame—more than the usual dose. But to my own surprise, Diane's comment did not trigger any of the old sadness. We were thinking the same thing: If the Game-Show Host had ever tried to put off Annie Truman with the high-handedness he'd shown me . . .

"She'd have kicked his ass," I said.

Here is my mother: Around 1977 or so, on a raw morning in early spring. The weather was damp. In our kitchen that morning, you could sense the dankness outside, the smells of rain and mud. Mum was at the table, reading a hardcover book. She was already dressed, her hair gathered at the back of her neck exposing the empty dimple-holes in her pierced ears. I was at the table too. And before me, my preferred breakfast of the moment, Apple Jacks and a glass of milk. The glass was a concession from my mother, who'd recently given up trying to force me to drink the unpotable milk in the bowl, with its filmy emulsion of cereal scum. There was still a lingering self-consciousness between us over this tiff. I had the strongest urge to drink the soiled milk for her, but I couldn't quite do it. (Those amoeboid globules of Apple Jacks oil . . .)

"What are you reading?"

"A book."

"What book?"

"A grown-up book."

"What's it called?"

She showed me the cover.

"Do you like that book?"

"Yes, Ben."

"Why do you like it?"

"Because I'm learning."

"About what?"

"It's a history book. I'm learning about the past."

"Why?"

"Why what?"

"Why would you want to learn *that*?"

"To be better."

"Better than what?"

She looked at me. Blue-gray eyes, laugh lines. "Just a better person."

Dad pulled up in his truck. The overnight shift was supposed to go from midnight to eight, but Dad always seemed to get home earlier. I heard him hawk his throat before coming inside. He sat down at the table with little mute greetings for Mum and me.

Look! I shot a glance at Mum: *Does he know?* There was a white patch in Dad's bushy brown hair! Right at the top of his forehead! It was white powder, like baby powder, I guessed. *Mum, do you see it?*

"Dad, there's—"

"Ben." My mother gave me a stern look to shut me up.

Dad said, "What is it, Ben?"

"Um, nothing."

Mum's face had gone a little white too. Her lips compressed into a line.

Dad offered around a box of doughnuts from the Hunny Dip doughnut shop in town. On the box was a cartoon of a brown honey pot brimming with thick, golden ooze. A doughnut floated in midair above the jar, dripping with the stuff. Dad said, "Here. From Hunny Dip's, like you like."

"No, thank you."

"Go on, Anne. It won't kill you."

"No, Claude." You could tell from Mum's voice she was angry about him bringing home those doughnuts.

I helped myself to a chocolate glazed, which pleased him. He cupped my jaw in his thick-fingered paw and shook it. His fingers had a weird, tangy chlorine smell. There was, I noticed, more white powder on his shirt cuff.

"Attsaboy. It's just a doughnut, for Christ's sake."

"Don't touch him, Claude."

"Don't touch him? Why not?"

Her blue eyes were squinched half-shut, as if she wanted to deny her husband the pleasure of looking into them. "Ben, take your doughnut and go in the other room."

"But I'm not done yet—"

"Ben."

"What about my cereal?"

Dad said, meekly, "You better go, Ben."

My mother was a small woman, maybe five-two and thin. But somehow she was able to dominate her husband. He seemed to enjoy submitting to her too. It was a game, a little joke of his: *Of all the people to boss around big Claude Truman, this little spitfire . . .*

When I was safely out of the room—and eavesdropping from the TV room next door—I heard her say, "—my house."

"What?"

"I said, get out of my house now."

"Annie, what the hell's wrong with you?"

"Claude, there's powdered sugar in your hair. This is a little town, Claude. Did you have to rub my face in it?"

"Rub your face—"

"Claude, don't. Don't talk to me like I'm stupid, like I'm the only one who doesn't know. I am not stupid, Claude."

I did not really understand what was going on that morning, but I knew—I think I always knew—their relationship was a precarious one. Dad's temper, his rabbity sexual habits, his ego, and Mum's own strong personality all made for a volatile marriage. Not a bad marriage, but an inconstant one. Sometimes they acted like lovers; they disappeared upstairs on Sunday afternoons for naps or kissed on the lips or laughed over obscure incidents in their secret history. Other times, the strain between them was obvious, like the creaking of a rope under a heavy load. As a kid I assumed this was what true love looked like—that love was inherently unstable above a certain temperature.

I pushed the door open a crack to spy and was immediately seen.

Dad spotted me—wide-eyed, the doughnut glutinizing in my fingers—and something, some small breath of shame, went out of him. To my astonishment, he surrendered to Mum immediately, asking only, "How long till I can come back?"

"Until I'm ready."

"Annie, come on. Just tell me how long."

"A week. Then we'll see."

"Anne, where am I supposed to go? I'm exhausted."

"Go to the station. Go wherever you want, I don't care. Except the doughnut shop."

Later that morning, after Dad had gone, Mum took me into town to return the box of doughnuts. Dad's friend Liz Lofgren was behind the counter that morning, and Mum waited until the store was empty to inform Liz that she'd better have nothing more to do with Chief Truman if she knew what was good for her. Liz pre-

tended not to understand for a minute, but when Mum
said, "You don't want to be on my wrong side," Liz
seemed to agree.

Anne Wilmot Truman was raised in Boston, and the im-
print of that city stayed with her. It was in her voice, in
the mangled *r*'s and odd archaic colloquialisms (she always called soda *tonic*; the dry cleaner, the *cleanser*; milk
shakes, *frappes*). But the deepest impression was left by
her father, a striver named Joe Wilmot.

Joe had clawed his way up from a Dorchester tenement. In the 1930s and '40s he built a small chain of
grocery stores in Boston, a respectable success if not a
spectacular one. It was enough to propel him out to the
suburbs, anyway. But even after he'd made it, Joe could
never quite shake the sense that his new neighbors—all
those WASPy Juniors and The Thirds with their tennis
games and rumpled clothes—possessed something he
did not, something more than money. It was an attitude
more than anything else, a sort of at-homeness among
the big green lawns and tree-shaded streets. For lack of a
better word Joe called it "class," and he knew it would
always be out of his reach. Of course, this is the frustration of arrivistes everywhere. They cannot acquire
"class" because they cannot envision themselves having
it. It is a failure of the imagination. They are anti-
Gatsbys.

So Joe did what would-be Gatsbys have so often
done: He tried to inculcate the elusive stuff in his only
daughter. After all, this was Boston in the age of that
real-life Gatsby, Joe Kennedy. And what had Old Man
Kennedy learned if not that class is granted only to the
second generation? So Joe Wilmot sent Annie to a private school, and when he deemed the education there
inadequate, he made up the difference by paying her directly for educating herself: nickels and dimes for good
posture, for reading Yeats or Joyce, for teaching herself a

Mozart *lied* on the piano. The payola did not stop when she got older either. Right through the Winsor School and Radcliffe—between ballet recitals and voice lessons and a semester in Paris—Annie could always earn a buck or a fin by reciting a speech from Shakespeare or some other feat of cultivation. It was a game father and daughter played on the road to refinement.

Then the unthinkable happened. Its name was Claude Truman.

He was a thick-wristed policeman—a policeman!—from some god-awful backwater in Maine. They were wildly mismatched. What Mum saw in him, nobody could understand. My guess is it was precisely his muscular rudeness that made Claude Truman appealing. He was cocksure and strong, a bull moose in springtime. He was different. Not dumb, far from it. But at the same time this was a man who thought John Cheever was a hockey player and Ionesco a corporation. It must have been a relief to Annie not to have to work so hard. Who knows? Maybe there was even an exotic appeal to Versailles, Maine. Of course, she'd never seen it, but the *idea* of Acadia County must have been romantic—*the forest primeval* and all that—especially to a young woman who had been literated to a fare-thee-well, educated beyond all reason. Her father forbade Annie to see Claude Truman, but she defied him, and the couple married three months after they met. He was thirty-seven, she was twenty-nine.

The price was high. Mum and her father had a ferocious argument, and the rift between them never healed. She called him every now and then; after she hung up the phone, she usually went to her bedroom to cry. When he died, Joe left his daughter enough to pay for my education and a little extra for herself, but not the lode she might have received if she'd stuck to the plan.

Mum did continue one Wilmot family tradition. When I was a kid, she'd pay me for various demonstrations of self-improvement. A dollar for learning the "we happy few" speech from *Henry V,* and another buck for reciting it before dinner. Fifty cents for reading a novel (if it was not "crap"), a dollar for reading a biography. Five dollars for sitting with her through all of *I, Claudius* on PBS.

The day Mum kicked Dad out for getting doughnut powder in his hair, she cleared aside the kitchen furniture and asked me if I wanted to dance for a one-time payment of one dollar. She put on a Frank Sinatra record in the TV room and left the door open so we could hear it, then she instructed me on the proper placement of the man's hands and the proper execution of the box step.

I laid my left hand on her hip and held my right hand up so she could rest hers in my palm.

"Now what?"

"Step with your outside foot."

"Which one?"

"Any one, Ben. I'll follow you."

"Why?"

"That's how it works. The man leads. Just keep stepping with your outside foot. Make the box."

We danced for a while, to "Summer Wind," then "Luck Be a Lady."

She asked, "Do you want to talk about what happened this morning?"

"No."

"Do you have anything you want to ask me?"

I was preoccupied with the complexities of the box step—*look up at your partner, never down at your feet; stand straight, as if there were a string coming out of the top of your head pulling you up, up*—and all the while I was con-cen-tra-ting-on-the-beat. So I said no, it was okay.

She clinched my head a little too tight to her tummy and said, "My Ben," which meant she was sad but didn't want me to know it.

▪ ▪ ▪

"You can't bet that. It's your badge."

"Of course I can. It's worth something, isn't it? It's gold."

"It's not gold. Besides, what am I gonna do with it? Melt it down?"

"No, you could wear it, Diane. It's jewelry."

"Ben, I'm not going to walk around wearing your damn badge."

"Why not? You can be the new chief."

She rolled her eyes, unamused. "Come on, bet money or fold. That's how it works. U.S. currency."

Bobby Burke added, "Legal tender for all debts public and private."

The pot was somewhere just south of fifty bucks, which is about as high as it gets in this game. I was sitting on three queens, with just Diane to beat. It was no time to drop out. I appealed to Dick: "Is this badge worth fifteen bucks or not? Tell her, Dick. These things cost twenty-five, thirty bucks. I can show you the catalog."

"That's if you buy it new," he demurred.

"Dick, it's not a Buick. It doesn't matter how many miles are on it."

"It's up to Diane. If she wants to take it, she can take it."

"Jesus, Dick, you have no backbone. You're like a . . . a squid. What, are you afraid of Diane?"

"Yup."

"Diane—"

"No."

"Diane, just listen."

"No."

"Look, if you take it, you can wear it around town and make me look like an idiot. Now, how's that?"

She shook her head no. "Throw in your pants. I'll take those."

"I'm not betting my pants."

"Must not be a very good hand."

"It's got nothing to do with that."

"Then throw 'em in."

"Diane, I'm not betting my pants."

"What else do you have?"

"That's it. It's all I got."

She picked up the badge and turned it over in her palm, frowning. I expected her to bite it to see if it was counterfeit. "I'll take it. Maybe I'll make an earring out of it or something. I'll wear it around town so everyone will know what a loser you are." She tossed it in the pot.

"Ben," Dick asked, "does this make Diane the new chief?"

"She hasn't won yet, Dick."

"Well, after. Will she be the new chief?"

"I guess so."

His mouth squeezed into a frown of deep concern.

Diane laid her cards on the table. Two pairs, kings and sevens.

The thought crossed my mind that all I had to do here was fold. Just put my cards down, let Diane have the pot and the badge with it. An ignominious end to my career in law enforcement, but what the hell, an end is an end. Then again, I don't get the chance to beat Diane very often. I put down my three queens and swept the pot toward me, forty-five dollars or so plus a gold-colored badge.

"You wouldn't have let me keep it anyway," she grumbled.

I shrugged. *Hey, you never know.*

Later, I watched Diane get out of bed to stand by the window. She was a big, haunchy girl with an athletic way of moving. I liked to watch her. The soles of her feet scuffed along the floor. At the window she lit a cigarette and puffed it distractedly, arms folded across her belly. She seemed lost in thought, her nudity forgotten, irrelevant. Outside, the hills were silhouettes against the moonlit sky.

"What's wrong, Diane?" I propped myself on an elbow.

She moved her head vaguely but did not answer. The tip of the cigarette glowed orange in the dark room. "Did you ever think that maybe this is all we're going to have?"

"What? You mean"—I wiggled my finger between us—"this?"

"No! Don't worry, Ben, I know what *this* is."

"I only meant—"

"I know what you meant." She shook her head. "I mean, what if this whole thing is all there is for me? Shitty little apartment, shitty little town. This whole shitty life. So-called life."

My neck began to stiffen and I sat up. "Well, you can change it. If this place isn't for you, you can go anywhere you want."

"No, *you* can go anywhere you want. It's different for you, Ben. Always has been. You could always go anywhere you want. I can't."

"Of course you can."

"Ben, don't. Just don't. I'm not asking to be cheered up."

"Oh."

I sneaked a glance at the clock. 2:17 A.M.

"We're not all like you, Ben. You've got choices. You're smart, you went to a fancy college, fancy graduate school. You'll be okay wherever you go. You're not even as butthole-ugly as I say you are. You're actually—" She looked back at me, then returned her attention to the window. "You're not that bad."

"You're not bad either."

"Right."

"I mean it, Diane."

"I used to be not bad. Now I'm not even not bad."

"That's just not true."

She dismissed this with a wave of her hand. "Ben, tell me what you're going to do when you leave here."

"Go home, I guess. I have a meeting in Portland to-morrow."

She shook her head again, the long-suffering Diane. "Not when you leave the room. When you leave this fucking town."

"Oh. I don't know. Go back to school, I guess. Maybe just go have an adventure somewhere."

"Right. Prague."

"You could come, you know. There's nothing holding you here."

"I don't know from Prague." She slid a hand over her hip, smoothing the clothes that were not there. A gesture to fill the space. When she was ready, she said, "I thought you were going to be a professor. Isn't that what you were in school for? English or something?"

"History."

"You've got a good name for a history professor. Professor Benjamin Truman. Very intellectual."

"It's probably not going to happen, Diane."

"Yeah, it will."

"I only got through one year of grad school. It takes a lot more than that."

"You say it like you flunked out. You got called back here. That's different. You came back to help your mother and now she's dead, so— You don't have to stay, you don't have to be here anymore. You should go back to school. It's where you belong. Join the chess club or the prom committee or whatever." She took a drag on the cigarette and looked out at the hills, then, as if she'd reached a decision, turned to me. "You should go to Prague. I have some money, if that's what's stopping you."

"No, Diane. It's not about money."

"Well, you just make sure you get there. Go to Prague, then get back to school. You know, those guys—Bobby and Jimmy, even Phil, all them guys—they look up to you. They want you to do all that shit you talk about."

I had no response.

"It'll make them happy to see you out there somewhere. Just to think of you out there, like, flying. It's important."

"How about you, Diane? Would it make you happy if I left?"

"I'd get over it. There'll be a new chief after you. Maybe I'll just use him for sex, same as I did you. Maybe he won't even be a prude like you."

"They might hire a woman. They do that now."

"That'd be just my luck."

Neither of us spoke for a while.

"Maybe we shouldn't do this anymore, Ben. It's starting to feel like a bad idea." The tip of her cigarette hovered at the window like a firefly. "We both got places to go."

5

Monday, October 13. 10:00 A.M.

We met at the Attorney General's office in Portland, a two-hour drive from Versailles. There were twenty or twenty-five people there, a number that necessitated theater-style seating. At the front of the room—onstage, as it were—was the Boston Homicide detective Edmund Kurth. He stood off to the side, arms folded, watching people find their seats. There was still that luminous intensity about Kurth. He looked like he was itching to knock somebody's hat off.

The audience consisted mainly of state troopers from Maine and Massachusetts, husky guys with buzz cuts and friendly smiles. There were prosecutors from the Maine AG's office too. It had been a long weekend for the lawyers; they had a gray, haggard look. Cravish, the Game-Show Host, stood off to the side.

I slipped into the back row of metal folding chairs, feeling vaguely like an eavesdropper. My invitation to this meeting was a formality, a courtesy extended to the locals. There were no illusions about that. My job was to show up, have my ticket punched, and go home. I hadn't even bothered to put on my uniform. I wore jeans and a sweatshirt. (The outfit was more than an expression of my outsider status, though. The truth is, the Versailles police uniform is pure hayseed and I try not to wear it any more than necessary. The uniform consists of a tan shirt, brown pants with a tan accent stripe, and a ridiculous Smokey the Bear hat, which my father insists on calling a "campaign hat." I dislike the whole getup, but it's the hat especially—no citizen could respect a policeman wearing that hat.)

Kurth struggled to remain still as the troopers and prosecutors found seats. The muscles in his face played under the skin. After a while—but before his audience had completely settled—he'd had enough of waiting. He walked to a corkboard at stage left, tacked a mug shot to it, and announced, "This is the man we're after: Harold Braxton."

I craned my neck to see the photos, the traditional twin frames showing the suspect face-on and in profile. Braxton looked to be in his twenties, African-American. The sides of his scalp were shaved and the remaining hair was pulled back tightly and gathered in a little tuft at the back of his head. The hairstyle seemed more Tibetan than hip-hop. His skin was as smooth and dark as a seal's.

Kurth added: "He's an absolute fuckin' animal and we're going to hunt him down."

The audience shifted uneasily. Kurth was from away, and the Maine troopers didn't like being lectured by him, much less informed what they were going to do. His melodramatic tone caused some eye-rolling too, even among the Massachusetts guys.

"Do you have some evidence?" an older guy finally asked. "Or should we just take your word for it?" He smirked, proud of the sarcasm.

Kurth tried to smile too, but the smile flickered and died on his lips. "Evidence," he said.

He went to his briefcase and fished out a bulging manila folder. He riffled the folder until he found a few photos, then returned to the corkboard. First a color eight-by-ten of Danziger's mutilated face, the right eye and forehead obscured by a dry cookie of blood. "Our victim, Robert Danziger." Then he added two rows of similar photos. "Vincent Marzano. Kevin Epps." With each name, Kurth punched a pin through one of the photos. "Theo Harden. Keith Boyce. David Huang." The victims were all young, in their early twenties. Marzano was white, Huang Asian, the rest black. All bore the same dark stain on one half of their face. Harden's features were a blur beneath the blood. "All shot in the eye with a high-caliber weapon, like a .44," Kurth informed us. "That's his signature." Kurth leaned against one of the tables. This was supposed to be a relaxed pose, but he managed to look like a two-by-four leaning against a barn. "Harold Braxton runs a crew called the Mission Posse. The Mission Posse moves a lot of rock, makes a lot of money, and they're willing to do just about anything to defend their business. All these guys here"—he gestured toward the photos—"threatened Braxton's business in some way. Some of them were cooperating with the police. Some tried to open up a corner in Braxton's neighborhood."

"Why a bullet in the eye?"

"It's a message. In Mission Flats everybody understands. It means, Close your eyes, don't see what we do." Kurth locked his gaze on the guy who'd needled him moments before. "That's called evidence."

"And Braxton's never been prosecuted for any of this?"

"Nobody talks."

"But why Danziger?" one of the troopers asked.

"Bob Danziger had a pending case against a member of Braxton's crew, a carjacking case. No big deal except the defendant was Braxton's second-in-command. The trial was scheduled to open a couple weeks ago, in early October, which is about the time Danziger was murdered. So that's your motive—no DA, no trial for Braxton's buddy. Braxton protects his own."

One of the prosecutors asked, "Why kill him in Maine?"

"That's where Danziger happened to be when they reached him. On vacation, apparently."

"It's all circumstantial," someone argued.

Kurth shrugged. "Of course it's circumstantial. It's a homicide; the best witness is dead."

Cravish stroked his chin and frowned. "I'm not convinced, Lieutenant Kurth. Why would a drug dealer murder an assistant DA? It doesn't make sense. There will always be another prosecutor to take his place, and another and another. The government is the biggest gang around. Why declare war on it? Besides, I've prosecuted guys like this before. They don't consider the prosecutor an enemy. It's all professional, they know that." The Game-Show Host was proud to announce he'd prosecuted tough guys. A supercilious look crossed his face.

"Mr. Cravish," Kurth drawled, "I don't think you've prosecuted anyone like Braxton."

"Oh, I'm quite certain I have."

"Are you, now?"

From his briefcase, Kurth plucked two more eight-by-tens, which he stuck to the board with the others. The first showed a jolly-looking man with an orange beard. The second image was harder to identify. It was a dark-colored object dangling from a rope over a crumbling driveway. It might have been a laundry bag.

"What the hell is that?" a trooper asked.

Kurth, thinking the question referred to the man with the beard—or pretending to—pointed to the first photo and said, "This is Artie Trudell. He was a cop. About ten years ago Trudell was on a drug raid in the Flats. Braxton was cornered inside an apartment. He was trapped, so he blew Trudell's head apart. Fired one shot through the front door, killing Trudell, then took off through a back door."

There was a moment of silence. Out of respect for the

fallen cop, everyone hesitated to ask about the second photo. Finally someone said, "What about that thing? What is it?"

"It's a dog," Kurth said.

The image came clear—the carcass of an animal suspended by its hind legs. The dog's head was hidden behind a flap of skin that hung from the back of its neck like Superman's cape. For some reason this photo seemed more gruesome than the others, whose subjects were merely human.

"Braxton and his crew had a pit bull. They wanted to see how mean he could be. So they tied up this dog and turned the pit bull loose on him. This is what was left."

"But . . . *why*?"

"Why?" Kurth shook his head. "Because Braxton's a fucking animal, that's why."

A rustle went through the room. The audience was visibly uneasy, but it took a few moments before anyone screwed up the courage to murmur, under his breath, "Come on."

Kurth fixed us with one of his reptile stares. "Listen to me, you can roll your eyes all you want, but this is what guys like Braxton do. Why? There is no why. It's like asking, Why do sharks eat swimmers? or, Why do bears eat hikers? That's what predators do. This guy is a predator."

Kurth removed the photos one by one and returned them to his briefcase. Then he paused to share a philosophical thought, or at least as nearly philosophical a thought as he ever voiced: "The system isn't built to handle a guy like this, who kills without even thinking about it. The system presumes that crime is logical, that people do it by choice. So we build prisons to deter them, or we offer programs to rehabilitate them. Carrots and sticks, all so these people will make the right choice. That whole model does not contemplate a Harold Braxton, because Braxton doesn't weigh the consequences in the first place. He doesn't choose to kill, he just kills. He doesn't think. He doesn't care. So there's only one thing to do with him: Take him out of circulation. We all know it, everyone in this room."

The audience, cops and lawyers alike, squirmed at Kurth's directness—the police because there was no ironic distance here, none of the cool cynicism that cops swaddle themselves in when confronted with the real danger of their job, the lawyers because Kurth did not share their genteel uneasiness with calling for Braxton's "removal from circulation." Kurth was too frank. Still, no one objected. None of us had wanted to be intimidated by Edmund Kurth, the flatlander, but we were.

After the meeting Kurth approached me and handed me a few mug shots, Braxton's among them. He asked me to show the photos around in Versailles, to find a witness who could place Braxton in the area. Someone must have seen Braxton or one of his crew. The request was delivered in Kurth's usual clenched manner. His body leaned forward, the little muscles of his face wriggling perceptibly. Most unnerving, he had a habit of locking his eyes on yours without glancing away or even blinking. My own eyes would sweep around the room just to avoid his, only to find upon returning that Kurth was still staring dead into my pupils.

So it may come as a surprise, given his overwound manner, that there was a strange attraction about Kurth too. He had a gorgeous purposefulness. In hindsight I see it was nothing more than the clarity of a man who is convinced his cause is righteous—*Get Braxton!*—but at the time he seemed to have been let in on some very profound secret. For Kurth, all the moral equivocation that underlies police work—that criminality is not the same as evil; that the criminal-justice system may be worse than the crime it is meant to cure; and therefore that policing itself is a morally ambiguous enterprise—all of it was washed away by Harold Braxton's overwhelming malignance. Braxton was evil, therefore Kurth must be good. Simple as that. It was this great moral reduction that allowed Kurth to speak in absolutes. Braxton was not merely troubled or desperate or suffering from some behavior disorder; he was an animal, a menace to be destroyed. I doubt that Kurth ever understood it was Braxton who gave him this gift of simplicity. In fact, I doubt Kurth ever fretted over the moral complexities in the first place. But without Braxton, Kurth would not have had that sense of crusade. He would have been an Ahab with no Moby Dick, no monster to hunt.

I did as Kurth asked. I showed the mug shots around Versailles for the next couple of days. I had mixed feelings about finding a neighbor to testify against Braxton, and it came as a relief when nobody in Versailles recognized his photo. I also did a check on the victim, with limited success. A few people remembered speaking with Bob Danziger, a few more recognized his photo. But none of the September renters in the lakeside cabins, now returned to their homes in New York and Massachusetts, remembered anything specific about Danziger. And no one had any idea how long the body had been baking in that locked cabin, although the ME later put it at two or three weeks. In the end, my investigation went nowhere. To all appearances, Robert Danziger had no connection with Versailles. It looked as if he'd come with the sole purpose of dying here.

But I was hooked just the same. Hooked on Kurth's narrative as well as the one I was composing in my own head, my own version of Harold Braxton the urban superpredator. I kept Braxton's mug shot in the case file, and over the next days I found myself studying it, trying to find hints of the lethal predatory stuff Kurth had described. I never did see it. In the photo, Braxton seemed harmless enough. He had not struck a pose for the camera. On the contrary, he looked passive, even sleepy. In a word, his appearance was ordinary, which only added to my fascination: How could Harold Braxton—Kurth's "animal" to be "hunted down"—look so unexceptional? Maybe that is always the case. Our villains always disappoint us. They never look the part. Remember the old news photos of Eichmann sitting in that Tel Aviv courtroom, blinking out from behind thick eyeglasses like some half-blind watchmaker? What a let-down, the world said. How "banal." We expect our monsters to make a better show of it.

6

During those first anxious days, the cabin on Lake Mattaquisett was guarded round the clock. Dick and I, with a couple of other officers, split the guard duty, rotating shifts so no one pulled two overnight watches in a row. There was not much to do out there, to be honest, especially at night. Once, some kids came driving down the access road, only to turn around the moment they saw the police Bronco parked out front. That was about it. There was no rush to contaminate this crime scene—Cravish would not be OJ'ed this time. I wasn't much of a watchman anyway. I tended to spend most of my time at the water's edge, listening to the plash and gurgle at my feet or gazing at the bare spots in the trees on the opposite side.

There are only a few months when we Versellians really get to see our lake. In summer, we are too busy making twelve months' worth of income in just twelve weeks. In winter, the lake freezes and is covered with snow. There are only these few precious weeks in between when the lake is there just for us. It is a magical time of year, late October, early November. Leaf season is over. The flashburst of red and yellow foliage has faded, and the leaf-gazers have moved on to southern Vermont, New Hampshire, and Massachusetts chasing the "high color." The air begins to take on the feel of winter. The water is a flinty blue. The lake is ours alone, briefly.

During these long quiet watches, my thoughts inevitably turned to my mother. I could envision her swimming here, arms turning in languid windmill strokes, far out into the lake where the white buoy of her bathing cap would vanish in the lambent cloud-shadows that slid across the water and up over the trees.

She used to swim in this lake nearly every day from May through September. That is no mean feat, mind you. In early spring Lake Mattaquisett is cold enough to shock your lungs into seizures. Joking about the water temperature (and, among men, about its effect on the genitalia) is a rite of spring around here. But Mum was fearless. She plunged in like an otter. She was a slippery swimmer too, the kind you stopped to watch. Her body glided along the surface, frictionless, back and forth, crisscrossing the lake at the pinch-point of its hourglass shape. You could tell she was proud of her swimming, all that naturalness achieved by hours of hard labor in the lap pool as a teenager. She would emerge from the water beaming and, between heavy breaths, challenge all comers: "Who wants to race me?"

It was for her that I came back to Versailles. I have said that I was trapped here, but that's not true, really. I chose to come back, and even in hindsight, even knowing where the decision led, I would do it again. It was a Hobson's choice, but all the same it was an easy choice.

In December 1994—not quite three years before the Danziger murder—I was a graduate student in history at Boston University. I was only in my second year, but already the academic world seemed everywhere and everything. I'd quickly joined in the death struggle with grad students nationwide over the usual desiderata: fellowships and grants and publications. The ultimate grail, a tenure-track faculty position, was an obsession—a measure of just how far I'd come from Versailles, Maine. Nothing else seemed to matter. I had a basement apartment in Allston, a horrible apartment even by grad-student standards—grungy, cold, damp. It had only one window, at sidewalk level with a view of legs scissoring past. A water stain ran along the bottom half of the wall like wainscoting, left by a flood who-knew-how-long ago. I had a girlfriend too, a fellow PhD candidate named Sandra Lowenstein. She was sallow and thin as a bird in December. Sandra talked a lot about Gramsci and Marx, and wore heavy black-framed eyeglasses to show her commitment to the cause. Maybe she dated me to show her commitment to the cause too: a bodily self-sacrifice to the lumpenproletariat of backwoods Maine. Which was hunky-dory with me because I'd put my prole past behind me. I was out. The big Venus's-fly-trap had not got me after all. Versailles was a memory, a quaint story I would tell my friends over cocktails in Cambridge or New Haven or wherever I was headed.

By this time I already suspected my mother had Alzheimer's. The disease can be difficult to diagnose, especially in early-onset cases like Mum's. The symptoms precisely mimic the ordinary prosaic effects of aging—forgetfulness, trivial sorts of confusion. Eventually, however, the signs become too obvious to ignore. In the fall of '94, Dad was calling every week to complain about her. She left the lights or the oven on overnight, he'd say. Once, she left the car engine running until it was out of gas and he had to go out to the station with a can to refill it. Exasperated, he told me, "Your mother's just not there anymore."

All of which I understood, and yet I was able to minimize it somehow. Or at least to compartmentalize it, as the euphemism goes. (We say *compartmentalize* when we mean *ignore* or *blow off*.) Maybe it was just the selfishness of a twenty-something; I could not bear to rouse myself from the hermetic life of a student. More likely, I could not accept that Mum was "not there anymore." The reports from Dad just did not fit. In my mind's eye, Annie Truman was always and very much *all there*.

But when I came home for Christmas break that year—after an absence of six months—I was brought up short by the reality of it. The slippage.

At first the changes were not startling. If you'd seen her, you would not have noticed anything obviously wrong. My mother was still an elegant-looking woman, effortlessly slim and "put together" (her phrase, not mine). She had a new pair of designer eyeglasses, for which she'd made the long trip to Portland twice, to order them and to pick them up. Those vivid blue eyes had not faded. Her face had aged a little. The skin had shrunk over the facial bones and you could just make out the longitudinal curve of the eyeballs. Still she was extraordinarily lovely.

To me, though, there were subtle but noticeable changes. She spoke less and resisted being drawn into conversation. She seemed to have determined that there was a risk of embarrassment in speaking and decided the safer course was to say as little as possible. There were occasional memory lapses, nothing shocking but unlike her. (Every morning she greeted me with the vague exclamation "Ben!" as if she were surprised to find me home.) What I saw at first was not a sudden, violent transformation in my mother, but a shift in mood. A sense of dullness and withdrawal about her, remarkable only because Anne Truman had never been remotely dull or withdrawn in her life.

Because the university virtually shuts down over the holidays, I was at home for several weeks that December. Family custom dictated that I work as a temporary at the department, but my real job was to look after Mum. By this point, Claude Truman had had just about enough of his wife. From the start, he was spectacularly

unfit for the task of caring for an Alzheimer's patient. He
was still The Chief, nearing the end of his glorious reign,
floating along on an argosy of self-satisfaction. Is that too
unkind? Maybe. Alzheimer's imposes a burden on the
spouse, and maybe it is unreasonable to demand that
every spouse be equal to the challenge. Better to say,
Claude had always been able to nourish himself from
within, and now he simply could not understand how his
wife, who'd once had the same knack, had mysteriously
become so ravenous.

So for a few weeks I put on a uniform and worked a
detail as Anne Truman's bodyguard, a happy enough
arrangement. I learned the various strategies Mum and
Dad had improvised for protecting her. There were yellow stick-on notes posted throughout the house—
CHECK OVEN, they said, or TURN OFF LIGHTS or KEYS
ON PHONE TABLE—and I began to add my own notes
rather than nag her, which wounded her leonine pride.
To prevent her from wandering, I took her on long walks
every morning and afternoon to tire her out. For good
measure, I was told, I should install a second lock on
each of the house doors, keyed from the inside. This I refused to do. It smacked too much of imprisonment. I did
hide the car keys, though, just in case.

The hardest moments were in simple conversation.

"Do you have . . . ?"

"Do I have what, Mum?"

"Never mind. It's not important."

"No, what is it?"

"I don't know—I can't—"

"Go ahead, Mum, it's alright. Do I have what?"

"Ben."

"Yes?"

"What do you . . . ?"

"I'm in school, Mum."

"Of course. Of course, I knew that."

Word-finding troubles were particularly infuriating for
her. Over and over, she would pause in mid-sentence,

suspended, unable to grasp the word she needed. If we were walking, she would stop and stare at her feet, fists pressed to her forehead, while she racked her brain for the missing tools. I learned not to guess at the next word, which frustrated her even more. "Shh! Shh!" she would hiss, and swing a stop-sign hand at me.

For all that, I still intended to go back to Boston when my break ended. I convinced myself that the Forgetting Disease was no more than an inconvenience. It was still in an early stage (she was only fifty-six), and Annie Truman would outwork it the way she'd outworked every other damn thing.

It took a calamity to open my eyes.

December 24, 1994, was absolute cold. At eight A.M., the temperature was five degrees above zero, fifteen below with the windchill. Gray, sunless, with a stabbing wind. The snow encasing us—on the roof, in the yard, in tree branches—made creaking sounds.

Mum and I did not walk that morning. Around eleven, Dick Ginoux called to say there was an impromptu Christmas party at the station. Sandwiches and beer (diet orange soda for The Chief). I declined, but Mum urged me to go. "It's Christmas Eve, Ben. Go have a good time for once." The kitchen thermometer had risen to ten degrees or so. Still, it was a forbidding day, and I hated like hell to leave her alone in that house. But it was only for an hour or two. "I'm not a child," she insisted.

When I got back around two, the house was quiet. An empty ticking sound in the halls. I called out and got no answer. Mum's bedroom was empty too, the bed made up neatly.

To ward off panic, I indulged the notion that she must be lost inside the house. I'd once found her standing in the hallway, confused about which doorway led to her room; maybe she'd fallen into a similar confusion now.

But racing around the house was just a waste of time. Her coat, hat, and knit mittens were gone.

In the front yard I shouted her name.

No answer. The wind loud in my ears.

Anxiety thickening into dread.

How could I have left her? Stupid stupid stupid stupid stupid.

I shouted her name. The cold swallowed my calls. There were no tracks. It was possible she'd walked off down the road, which had been plowed clear.

Or into the forest. On our little street the forest crowds right up to the road's edge. The curtain of trees is pushed back as if by an invisible arm to reveal the house in its shadow. She might have wandered anywhere in these woods.

Stupid stupid.

I phoned the station. No one in town knew where she was. Within minutes there were twenty guys out looking for her, then fifty.

"She'll be fine, Ben," Dad said.

"The sun sets at five," I reminded him.

Why didn't I insist we walk that morning, cold or no cold? We should have walked till we were both exhausted.

I set out along the unmarked trails in the thick woods around our house where we often walked and where my mother had been hiking for as long as I could remember. It was gloomy among the trees but warmer since the wind was somewhat subdued here. My undershirt was soon clammy with sweat as I ran along shouting for her.

No answer. Just the crunch of my boots in the snow.

I had a radio on my belt. Now and then a searcher would call in to report he'd seen no sign of her.

I receded into the forest along familiar trails until each ran out, then doubled back until I reached a new spur to follow. Others were searching near me. I could hear their shouts—"Anne!"—and my own, more frantic—"Mum!"

The light became shadowy and dull as afternoon began to dim.

How ridiculous that she might die this way. That an entire remarkable life could arrive at such an abrupt and stupid terminus.

I scrambled through the forest for two hours, through the bare pines growing thick like hairs on a vast scalp. Dusk was coming. It was foolish to run around this way, calling crazily into the trees. The search needed better planning, better organization. Who the hell was in charge here? Didn't they realize? These woods stretched for miles in all directions, thickening into impenetrable old growth. We would never find her by trial and error. We would run out of light and time long before we ran out of trees.

I stopped to think. Where did we walk? Where would she go?

Think.

An idea crowded in: This was what Alzheimer's disease meant. This was the lethal danger behind that austere Teutonic name. She had *wandered*, in the clinical parlance; she'd had a *catastrophic event*.

Control your emotions. Where would she go?

A blackbird flitted in the trees, unsettling the branches.

She would go to the lake. I knew it with a crashing certainty. She would follow the road to Lake Mattaquisett, lured by some memory of a vanished summer—an engram not quite expunged, a nano-thought surviving as a skittery arc of electrical current jumping across a damaged synapse somewhere. The lake, *her* lake. Had the weather not been so extremely cold, or had it not been Christmas Eve, maybe the roads would not have been empty and someone would have seen her walking. She'd have been picked up on small-town radar and her whereabouts would never have been a mystery. But she'd chosen a bad day for wandering.

I ran up the trail, scrabbling past the fingers of the trees.

To the house, the car.

Driving, I felt this adrenalized sense of certainty grow. She was there, I knew it. I raced along the Post Road. I was a policeman, a real one this time, rushing to an emergency.

At dusk I found her curled on the dirt road that rings the lake. The sports use this road to reach their summer rentals. In winter it is abandoned, and far enough from the house that no one had thought to search there. No one thought she could walk that far.

I knelt and put my arms around her. Her body trembled. She pulled her arms against her chest so I could hold her. I squeezed tight to stop the shivering. Her lips were blue, her eyes frightened.

In the gloom, the water beside us looked black. This lake had been the scene of so many blithe sunny afternoons. Now it was transformed into a forbidding place. Deep, glacial, primal.

I carried her to the car to warm her up. Her cheek against mine was cold rubber.

"I . . . I got lost." Her jaw chattered, her lips and tongue were thick.

"Mum, you've been on this road ten thousand times."

"I got lost."

I understood she meant more than she'd said. It was not simply that she'd got lost or even that she'd had such a dangerous close call. She'd glimpsed the horrifying course of her disease. The illness was no longer theoretical. It was the inescapable future: erasure of everything she had ever learned—even near-instinctive ideas like how to chew and swallow food, how to speak, how to control bowel movements—and the inevitable end when the brain would lose its ability to regulate essential bodily functions, when she would become bedridden and at last perish from diseases common to the bedridden, heart failure, infections, malnutrition, pneumonia. Mercifully—and it was merciful—my mother died before experiencing the full devastation of Alzheimer's. But what she did experience—starting that Christmas Eve, I think, as she lay shivering on the frozen dirt road—was almost worse: the foreknowledge that this would be her end, the awareness that her brain had begun to clot with plaque and fibrous tangles, that neurons had begun to shut down by the tens of thousands, winking out like lights on a sinking ship. She would be stripped. Her body, unbrained, would continue to operate for years, maybe decades. Babbling, demented, incontinent. A fool.

"What will . . . I do?"

"I don't know, Mum."

When Dad arrived a few minutes later, he opened the passenger door of the car as if he meant to tear it off the hinges. He buried his head in her neck and kissed her and muttered, "Jesus, Annie. Jesus."

The next morning I withdrew from school and joined the Versailles Police Department.

7

I t was inevitable, I suppose, that I would look inside the cabin. It was a constant temptation, wrapped in that cheerful yellow crime-scene tape like a big gift just waiting to be opened. The Game-Show Hosts had already swarmed over it and taken anything that was remotely relevant. What harm could there be in having a little peek? I gave in, finally, on a sunny Wednesday afternoon, October 15.

Of course, I had broken the door lock myself when I found the body, so it was easy to pull off the tape and swing the door open. The sour stench scratched in the nostrils but did not send me reeling into the woods to vomit, as it had four days earlier. The techs had done a job on the interior. There were gaps in the floor where floorboards had been sawed out and removed for testing. An outline had been marked where the body fell, not in chalk but with little cones, presumably to preserve the surface underneath. As my eyes grew accustomed to the gloom, I saw the blood spatters. Blood was everywhere, an incomprehensible amount, a flood of it, too much to have been contained in one body. There were smudges on the walls too, from the powders used to illuminate fingerprints and hidden speckles of blood. Somewhere in the shadows an insect buzzed intermittently, like a small plane with engine trouble.

I walked around the cabin, being extremely careful not to disturb any of the cones or markings. Until you have seen something like this, you cannot appreciate how much fluid a human head contains. Danziger's had burst like a water balloon. Near the body, the floor was painted thick with it in an immense dark oval. At the edges this stain gave way to heavy splats, which in turn gave way to shapely teardrops. Furthest from the body, the blood was no more than a mist on the wall. Delicate micro-droplets with an irresistible needle-fine texture. I lifted a finger to touch them, to feel the tiny Braille bumps they'd formed.

"Unh-unh-unh." This was a voice behind me. "I wouldn't do that."

An inch from the blood-spattered wall, my hand froze.

I turned to see a very tall, lanky man in the doorway. Backlit, his features were difficult to make out. He wore a flannel jacket and a scally cap, which made him look like a longshoreman, one of the tough guys who beat up Brando in *On the Waterfront*.

"It's okay. I'm a cop."

"I don't care if you're J. Edgar Hoover. You touch that blood, you'll be tampering with a crime scene."

"J. Edgar Hoo—I didn't touch anything."

"Didn't touch anything? Son, you're marching around in there like it's a parade ground. You have no blessed idea what you've touched."

I exited, retracing my steps with the same exquisite care I'd used in entering the cabin.

"Don't knock anything over," the tall man advised, unimpressed.

In the pine-needle yard, I told him, "I'm Ben Truman. I'm the chief here."

"Well, Ben Truman, you won't be chief for long if you keep this up. Didn't they teach you anything in school?"

"History."

"History. Ah."

Neither of us spoke for a moment while we considered the irrelevance of my education.

"Did you want something here?" I asked him.

"Just to have a look."

I hesitated.

"It's alright. I'm a cop too."

"Are you working this case?"

"No, no. Just came to scratch an itch."

"Alright. Just don't go inside. It's not a parade ground, you know."

He stepped to the threshold of the cabin, where he stood stiffly, scanning the one-room interior. His hands never emerged from the pockets of his coat. The inspection took only a minute or two and when it was concluded the tall man abruptly turned, thanked me, and walked off.

"Wait a minute," I called after him, "wait a minute, that's it? I thought you wanted to look at it?"

He turned back. "I just did."

"But you can't see anything from there."

"Of course you can, Ben Truman." He gave me a little wink and turned to go.

"Hold on a second. You came all the way out here just to— Who are you, anyway?"

"I told you, I'm a policeman. Well, a retired policeman. But as they say, a retired policeman is like a retired whore—she can stop working but she'll always be a whore. We'll always be policemen, you and I. It's the nature of the job, Ben Truman."

He stood there, hands in pockets, waiting for another question.

I was distracted, though, first by the joke—the wisdom of which eluded me, as did the humor—and then by the archaic term *policeman*. When had *policeman* been laundered out of the language, replaced by the antiseptic but gender-neutral *police officer* or the slangy, vaguely disrespectful *cop*? *Policeman* belongs to a more prosaic past—Officer Friendly in a brass-buttoned tunic, that was a policeman. But this man had used the term without self-consciousness. He was an older guy, maybe sixty-five or seventy, and I had the feeling he used other anachronisms as well, *girl* to refer to a grown woman, or *tennis shoes* for sneakers.

"Well," he said. "Good luck with it."

Evidently he thought this was my case. It was a welcome misapprehension at first. Flattering. But I knew I had only the faintest idea what a homicide detective actually does. And if this guy was a detective . . . well, what harm in asking?

"What did you see in there?"

His face registered the realization that I was no homicide detective, nor any other species of detective. He frowned. Whoever he was, he had not come out here to hand-hold a novice. "The same things you did. I just didn't step on them."

"I told you, I didn't step on anything. Anyway, there was nothing to see."

"Nothing to see? So tell me, what happened in there?"

"A guy got shot."

"Well, of course. But what then?"

"What then?"

"A guy got shot—then the body was moved. You'll have to figure out why."

"How do you know the body was moved?"

"I know because I looked. Keep looking, Ben Truman. Figure it out."

"No, show me. What did you see in there? Show me."

"Show you, why?"

"Because I'm curious. I'm just—I'm curious about things."

"I thought you said you were a policeman." He regarded me a moment before saying, "Come here." We moved to the doorway, where he stood behind me. "Tell me what you see."

"I see a cabin with a lot of blood all around. Some cones where the body was. Little signs to show where things were found."

"Yes, those are the obvious things. But what's wrong here? What's out of place?"

I looked.

"Look at the blood. The spatters."

I stared obediently at the whole baroque pattern of blots and curlicues.

"Do you know anything about blood-spatter patterns?"

"No. I've never—"

"Well, there's nothing mysterious about it. When blood or any other fluid falls straight down, it spatters evenly. You get a stain that's a round circle with splashes of blood around it, the same in all directions. But when it strikes a surface at an angle, the blood's own momentum makes it spread across the surface. So, instead of a round stain, it leaves a stain the shape of a teardrop. The fat end of the teardrop is where it hits first, then it tapers off, thinner and thinner as it moves away from the point of origin. You can tell all kinds of things from stains. If you get a round stain on the floor, you know the blood probably just fell with gravity rather than being projected by force. That's called passive bleeding. A wounded victim will leave a lot of stains like that as he moves around and blood drips from his wounds. There's not much of that here, of course, because your victim died instantly. But look at these stains, the ones like little comet trails. The blood was spattering out"—he gestured—"this way. You see, those cones are *behind* the blood spatters. The body couldn't have fallen there. The way those cones are placed, it looks like the blood came flying *toward* the victim, and of course that's impossible. So this body was moved after it hit the ground."

"Maybe he didn't fall straight down," I argued. "Maybe the bullet pushed him in that direction after the blood sprayed out, so he just landed on the wrong side of the spatters."

"No, no." He shook his head—but patiently, even respectfully, with no suggestion that I was some hayseed sheriff from Acadia County. He seemed to take me for what I was, a young cop with a lot to learn. He seemed to enjoy playing the professor too, for a while at least. "You've been watching too many movies, Ben Truman. In movies, you see a man standing stock-still, and when he is shot the bullet sends him flying against the wall. Pure bullshit. It doesn't work that way. A bullet can't do that. Shooting into a human body is like shooting into a bag of sand. The bullet pierces the surface, and the sandbag, which is much heavier than the bullet, just absorbs the impact. Same with a person. The bullet is too small and too penetrating to shove him in any direction. So in real life, if a person is standing still and he's shot, he falls straight to the ground. Now, if a man is moving—if he's running, say—and he gets shot in the back, then yes, he'll fall forward. But that's not because the bullet knocked him forward; it's because his own momentum carried him in that direction. Even allowing for Danziger's height, he could not have landed that far on the wrong side of the spatters. So this body was moved, we presume by the shooter."

He punctuated all this with a modest little shrug. *Obvious.*

"Who are you?"

"My name is John Kelly."

"No, I mean who *are* you? You were a policeman—okay, where? How long?"

"Boston. Thirty-seven years."

"You were a homicide detective."

"Among other things."

"And you knew this guy Danziger? Is that why you're here?"

"We met. May he rest in peace."

"What do you do now?"

"I told you, I'm retired. I watch baseball on my satellite dish. I call my daughter on the phone. At five o'clock
I have a whiskey."

"Tell me more." I waved my thumb toward the blood-
stained cabin.

"What is it you want to know?"

"Everything. I want to know everything."

"Everything. Hmm. Well, usually if you see a body
moved this way, it means your scene was staged. The
killer tried to make it look like something other than
murder: accident, suicide, anything that will throw the
investigator off. They always get it wrong, of course, because very few people have actually seen what it looks
like when someone dies by suicide or by accident.
They've seen movies so they think they know, just like
you thought you knew, but they don't know. That's how
you catch 'em, see. You look for the detail they got
wrong—in this case, the blood spatters."

How to explain the quickening I felt, the tremor?
Kelly seemed to be able to read the environment in a
way that no one—not Kurth, not the Game-Show Host,
and certainly not I—had done. The resolution of this
murder, with all its evident danger, seemed suddenly
closer. Listening to him analyze the killer's mistakes, I
felt certain the truth would come out quickly, that the
whole thing must look clumsy to an expert. Amazingly,
given the circumstances, I enjoyed it.

"What else?"

"Well, you know someone jimmied the scene; he
moved the body. So the next question is why? He didn't
try to stage it as something other than a murder. There's
no phony suicide note or anything like that. That's why I
say he must have been looking for something—it's the
only reason he'd have risked moving the body. Was
there any sign of a motive?"

"No."

"Anything obviously missing?"

"No. In fact, the wallet was left on the floor, in plain sight."

"Well, he was after *something*. Otherwise he would have run. From the looks of this place, the guy must have used an elephant gun. It was loud. You ever hear a gun go off in a small space like this? Deafening, blows your ears out. The blood sprays, too, remember. So picture him: His ears are ringing, he's covered with blood, he's agitated. He ought to be thinking one thing—run. But he doesn't run, this guy. He sticks around, he even touches the body. He moved it so he could search the thing without standing in all that blood. That's an awfully big risk. Whatever Danziger had, your shooter wanted it bad. Prints?"

"No prints."

"Well then I'd guess your man knew what he was doing. This wasn't his first time. He may have planned the whole thing too. No other way to account for his bringing gloves in September. It hasn't been that cold yet."

I'd been standing with my back to Kelly, looking into the cabin, and now I turned toward him.

Kelly immediately stepped back. I later realized this was a habit of his. He stood well back from whomever he spoke to, presumably to muffle the effect of his height. Big men usually do just the opposite. They crowd you, they loom. They stand close enough that you—and they—are always aware of their superior size. It is an obvious advantage in conversation literally to look down on someone, and tall men tend to exploit it. But Kelly purposely renounced the tall man's advantage by standing back, by burying his big hands in his pockets. At the time, all I can say is that I sensed a gentleness about him but could not explain why. Now, in hindsight, I realize that John Kelly wore his height modestly, as if that lanky body were two sizes too big for the man inside. Also, let me confess here, right at the start, that my image of Kelly is probably not an accurate one. To me, he is the hero of this story—though you might disagree—so I have to remind myself that there was nothing heroic about his appearance.

"Well, you figure out what your man was looking for—why he moved that body—and you'll find him."

I shook my head. I felt at a loss, unnerved by the whole thing. The reality of it, the nearness.

"Don't look so hopeless, Ben Truman. It's not rocket science. You'll figure it out."

"Doesn't matter anyway, it's not my case. It's just, you have to wonder how anybody could do this. Not how—I guess we know how. I mean *why*?"

"Why indeed." Kelly gazed at the cabin. "Well, here's your first lesson. There are only six motives for murder: anger, fear, greed, jealousy, desire, revenge. Your first job is just to figure out which one fits your case. There's no such thing as a murder without a motive. Even psychopaths have a motive that makes sense to them. Every murder has a motive," Kelly said. "That's the golden rule."

"I thought the golden rule was 'Do unto others.' "

"For priests, not policemen." He winked. "We have our own golden rules."

He turned and headed for a tiny Toyota Corolla, a car so small it was hard to imagine Kelly folding himself small enough to fit into it. But he fit.

8

My father was at the stationhouse when I got back that afternoon. He was massaging the back of his neck as his head tilted left and right like a slow metronome. He didn't greet me when I came in, just said, "What did you do with my chair?"

The chair in question was a leatherette, brass-riveted swivel chair of monumental proportions. The Chief had ordered it from someplace in New York and over the next twenty years or so had literally left his impression on it.

"I sent it back to the Lincoln Monument. Mr. Lincoln said he was tired, he wanted to sit down again."

"I'm being serious." His tone was don't-fuck-with-me belligerent. "Where's my chair?"

"I gave it to Bobby Burke. He'll find a taker for it."

"That was my chair."

"No, that was the department's chair."

He shook his head, disappointed. His son just didn't get it.

I had not seen much of Dad since the body had been discovered. He hardly left the house, as far as I could tell. He busied himself with chopping cords of wood—

enough to heat Manhattan through several winters—
and staring at the TV. I had not found any more bottles,
nor had I ever gotten the impression he was truly drunk.
That said, these days The Chief never seemed quite
sober either. Of course I can't rule out the possibility he
was sneaking more 40s of Miller (or worse), but I suspect
that Mum's death had more to do with it. I think he was
just shocked. Shocked not by her dying—we'd both
known all too well her death was coming—but by the
continuing reality of her absence. It is a recognition that
strikes the bravest mourners sooner or later: The dead
are truly vanished. I'd been feeling it too, and I can attest
the mood was a little like drunkenness.

I sat down at the desk. For years this had been my father's desk and, other than the chair, I'd made few
changes since taking his place as chief of police. I'd removed the plaque he'd posted, which read PLEASE
INSERT COMPLAINTS IN SLOT AT REAR—Dad's idea
of humor—otherwise the desk was essentially as he'd
left it.

"So," I said, "did you come down here to visit your
chair? Or was there something else you wanted to talk
about?"

"You know what I came to talk about."

But the next moment he seemed to forget what that
urgent errand was. He wandered around the perimeter
of the station's one dismal room. "A lot of years I busted
my ass in this place."

I rolled my eyes. Self-pity did not suit Claude
Truman, even in his ravaged state. Besides, in all those
years it was generally other people's asses he'd busted,
not his own.

He shuffled around some more before coming to the
point. "What's going on with that case?"

"The AGs have it. They think it's some gang kid."

He grunted.

I said, "This guy Danziger was getting ready to prosecute him."

"What about you? They give you anything to do yet?"

"No. They have jurisdiction."

"Well, you've got to stay involved, Ben, you have no choice. You can't just do nothing."

"I know."

"You're the goddamn chief of police. Some flatlander comes up here and gets his head blown off—"

"Alright, Dad, I got it."

"What else do they know?"

"Dad, this has got nothing to do with you. Stay away from it."

"I'm just asking. Can't I take an interest in my son's work?"

"I'm not sure what they know. They don't report to me; they tell me what to do."

He smirked.

"Don't start with me, Dad."

"Who's the suspect?"

"His name is Harold Braxton. Here, they gave me a mug shot."

He glanced at the photo. "Who is he?"

"All I know is he's a gangster down in Boston. Deals drugs, I guess. One of the detectives from away said this looks like his"—I was about to say "M.O." but the term would have sounded cop-show phony coming out of my mouth—"it looks like his style."

"What else?"

"Why?"

"Because I want to know."

"Dad, why don't you just let me do my job."

"Because you don't know how."

His arms stiffened as a little flume of adrenaline released somewhere. There was no Anne Truman anymore to soothe him, to coo "Claude" in a way that both reassured and warned.

"Alright, Dad, look: There's another cop I just met; he

thinks the crime scene has been set up somehow, that the body was moved, like maybe the killer was looking for something. That's really all I know."

"You've got to stay on top of this."

I gave a little salute.

"Don't let 'em walk on you, Ben."

"I know, Dad. 'Nobody's getting through us.' "

"That's right," he said, "nobody's getting through us."

"Okay, Dad, don't worry, I'm on it."

I watched him move toward the door. From behind, his clothes looked too big. The seams of his work shirt sagged over his triceps, the seat of his pants drooped. He was shrinking, contracting in the airless atmosphere of his wife's absence.

"Hey, how you holding up, Claude?"

It was the first time I'd ever addressed him by his first name. I don't know why I did it. Maybe there was a thought that I'd detected some movement, a low seismic groan in that Yankee limestone. It was a thought he quickly quashed.

"Don't you worry about me, Ben. Just do your job."

I waited till he was gone before shaking my head at the old man. Unnerved as he was—and who wouldn't be, in his shoes?—deep down he was Claude Truman right to the end.

Nobody gets to you without going through me—and nobody's getting through me. It was one of my dad's favorite expressions. And mine too, because I understood it was Yankee code, I understood it was his big-fisted way of saying *I love you.* After I returned to Versailles, as my mother's illness worsened, it became the family ethic. We would circle the wagons. Dad and I would protect her together. *Nobody gets to her without going through us. And nobody's getting through us.*

Why did we have this sense of siege? Most people in town were eager to help take care of Mrs. Truman. They called the station to update us. "Annie's out sitting in the gazebo," they'd say, or "I just seen your mother out walking toward the lake." We could track her movements without leaving the stationhouse. To be frank, until she got sick, Mum had never been especially beloved in Versailles. She'd lived there some twenty-odd years, yet most Versellians were still skeptical of her Massachusetts roots and her Massachusetts attitude. With her illness, though, all suspicions and grudges were swept away, and the town showed its quiet, prickly brand of kindness—true kindness. If we found a supper in tinfoil left at our front door, there wouldn't be a card to identify who'd put it there, as if claiming credit would be showoffy and uncharitable.

Of course, there is a limit to what others can do. Illness imposes on a family in ways no outsider, however well-intentioned, can truly understand. The family is isolated until it is over, one way or the other. In the solitude of our little house, Dad and I were forced to work together for the first time. This meant, predictably, that The Chief assigned me 90 percent of the household chores. With Mum, I folded the laundry and cooked the dinners and lugged the groceries, all activities she seemed to enjoy because they prolonged the illusion of ordinary life. But as her condition deteriorated—as her thinking became more chaotic, a devolution that occurred much faster than I thought possible—Dad showed a side of himself I'd never seen. I don't want to make too much of this. People are what they are, after all. But here was Claude Truman holding his wife's hand in public. And carrying her upstairs if she fell asleep on the couch. And driving her all the way to Portland to get those damn designer eyeglasses.

One afternoon—this was a couple of years after I came home—I found Mum in the TV room. "What's going on?" I asked.

"He was just here."

"Who?"

"Kennedy."

"Kennedy was just here?"

She shook her head in little circles that seemed to mean yes.

"Which one?"

"Bobby." (Bobby was always her favorite Kennedy.)

"Bobby Kennedy was just here?"

More nodding.

"Meaning he was on the TV, right? You saw him on TV."

"Here."

"No, Mum, you mean on the TV."

"No!"

I should have let it go. Who knows what was really in her head? It was just as likely she'd meant to say something else, or not meant to say anything at all. But I didn't. I laughed at her and made an obvious smartass joke about seeing him drive off with Marilyn Monroe.

Her face fell. With an exasperated flounce, she twisted away from me.

"Oh, come on, Mum, it's a little funny, isn't it?"

"Shush!"

"Come on, I didn't mean anything."

"Shush!" She stared at the TV. (It was tuned to CNN, the twenty-four-hour newsathon. Some talking head bloviating about some crisis or other. Had he mentioned Kennedy? I don't know.)

Dad must have heard her shushing me. He stormed in and demanded to know what I'd done. When he got no answer, he knelt beside her and whispered into the swirl of her ear. She made a coy little smile and hunched her ear down against his face, as if his breath was tickling her. They looked like teenagers.

That he was capable of such tenderness was a revelation to me, though I think Mum knew it all along. Once, during one of our daily walks around the circumference of the lake, I asked her what she'd first seen in Claude Truman—his strength? his looks? his aggressiveness?

"No, Ben, his heart. I saw it right off. That man didn't fool me for a second." I snorted. You might as well say you liked the Venus de Milo for her lovely arms. "Don't talk like that," she said. "He'd die for you, Ben. You should know that. Your father would absolutely lay down in traffic for you."

9

Twenty-four hours after John Kelly's visit, I was sitting in the Bronco trying to tune in WBLM, The Blimp, 102.9 in Portland. The signal was staticky, blocked by the hills around the lake. It came and went. Mick Jagger doing his white-boy rap about *rats on the West Side, bedbugs uptown*. While my fingers toyed with the dial, my eyes took in the view from the windshield: the shore access road that sloped downhill and disappeared into the water. This was a boat launch where, in summer, the sports put in their Sunfishes and Whalers. But it looked like an entrance ramp to an underwater road, a shortcut along the lake bed that would reemerge on the opposite shore. My attention wandered down this road and out to the water. The surface rippled when the wind kicked up, then, when the wind died, it fell smooth again, like a tablecloth skimmed by the palm of an invisible hand. It was in one of these windless moments that a pale yellow patch appeared. I tried to fix on the spot, but the wind riffled the surface again and the yellow object disappeared. I switched off the radio and stared, chin resting on the steering wheel. But it was no good. The lake surface would not come clear.

I walked down to the edge. The water sploshed against the shore. In the shallows, a fish basked in the sun. He was eighteen inches long, dark, with black leopard spots on his back. He lolled, all fat and lazy, waiting for winter. I could have reached in and grabbed him if I'd wanted to. A few yards beyond the fish, a white rock jutted from the sand like a bone. Then the water went black.

I stood there for some time, trying to see the hidden picture. It was important to be careful here, to get it right. I had to be sure I could see the object clearly before I went any further. The yellow spot appeared occasionally, opaque and formless. A rock maybe? It was some time before the lake decided to open up and show it to me clearly—the back end of a Honda, dull yellow, with a Massachusetts plate, ten or fifteen feet from shore.

Dick Ginoux managed to drift above the submerged car in a little rowboat and hook it with a thick, frayed rope. We hitched the rope to the rear tow ball of the Bronco, but, filled with water, the Honda was heavy as cement. The two vehicles pulled against each other in a tug of war. The Bronco strained. Its wheels spun on the sand and pine needles before it finally gained purchase and the two began to move in tandem away from the lake. The Honda surfaced about eight or ten feet from the bank and rolled backward. Water cascaded from the open windows. At the Bronco's wheel, I dragged the car all the way out until it sat on the access road, then hurried around to block the wheels before gravity pulled it back into the lake.

The Honda continued to shed water. The surface level in the passenger compartment dropped to the windowsills, then the water sought out leaks in the door seals and in the floor. Rivulets squirted through the bottoms of the doors and from the undercarriage. The draining slowed, however, so that the steering wheel remained half submerged. Black mud and lake grass clotted the exterior.

Dick studied the pool of water still trapped in the car and remarked, "Look at that seal. These Japanese cars are something."

"Dick, they make these in Ohio," I informed him.

"Still Japanese."

Dick pulled open the driver's door, releasing a wave of water over his shoes. He stamped around, angry.

Inside the car, a lawyer's boxy trial case was wedged in the foot well behind the driver's seat. I pulled it out and held it sideways so the water could run out of it, then set it down on the back gate of the Bronco. The case was filled with manila folders.

Dick looked over my shoulder. "You better pull them out yourself, Chief," he told me. With Dick, it was always *Chief* when he wanted me to do something, *Ben* when he wanted to do it himself.

I peeled the fattest folder away from the others and extracted it. The beige cardboard was sopped. I laid it on the carpeted back gate, gently, like a relic. On the front cover, a form was printed with blanks for *Defendant, DOB, SSN, Address, Charge(s), Bail, Next Date,* and *Comments.* It was rubber-stamped SPECIAL INVESTIGATIONS UNIT. The handwriting on the file was barely legible, since much of the ink had dissolved.

Dick squinted to read the defendant's name out loud: "Gerald McNeese, a.k.a. 'G,' a.k.a. G-Money, a.k.a. G-Mac. That's a lot of names. He ought to pick one and stick with it." In a section marked *Codefendants,* Dick read out more names: "Harold Braxton. June Veris." He added, "You figure that's a man or a woman, June Veris?" Next to each name were the handwritten initials *MP,* circled. In large print at the top of the file someone had written, *Trial Date: 10–6.*

The papers inside the folder were mostly illegible. These included Boston Police incident-report forms, which were printed on pink paper, and a few yellow legal sheets. In a subfile marked *Opening* were several soaked yellow pages. Most of the ink on these pages had rinsed off, but you could make out a few faint words: *Echo Park, heroin.* The signature on court pleadings was legible too; it looked like *Danzig.* The notes Robert Danziger left on the cardboard file folder had held up better. One read clearly, *Call Gittens re. Where is Ray Rat?* On the inside cover was a handwritten organizational chart:

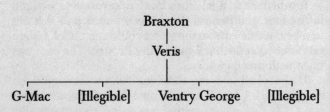

Braxton
|
Veris
|
G-Mac   [Illegible]   Ventry George   [Illegible]

A series of arrows pointed from G-Mac to Veris to Braxton. That was apparently the route Danziger intended to follow: straight to the top.

The keys to the Honda were still in the ignition, still attached to a two-inch ring holding ten or fifteen other keys. Driver's seat pushed as far back as it would go, although Danziger could not have been more than five-ten. Other flotsam in the car: a pair of running shoes, an oversize road atlas, a suitcase.

Dick ran the plate. It came back to Robert M. Danziger of West Roxbury, Massachusetts. He ran the names on Danziger's folder through the NCIC computer too. The computer reported a substantial record for Harold Braxton, including a conviction for assault with intent to murder (five to seven years at MCI–Cedar Junction) and a dismissal on a charge of first-degree murder. Nothing on the other names. Of course, the NCIC computer was notoriously unreliable; submit the same suspect's name ten times and you could get ten different results. I would have to call Boston to confirm the criminal records.

My eye was drawn to two stickers on Danziger's back bumper. One was for a political campaign. Its message was simple enough: ANDREW LOWERY, DISTRICT ATTORNEY. The other featured the crest of the Boston Police Patrolmen's Association and the motto I SUPPORT THE BOSTON POLICE.

Of course, I ought to have turned all this over to the Game-Show Hosts. The car, the files, everything. It was their case, not mine. But I decided to keep them to myself for a little while. In the last twenty-four hours, my father's command had taken root. Or perhaps it was my idea—in a sense, this *was* my case. I could not simply do nothing. I had a duty. Like it or not, I would have to see this through.

10

By a little pond near Sebago, John Kelly's cottage hid in the selvage of the forest, with unpainted cedar shingles that mimicked the brown setting, tree bark and a bristly carpet of pine needles. The structure might have disappeared altogether into the piney gloom, camouflaged like a green toad on a green leaf, if not for Kelly's white Toyota and a satellite dish—the state flower of Maine—out front. I drove past the house twice before I found it, and when I did finally track it down, it occurred to me that this hermit's cave was not a fit home for Kelly, to whom I'd already ascribed any number of heroic characteristics. It seemed to represent a sort of failure on his part—a fatigue of the spirit, a retreat from the world.

I hauled Danziger's briefcase, still heavy with lake water, to the front door. A window at my right was bearded with pollen and dust. I tried to peek in and still had not got around to knocking when Kelly came around the side of the cottage. He held a newspaper rolled into a tube.

"Chief Truman," he said.

"Can I show you something, Mr. Kelly?"

"Depends what it is."

I held up the ruined bag. "Danziger's briefcase."

"Hmm."

"Want to have a look?"

"No."

"Really?"

"Why do I have this feeling you're about to convert me into a witness, Ben Truman? I'd rather not be."

"No, I—"

"Where did you get that bag, anyway?"

"We found Danziger's car. It was sunk in the lake. The bag was inside."

"And now you're just carrying it around? Please tell me you didn't go rummaging around inside it."

I did not answer.

Kelly kneaded the hollows of his cheeks then his jaw with one long-fingered hand, a gesture of checked frustration. He looked like a father whose son has just cracked up the family car.

"I know where the case is going. I have a lead."

"A lead. May I make a suggestion, Ben Truman? Go back to Ver-*sigh*—"

"Ver-*sales*."

"Go back to Ver-*sales*, call the AG, tell him you found Danziger's briefcase and car and he should send somebody over to pick them up."

"Don't you want to know what we found?"

"No. I'll read about it in the newspaper, thank you."

"I've already handled the thing. Whatever damage I might've done is already done."

He shook his head no. "I thought this wasn't your case."

"It's not."

"So you're playing detective."

"No, just an interested observer."

"And what do you intend to do now, as an interested observer?"

"I'm going to Boston."

"To observe."

"To stay informed, yes. I have to. The murder happened in my town. I have a responsibility."

Kelly gave me an indulgent paternal smile. He swung the door open. "Perhaps we'd better have a chat, Ben Truman."

Inside, the rooms were furnished with delicate pieces, all spindle legs and needlework pillows and flowery chintz. I assumed his wife had picked them out many years before. There were no signs of a wife now, though. Kelly appeared to live here alone, still sitting on his wife's furniture. I tried, as guests invariably do, to gain some glimpse of my host's inner life from the belongings on display, but Kelly wasn't giving much away. There were very few pictures and no books at all in the living room where we settled. Kelly did have a collection of old vinyl LPs. His tastes ran toward big bands and mainstream jazz: Bing Crosby, lots of Sinatra, Dean Martin, Perry Como, Louis Prima, Louis Armstrong, with a few Aretha Franklins thrown in. There were two photos on a low chest. An older, faded picture showed a little girl, one of those grade-school portraits with a marbled blue sheet for a backdrop. The girl in the picture was strikingly pale. Her dark hair draped around her face like a cowl. She stared out with a grave expression. The newer photo showed a woman in her early thirties, pretty in a stern, dark-browed way.

"Is this your daughter?" I gestured to the photos.

"Daughters. That's Caroline on the right. And this"—he picked up the older photo, dragged the top of the frame across his shirt to dust it, then replaced it—"this is Theresa Rose. She passed away."

"Jesus, I'm sorry."

"It was a long time ago."

Kelly poured himself a tumbler of brown whiskey. He offered me one, which I refused. He gave it to me anyway. "Take it," he said. "It sounds like you need it." I sipped, and struggled to keep a poker face while the whiskey scalded its way down my throat.

"Now, what are you talking about, Ben?"

From the briefcase I pulled out the file on Gerald McNeese and laid it on the coffee table. The file was corrugated from soaking in the lake. It looked like a napoleon.

"Danziger was getting ready to prosecute this guy Gerald McNeese, or G-Mac, whatever his name is. But that was just the start. Really Danziger was going after Braxton. He was starting with one of the low-level guys in Braxton's gang, then he was going to work his way up the ladder to Braxton. He drew this chart here. Look."

Kelly made a skeptical grimace, as if I were a kook insisting that the end of the world was nigh. "Chief Truman, am I correct in assuming you've never handled a case like this before?"

"Yes. Well—yes."

"What is the most serious case you've had?"

"I had a mayhem once."

"Mayhem."

"It was a fight. Joe Beaulieu bit off Lenny Kennett's pinky finger. They were drunk. It never got to trial. Lenny refused to testify. Joe was a friend, and there was a rumor he paid Lenny a fair price for the finger—"

Kelly held up his hand. He got the picture.

"Look, I know I'm a little green. But I do have this job. In my town I'm the chief, for better or worse. I'm the only one they've got. I didn't choose this."

"You're green as grass," he said, as much to himself as to me.

"Okay, well, thank you, I guess."

"There are hundreds of cops already working this case. You do know that, don't you?"

He glanced at the newspaper he'd been carrying, the *Boston Herald,* then went to the breakfast table for the other morning papers, which he tossed one by one on the coffee table in front of me. *The Boston Globe* led with the story on page one. A two-column headline read,

SEARCH FOR PROSECUTOR'S SLAYER CONTINUES. A color photo showed Danziger smiling behind his red mustache and owlish glasses. The caption identified him as *Robert Danziger, led anti-gang unit.* The *Herald,* Boston's bad-boy tabloid, was more histrionic. It had a one-word banner headline, DRAGNET!, over a photo of detectives in BPD windbreakers questioning a group of black teenagers on a street corner. A local paper, the *Portland Press Herald,* and even *The New York Times* had picked up the story.

But the notion of following the case to Boston seemed logical, even inevitable. My response to the newspapers was a mute shrug and a manful sip of whiskey.

"So what do you want from me?" Kelly asked.

"I thought maybe you'd like to come along."

"To Boston?"

I nodded.

"I told you, I'm retired."

"Yes, but you knew Danziger. Besides, you said yourself, a retired cop is still a cop. You said you never stop being a cop."

"Yes, but even cops get old."

"You could teach me. You could help me."

"Help you what?"

"Help me follow the case. Stay informed. Maybe get involved somehow if we can."

Kelly shook his head and paced with his drink. He wandered over to the chest, where the photo of the dark-haired girl stared back at him with a somber expression. "Ben, look at me. I'm sixty-six years old. I came up here just to get away from this bullshit." He turned for assistance to the little girl in the photo, the late Theresa Rose Kelly. She seemed to shake her head at me too. "I'm sorry," he said finally.

"Me too."

"You'll be alright, Ben Truman. You're a good cop, deep down."

"I'm not really a cop at all. It's just a job."

"That's how it always starts."

The next morning, Kelly knocked and opened the stationhouse door, tentative and polite, wearing his ever-present flannel jacket and scally cap. "Can I have a word with you, Chief Truman?" He glanced at Dick, who was working a crossword puzzle at the dispatcher's desk. "Alone?"

I slipped on my jacket, and Kelly and I walked down Central Street. He produced a wooden billy club, which he had tucked in his belt. It was coffee brown with a leather wrist strap. Every inch of the wood was nicked and scratched. As we walked, Kelly twirled the thing absentmindedly. There seemed to be two ways to do this: a propeller sort of motion directly in front of the belt buckle; or at the hip, like a floozy spinning her feather boa. Kelly executed both maneuvers with incredible dexterity. Who knows how many years of practice he'd had, how many beats he'd walked with that truncheon. Our steps fell in with the rhythm of it—*spin, slap! spin, slap!*—and I understood why they call it "walking a beat."

"Did they give you that thing at Central Casting?"

"Standard issue, Ben Truman. Every good policeman carries one." He gave me a once-over, ascertained that I was not carrying one, and made a face.

"Well, you can put it away. I don't think you'll need to whack anyone with a billy club in this town."

"It's called a nightstick. And the point is not to whack anyone. It's part of the show." *Spin, slap.* "People have certain expectations. That's why doctors wear white coats."

"So you've never whacked anyone with that thing?"

"I didn't say that. I said the point of carrying a nightstick is to *not* use it. If you carry it right, you'll never have to."

"Never?"

"Never."

"Then how did all those dents get there?"

"Okay, almost never. Still, it's best not to." He inspected the truncheon briefly, as if he'd never noticed all the dents and dings in it. "If you are going to be a cop, Ben Truman, you can either be a fighter or a talker. I have always been a talker."

We strolled along. From the window of the Owl, Phil Lamphier stared out at us. He was holding a coffeepot, swirling the coffee in the glass bulb. Hard to know what Phil made of the sight—a very tall stranger spinning a cop's nightstick, walking a beat in a town that had never seen a beat cop; and me, hands in pockets, listening intently. I could imagine Phil passing along the intelligence over the lunch counter: "Ayuh, saw Ben walking with a tall fella this morning, 'round nine-thirty 'twas . . ." In the hothouse atmosphere of those days, any rumor that concerned the body in the cabin was snapped up and analyzed ad nauseam. I waved to Phil, and he lifted the coffeepot toward me in a sort of salute.

"What does a cop do," Kelly asked, "in a place like this?"

"Wait, mostly."

"Wait for what?"

"For something to happen. Something different, I mean."

"So how long have you been waiting?"

"Three years, give or take."

"You've only been a cop three years and already you're the chief?"

"They weren't exactly standing in line for the job."

Kelly stooped to pick up a stray piece of paper, slipped it into his back pocket, then resumed his twirling, *spin, slap!* "You know, when I started out, there was a sergeant in my precinct named Leo Stapleton. Leo was my first watch commander. He introduced me around, kept me out of trouble, showed me how things worked. Do you have anyone like that, a guy like Leo Stapleton?"

"No." It occurred to me that I did have Dick Ginoux and my father. "Definitely not."

"So this idea about going down to Boston, you came up with that on your own. You haven't discussed it with anyone."

"Right."

"Boy-o, do you have any idea what you're getting into?"

"I'm not sure what you're asking."

He stopped and poked me in the sternum with the nightstick. "What I'm asking is, do you know what it means to tangle with a guy like Braxton? Do you know what's involved? Chief Truman, have you ever put physical pressure on a suspect?"

" 'Physical pressure'?"

"Yes. Have you used physical pressure to obtain information?"

"No! Of course not."

"Of course not? What if it were the only way to protect innocent life? Let's say there was a bomb, and the suspect knew where the bomb was planted. Would you use force to make him talk, knowing it would save thousands of innocent people?"

"I don't know. Maybe."

"Maybe. Well, would you endanger an innocent person in order to get a conviction?"

"What?"

"Would you force a witness to testify, knowing his life would be in danger if he did so, but also knowing that a conviction might save many lives?"

"I don't know. I never—"

"Well, you'd better start thinking about it, Chief Truman, if you want to get a guy like Braxton. You'd better think about what you're willing to do." Kelly gave me a long look.

He withdrew the nightstick from my chest. "Because

there's no other way. You can't be a good cop and obey all the rules. That's the dirty little secret."

We started walking again.

"Good cops do bad things for good reasons. Bad cops do bad things for bad reasons. Most cops want to be good, that's the truth. But it takes experience to know how. Do you see what I'm getting at?"

"You're saying I don't have the experience to work this case. But all I want to do is observe—"

"I'm saying, if you get mixed up in it, you'll probably get hurt. Or worse."

"When you say *worse*—" Another of Kelly's looks. "Ah."

We went on walking.

"Chief Truman, I came here to tell you what Leo Stapleton would have told me: Don't be in such a hurry to meet the Harold Braxtons of the world. They'll come to you when the time is right."

"In a town like this, I'm more likely to meet a woolly mammoth than a Harold Braxton. I need to do this. I need to. You'll have to trust me on that."

Kelly stopped to look up at the sky. It was a clear-blue fall day. He puffed out his cheeks, then released a long sigh. "Well," he concluded, "two dead boys is enough."

He was referring to Braxton's police victims, Danziger and the narcotics officer Artie Trudell. At the time, they were the only two we knew about.

There is no official oath for police officers in Versailles, Maine, so I had to make up some malarkey about "faithfully protecting and serving the people" of the town "so help you God." It fell somewhere between the presidential oath of office and the Boy Scouts oath, but it did the trick. John Kelly, age sixty-six, was now the junior officer in the Versailles Police Department.

We decided to leave first thing Monday morning. That gave me a couple of days to make arrangements and pack my car, an old Saab 900 with a crack in the steering rack and a number of cancerous rust stains. I told everyone where I was going, although I described the journey in the sunniest possible way. I did not mention the Mission Posse or the gunshots to the eye. I was just going down to the city to observe, to keep tabs on the case. No danger 't'all. Diane and Phil and the rest all pretended to understand and believe me, and in the shadow conversation of things unsaid—the habitual language of Maine Yankees—I understood that they knew enough about Harold Braxton anyway and were worried for me.

I left Dick Ginoux in charge of the station while I was gone. It was not an ideal choice. Dick was the kind of guy who would prop his eyeglasses on his forehead then spend the better part of an afternoon looking for them. But he was the senior man in the department, and besides, there were no Eliot Nesses among the other candidates.

The morning of my departure, my father got up early to see me off. "I know why you're doing this," he told me. "I'm not so old I don't understand what you're doing. Just you be careful." His beard was growing in. It was almost pure white. "Well, you'd best get going, Ben. It's a long ride." I hugged him. His body was almost exactly the size of my own now, even a little smaller. It came as a surprise. I still thought he was a giant. He endured the hug as long as could be expected. "Look at us," he said, pulling away, "couple of fruitcakes."

As for me, I had an inchoate sense that my life was veering, that from now on events—my personal history—would move along a different vector. For the second time in my life, I was getting out. I was leaving Versailles behind.

In a way, I'd already left—the moment I first learned of that dead man by the lake.

PART TWO

"What have we better than a blind guess to show that the criminal law in its present form does more good than harm? . . . Do we deal with criminals on proper principles?"

Oliver Wendell Holmes

11

In the year and a half I lived in Boston as a graduate student, I never went to Mission Flats, not once. The neighborhood was mentioned often enough around BU. The savvier students, native Bostonians especially, referred to it in a smirky, knowing way, but always with fearful reverence. The name Mission Flats was shorthand for them. It meant all the things dreaded by city dwellers: a place where one would not want to get lost on a dark night, a place where stolen cars turned up abandoned, where stray bullets passed through kitchen windows, a place to score drugs (if you were so inclined). But for all the talk, few of them had actually seen it. I suppose every city has its isolated, run-down districts. Still, it was surprising how few Bostonians—white Bostonians especially—had ever been to Mission Flats. To them, it was as remote as the Gobi Desert. To be fair, there is no real reason to visit the Flats unless you live or work there. The neighborhood is small. There are no shops or sights. The only institution of any distinction is the New England Presbyterian Hospital, which found itself marooned in the Flats when the tide of wealth receded in the 1930s, '40s, and '50s. Even the picturesque

features for which Mission Flats is named have been
erased; there is no longer a mission or a flat there. The
mission, where John Eliot preached Christianity to the
Indians in the seventeenth century, vanished long ago.
And the flats—a marshy, pestilential fen surrounding the
Little Muddy River—had already been drained and
filled by 1900. The district is adjacent to nowhere and on
the way to nowhere, dangling beneath Franklin Park like
a rotten pear. It exists in near-perfect isolation from the
rest of the city, a sort of blighted Brigadoon. But it had
taken up a spot in the ether of the imagination, especially among white suburbanites who knew nothing
about Mission Flats except that they did not ever want to
be there.

Kelly and I reached the eastern edge of the Flats
shortly before noon. "You want to look around a little?"
he offered, and as I drove, he directed me down a broad
avenue called Franklin Street. Here the sidewalk was
lined with the same red-brick row houses that fill the
Back Bay and the South End. Proceeding north, though,
the street wall began to falter. Burned-out and abandoned buildings cropped up between the occupied ones.
Here and there a tenement would simply have vanished,
leaving a gap between the rough interior walls of the adjacent buildings. These vacant lots were strewn with
stones and bricks. Eventually the row houses gave way
to larger apartment buildings, then the desolate Grove
Park housing project, then a commercial strip: auto-
body shops, check-cashing services, convenience stores,
tow lots.

"The tour buses don't get out here much," Kelly remarked dryly.

We turned off Franklin Street into a maze of side
streets with tranquil names, Orchard Street, Amherst
Street, Willow Street. The apartment buildings fell away
and one-, two-, and three-family homes lined the sidewalks. Cracked driveways, sagging porches, peeled
paint, even a few broken windows. The well-kept houses

served only to highlight the decay of the surrounding ones. Yet for all that decay, on a sunny autumn day the neighborhood did not look especially threatening. Everywhere I looked, there seemed to be cheery details: a milk crate nailed to a phone pole as a makeshift basketball hoop, flower boxes, little girls skipping rope. This was no underworld, just poor. I had seen poverty before. There is no shortage of dirt-poor swamp Yankees and Québécois in Acadia County. I imagined people here felt the same sense of diffident yearning. Poor is poor.

We emerged from the winding side streets and Kelly announced, "This is Mission Ave."

(Bostonians reflexively shorten the word *avenue* to *ave.* A New Yorker sees the abbreviation *5th Ave.* and says "Fifth Avenue"; a Bostonian sees *Massachusetts Avenue* and says "Mass Ave." I don't know why. In any event, in Boston the road is generally referred to as Mission Ave.)

The main artery through the Flats was a wasteland. Looking north, Mission Avenue was a corridor of empty lots strewn with rubble and garbage. Tenements stood here and there, listing like punch-drunk boxers. The pediments above each door had been stripped away along with any brass or metal trim, drainpipes, mail slots, street numbers—anything that could plausibly be carried off and sold. Someone had erected a chain-link fence around one of these buildings to define a sort of yard; scumbles of garbage were caught in it like fish in a drift net.

"These row houses used to stretch for miles," Kelly said. "Used to be a nice place. Italians lived here, Irish, Jews. They all got out."

We passed the Winthrop Village housing project, a cluster of concrete bunkers set in a landscaped park. A Boston Housing Authority Police cruiser sat idling near the entrance, and the cop, an enormous black guy with a badass goatee and wraparound shades, watched us drive past.

Kelly pointed to graffiti, the same insignia recurring

over and over: two interlocking letters, MP, artlessly spray-painted in childish lettering. "Braxton's crew," Kelly said. "Mission Posse." The Posse had tagged everything: MP on telephone poles, MP on sidewalks, they'd even painted over street signs with it.

"Pull in here, Ben Truman." Kelly was pointing at a little market called Mal's. "I want to use the phone."

Kelly disappeared into the store, and after flipping through the radio stations for a minute, I decided to get out of the car, take in the sunshine and the view. There was not much to look at. The oatmeal shade of the sidewalk nearly matched Mal's storefront. Even the signs in the window had been bleached by the sun. I stood on the sidewalk, crossing and uncrossing my arms, leaning and unleaning against a parking meter.

People stared. A kid hanging in a doorway, sagging against the doorjamb like an empty set of clothes. An overweight woman in Adidas shower sandals. Were they staring? What were they staring at? Mine was the only white face on the street—was that enough to draw attention?

The kid draped in the doorway roused himself to approach me. His face was the color of caramel, almost as fair as my own. He wore new-out-of-the-box white sneakers and a loose hockey-style shirt that hung off his bony shoulders.

A second kid joined him. A huge, plump kid I had not noticed before. There was a cretinous quality about him. He had narrow eyes incised into a bloated, doughy face.

"What are you waiting for?" the first kid said.

"Just waiting on a friend. He's inside."

The kid studied me, as if my answer were suspicious.

"This is a nice car," the slit-eyed guy said.

The first kid was still staring at me. "You got any money?"

"No."

"We need some money to go to the store."

"Sorry."

"You lost?"

"No. I told you, my friend is in the store."

"All we need is like a dollar," said Slit Eyes.

"I told you—"

"Come on, a *dollar*?"

I gave them a one-dollar bill.

"Thought you didn't have any money."

"I didn't say that. I said I wasn't giving you any."

"Only now you did. You gave us some."

"So?"

"So, a dollar? That's like, why don't you just give us a fuckin' penny?" The skinny kid watched me for a reaction. "Come on, you got a whole walletful. I just seen it. We need it to go to the store."

"No. Sorry."

"We need to get something to eat."

"Yeah," agreed Slit Eyes, "something to eat."

"I'm not giving you any more."

"Why not? I told you, we need it."

I shook my head. Maybe it was time to announce that I was a cop. But these were just kids, it was under control. Besides, I was not a cop here. I was outside my jurisdiction, I had no police powers. Just another tourist. "I gave you a buck, fellas. That's all you're gonna get."

Slit Eyes edged beside me. "But I just seen your wallet." He was taller and heavier than me. His eyelids squeezed tight as clams.

"Come on," the first kid wheedled, "just help us out."

He stepped toward me, not aggressively—or maybe it was aggressively, I'm still not sure. I raised my hand to hold him away. My five fingertips pressed lightly on his breastbone.

"Hey, don't touch me!" the skinny kid said softly. "You don't want to get physical."

"I'm not getting phys—"

Slit Eyes cut me off: "Hey, yo, don't go getting physical. There's no need."

"Look, you asked for a buck, I gave it to you."

"Yeah," the skinny kid said, "but now you went and started getting physical. What's up with that?"

"I didn't get physical."

"Have I disrespected you?"

"No."

"No, we're just talking here. I just asked you for some help. How come you're all mad?"

"I'm not mad." I pulled my hand back down. "I'm asking you nicely now, respectfully: Step back."

"It's a public sidewalk. You think you can tell me where to go just 'cause I asked you for help? It's like that? I got to step back because you gave me a *whole dollar*?"

"I didn't say that."

"You thought it. I can see."

"I didn't think anything."

"Yes, you did." The skinny kid reached out and tapped my front pants pocket with his knuckles, apparently to feel my wallet.

I brushed his hand away, gently. "Don't touch me."

"Hey! I told you, you don't have to push. I'm just talking to you."

Kelly emerged from the little market. He glanced at the three of us, then said, in a peremptory way, "Come on, Ben, we don't have time to fool around. I want to see my daughter." He brushed between us and climbed into the passenger seat. "Well? Let's go."

I stepped around the two kids without a word, and they offered not a word to me.

"It's like another country," I said in the car, but Kelly did not respond, and saying it did not dispel my uneasiness.

12

Mission Flats District Court, First Session.

By 12:45, Judge Hilton Bell was no longer sitting at the judge's bench but pacing behind it, his black robe unzipped to the navel. The judge had been processing arraignments since nine o'clock sharp, and still his courtroom was packed. There were occasional shouts of protest from the holding cells in the basement; they, too, were still crowded.

I sat on a front bench, wedged between an armrest and a young woman who smelled, not unpleasantly, of Dune perfume and armpit. For reasons I can't begin to explain, this woman clutched a plastic baggie containing dark curls of what appeared to be human hair.

(John Kelly had the good sense to avoid the courtroom. He waited outside on the street, where it was cooler.)

Judge Bell looked out over the audience, apparently considering his plight. The judge was quite literally overheating. Somewhere in the intestines of the courthouse, an ancient furnace was huffing hot air into the first-session courtroom, where the temperature was already near eighty oxygenless degrees, and the goddamn

Boston police had placed the entire population of the city under arrest, and here they all were, these huddled masses, turning Judge Bell's courtroom into a great sweating steerage compartment, exhaling more and more of their steamy vapor toward the judge's bench, a sirocco of unminty breath. The judge fiddled with his bow tie. He looked up at the ceiling for heavenly assistance. The audience looked up along with him, but all we saw were water stains.

Then the pensive moment was over and it was back to work.

"Next case!" Judge Bell bellowed.

"Number ninety-seven dash seven-seven-eight-eight," the clerk read out. "Commonwealth v. Gerald McNeese the Third, also known as G also known as G-Mac also known as G-Money also known as Trey McNeese."

"Custody!" the clerk sang.

"Custody!" echoed one of the court officers.

By now the audience had learned the drill, so like spectators at a tennis match we right-faced in unison toward a rectangular cutout in the wall. On the other side of this glassless window were the arrests from the previous weekend who had not posted bail. They crowded together, visible from the waist up like puppets in a shadow box. The men shuffled about until one was able to squeeze to the front and wordlessly identify himself as Gerald McNeese.

"Commonwealth!" the judge said.

A young assistant DA riffled through his files. The kid's face was sweat-shiny from the heat. Two round coins of red flushed his cheeks. At length, he pulled out an empty file folder and held it open for the judge to see. "Your Honor, I don't have anything on this one. It's Ms. Kelly's case."

The clerk rolled his eyes.

Judge Bell shook his head. It was hopeless. "So where is she?"

The kid made a face. *Beats me.*

"Well?"

"I don't know, Your Honor."

"Why don't you know?"

"Um, I don't know . . . why . . . I don't know."

The kid could not have been more than a year or two out of law school. Now here he was, reddening in the heat of Mission Flats District Court, buried in files, no doubt counting the days till his tour of duty was up and he would be transferred somewhere—anywhere—else.

"You don't know why you don't know?"

"I don't— I don't know. Your Honor."

"Next case!"

There followed a few desultory arraignments on charges that, even to me, seemed petty: possession of marijuana, disorderly, simple A&B. With each arraignment, the audience gave a little respiratory heave of relief as the defendant and his supporters were exhaled from the courtroom. Each time, though, the void was filled by others. They pushed in from the hallway, and the benches were squeezed tight, the room repressurized.

"Call the McNeese case again." The judge was smoldering.

"Your Honor, I still have not heard from Ms. Kelly."

"Then turn around and tell *them.*"

"Tell who?"

"Turn around and explain to all these people why you're unprepared, why you're wasting everyone's time."

"Your Honor?"

"Turn around, Mr. Prosecutor." The judge swept his arm toward us, the groundlings in our damp shirts. "Tell it to them, not me."

The kid turned slowly, penitently. The red stains on his cheeks seeped over his ears and down his neck. He stood with a self-effacing turtle-backed slouch, scanning the crowd. But when his eyes reached the doorway, he managed a wan smile. He'd found an ally.

A woman entered the courtroom and pushed and excuse-me'd her way forward. She was dressed in a sleek black skirt suit. The jacket had a band collar with an open tab at the hollow of her neck. It looked a little like a priest's collar.

"Ms. Kelly!" the clerk blurted, and the entire court staff repeated "Ms. Kelly!" as if they'd all been trying to think of a forgotten name and it had just come back to them.

Caroline Kelly stood at the prosecutor's table next to the young ADA. Unseen by the judge, she put her hand on the kid's shoulder blade. The point was not so much to reassure him, I think, but to get him to stand up straight. She stretched her thumb to touch his spine just as a stern mother would press on the backbone of a slouching child. And it worked; the kid did stand a little straighter. Kelly left her thumb on his weakest vertebra for good measure, to prevent a relapse. She leaned over and whispered in the kid's ear, but loud enough for us in the front row to hear quite clearly, "Fuck him."

Those were the first words I ever heard Caroline Kelly say, *fuck him,* and she loaded a little extra sauce on the *fuck* to show she meant it.

From my seat in the front row, I studied the details of her posterior side. Her hair was dark brown, clipped loosely at the back of her neck with a gold clasp. The twill fabric of her skirt was slightly but discernibly taut around her hips, which were not thin. She stood with her anklebones nearly touching, so that a flame-shaped gap was formed between the inner curves of her calves. A soft leather briefcase slumped against her ankle when she set it down.

"Ms. Kelly," Judge Bell said. "The prodigal daughter."

She held out her free hand, palm up. The gesture said, *Here I am.*

"Was there something you'd like to share with the court?"

"Not really."

The judge regarded her. "Perhaps you can help us,

Ms. Kelly. We have a little mystery. Last weekend there were—Mr. Clerk, how many arrests?"

"Two-oh-five."

"Two hundred and five arrests. All for this one humble court. I believe that must be a new record."

"Congratulations, Your Honor."

"Enlighten me, Ms. Kelly. How do you explain such a burst of zealous law enforcement? Was there a sudden spike in the crime rate? These must be serious cases, I'm sure. Let's see"—he thumbed through the case files—"one marijuana cigarette; trespassing; ooh look here, defacing public property."

"Defacing public property is a crime, Your Honor."

"He urinated on the sidewalk!"

"Well, if it left a mark, then technically—"

The facial muscles around Judge Bell's jaw and temples tightened visibly. Evidently you just did not bother with these sorts of offenses in Mission Flats. They were clogging the docket; they were sand in the gears. It wasn't funny, dammit. "Ms. Kelly, is it the District Attorney's intention to punish a whole neighborhood for a single homicide?"

"I'm sure I don't know what you mean."

The judge told the young ADA to sit down. Before the kid moved, Kelly patted him twice on the shoulder blade, once again unseen by the judge.

"Call the case," the judge said.

"Number ninety-seven dash seven-seven-eight-eight," the clerk announced a second time. "Commonwealth v. Gerald McNeese the Third, also known as G also known as G-Mac also known as . . . whatever. Intimidation of a witness. Assault and battery. Assault with intent to maim. Assault and battery with a dangerous weapon, to wit, a sidewalk."

Beside me, the perfumed girl confided, "He hit somebody with a friggin' sidewalk? I don't *think* so."

"Assistant District Attorney Caroline Kelly for the Commonwealth. And Mr. Beck."

The players all stepped forward, forming a triangle before the judge.

Along with Kelly, there was Attorney Max Beck, who marched over to the hole in the wall. Beck had the look of a True Believer. His hair was a snarl of salt-and-pepper curls that tumbled over his collar. Plastic pens poked out of various pockets. His necktie was wrenched loose. The message in all this anti-fashion seemed to be: *Citizens, fighting Government Oppression is hard work! I have no time to worry about clothes!* It was pretty effective, actually.

The anchor of the triangle, however, was the defendant. Gerald McNeese radiated a sinewy, menacing aura. He leaned his forearms on the sill of the prisoners' dock and laced his fingers. The pose was so perfectly casual, so lazy-cool, you almost forgot there were handcuffs on his wrists. Tall and very thin, the points of McNeese's clavicles protruded under his shirt. His head was shaved, revealing a lumpy cranium.

At the prisoners' dock, Max Beck laid his hand on McNeese's forearm—*Fight the power!*—but McNeese pulled his arm away.

"Commonwealth," the judge said.

"Your Honor, this is the man Assistant DA Bob Danziger was preparing to prosecute when he was murdered."

"Objection!"

"Overruled. I want to hear this."

"But my client is not charged with killing Bob Danziger! This has nothing to do with Bob Danziger!"

The judge flippered his hands, brushing Beck off. "I said I'll hear it." Suddenly we were no longer talking about a garden-variety A&B. The mention of Danziger's name changed everything.

The prosecutor continued: "The defendant's gang—"

"Objection!"

"Overruled."

"But my client is not a member of any gang!"

"Yes, he is," Caroline Kelly assured. "And it goes to motive."

"Overruled," the judge said again.

"The defendant's gang, the Mission Posse," Kelly said, "was anxious that Danziger's case against this defendant not come to trial. Gerald McNeese is believed to be a close associate of Harold Braxton, the gang's leader. In the case Mr. Danziger was prosecuting, the key witness had gone into hiding, and the Posse could not locate him to . . . dissuade this witness from testifying."

"Objection! Pure speculation."

"Overruled. I'll hear it."

"Over the weekend," Caroline Kelly said, "Mr. McNeese—who is known as G-Mac on the street—finally did locate the informant, a man named Raymond Ratleff. The defendant was eager to convince Mr. Ratleff not to testify in Mr. Danziger's case. Around midnight on Saturday, the defendant was seen beating Mr. Ratleff on Stanwood Street in the Flats, smashing his face against the curbstone at least a half dozen times. According to one observer, it looked like the defendant was driving a nail into the sidewalk with Mr. Ratleff's head. Mr. Ratleff suffered broken bones in his face, including a fractured eye socket. He may lose the use of his right eye."

Gerald McNeese pursed his lips and sniffed disdainfully.

"Mr. Beck?"

"Your Honor, with all due respect to Ms. Kelly, the police have been sweeping through this neighborhood, rousting young African-American men for weeks because of the Danziger case."

Kelly glared as Beck dropped the firebombs of race and police misconduct, and her stare only darkened as Beck went on.

"—young black men in this neighborhood have been targeted—"

The prosecutor's eyes narrowed to a high-noon stare.

She seemed to be trying to vaporize poor Max Beck with those lasers.

"Mr. McNeese in particular has been targeted," Beck persisted. "He certainly has no link to the Danziger murder. That is just a smear against my client. The police have nothing, so they're conducting a witch hunt."

The judge groaned. "Not the witches, not today."

"My point is, this is just the kind of hysteria—"

"Mr. Beck, I have a crowded courtroom. We're not going to do the thing with the witches."

Beck made a face to show there was a valid point to be made about witch hunts, if only the judge would let him. "Judge, then I'll simply say there is no evidence against my client, there is no witness, therefore there's no possibility of a conviction. Under the circumstances, he must be released on personal recognizance."

"What about it, Ms. Kelly? Do you have a witness?"

"Yup."

"Can this witness make the I.D.?"

"Yup."

"And he's willing to go forward?"

Kelly hesitated. She tilted her head left and right, a gesture of uncertainty. "Your Honor, we believe the witness will go forward. We're requesting the defendant be held without bail."

Judge Bell frowned. The prosecutor was pushing a case with a reluctant witness—more likely, no witness at all—and putting the judge on the spot by tying the case to a more sensational one, the murder of ADA Bob Danziger. He studied a fanfolded printout of McNeese's record while his fingers worked the bow tie. At last he announced his decision: "Fifty thousand cash, five hundred thousand surety."

The clerk repeated this information to the defendant, but G-Mac did not seem to be listening. He was glaring at Caroline Kelly.

The judge had a message for the prosecutor too. "Ms.

Kelly," he said, "find your victim and indict this case, or I'll cut him loose."

When the McNeese arraignment had been wrapped up—with the droning incantation "Gerald McNeese, this honorable court has established bail in the amount of fifty thousand dollars cash or five hundred thousand dollars surety . . ."—the judge looked at his watch and announced, "Two o'clock," which signaled the lunch break. The atmosphere in the room instantly relaxed, in large part because Judge Bell himself departed. In the lawyers' area, ADAs and defense attorneys chatted like weary comrades-in-arms. Among the spectators, there was a riotous push toward the door.

Caroline Kelly lingered at the prosecutors' table for a few moments, arms folded, greeting some of the lawyers. It was interesting to watch her after seeing her photo in Kelly's cabin in Maine. I realized immediately that I had misimagined Caroline—that she was both more formidable and much, much prettier than I'd presumed. Which is not to say she was conventionally beautiful, because she was not, quite. She had not inherited her father's lanky frame or his narrow face. Caroline's features were more generous: broad, prominent cheekbones, dark brows separated by a twice-creased spandrel, a slightly too-soft chin. Her nose was prominent too, with an aristocratic little Bourbon bump at the bridge. Caroline's mouth was her only delicate feature. She had thin, expressive lips and small teeth, which she seemed reluctant to reveal. All of it fit somehow, and anyway the alchemy of attractiveness is more mysterious by far than a simple accounting of facial features; there are many more ways to be attractive than to be beautiful. What Caroline Kelly had that her photo did not and could not capture was *presence*. She had a worldly manner. She met events and people with a sidelong glance, with the left corner of her mouth curling upward like a cat's tail. That smirk suggested not the usual acid cynicism of young people, but a gentler and healthier sort of knowingness—a comfortable skepticism from which, one suspected, she did not exempt herself.

When I reached her, Caroline was chatting with Max Beck. Or, to be accurate, Beck was attempting to sustain a chat with her.

"How is your father?"

"Oh, he's unchanged, Max."

"Unchanged! Precisely!"

Caroline gave him one of those wiseguy smirks, then turned to me. She was not as tall as I am, but she managed to convey the impression of looking me level in the eye. "Ben Truman. What did you think of this place?"

"Have we met?"

"No."

I glanced down to see if I was wearing one of my uniform shirts, which identify me variously as *Officer Truman* and *Chief Truman*. I was not. "How did you . . . ?"

"My father called to say you'd be here. Weren't you with him?"

"Sorry. I'm an idiot."

Her lips unfastened into a lopsided Elvis-like smile. "So what did you make of all this?"

"It was interesting."

"Interesting!" Beck said, delighted again. "It is that!"

Caroline still had not unfolded her arms. "Max Beck, this is Benjamin Truman. Mr. Truman is the chief in Versailles, Maine."

Beck pumped my hand up and down. "We're all so upset about what happened."

I offered my hand to Caroline, and she gave it a dry, businesslike shake.

"Max, I should warn you, Mr. Truman came down to look into the Danziger case. You'd better hope he strikes out, otherwise you'll lose a few clients."

"Oh, I'm not too concerned." Beck gave me a look,

rolling his eyes up toward that inverted bird's nest of hair: *Typical Caroline*. Having imparted that mute warning, he drifted off.

"I don't think he thought that was funny."

"That's because it wasn't a joke."

Caroline gathered her papers into her briefcase. Up close, I could see there were undyed gray strands whipstitched through her dark hair. I wondered if she'd missed these while removing the other grays or if she'd decided to leave them. The latter seemed more likely. Caroline obviously paid too much attention to her appearance—she wore very light makeup, artfully applied, and her suit and shoes looked stylish and expensive—to have overlooked them.

"*Interesting* is a pretty noncommittal word, Chief Truman. Is that all you have to say about this place?"

"There was one thing. When you said . . . what you said to that DA, we could all hear you."

"So?"

"Well if we could hear you, the judge could probably hear you too."

"Good. He needed to hear it. You didn't expect that kid to say *fuck you* to a judge, did you?"

"Actually it hadn't occurred to me that anyone was going to say it."

"Maybe not out loud," she sighed.

"And the bit about the witch hunt?"

"Oh, that's just Beck. He tends to be dramatic."

"Is he right?"

"About the witches? No, we've got a pretty good handle on the witch problem." Another Elvis smile.

"I mean about the hysteria. Are the cops panicking, making crazy arrests?"

"Maybe. Probably. But in G-Mac's case, they got the right guy. We've got a victim who knows him personally and can make the I.D. There's no issue. McNeese is guilty and Beck knows it."

"He also seems to know McNeese is going to get off."

"Right. Well, there is one issue: whether the victim will show up to testify."

"What are the odds?"

She shrugged. "This case is less important than the Danziger investigation. I won't push the witness on this case; I may need him later. Besides, if McNeese gets off, we'll get him next time. Guys like him always come back. The statistics say 5 percent of the criminals commit 95 percent of the crimes. G-Mac's a five-percenter."

"Sounds like a witch to me."

"I think so too."

Outside the courthouse, a four-story cube at the southern end of Mission Ave., Caroline stood on the second step so she could look her father, John Kelly, in the eye. She kissed him, then wiped his cheek with her thumb to be sure she had not left a lipstick mark. It was a motherly, muscular gesture, but John Kelly seemed to enjoy it.

"Thanks for helping us, sweetheart."

"Don't thank me, Dad, thank Andrew Lowery. He's the DA. It was his call."

"But you gave him a nudge, I'm sure."

"Actually I told Lowery to send you right back where you came from."

"Now, why would you do a thing like that?"

"Because I don't want you screwing up my case."

"I thought it was Maine's case," I said.

"It is, but I'm coordinating the investigation here. Frankly, I don't understand why you can't just monitor the case from Maine, Chief Truman. But if you feel it's important to be part of it . . ." She shrugged. "Well, it's none of my business. I suppose you have your reasons. Anyway, DA Lowery says I should extend our full support, as a courtesy."

"Imagine," Kelly grumbled, "my own daughter needing to be told—"

"Dad, spare me. You're supposed to be retired."

"I'm too young to retire."

"You're sixty-seven years old."

"Sixty-six."

"It's old enough."

"For what?"

"Don't ask." She scribbled something on a scrap of paper and handed it to her father.

"Martin Gittens," he read. "Who's this?"

"A cop. He's been detailed to help you out, courtesy of Mr. Lowery."

"Very courteous, our Mr. Lowery. What do you know about this Gittens?"

"He's a detective. He's supposed to be wired up in Mission Flats. And he's been calling me begging for a piece of this case. Other than that, not much."

"Do you trust him?"

"Dad, it's like you always say: Trust everyone—"

"Trust everyone but cut the cards. Good girl."

"Thank you," I interjected, "for helping."

Caroline leveled an index finger at me. "Chief Truman, so help me, if anything happens to my father . . ." She didn't feel constrained to fill me in as to the precise consequences.

"Um, what if anything happens to *me*?"

She ignored me. "One more thing. You two have to promise to share whatever you find with me. If you hold anything back, and I mean even the smallest detail, the arrangement is off. You'll be on your own. That's straight from Lowery."

"Of course," Kelly *père* assured.

"Alright then." She kissed her father again and wiped his cheek again with the pad of her thumb. "You two make some team."

"Like Batman and Robin," John Kelly suggested.

She sniffed and made that sardonic Elvis-smile. "Yah, right."

13

The Grove Park housing project was a collection of six ugly, yellow-brick apartment buildings. They were arranged asymmetrically, like blocks dropped here and there by a careless giant.

We caught up to Martin Gittens on a rooftop. He was bending forward with his hands on his knees like a running back before the ball is snapped. At Gittens's feet, an African-American man in his mid-twenties sat splay-legged, his back slumped against the concrete parapet. He had a forlorn look on his face. "You can stop this any time, Michael," Gittens was telling him. "Just say the word. I'm not gonna make you do anything you don't want to do." The man just sat there, in a daze. Gittens hunched over him, waiting for a response, then straightened and said, "Your call."

Nearby, a couple of plainclothes cops monitored the conversation. They seemed anxious to just get on with it already.

But Gittens was in no hurry. He came over and shook our hands. Martin Gittens was not an imposing guy. His face was unlined and pleasant, even bland. The forgettable face in the crowd. A receding hairline and prominent forehead—which together formed a headland, a tall forehead shaped like a sperm whale's brow—were Gittens's only irregular features. He wore khaki pants and sneakers. If not for the small nylon holster and badge on his belt, you might have taken him for an accountant or a high-school teacher, if you remarked him at all.

"This kid is getting ready to make a buy for us," Gittens said. "He's almost there."

"Should we come back?"

"Nah. This isn't a bad kid. He's just having a little crisis. He'll figure it out. Then we can talk." He gave us a knowing look, letting us in on the game. *You know how it works; you know the score.*

A few feet away, the kid let out a sigh. It seemed to take all his strength to look up at Gittens and say, "I can't do it."

Gittens went back to him. "Alright, Michael, no problem. If that's what you want."

"So what happens now?"

"Well, I'll file my report with the DA, see how they want to handle it. When they get around to it, they'll indict you. Couple of weeks maybe. They're busy. It's just a drug thing."

"I can't believe this shit."

Gittens nodded sympathetically.

"What would you do, Detective?"

"It doesn't matter what I would do. It's your life, Michael. I can't tell you what to do. I'm not your lawyer."

"Well guess what: My lawyer isn't here at this particular moment. Just tell me, what am I supposed to do?"

Gittens knelt beside him. "Look, I gave you this opportunity because I thought you deserved it. I don't see you in state prison, Michael, I really don't. But what am I gonna do? I've got a job to do, right? I can't just shitcan the thing without a reason. I need you to give me something in return. Tit for tat."

"Where will I do the time? Walpole?"

"No, Concord probably."

"What's Concord like?"

"What do you think, Michael? It's state time, it's bad."

The kid sagged against the wall, disconsolate. "I don't know how I got here. I really don't."

"You don't know how you got here?"

"No, I mean I *know*. But it was a fucking dime bag. What the fuck! Three years for a dime bag? Mother-*fucker*!"

"It wasn't a dime bag, Michael. It was sixteen grams."

"I didn't weigh the shit! I told you, it wasn't mine."

"Michael, you put yourself here. You should learn to take responsibility."

"I told you, I was just holding it."

"Holding it, selling it, putting it on a hot dog, whatever—if you have sixteen grams, that's trafficking, end of story. You have to own that."

The guy made a face. He wasn't up for the lecture.

"Look, Michael, you want to try and beat it? Go for it, take a chance. I'll be rooting for you. Hey, you never know, right? Maybe you'll walk."

"And if I don't?"

"It's a three-year minimum, and that's day-for-day—no parole, no good time, no work release, no nothing. You sit there. There's a war on drugs, maybe you haven't heard."

"I got two kids, Gittens, you know that. I can't go away for three years. I can't go away for three *days*. You got kids, Gittens?"

"Yeah, I've got kids."

"Then you know how it is."

"I'm offering you a way out, Michael."

"A way out with a fuckin' cap in my head."

"I told you, they'll never know who you are."

"They'll know."

"No. You won't be named in any of the reports; no one will ever name you in court. You have my word on that. What's between you and me stays between you and me. Have I ever broken my word to you?"

"They'll know."

"Not if everybody does their job."

The man breathed deep, considering his options. "This is the last one. I can't take no more of this shit."

"Last one, Michael."

"After this, I'm out."

"After this, you're out."

"What about the DA? What's he gonna do with my case?"

"There won't be any case. The DA doesn't have a case until I bring it to him. Until then, it's my case. This is between you and me, Michael. I'll take care of you. You know you can count on me."

"Truth?"

"Truth. The DA will never hear your name."

"Last time," Michael warned, relenting.

Gittens nodded. "Last time. Alright, you know the drill. Stand up, empty your pockets. Detective," he called to one of the plainclothes guys, "will you come witness this?"

The kid emptied his pockets and turned them inside out for good measure. He left his things in a tidy pile on the rubbery surface of the roof, then raised his hands and allowed Gittens to frisk him. Boredom registered on both their faces. The procedure had become routine for them. Gittens carefully copied down the serial numbers from two twenty-dollar bills and handed them to the kid with the advice, "Knockout, Michael, nothing else. Tell him it's got to be Knockout. And make sure the money goes to Veris himself. Big guy in the red FUBU shirt."

"I know who the motherfucker is."

"Alright, Michael. We'll be watching."

"That makes me feel much better," the kid sniffed, and he disappeared down the stairs.

Gittens invited us to watch. "Step right up, men. Showtime at the Apollo."

We moved to the edge of the roof, which overlooked Echo Park five stories below. Like so many things in Mission Flats, Echo Park was not what its name suggested, a rolling green meadow where sounds echoed off trees and hills. Instead, it was a crooked pie piece wedged into the joint where North Tremont Street branched off from Franklin Street. Gittens said the locals called it Hypo Park for the hypodermic needles found there. Inside were a few stringy trees and some park benches—the unfancy kind, green slats in concrete bases. A Y-shaped walkway connected the three corners of the park. Graffiti on the walkway read, *Fuck the PoPo, DeeZee,* the ubiquitous *MP,* and some markings I could not interpret.

Gittens looked down at this scene, rapt. He held a pair of binoculars, which he passed to me occasionally.

I mimicked his posture, craning slightly, forehead creased with concentration.

I tried to detect something more than a few kids hanging out in a ratty park. There wasn't much going on, though. A half dozen young guys—kids, all of them black, wearing baggy hip-hop styles—were draped over the benches. A few people came and went, loitering, talking, moving on. From all appearances, the Echo Park drug trade had shut down for the day.

"What's Knockout?" I asked Gittens.

"Heroin with some other garbage in it. It's been turning up the last few weeks. We had a kid die from it."

One of the cops with us muttered, "Come on, shithead."

"Give him a minute to get down the stairs," Gittens soothed. "Be patient."

Echo Park struck me as an indiscreet place for a drug market. There was nothing to hide behind, no privacy from the heavy traffic on Franklin Street. "Isn't this place a little . . . exposed? You can see everything."

Gittens shrugged. "It's not enough to see. We have to get the stuff, we have to catch them with the dope in their pockets, otherwise there's no case. And we can't get close enough for that. There are lookouts all up and down the block. You go down there, you'll hear them whistling signals to each other. It sounds like a birdcage."

A woman was entering the park now, at the corner closest to us, the narrow tip of the pie wedge. She was black, rail thin, with a knock-kneed walk and a rainbow-colored knit hat. A kid greeted her just inside the park. He seemed glad to see her, greeting her as an old friend, laughing, clasping her hand, pulling her close for a hug.

"That kid's a sweeper. His job is to steer the buyers to the right place. He'll hang out near the entrance to the park, ask you what you're looking for, figure out if you're a player or a cop or just someone walking through the park. If you're a buyer, he'll tell you to go sit on one of those benches and he'll give one of those whistle signals." Gittens whistled a little bird call, soft, under his breath, low-high-high-high.

The woman moved on. She sat on one of the benches next to a guy in a red FUBU baseball shirt.

"FUBU," Gittens said, "For Us, By Us. Those FUBU clothes went big-time and they started telling white kids it meant For U, By U." He shrugged. "That's June Veris in the red shirt. He's original MP. Used to run with Braxton when they were kids. Now Braxton just uses him as muscle."

June Veris had muscle to spare. Big guy with massive shoulders that tapered down to a narrow waist. Veris sat a level higher than the buyer, his butt on the backrest, feet on the seat of the green bench. He chatted with the woman for some time before she reached into her pocket and slapped her hand down into his. The gesture was a sort of exuberant handshake. From our position, you could not see any cash being passed. Then Veris disappeared and a kid walked toward the woman.

"That's the slider," Gittens narrated.

The slider sauntered right past the woman. There was a little seesaw in his walk, a flourish. It was a walk the kid probably practiced, checking himself out as he passed store windows. He dropped something in a garbage can and kept walking. When the woman retrieved it, the three guys who'd been so friendly with her a moment before were nowhere to be seen. They'd melted away to the edges of the park. She hurried out of the park with anxious, bird-like glances.

"The slider has the most dangerous job," Gittens said. "Nobody touches the dope but him. That way the risk to everyone else is minimized. Even if we catch the others, there's no case because there's no dope on them. Without an informant or an undercover buy, there's no way to tie the sweepers or anyone else to the drugs. But the slider has to carry the drugs on him, so if he's caught . . ."

There was a lull in the sliders' business.

"There's a stashpad around here somewhere," Gittens lectured to fill the downtime, "to replenish the sliders. The kitchen will be somewhere else. It moves around. We close one down, another one opens somewhere else. It's like Whack-a-Mole, you know that game? It'll never end."

"What about Braxton? What does he do?"

"Braxton designed all this. He runs this whole thing. If things were different, he'd have gone to Harvard Business School. As it is, he runs a damn good business. He doesn't need Harvard Business School. Harold's a player. He's a damn smart guy."

"And a murderer."

"Yeah, but it's not like that," Gittens said.

Our man Michael finally emerged. He moved casually between the buildings, entering at the near corner of the park.

This time I did not need Gittens's narration to follow the process. Michael was met by the same sweeper, who approached him tentatively. There were no smiles, no hugs. Presumably the sweeper did not know him, maybe even suspected he was a snitch. Whatever the reason, their chat took a little longer than the previous one. But the informant bluffed his way by the sweeper and made his way to a bench. Veris sat down next to him, easy to pick out in his cherry-red shirt, and it was Veris who actually took the cash. Gittens's two twenties, the serial numbers recorded, disappeared into his pocket. After the money was passed, less gracefully this time, Veris moved off. A slider walked past to drop a plastic envelope in a trash can for Michael to retrieve.

"Another satisfied customer," Gittens drawled as the informant quick-stepped out of the park.

Echo Park was quiet again. June Veris sat alone on his bench and soon was joined by another guy, who talked to him in an animated way. The sweeper loafed near the entrance awhile, then drifted back to his friends on the benches. Kids hanging out, nothing to do but yack with one another. If Gittens had not explained what I'd just seen, I wouldn't have recognized it as a drug sale at all.

Michael emerged on the roof again and the search procedure was repeated. He emptied his pockets to reveal no money and a little plastic envelope that had not been there when he left. The "controlled buy" was complete.

Gittens displayed the little opaque plastic square to me. There was a red boxing glove rubber-stamped on the package—Knockout.

"Send them," one of the cops urged Gittens. He was watching the park, apparently anxious that June Veris—the target of this whole operation—would leave or simply pass the marked twenties to someone else. If that happened, there would be no way to tie him to the drugs. It was essential the cops arrest Veris while he had the sting money in his pocket. "Let's go, Martin," the cop urged.

"Not yet," Gittens said.

"Let's go! Send them now!"

"I said, not yet."

We waited through several more purchases, maybe twenty or twenty-five minutes in all. At one point a white kid in a Volvo pulled up to the park. He had shaggy red hair and a goatee. The Volvo had a Yale sticker in the rear window. "Hello there, Skippy," Gittens muttered. Only after a handful of others had scored their drugs—that is, when it was no longer obvious that our informant was Michael—Gittens murmured into his walkie-talkie, "Okay, go."

Within seconds, four unmarked black cruisers converged on the park, pulling right up onto the curb to block the three gates. The kids in the park scattered. Cops ran after them, caught and tackled a few, disappeared down side streets chasing others. It was a joyful chaos.

As it turned out, Veris escaped. The operation failed. But as I think back on that day—even knowing, as I do, that Gittens probably expected Veris would escape, maybe even warned him of the raid—what I remember is that Gittens kept his word. He protected his informant. I remember, too, how it felt to watch that wonderful anarchy in the park, the riot of police and sliders all running, all shouting. From above, through binoculars. How I smiled. It was exhilarating. It was fun.

"Listen," Gittens told Kelly and me afterward, "the question isn't Who killed Danziger? Everybody knows who killed Danziger. The problem is What do you do about it? Nobody in this neighborhood will even talk about Harold Braxton, let alone testify against him.

"To tell you the truth, I don't know what Danziger thought he was doing. That case he brought against Gerald McNeese was an old beef, just stupid crackhead stuff. Ray Ratleff was a slider who came up short on a bundle the Posse gave him to sell, so McNeese tried to collect the debt. That's all there was to it. Ray probably did the coke himself, then he told McNeese he got robbed. Ray Rat's a pipehead. He's not a bad kid. I mean, I like Ray. But he's been on the pipe a long time, he just can't help himself. Harold shouldn't have trusted him with the stuff in the first place. It was his mistake, really."

We were in Echo Park, where the drug market was closed until all these cops decided to go home. The three of us sat on a bench as Gittens illuminated the secret history of Mission Flats. There was none of the wiseguy Boston accent in the detective's voice. He spoke in an adenoidal, Midwestern tone that matched his white sneakers and home-ironed khakis. The story he told was a different thing.

"Ray gets into a hole and the debt piles up. So now Braxton has to respond. He can't allow that kind of thing to go on, he's got a business to run. He can't just get ripped off and do nothing about it.

"So Harold sends out McNeese to square the thing away. But G-Mac was a bad choice. McNeese has killed guys for way less than what Ray Rat did, and Ray's basically harmless. It was like dropping a bomb on a mosquito. Maybe Braxton figured G-Mac would scare Ray Rat into paying, but Ray just didn't have the cash because, like I said, any money Ray gets goes straight into the pipe.

"Anyway, the only thing Ray has is this piece-of-crap Volkswagen Jetta. So one day G-Mac sees Ray driving the Jetta. Ray comes to a light, G-Mac walks up, sticks a gun in his ear—this is right on Mission Ave.—and he tells Ray he's taking the car on account of the money Ray owes the Posse. Just like that. So that's the carjacking—boom, life felony, right there.

"Now, Ray's not a bad kid, like I said. But let's be honest: Ray did owe the money. Plus, he was lucky McNeese didn't cap him right there, being the way he is. So the whole thing should have been over and done with—Ray Rat screwed up, so G-Mac took the Jetta, case closed. Ray should have walked away.

"Okay, so at this point somehow Danziger got Ray Rat to agree to testify about the whole thing—which is unheard of. These DAs can never find a witness in a

gang case. I don't know what the heck Danziger promised him. I don't even know why Danziger was pushing
the case in the first place—and I liked Bobby Danziger,
believe me; we were in SIU together a long time—but
no jury in this city was going to send anyone to jail over
a drug beef, not when the only witness was a crackhead
like Ray Ratleff. Even if Danziger could get Ray into the
courtroom, he'd have to strap him to the chair to keep
him from falling off. I mean, you could have tried this
case in Beijing, it still would have come back not-guilty.

"Anyway, predictably Ray Rat boogies, and now
things get really crazy. Braxton can't find Ray Rat; and
G-Mac's all hot and bothered because Danziger is pushing this thing about Ray Rat's Jetta. And if it gets to trial,
who knows? There's always a chance a jury will believe
Ray because, crackhead or not, you know Ray *is* telling
the truth. So, long story short, everybody's looking for
Ray Rat—cops, gangsters, everybody—and nobody can
find him.

"So what happens is, the trial is coming up and Braxton's crew can't reach the witness. Well naturally something has to be done to stop that trial. So Braxton goes
up to Maine and caps Danziger. I mean, maybe he
didn't actually pull the trigger, but he sure as hell gave
the order."

I asked, "How do you know all that?"

"Chief Truman, everybody knows all that. There's no
great mystery here, fellas. Half the people in this neighborhood could tell you what happened. But go prove it."

Kelly frowned at this version of events. It was all
hearsay, of course. Rumor, not evidence. Or maybe it
was Gittens himself that Kelly did not approve of. But to
me, this was all good news. Gittens represented something more important than evidence: an insider, a skeleton key.

"Where is this Ray Rat now?" Kelly asked.

"Who knows? The whole department's out looking

for Braxton. Nobody's thinking about Ray right now, because Ray didn't shoot Danziger."

"But you could find him?"

Gittens shrugged. "I've got some friends around here who might know something."

Friends? What to make of this guy? If Kelly was right that there are two kinds of cops, talkers and fighters, then here was the beau ideal of the talkers. But there was no way to know how much of Gittens's talk was just that—talk.

Kelly and I exchanged a glance. *Why not?*

"You can really find Ray Rat?" I asked.

"Chief Truman, I found you, didn't I?"

14

The radio is the soundtrack of every cop's working life. *Bravo six-five-seven, adam-robert . . . Acknowledge, bravo six-five-seven . . .* It is a constant presence in police cars, the voices almost indecipherable, a blizzard of information. Gittens and Kelly had acquired the ability to filter out the white noise, to hear selectively. But my ear constantly sought out the pidgin messages. *One-five, could you swing by 75 Leinengen Road. We have a report of a stripped car . . . One-five, we have it, sir . . . Bravo K-one, I'm ocean-frank . . .*

"Where are we going?" I asked Gittens.

"This place Ray hangs out. Kind of a social club."

We drove south on Mission Ave., past a series of parking facilities. On the sidewalk, people eyed us. Suspicion naturally attached to three white guys in a Crown Victoria—as suspicion always seemed to attach to racial difference in the Flats. It was in the air here. You were conscious of your race, you wore it like new clothes.

Bravo four-three-one. Tremont and Vannover with a hot box, Mass. two-six-oh-paul-victor-john, beige VW, two Hispanics.

Gittens parked in front of a massive industrial plant

just off the avenue, one of the only thriving businesses
I'd seen in the area. A sign read,

ZIP-A-WAY WASTE DISPOSAL SERVICES, INC.
BOSTON CENTRAL RECYCLING CENTER

Bound by high fences topped with cyclone wire, the
plant consisted of three enormous warehouses. A con-
veyor rose out of the roof of the largest, hauling plastic
bottles and containers up and dumping them into a
shredder. There was no activity outside the building,
though. You got the impression the plant was empty, op-
erating on its own, robotically.

"This is the place," Gittens announced.

He led Kelly and me through a gate at the front of the
complex, and once inside we walked along the fence to a
back lot. Here great driftpiles of garbage were sorted by
type, newspaper, metals, plastic. Gittens guided us
through the garbage dunes to a forty-foot industrial
Dumpster. The enormous container sat in a corner,
seemingly abandoned. Nearby were piles of old bricks,
all sorted and mounded up. I presumed that the Dumpster contained more of the same: construction materials
or other junk. It was impossible to imagine why Gittens
had led us here. There was a narrow corridor between
the Dumpster and the heavy-gauge chain-link fence, and
we had to edge in sideways to reach the rear corner of
the Dumpster.

"Let me go first," Gittens whispered.

"Go where?"

Gittens winked and promptly disappeared through
the wall of the Dumpster. More precisely, he pulled back
a rough cloth curtain that was hanging against the steel
sidewall, and he stepped through a gap in the wall.
There were voices inside, and after a moment Gittens
poked his head back out. "Come on," he encouraged us,
"it's not as bad as it looks."

Kelly and I looked at each other. "You first," I said.

Inside the Dumpster was perfect darkness. Blind, I
was acutely aware of the smell—rotting garbage, urine,

the musky smell of sweat, and a more acrid odor, burned plastic maybe. After a few seconds, I was able to make out a little sitting area. A wooden cable spool had been turned on end to make a table. It was flanked by two battered chairs, one of them missing a leg. Sunlight filtered through the curtain and dimly illuminated the table and chairs. The tabletop was cluttered with needles, a lighter, scraps of blackened tinfoil, discarded containers of heroin and cocaine. The drug packages—plastic envelopes about one inch square—were ink-stamped with two different symbols. One showed the black silhouette of a dog, the other a red boxing glove—Knockout. From the looks of the table, Knockout and Black Dog seemed to be the Coke and Pepsi of the local heroin world. The table was also littered with tie-offs, cheap packages of cocaine formed by placing the rocks or powder in a corner of a plastic sandwich bag then twisting the corner off to form a little sachet. The drug packets were all empty. The party was over, for the moment.

In Versailles there is a lot of pot, misuse of prescription drugs, and a tsunami of alcohol. Occasionally a few bags of cocaine will turn up at the high school and I go over to Mattaquisett if the kid is from Versailles. There is a rumor that Joe Grasso, who drives an eighteen-wheeler between Montreal and the Florida Keys, keeps a stash at his house out on the Post Road, but there's never been any evidence to support a search there. Freebasing, speedballing, these things I'd never seen.

Gittens poked through the empty packets on the table. He pocketed one with the Knockout label on it, but it was obvious he had no intention of making any arrests or even searching for more drugs. The drugs were beside the point.

Something shifted in the dark interior of the Dumpster. Then a groan.

I jumped back from the table, startled. Squinting into the gloom, I could just make out the contours of three or four men—impossible to see exactly how many—lying on the floor. Their movements were languid, heads and shoes lolling, shadows, no more.

"Jesus," I hissed, feigning anger to mask my embarrassment.

"Hey, that's my works, brother," a voice said.

Gittens pointed to a needle and syringe on the table: a *works*. "No one's touching your works, brother. Everything's okay."

Kelly, who had to stoop to avoid bumping his head, poked at the things on the table with his nightstick, careful not to touch anything bare-handed.

Meanwhile Gittens moved into the darkness at the other end of the trailer. "Everything's fine," he cooed to the men who lay on the floor side by side, "everything's peachy." He snapped rubber gloves onto his hands and straddled the first of the sleepers, bending over and laying a latex hand on the man's side. "How you doing down there, my friend?" There was no response. "Who do we have here? Come on, Sleeping Beauty, show me that pretty face. Any of you fellas seen Ray Ratleff? Huh?" He stepped across the bodies as if they were fallen logs. "Who do we have here? Bobo! Hey, pal. Come on, Bobo, wake up a minute, I need to talk to you." The figure groaned and tried to push Gittens away. "Come on, Bobo, nap time's over." He reached under the guy's armpits and pulled him up to a sitting position. While Gittens steadied Bobo with one hand, he reached into his coat pocket and fished out a pair of rubber gloves for me. When I'd stretched the gloves over my hands, Gittens and I walked Bobo over to the table.

Bobo turned out to be a frail, bone-thin man in his late twenties. Lifting him was like lifting an old woman. Bobo wore filthy work pants and a Lakers sweatshirt. On his head was a Greek fisherman's cap, though Bobo's cap was made of black leather, a design modification no Greek fisherman would approve. He was suffused in body odor.

We deposited Bobo in the good chair, and Gittens

perched on the three-legged one, bracing himself to keep from toppling forward. He slid the empty drug packets to one side, careful not to drag the sleeve of his sweater on the tabletop.

"Bobo, we need to find Ray."

Bobo groaned sleepily. His head slumped. I held his shoulders so he wouldn't slide right off the chair.

"Bobo, come on, I know you can hear me. Have you seen Ray Rat?"

Bobo managed to force an eye open a crack. "Gittens," he moaned.

"Bobo, have . . . you . . . seen . . . Ray . . . Ratleff?"

"Gittens." Bobo laughed at a joke that only he'd heard. "Gittens, what are you doing here?"

"Where's Ray?"

"I don't know no Ray."

"Come on, don't fuck around. You know who Ray is."

Bobo thought it over. "Oh, *Ra-a-ay*. With like a big 'fro? Doctor-J-lookin' motherfucker?"

"Yeah, Bobo, that's the one. You seen him?"

"No, man, he gone away. Ray's away." He laughed. "Ray zway."

"Where's he away to?"

"I think he's in that—whaddaya call it?—witness p'tection program."

"Yeah?"

"Yeah. They made him, like, a farmer."

"Bobo, we don't have a witness protection program. That's the feds."

"No, it's true. He lives in Connecticut someplace."

"Bobo, Ray can't even spell Connecticut."

"Enough of this bullshit," Kelly cut in. "Detective, may I?"

Gittens gestured with his arm, *Be my guest.*

Bobo sensed what was about to happen. He struggled to his feet, ready to defend himself.

"Sit down," Kelly ordered.

Bobo did not sit down—unwisely, as it turned out.

Kelly's baton whirled squarely into Bobo's crotch. There was a liquid *thwop!* and Bobo dropped to the floor.

"There," Kelly announced, "I think we have his attention now. Ben, put him back in the chair. Detective Gittens, you can ask your questions now."

"My balls!" Bobo gasped. I said, "I know. Your balls." I stole a glance at Kelly, who was wiping the nightstick on the leg of his pants. He saw me looking but avoided my eyes.

Softly, Gittens asked, "Bobo, have you seen Ray?"

"Yeah. I seen him." Bobo was still bent over, wheezing, cupping his genitals.

"When was that?"

"I don't know, like a couple nights ago. He come here looking for a package. He was all like, can I help him out?"

"Did you sell him the package?"

"You want to read me my rights, Steve McGarrett?"

"What time did he show up?"

"I don't know. Late. I was occupied."

"Did he say where he was staying?"

"No."

"How did he get here? Did he walk, drive?"

"He drove."

"Drove what?"

"Some Japanese thing. Shitsu, something like that."

"A Shitsu?"

"Yeah, Shitsu."

"What the hell's a Shitsu?"

"It's a car."

"There's no car called a Shitsu."

"What can I tell you? That's what the man had."

Gittens frowned. "What color?"

"I don't know. Brown, orange maybe. I couldn't see."

"A brown Shitsu. That's very helpful. Was anyone with him?"

"I don't know, Gittens. It's getting hard to remember."

Gittens pulled out a roll of cash in a money clip. He

peeled off two twenties and dropped them on the table.
"It's important, Bobo."

"How important?"

Gittens threw another twenty on the table. "Bobo, I
need to find Ray Rat before Braxton does."

"This is me and you, right? 'Cause me and Ray, we go
back, alright? Back in the day we was—" Bobo held up
two fingers together to indicate how tight he once was
with Ray Ratleff.

Gittens nodded but gave no assurance he would keep
the tip confidential. "Ray's dead, Bobo. Braxton's looking for him. Unless I find him first, Ray's dead."

Bobo studied the three bills on the table. "Ray's got a
sister lives in Lowell. The cops already talked to her,
only she told them Ray wasn't there. I don't know her
name. She stays with this guy Davy Diaz. He drives a
Harley. Ray might be there."

Gittens nodded again to signal he understood.

"I said he *might* be there, right, Gittens? You remember that."

"I'll remember, Bobo. It's alright." Gittens dropped
another twenty on the table, like an afterthought.

"Gittens, you find Ray, you'll help him out, right?
Ray didn't do nothing. It was that DA put him in the
middle of all this. The DA was the one put all these ideas
in Ray's head."

"I know, Bobo."

"You can see what's happening here, right? You can
stop this, I know you can. You help him."

"Gittens, you just gave that guy eighty bucks."

"Not a bad five minutes' work for Bobo."

"Where did you get the cash?"

"It's drug money. We forfeit it from dealers. Let the
bad guys finance our investigations. It's only fair. Hey, if
there were no bad guys, we wouldn't need cops in the
first place, right?"

"How do you get it, though?"

"Oh, Ben, if you work narcotics, money's every-where. You raid a place, there might be five, ten, twenty thousand dollars sitting on a table, all cash, all banded-up like a bank. You make a pinch on a street corner, some slider will have a pocketful of tens and twenties. So we take it."

"Nobody ever fights it?"

"Of course not. What are they gonna say? If a dealer shows up in court and says, 'That's my money,' then he's got to explain why he has so much cash, or why he keeps his money in a stashpad full of coke, or why he only car-ries tens and twenties. The cash is evidence of the crime, see. If they claim the cash, they're admitting the crime. So they never say boo about it."

We were speeding along I-93 on the way to Lowell, the decayed mill city forty-five minutes north of Boston. Gittens had the wigwags on but no siren, and we glided past miles of stalled commuter traffic.

"We don't do many forfeitures in Versailles," I of-fered. "It's never worth the effort."

"Well, Ben, I'm talking about a more informal proce-dure here." He looked at me to see if I understood. "We don't always actually report it."

There was an awkward pause.

"I've got to pay these guys somehow," Gittens said in his uninflected tone. "That's just the way it is."

Lowell seemed a good place for Ratleff to hide, just far enough from Boston that word of his location would not filter back, yet not so far away that he had no one to sup-port him. It was a grim place, though. Downtown, the old mills had been converted into shopping malls and muse-ums as the city tried to Disneyfy its industrial past. What-ever effect these cheerful renovations may have had on the downtown area—and even downtown the act was not completely convincing—the cheer quickly evaporated as we worked our way toward the city's grimier precincts. On Shaughnessy Garden, the street where Ray Ratleff had holed up, the earth's natural color was utterly smeared away. The neighborhood was one long smudge—the world through a dirty windshield. Davy Diaz's place was in one of these monochrome buildings, a two-family built on a crumbling concrete foundation. There was a Harley and an old Mitsubishi—a Shitsu—parked out front. A dog's chain lay in the front courtyard. It looked heavy enough to hold a destroyer at anchor; I was not sorry the dog it belonged to was absent.

A woman answered the door. She was a very tall, very dignified black woman. "Can I help you, officers?" she said, though we wore plain clothes.

We could hear the dog barking inside.

Gittens asked for Ray Ratleff, and the woman politely told him he was not there. "I haven't seen Ray in years," she demurred.

Gittens looked at her a moment, taking her measure. "I tell you what," he said, "tell Ray it's Martin Gittens. I just want to talk to him. Tell him 'Martin Gittens,' and if he's still not here, we'll be on our way, alright?"

The woman studied Gittens, taking his measure now, then disappeared behind the door.

A moment later, Ray Ratleff came to the door. He was tall, nearly as tall as Kelly, and his head was haloed by a great airy Afro. It floated over him like an atomic cloud. He wore a T-shirt with the sleeves cut off, accentuating his long, muscle-less arms. The right arm had a horrible scar just below the elbow where the forearm muscle was simply missing, torn away. It looked like something had taken a bite out of his arm. Tracks scored the underside of his forearms, the stigmata of needle use. A bandage covered his forehead and right eye. I recalled that Danziger's file listed Ratleff's date of birth as July 25, 1965, but it was impossible to believe this man was only thirty-two. He looked fifty.

"Gittens," Ratleff sighed in a deep bass.

"Hey, Ray." Gittens's tone was not threatening. "You got a lot of people looking for you."

"Looks like they found me."

"Well, someone was going to find you eventually. Lucky for you, it was me."

"Yeah, lucky me. Am I under arrest?"

"No. You haven't done anything wrong."

Ratleff nodded, slowly.

"If you want, I can take you in, charge you with something or other. It'd keep you off the street for a while, away from Braxton."

"Nah, that's okay."

"You need anything up here, Ray?"

Ratleff crossed his arms. He looked like a cigar-store Indian. "I'm alright."

Gittens stood beside him, staring out at the sway-backed buildings on Shaughnessy Garden. "This is some shit-storm, Ray."

"You going to tell them where I am?"

"I guess I'll have to," Gittens said. "How's your head?"

"I'm alright." Ratleff patted the bandage on his eye as if he'd forgotten it was there. There must have been panic and confusion behind that bandage, but he managed to mask it all. "I didn't do nothing wrong."

"I know, Ray."

"I didn't do nothing wrong," Ray repeated.

Gittens nodded his understanding.

Ratleff continued to stare, and you could practically hear him repeating the phrase like a mantra: *I didn't do nothing wrong, I didn't do nothing wrong.*

"Ray," Gittens said gently, "these guys want to ask you some questions. They're working the Danziger case, the DA that got shot."

"Mr. Ratleff," Kelly said, "did Gerald McNeese or anyone from Braxton's crew ever talk to you about the carjacking case? About dropping it?"

"They didn't have to talk to me. I knew what they wanted. They wanted me to drop the case."

"How did you know that?"

"It's MP. That's just how it is."

"But you decided to go ahead and testify anyway?"

"DA told me just go and tell the truth."

"But you knew about Braxton, about what he might do?"

"Everybody knew. The DA knew too."

"You mean Danziger?"

Ratleff nodded.

"Danziger knew you were in danger?"

"Course he did."

"So what did Danziger say to you? How did he convince you to go forward?"

"He had a case on me. I sold a bag to a cop."

Gittens snorted. "One bag? Ray, that's just distribution! It's a few months of house time. You could do that standing on your head. You did all this just to avoid a six-month ride in the house?"

"It wasn't like that."

I put my foot up on the bottom step, which left me looking straight up at Ratleff. "What *was* it like, Ray? What was going on?"

He looked down on me.

"What was going on?" I repeated.

"I couldn't go to the house. I didn't have the time. Besides, the DA, Danziger, said it wasn't going to happen anyway."

"What wasn't going to happen?"

"There wasn't going to be no trial. The DA had some kind of deal. He said all I had to do was say I was going forward, let it keep going till we got to the trial, then the whole thing was gonna go away."

Again Gittens was surprised. "G-Mac was going to plead?"

Ratleff shrugged. "That's what the DA said."

"I don't believe that, Ray," Gittens said. "Those guys don't plead. You know that."

Ratleff just shrugged again. *I don't know, I don't care.*

I coaxed him, "Ray, what was going on, do you know?"

"All I know is Danziger told me if I just stuck with the program, let him work on G-Mac awhile, he could get G-Mac to do what he wanted. I told him McNeese wouldn't give anybody up or nothing like that, but Danziger kept saying it wasn't like that. He said he had something G-Mac would want."

"And what was that, Ray? What was Danziger doing?"

"I told you, I don't know."

"Ray," Gittens said, "what are you gonna do when Braxton comes after you?"

"Let him come. I didn't do nothing wrong."

"That doesn't matter, Ray. You know what he's gonna do."

"Let him come. Doesn't matter what he does to me. I got the bug."

We looked at him, uncomprehending.

"I got the bug." He injected his arm with an imaginary needle, presumably to signal needle-borne AIDS. "I've got no time to go to the house or noplace else, and I got no time to waste on Braxton and his foolishness. There's nothing Braxton can do to me now."

15

If there is a heaven for cops, it looks like the J. J. Connaughton Cafe. The interior consists of a wood-paneled room, a long, plain bar running the length of it. The bartenders wear white short-sleeve shirts and solid black clip-on neckties. On the wall behind them hang a large American flag and a much larger Irish tricolor. There are no stools, just a rail along the base of the bar to rest one foot on, and when Gittens, Kelly, and I got there—around seven-thirty that evening, after we returned from Lowell—men were lined up along the bar with one foot up like pelicans.

We settled in at a table in the back with three sweating bottles of Rolling Rock.

"A lot of cops hang out at this place," Gittens said. In fact, nearly everyone in the place seemed to be a cop. There were cops in blue uniform pants, plainclothes cops in nylon windbreakers, cops with potbellies and cops with handlebar mustaches, short cops with Popeye forearms and lanky cops with John Wayne walks.

Before long, cops began to drift up to greet Gittens. They shook his hand and said, *howahya Mahtin*. Several knew Kelly too, and most of those that didn't at least had heard his name and seemed happy to see him. They seemed happy to meet me too. They brayed *howahya* to me and shook my hand vigorously. They sat down with their beers, and soon we were one big group of six or eight or ten or twelve, depending on who was standing and who was off milling around at any given moment. There was an infectious, pleasant sense of testosterone in low idle with these guys. It didn't take long before I was telling people *howahya* just like the rest of them.

After we'd been there awhile, one of the younger guys—he had an open, pink face—asked, "Any word on the Danziger thing?"

Silence. Danziger's murder was a close cousin to a cop killing, and it was treated accordingly, with reverence.

"Nothing," declared Gittens, flatly lying. "Nobody's talking."

"I've never heard anything like it. *Nevah.*"

"It's like Colombia, y'know? Some fuckin' banana republic? I mean, killing the lawyers? It's crazy."

"—or Sicily. That's how they do it—"

"—they'll kill that kid Braxton too. You watch."

"Who?"

"Up in the Flats, those people'll kill him."

There was a low growl—"he-e-ey"—emitted by the only black cop at the table.

A pause.

"Oh, come on, he didn't mean *that,*" one of the white cops said. He held out his beer bottle and grinned. "Come on. To Al Sharpton."

They clinked bottles.

"To Rodney King," the black cop said. He managed a fractional smile.

"Whoo! Rodney King!"

The crisis seemed to have passed. The monster's head sank back under the surface of the loch, and the banter resumed as before.

"Remember Braxton threw that kid Jameel Suggs off the roof?"

"That was a long time ago."

"I remember that. Like '92 maybe? '93, something like that?"

I asked, "Who's Jameel Suggs?"

One of the cops clued me in. "Suggs raped a little girl in the Grove Park project there. Hey, what was her name? Something Wells?"

"It was like some African name, I think."

"Nikita—"

"Nikisha."

"Nikisha Wells, that's it. This little girl, she was like seven years old. Suggs raped her then he threw her off the roof so she wouldn't tell nobody. So a few days later somebody went and threw Suggs off the roof too. They say it was Braxton."

"Hey, Maine, that's called a misdemeanor murder."

"That's the story anyway. Nobody knows if it was really Braxton."

"Hey, I say if Braxton really killed Suggs, let's give him a fuckin' medal."

"—Did he really do that?—"

Gittens broke in. "Yes, he did."

The table got quiet again.

"Harold threw Jameel Suggs off the roof." With his storyteller's instinct, Gittens took a moment to wipe the condensation off his beer bottle with a napkin. "He told me so himself."

" 'Harold'?—"

"—get the fuck out!—"

"—what is this with 'Harold'?—"

"—what, you know him?"

"Course I know him." Gittens shrugged. "I've known him since he was a kid. I was up in A-3 a long time chasing those kids around."

"Get the fuck out. Why don't you go find him then?"

"He doesn't want to be found. No one's going to find Harold till he's ready to be found."

The cops all studied Gittens. Some found the association with Braxton suspicious, others were impressed, others simply didn't believe it. But all were curious. Martin Gittens had a way of making people curious.

"Stop calling him Harold," said one. "You're weirding me out with that shit."

"Hey, Gittens, if you do know him, you better tell Maine here what Braxton's like so he knows what he's getting into."

Gittens smirked at me. "Well, he's smart, I'll tell you that. Smarter than any of these guys. Harold put together that whole Hot Box Boys thing in high school. You go up to the Flats now, half the guys there will claim they were in Hot Box Boys. But there were really only six or seven of them, and Harold ran the whole show."

I asked, "What does that mean, 'Hot Box Boys'?"

"A hot box is a stolen *cah*," one of the cops informed me.

"Ah," I said, "a stolen *cah*."

Gittens continued: "They were grabbing cars left and right. Fifty in one night off the lot at Hub Nissan in Dorchester. Fifty! They never did any time for anything. They'd get sent to DYS and they'd be out the same night. It was ridiculous."

"It's a revolving door—"

"—see, that's what happens," one of the others scoffed. "You've got to nip this stuff in the ass. This juvenile shit—"

"What, are you gonna lock up every kid who steals a car?"

"Yes! Every one! That's what you do—you hit 'em hard right away so they learn. They've got to know this shit isn't gonna flush."

"Doesn't matter. These kids have brass balls, they don't care."

"You know what I don't get?" said another, in a puzzled tone.

"We all know what you don't get."

Guffaws and high fives all around.

"No, listen. The thing . . . the thing I don't get is, Gittens, you said Braxton *told* you he threw Jameel Suggs off the roof. So if he admitted it to you, why didn't you do anything about it? I mean, he confessed. You had him on a murder."

"Yeah, Jesus, Gittens, what are you, protecting this piece of shit?"

Gittens allowed the question to hang there a moment. "I did report it. The DA said it wasn't enough to indict. They didn't have anything else, and they said a confession alone wouldn't support a conviction. They didn't want the case."

Another pause. We waited, uneasily, for the next gust of conversation.

"I heard a rumor Braxton was a rat," said one.

"No way—"

"—Who would he give up? Himself?"

"—How do you turn a guy like that anyway? Braxton's a murderer. Even if he wanted to flip, you couldn't give him a deal. No DA would go for it."

"Hey, the feds flipped Whitey Bulger. He was a murderer."

"That's different, it was a Mafia thing. Whitey was a mobster."

"Yeah, and Whitey fucked them anyway. He didn't give them jack shit. These feds are complete shitheads."

"Tell you what, if anybody ever did flip Braxton, he'd be a great rat. Imagine the shit Harold Braxton could tell you."

"Lowery'd never give him a deal. He'd never get elected again."

"Hey, you never know. It's like the man said: Whitey Bulger got his deal."

"That's because he's white." This was the black cop. He delivered the statement in an even tone. It was a fact, take it or leave it.

"Oh, Jesus, here we go—"

"—Why are you always starting with that shit?—"

The black cop shrugged. "You all know if Whitey Bulger was black, the feds never would have let him flip, Mafia or no Mafia."

"What do you mean? Lowery's black and he's the DA."

"Yeah, what's he, a black racist?"

This last comment was pushing. The monster's eyes appeared on the surface of the loch and lingered there a moment before submerging again.

"Andrew Lowery wants to be the first black mayor," the black cop said. "He can't afford to be associated with a thug like Braxton. An African-American DA protecting an African-American gangster? No way. Braxton scares white people, and white people vote."

Gittens said, "Yeah, well, just the same, I'd try and flip Braxton if I could. That's the job."

"It'll never happen. Braxton'll never rat out anyone."

Gittens inclined his head as if to say, *Hey, you never know.*

Much later, I learned that Gittens kept a photo in his office of Nikisha Wells, the little girl who had been raped and thrown off the roof in the Grove Park project. In the photo, she wore a red dress and white blouse. Her frizzly hair was arranged in two pigtails, which stuck out from her head at ten o'clock and two o'clock like antennae. There was a red ribbon at the end of each pigtail to match her dress. The photo showed Nikisha leaning forward and laughing as if she'd just heard something very funny. *What time is it when an elephant sits on your fence?* Typical third-grader. I asked Gittens why he kept the photo. He said he'd known Nikisha from his years in the Flats and he kept it "to remind me—this is who we work for." At the time it seemed like a full enough explanation. In hindsight, though, I wish I'd probed further. I wish I'd asked what he thought of Braxton throwing Nikisha's murderer off that same roof. It would have been interesting to know Gittens's answer.

16

The next morning, a little the worse for wear after a night at Connaughton's Cafe, I showed up at the DA's Special Investigations Unit. John Kelly did not accompany me, pleading a personal errand of some mysterious and unexplained kind. I did not ask him about it. It was plain that he did not want to discuss what he was doing.

The Special Investigations Unit was in a nondescript seventies-modern office building, separate from the main District Attorney's office, which was housed in the Sussex County Courthouse. And lest you imagine the SIU office as one of those movie-ish gritty urban police stations—phones ringing, typewriters clacking, "perps" handcuffed to chair legs—let me tell you up front that the SIU looked more like an accountant's office. In fact, several accountants and even a dentist shared the same third-floor hallway. The office was furnished with cloth-walled dividers and industrial carpeting, all in shades of tan. The only concession to law-enforcement gung ho was a poster pinned to one of the cubicle walls: A SOCIETY THAT DOES NOT SUPPORT ITS POLICE SUPPORTS ITS CRIMINALS.

With Bob Danziger's murder, Caroline Kelly had ascended to the head of this unit. Caroline greeted me at the reception area and ushered me around the place, introducing me to several state troopers and to one lawyer, a bowling ball of a man named Franny Boyle.

Boyle came out from around his desk and gave my hand a bone-crushing squeeze. He said, with a Boston accent so thick it sounded like a put-on, "So yaw the guy from Maine." I admitted I was, then stretched my fingers to peel them apart. Boyle looked like he'd been a football player once, a linebacker maybe, though now, at age forty-five or so, he was going soft. The skin of his face sagged. His belly ballooned over his belt buckle. He was nearly bald, with even the sides of his head shaved virtually to the scalp. Still, he was formidable enough. It was difficult to tell where that hairless head ended and his thick neck began. "Anything you need, Mistah Truman, I mean any fuckin' thing . . ." Boyle didn't finish the sentence, but stood there nodding to signify *Just ask*. He pointed a meaty finger at me: "Remembuh." I told him I would.

Caroline asked Boyle if he was feeling alright. The smell of alcohol hung about him—it was ten A.M.—and his face was mottled with a drinker's flush. A fine mesh of red, threadlike veinules netted the skin of his nose.

"I'm okay, Lynnie. Just upset, is all. The funeral's coming up, you know. Autopsy took forever."

"Franny, maybe you'd better go home. You don't look so great. It's alright, we're all upset."

After a moment's hesitation, Boyle grabbed his coat, gave me another knuckle-cruncher, and shuffled down the hall. With his overcoat on, the man's neck all but disappeared; his head seemed to be attached directly to his back like a bullfrog's.

When he was out of earshot I said, " 'Lynnie'?"

Caroline shook her head with an expression that said, *Don't even think about calling me Lynnie.* "Franny's a long story," she said, and left it at that.

She brought me to Danziger's office, where two strips of yellow crime-scene tape were strung in an X across the door frame. A glossy peel-and-stick label on the door predicted dire consequences for anyone who entered (. . . *under Massachusetts law it is a felony to enter, tamper with, or otherwise disturb a crime scene unless explicitly authorized* . . .). Caroline paused to run her fingertips over the plastic nameplate with its impressed letters, ROBERT M. DANZIGER, CHIEF, then she pulled off the tape as if she were clearing away cobwebs. Inside, the office was neat and organized. A half dozen files stood at attention in a rack on the desk, their edges aligned. The phone, Rolodex, stapler, everything was arranged just so. You half expected Bob Danziger to walk in through a side door and take his seat at the desk.

"I don't think you'll find much in here," Caroline cautioned. "We took out the files on all Bobby's open cases."

I stopped at a small photo on the wall. It showed a group of men posing on the steps in front of a courthouse. "That's the original SIU crew," she explained. "It was just an anti-narcotics unit then. DAs and cops working together, that was the idea. That must be '85 or so. Your tour guide, Martin Gittens, is in there somewhere." The photo conveyed a feeling of jock comradeship. It reminded me of one of those old photos of a B-52 crew, a bunch of cocky young guys grinning and hanging on one another. Gittens was in the front row. He had a cheesy mustache and thick hair, both gone now. I had to look closer to find Danziger. He was in the back, smiling. A burly redheaded cop with a full beard had his arm over Danziger's shoulder, and together the two redheads looked like brothers—Danziger the studious firstborn son, this big cop his mischievous younger brother.

"Who's this guy?" I asked.

Caroline stood next to me. (She smelled faintly of soap and powder, and my eyes pulled toward her.) She followed my pointing finger to the big guy with the beard. "That's Artie Trudell. He was killed a long time ago. Harold Braxton was charged but he got off." She continued to scrutinize the photo. "Look how young Bobby was."

Robert Danziger must have been in his late twenties, early thirties when the picture was snapped. Not more than a year or two out of law school, with no idea what lay ahead. He probably felt bulletproof with the weight of Artie Trudell's arm on his own bony shoulder. There was no way to predict the countless branchings that would lead to his own death. Was Danziger already moving inexorably toward that cabin in the Maine woods? Or was there still time to pursue an alternate fate? To leave the DA's office, say, or stop practicing law altogether. Or simply to leave Boston—to remove himself from Harold Braxton's murderous path. Every life carries an allotment of what-ifs, but the questions become more fraught when a life ends badly. Of course, no one predicts a bloody death for himself. We all expect to die in bed. But a percentage of us will not; a percentage of us will die violently or too soon. Those people are traveling along their own chain of incident right now, ignorant, free to alter their fate if only they knew it. We are all blithe and unaware, as Danziger had been when he posed for this picture twelve years earlier, and some of us will die just as he did.

"So what does SIU do now if it's not an anti-narcotics unit anymore?"

"Complex investigations. We still do narcotics stuff, but we handle other things too. White collar, public corruption, gang cases, cold cases. We also handle cases where BPD has a conflict of interest."

"I thought cops were supposed to have a conflict of interest with bad guys."

"I mean where the cops are the bad guys."

"Oh."

Caroline straightened the photo on the wall.

"What about Danziger?" I said. "What kind of cases did he do?"

"A little bit of everything. When you're in a unit this small, that's how it works; everybody does everything. Bobby coordinated all the anti-gang stuff, but he took other cases too."

She led me to a conference room next door to Danziger's office. Manila folders and cardboard boxes were stacked along a wall. The waist-high pile of papers stretched six or eight feet across. "These are Bobby's files, everything he was working on when he died. If Braxton had a reason to kill him, there ought to be something relevant in here . . . somewhere. It's kind of a needle in a haystack."

"That's not a haystack," I sighed, "it's a farm."

"Well then, you should feel right at home." She smirked.

"I'm from Maine, not Kansas."

"Whatever."

I spent the rest of the afternoon in that conference room, sifting through Danziger's case files. It made lurid reading. There were a dozen or so files involving police corruption of one kind or another—a cop charged with extorting blow jobs from prostitutes in the Combat Zone (the report quoted him, *Don't you say no, don't you say no to me*); a half dozen narcotics detectives who helped themselves to $30,000 from a stashpad in Mattapan; an evidence officer who got hooked on the cocaine that passed under his nose every day on its way to the evidence locker; another group of narcotics detectives who beat up an African-American drug dealer, only to find the dealer was actually an undercover Boston police officer (*I'm a cop! I'm a cop! Look at my badge!*). Among the crooked-cop files, there was one that stood out, not because it was so serious but because it was so trivial. *Commonwealth v. Julio Vega* was a perjury case in which the defendant pleaded guilty and accepted a year probation. The case had been closed five years earlier, in 1992, and the file jacket was empty. Why would Danziger still be monitoring a case so petty, years after it had been closed? I set the empty file folder aside.

The bulk of Danziger's case load was in anti-gang prosecutions. So I began looking for defendants I recognized as members of Braxton's gang: Gerald McNeese, June Veris, Braxton himself. The cases ranged from ordinary drug pinches to more chilling crimes. June Veris, the guy I'd seen dealing in Echo Park the day before, emerged as a particularly sinister character. In one incident, Veris had used a chunk of concrete to crush the hands of a member of the Mara Trucha, a Salvadoran gang. Both hands were reduced to a mash; all the tiny bones were shattered. The attack was payback for Mara Trucha's selling rock in Echo Park, clearly Mission Posse territory. Veris was never prosecuted, because there were no witnesses, including, miraculously, the man whose hands were flattened. That pattern—an outrageous crime followed by an acquittal or even an outright dismissal of charges—was repeated over and over again. Whatever mayhem the Posse was responsible for, so long as they confined their activities to Mission Flats, charges were rarely filed. Witnesses who lived there simply refused to testify.

As the hours passed, my sense of outrage over the goings-on in Mission Flats began to wane. It became easier to blame the victims who would not come forward to testify. How could Danziger or anyone else help them if they would not help themselves? To judge by these documents, Braxton's name rarely appeared in the files. Danziger had no open cases pending against him and none in the offing.

By two o'clock, my eyes were fogged over. Caroline came by to check on me and deliver a can of Coke.

"You read enough police reports yet, Ben?"

"Let me ask you something: Where do cops learn to talk this way? *I alighted from my vehicle.* Who the hell alights from a vehicle? Why can't they just say they got out of the car?"

"It's cop-speak. All police reports sound like that."

"Mine don't. My reports are beautiful."

"Chief Truman, you sound like a crotchety old Down-easter."

"I'm no Down-easter. Just crotchety."

She smiled, though it appeared to be against her better judgment.

"Who's this Julio Vega? There's a file here with nothing in it."

"Julio Vega? Come here, I'll show you."

I narrated in cop-speak: "The law-enforcement personnel alighted from their chairs and initiated foot traffic to the office of the victim."

"Enough," Caroline called over her shoulder.

"Sorry. It's catchy once you get started."

In Danziger's office, she stood before the photo of the Special Investigations Unit circa 1985 and pointed to a handsome Hispanic man sitting in the front row, right next to Gittens. "That's Julio Vega."

"He was a cop?"

"He was in Narcotics in Area A-3, which is basically the Flats."

"Why did Danziger have a file on him?"

Her finger moved from Vega to Trudell, the red-bearded giant who had his arm draped over Danziger's shoulder. "Vega and Artie Trudell were partners. Vega was standing right next to Trudell when Trudell got shot."

"Shot by Braxton."

"Right. Vega saw his partner get killed. It was a terrible case."

"What does that have to do with a perjury file on Vega?"

"It's a very long story."

"I've got time."

"It's a big file, I'm warning you."

"How big could it be?"

Caroline's mouth turned up in a smile. She looked like a cat who has just noticed the canary's cage is open. She went to a cabinet and began unloading boxes, folders, transcripts, notebooks. We lugged the papers to the conference room, where they swamped the surface of the table.

"I thought you said it was big," I cracked.

She left me there with the file on Artie Trudell's murder, a case that had been closed nearly a decade. Why Danziger had kept all these materials—other than his friendship with the victim—I did not know. But I quickly fell to the task of sifting them and, out of old habit, trying to see the events in real time. To *be there*. I'd done similar reconstructions before, as a would-be historian, before my life was interrupted—before my mother's illness mooted all my own plans for the future. This was the essence of historiography, piecing together a moment in time from primary sources. I had done it a hundred times. When I was in school, it had all seemed like a very romantic adventure: I was a time traveler, riding the matrix of time and place. Poring over the ten-year-old file on Artie Trudell's murder, that adolescent, almost physical sense of transport did not return, but some of the old pleasure did. For the next few hours I was lost in the events of a decade earlier. There was even a little flush of confidence about my abilities as a policeman, for what is a detective but a species of historian?

17

From the prosecutor's file in the case of *Commonwealth v. Harold Braxton* (1987).

Transcription of Turret Tape, Area A-3 Station, August 17, 1987, 0230 hrs.

Unit 657 (Det. Julio Vega): I need an ambulance!

Turret: Identify yourself.

Vega: Bravo six-five-seven! Get an ambulance up here! It's Artie! I need an ambulance right now! An ambulance!

Turret: Five-seven, I need your location.

Vega: Jesus, he's dying! Artie!

Turret: Bravo six-five-seven, I need your location. Clear the air, please. Five-seven?

Vega: Fifty-two Vienna Road, five-two Vienna, third floor.

Turret: Acknowledge, five-seven. I need an ambulance, code seven, at five-two Vienna Road. All units, there is an officer down.

Unit 106: One-oh-six, adam-robert.

Turret: Alright, one-six.

No ID: We're heading in there.

Unit 104: Four's on the way.

Turret: One-oh-seven and one-oh-one, where are they? Acknowledge.

Unit 107: Bravo one-oh-seven. We're on Mission Ave. We're on the way. Adam-robert.

Turret: One-oh-seven, adam-robert. All units, five-two Vienna, third floor. Officer down. Hang on, Julio, the cavalry's coming.

Unit YC8 (Det. Sgt. Martin Gittens): Yankee C-eight. Take me off at five-two Vienna. Charlie-robert.

Turret: Yankee C-eight, repeat, sir. Did you say you're there?

Gittens: I'm here. I have the five car here with me too. I'm going in.

Turret: Detective Gittens, wait for arriving units, sir.

Gittens: [unintelligible shouting]

Turret: C-eight, I said wait for arriving units. Acknowledge, C-eight?

Gittens: No time. Tell Julio we're coming up.

Turret: Gittens, wait. Gittens, go to channel seven, please.

Vega: Where's that fucking ambulance!

Turret: Hang on, five-seven.

Memorandum Dated August 17, 1987.

To: Andrew Lowery, District Attorney

From: Francis X. Boyle, Assistant District Attorney, Chief of Homicide Division

Re: Homicide of Arthur M. Trudell, #101, Preliminary Report

At 3:00 A.M. this date I was notified by the
   turret of a shooting at 52 Vienna Road in
   Mission Flats. I responded to the scene,
   arriving at approx. 3:30. . . . Numerous
   officers report shooter escaped through back
   stairway and has not been found. No I.D. or
   description of shooter available. Shooter was
   not seen because door remained closed. . . .
   Det. Julio Vega of A-3 Narcotics stated he
   cradled victim's head "to hold it together."
   Vega's arms were covered in blood. He
   appeared to have dipped his arms up to the
   elbows in red paint. Vega was distraught and
   refused to clean his arms. . . . Det. M.
   Gittens states he found a Mossberg 500 12-
   gauge shotgun in back stairwell of 52 Vienna
   Rd. and no other guns in building after
   thorough search of all hallways, stairwells,
   and apartments. Gun sent for I.D. and
   ballistics.

*Transcript of Probable-Cause Hearing in
   Mission Flats District Court,
   September 3, 1987.*

*Cross-Examination of Det. Julio Vega by Attorney
   Maxwell Beck.*
Mr. Beck: Detective Vega, what was your
   purpose in raiding the apartment at 52
   Vienna Road, the so-called "red door"
   apartment?
Det. Vega: My purpose? It was known to be
   part of a drug operation.
Mr. Beck: Known by whom?
Det. Vega: It was common knowledge on the
   street.
Mr. Beck: Yes, but how did you confirm it?

Det. Vega: I investigated, with Detective
   Trudell. We personally made two
   undercover buys there. Plus we had received
   information from a confidential and reliable
   informant.

Mr. Beck: A tip.

Det. Vega: Yes.

Mr. Beck: Now, this "confidential and reliable
   informant"—when you applied for the
   search warrant, you did not identify this
   person for the judge.

Det. Vega: As I have the right to do. If I'd
   named him, your client would have killed
   him.

Judge: Detective Vega, please just answer the
   question.

Det. Vega: Sorry.

Mr. Beck: Detective, in your affidavit, you did
   not reveal your informant's name, did you?

Det. Vega: For the witness's protection, I did
   not use his real name, no.

Mr. Beck: Instead, you referred to him by a
   pseudonym, "Raul," is that right?

Det. Vega: Yes.

Mr. Beck: And of course you know who "Raul"
   is?

Det. Vega: Of course.

Mr. Beck: So if you had to find him again, you
   could.

Det. Vega: Yes.

Mr. Beck: And "Raul"—whoever that is—gave
   you this case, didn't he? He handed it to you
   on a silver platter.

Det. Vega: I don't know about a silver platter.
   He gave us a heads-up about the apartment;
   he said Braxton was dealing out of there.

Mr. Beck: And the judge took you at your

word. The judge believed what "Raul" told you, and he gave you the warrant, isn't that right?

Det. Vega: That's right.

Mr. Beck: Now, after Detective Trudell was shot, you went in and searched the apartment, didn't you?

Det. Vega: Yes.

Mr. Beck: But you didn't get a new warrant for that search, did you?

Det. Vega: We already had a warrant.

Mr. Beck: The one that relied on the tip from "Raul."

Det. Vega: Exactly.

Mr. Beck: So if that warrant is thrown out, then everything you found in the apartment—the gun, a sweatshirt—has to be thrown out too?

Det. Vega: That's for you lawyers to decide, not me.

Mr. Beck: Well, then, let me put it in terms a non-lawyer can understand. If "Raul" doesn't exist—

Det. Vega: What do you mean "if he doesn't exist"?

Mr. Beck: If "Raul" doesn't exist, then the entire case against Mr. Braxton has to be thrown out. Doesn't that sound right?

Det. Vega: [No response.]

Mr. Beck: Detective, do you want to tell us who "Raul" was?

DA: Objection! The informant's identity is privileged information necessary to protect the safety of the witness and other police-informant relation—

Mr. Beck: Detective, who was "Raul"?

DA: Objection!

Judge: Yes, that's enough, Mr. Beck.

Grand Jury Minutes, September 21, 1987.

*Direct Examination of Detective Sergeant Martin
Gittens by Assistant DA Francis X. Boyle.*

ADA Boyle: Detective, are you familiar with an
apartment on the third floor of the Vienna
Road address?

Det. Gittens: Yes, I am. It is a stashpad used by
a gang called the Mission Posse.

ADA Boyle: Would you explain to the grand
jury what a "stashpad" is?

Det. Gittens: A stashpad is an apartment where
drugs and money are kept to be used for
restocking the street-corner dealers. To
minimize risk, the managers only give the
sliders—that's the dealers—a little bit at a
time, usually one bundle. A bundle is one
hundred vials. They come wrapped in a long
piece of tape, and the sliders peel off the
vials one by one as they sell them. In this
case, they were selling drugs directly from
the apartment as well.

ADA Boyle: What else can you tell the grand
jury about that apartment?

Det. Gittens: The apartment is known on the
street by its bright red door. Junkies
sometimes refer to the crack sold there as
"red door" cocaine. The color is significant
for two reasons. First, in this neighborhood
red is recognized as the color of the Mission
Posse. Only Posse members wear it, often
with a red bandanna hanging from a pocket
or worn as a belt. The use of red on the door
is also significant because the crack sold by
the Posse comes in vials with a red plastic
top. That brand has the street name "red
top." You hear kids talk about a "bottle of
red top."

ADA Boyle: And the red-top vial is recognized as the Mission Posse's packaging for crack?

Det. Gittens: In this area of the city, yes.

ADA Boyle: Now, Detective Gittens, you personally responded to the scene on the night of the shooting, correct?

Det. Gittens: Correct.

ADA Boyle: Did you find any weapons there?

Det. Gittens: Yes, in the back stairwell I found a Mossberg shotgun. I submitted the gun for forensic analysis. Ballistics was able to confirm that the shotgun was the murder weapon. I.D. also was able to identify Harold Braxton's fingerprints on the gun in four different places. I also found a hooded sweatshirt of Harold Braxton's in the apartment. I recognized it as his by a distinctive rip and a logo for St. John's University.

ADA Boyle: Was the shotgun tied to Harold Braxton in any other way?

Det. Gittens: Yes, we later spoke to a witness who admitted selling it to Braxton several months before. The witness claimed he'd brought the gun up from Virginia.

ADA Boyle: Detective, based on all this evidence, do you have an opinion as to what happened at 52 Vienna Road last August 17?

Det. Gittens: Yes. In my opinion, Braxton was at the apartment alone that night managing the Mission Posse's cocaine operation. The Narcotics team surprised him when they showed up at the red door. He was trapped inside. Braxton panicked, grabbed the gun, and fired through the door, then he fled down a back staircase, dropping the gun as he ran.

ADA Boyle: And how certain are you of this
    opinion?

Det. Gittens: Very, very certain.

*Transcript of Hearing on Defendant's Motion for
Court Order Requiring Prosecution to Disclose the
Identity of the Confidential Informant "Raul."
Sussex Superior Court, March 7, 1988.*

*Cross-Examination of Det. Julio Vega by Attorney
Maxwell Beck.*

Mr. Beck: Detective, can you describe "Raul"
    for us? What does he look like?

Det. Vega: Medium-build Hispanic male,
    medium complexion, brown hair, brown
    eyes.

Mr. Beck: Oh, come on, you can do better than
    that. You've met with him many times,
    right? Can't you tell us anything particular
    about him? Does he have a scar? A tattoo, a
    lisp, a wooden leg?

ADA Boyle: Objection.

Judge: Sustained.

Mr. Beck: Do you even know "Raul's" name?

Det. Vega: His street name is "OG," for "Old
    Gangster."

Mr. Beck: But what's his real name?

Det. Vega: I don't have that information.

Mr. Beck: You've known him for years and you
    don't even know his name?

Det. Vega: On the street, that's not unusual.

Mr. Beck: Detective Vega, do you know what a
    buy log is?

Det. Vega: It's a log at the Narcotics unit where
    we keep a record of any drug buys we do.

Mr. Beck: So every controlled buy is recorded
    in the log, correct?

Det. Vega: Every drug buy, yeah. It doesn't
    matter if it's a controlled buy or an
    undercover buy.

Mr. Beck: And what's the difference?

Det. Vega: Well, an undercover buy is just a
    drug purchase made by an undercover
    police officer. But we can't do all our own
    buys, because the dealers get to know our
    faces. So we do controlled buys, which is
    where you get somebody to make the buy
    for you.

Mr. Beck: I see. So if you ever did an
    undercover buy yourself, you would have
    recorded it in the buy log, correct?

Det. Vega: Correct.

Mr. Beck: And when you applied for the search
    warrant in this case, you stated that you
    made a buy at the red-door apartment that
    very afternoon, did you not?

Det. Vega: I did.

Mr. Beck: And was that statement true?

Det. Vega: Yes, it was.

Mr. Beck: But you did not record that buy in
    the log, did you?

Det. Vega: I don't recall.

Mr. Beck: Would you like to look at the buy log
    for August 17, 1987?

Det. Vega: Yes.

*[Mr. Beck shows the witness a log book marked
    Exhibit 14.]*

Det. Vega: I guess I did not put it in.

Mr. Beck: But you're sure you made the buy?

Det. Vega: I'm sure.

Mr. Beck: Well, if you made the buy, then you
    must have come away with some drugs,
    right?

Det. Vega: Of course.

Mr. Beck: And this was . . . ?

Det. Vega: Crack cocaine. We bought one
bottle.

Mr. Beck: By a "bottle" you mean a little plastic
vial?

Det. Vega: Yes.

Mr. Beck: And by department regulation,
evidence like that has to be turned over to
the evidence officer and logged in as well,
right?

Det. Vega: *[No response.]*

Mr. Beck: But you did not log this vial of
cocaine into the evidence room, did you?
Would you like to see the evidence log?

Det. Vega: Sometimes—

Mr. Beck: Detective Vega, if you really made a
buy from the red door that afternoon, why
wasn't the evidence recorded in the
evidence log?

Det. Vega: *[No response.]*

Mr. Beck: Detective?

Det. Vega: Sometimes when we seize drugs we
just throw it out so no one can use it. We
didn't have a defendant at that point. We
needed the search to have a case. There was
no case yet, so the drugs weren't evidence
against anyone. So I must have just tossed
them.

Mr. Beck: You just tossed them. How often do
you just toss evidence?

Det. Vega: All the time. I mean, not evidence.
We seize stuff—if there's no case to tie it to,
what else should we do with it? Leave it
sitting there for some kid to find?

Mr. Beck: Detective Vega, let me pose a
hypothetical to you. Let's assume, just out of
curiosity, just for fun, let's assume there
really is no "Raul." "Raul" doesn't exist.

ADA Boyle: Objection.

Judge: Overruled. Mr. Beck, you're on very
thin ice.

Mr. Beck: I understand, Your Honor. Detective
Vega, let's assume there is no "Raul," just
hypothetically. A couple of young Narcotics
detectives hear a rumor on the street that
somebody is selling crack from a certain
apartment. It's just a rumor, though. Maybe
it comes from a junkie. Do you understand
that premise?

Det. Vega: Yes.

Mr. Beck: And does that sort of thing happen?
You hear a rumor about drug dealing here
or there?

Det. Vega: Every day.

Mr. Beck: Every day, excellent. Now, these two
young detectives know the information is
true, the tip is correct. But the source is
shaky. They know a judge won't issue a
warrant based on a tip from a junkie. But
these two young detectives want to raid this
place and shut it down, they want to get that
warrant and get into that apartment, they
want it so bad—

Det. Vega: That's not what happened.

Mr. Beck: I understand. It's a hypothetical.

Det. Vega: That's not what happened.

Mr. Beck: Yes, I understand. We're just
assuming for a moment. These two young
cops with the shaky tip, they need to dress it
up a little in order to convince a judge to
give them the warrant, right? So instead of
saying, "This tip came from a junkie," they
say, "This tip came from a guy named Raul,
who is one hundred percent reliable."
Maybe they even go the extra mile and they
invent an undercover buy, just to be sure

they get the warrant. Who'll question it,
right? It's just another drug raid. How many
drug raids do you make in a year, Detective?

Det. Vega: Dozens, hundreds maybe.

Mr. Beck: So these officers, they lie to get the
warrant. Not a big lie. After all, their hearts
are in the right place. They know there
really is a drug dealer behind that red door,
right? It's just a white lie. Do you know what
a white lie is, Detective?

Det. Vega: *[No response.]*

Mr. Beck: Detective, do you know what a white
lie is?

Det. Vega: It's when you tell a lie for the right
reasons.

Mr. Beck: Precisely. It's a lie you tell for the
right reasons. But then it all blows up. One
of the cops gets murdered and suddenly
everybody wants to know, Who is Raul?
And where is the evidence from that
undercover buy?

ADA Boyle: Objection. If there is a question
here, I wish Mr. Beck would ask it.

Judge: Sustained. Pose a question, Mr. Beck.

Mr. Beck: Detective Vega, my question is this:
Wouldn't that scenario account for all the
irregularities in this case?

ADA Boyle: Objection!

Mr. Beck: Detective, wouldn't that explain why
no one can find "Raul" and no one can even
tell us what he looks like?

ADA Boyle: Objection!

Mr. Beck: Detective, wouldn't that explain why
the controlled buy never got logged in?

ADA Boyle: Objection!

Judge: Sustained! Mr. Beck—

Mr. Beck: Detective, there is no "Raul," is
there?

Judge: The objection is sustained, Mr. Beck!

Mr. Beck: Detective, if there really is a "Raul,"
   why won't you produce him? Where is he?

Judge: Mr. Beck, I said that's enough!

Court Order Dated April 4, 1988.

... It is hereby ORDERED that the prosecution
   locate and produce the witness referred to in
   court papers as "Raul" within seven (7)
   business days. The prosecution will satisfy
   this order by the production of "Raul's" full
   name, date of birth, current address, Social
   Security number ...

Police Report Dated April 5, 1988.

Reporting Officer: Det. J. Vega (badge 78760)

Spent double shift (1600–2400, 2400–0800)
   searching for CRI "Raul" but have been
   unable to locate him. Have informed ADA
   Boyle of this fact. It is my belief that "Raul"
   has purposely removed himself from the
   area out of reluctance to become involved in
   the prosecution of Harold Braxton for the
   murder of my partner, Det. Arthur Trudell.
   This officer will continue the search.

Court's Memorandum and Decision Dated June 1, 1988.

... Whether "Raul" actually exists or, as now
   seems likely, he does not, the
   Commonwealth has committed deliberate
   and egregious misconduct depriving the

defense of an essential witness and resulting
in irreparable harm to the defense. . . .
It is therefore with a heavy heart that the Court
reaches its decision.
The indictment alleging that the defendant
Harold Braxton did commit murder in the
first degree against Arthur M. Trudell is
hereby DISMISSED.

News clipping: "Officer in Murder Controversy Retires,"
The Boston Globe, *January 17, 1992, page B7.*

Detective Julio Vega, the partner of slain
Narcotics detective Arthur Trudell and a
central figure in the controversial trial of a
Boston gang leader for that crime, has
quietly retired from the Boston Police
Department. Vega was removed from active
field duty following the dismissal of the
Trudell case in 1988.
According to a police spokesperson, Vega
retired one day after reaching his fifteenth
year on the force, a critical date for purposes
of his retirement pension.
The department provided no information as to
Vega's future plans or whereabouts.
Vega, 41, could not be reached for comment.

18

A key scraping in the lock startled me, breaking the spell. A glance at the clock: nearly seven at night. Was that possible? Had I been sitting there for five hours? Lately I had begun to wear reading glasses, little wire-rimmed jobs with round lenses, and I twisted them off to rub-rub-rub my eyes like a kid. My muscles and spine and eyes all ached, but there was more than just exhaustion. Something in the Trudell file had spooked me. Something I could not quite name.

More clumsy scratching at the front door lock. Then it was quiet again. Background noises sounded clearly—the buzz of fluorescent lights, the clicks and creaks of the building, a car horn.

At the reception area, I coughed to test my vocal chords, then announced, "Who is it?"

"Who is it? Who the fuck ah *you*?"

"Ben Truman."

"Ben Truman? Who?"

"Franny, is that you?"

"Yeah. Open the daw, would'ja?"

I opened the door and there was Franny Boyle, the SIU prosecutor, a foggy-drunk look on his face. He clutched his keys in his left hand. His right hand shook visibly. Franny's tie was stuffed in his coat pocket, and his shirt was open, revealing a frayed T-shirt collar. "You scared the piss outa me, pal," he grumbled. Booze had thickened his Boston accent, which I would not have thought possible. "Just gonna grab a little snooze here, a'right? I'm not payin' for a cab and I can't deal with the fuckin' T." He brushed past me.

"Sure. Whatever, Franny."

He shuffled down the hall. His thick torso rolled with each step so that he rocked like a little tugboat. "It's alright, Opie, I do it all the time."

"You sure you're alright, Franny?"

"Swell."

"Where's Caroline?"

"How the fuck should I know?"

"I was just . . . She didn't say good-bye."

He stopped, then turned to face me. "Are you porkin' her?"

"No!"

"You sure, Opie?"

"Pretty sure, yeah."

"Why aren't you? You don't like her?"

"Do you always cross-examine people this way?"

"She's divorced. Did ya know that?"

"No, I didn't."

"Well it's true."

Boyle nodded as if we'd just cleared up a misunderstanding, then he moved off again. At the conference-room door he stopped and stared. The file boxes—shit! Boyle regarded the conference table, piled with papers and boxes. *Comm. v. Braxton* was written on each box in thick Magic Marker. He puffed his cheeks with a sort of sigh. "What are you doing, reading that shit?"

"Reading about Braxton, that's all."

"You want to hear the truth someday, you come ask me."

"Sure, Franny."

Boyle gave me an exhausted look and continued down to his office, where he promptly tumbled onto the couch. "Hey, don't tell Caroline I said she was fuckin' you, alright? She might take it the wrong way."

"Oh, I don't think she'd take it the wrong way, Franny."

"She's not wild about me anyway. She thinks I'm crooked."

"That's not true." I dragged an old wool blanket over him.

"She hates me. She wants to get rid of me but Lowery won't let her."

"Just sleep it off, Franny. I'm sure she doesn't hate you."

"She told some people once, 'Franny's so crooked he has to screw his hat on.' Like it was a joke. She doesn't think I know that, but I heard about it. She said, 'Franny's so crooked he has to screw a rubber on.' "

"She said that?"

"Yeah. Charming, isn't she? It's not true anyway."

"About the hat or the rubber?"

"You know what I mean. I'm not crooked. I'm not crooked. . . ."

I was prepared to reassure him again, but Boyle was asleep before I could get the words out.

Back in the conference room, I gathered up the papers, put them back in the boxes, and moved the whole mess into Danziger's office. Boyle's snuffling snores carried from the next room.

And then I had it. I saw the importance of the Trudell case.

Now, when you're exhausted, it's easy to mistake ordinary thoughts for profound ones. This trick of the tired mind explains why our deepest insights always seem to arrive at three A.M. and why there is such exquisite, tantalizing pleasure in trying to recover those three-A.M. thoughts the next morning. It is a pleasant misperception to think yourself profound, and tired as I was that evening, well . . . I thought I understood the situation.

The Trudell case—all the hidden acts and secret motives became clear. I knew that Raul did not exist—not the Raul described in the warrant, anyway. Detective Julio Vega had invented Raul as a well-intentioned scam to trick judges into issuing search warrants. The courts had insisted that Vega do better than the junkies and rats who fed him information on the street, so Vega invented the informant to end all informants, a street-corner oracle so reliable he could exist only in a judge's fantasy. And then it all blew up. With one shot, Harold Braxton not only murdered Vega's partner, he exposed the whole fraud. He converted a routine bogus search warrant into a cause. And he converted Julio Vega from an obscure and unexceptional cop to a bumbling, lying villain with his face on the front page of *USA Today*. That's how Harold Braxton got away with murdering Artie Trudell.

In Danziger's office I stood in front of the photo of the original SIU team, the photo showing Artie Trudell with that big rump roast of an arm on Bobby Danziger's shoulder.

And I knew.

With three-A.M. certainty, I knew how it galled Danziger to see Braxton on the street after he'd killed Trudell. I knew that was why Danziger had kept the file—he wanted to reopen the case. And I knew whom Danziger must have contacted. Not Franny Boyle or Martin Gittens, neither of whom seemed to be aware that Danziger had revived the old case. No, it had to be the only other member of the old guard who knew what really happened that night: Julio Vega.

19

It was not Caroline but a little boy who answered the door. He was nine or ten, and his manner suggested that the doorbell had interrupted some very important activity in the life of a nine- or ten-year-old. Before I could open my mouth, the kid moaned, "Mom, there's a cop here for you."

"What makes you think I'm a cop?"

"You're here to see my mom, aren't you?"

"Your *mom*?" It occurred to me I might be at the wrong apartment. I actually checked the number on the door to be sure.

Caroline came around the corner, wiping her hands on her jeans and pushing the hair off her forehead with the back of her wrist. "Ben! What are you doing here?"

"I need to talk to you about something. I was looking through Danziger's files—"

"This is Charlie," Caroline interrupted, with a pointed look. "Charlie, this is Ben Truman. Ben is a friend of your Grandpa's, and that's why Grandpa's in trouble."

The kid mustered a little wave.

"Charlie, you know better than that. What do you do when you meet a new person? Go on."

Charlie rolled his eyes, then extended his hand. "It's very nice to meet you, Mr. Truman." He gave my hand a firm squeeze, just as Caroline had instructed him, I'm sure.

"Ow, ow." I fell to my knees and grabbed my hand as if the kid had broken every bone from wrist to fingertip.

Charlie's eyes widened, then he smiled. Boys are nothing but very small men (and vice versa); the surest way to their hearts is through their egos. He stepped back and leaned against Caroline, who crossed her hands over his chest.

"Go do your homework," she said, with a pat on his chest.

"I don't have any homework."

"Then go do tomorrow's homework."

"How can I do tomorrow's homework if I don't have it yet?" He twisted his neck to look up at her, but she would not listen to reason. Charlie emitted a world-weary groan, then padded off.

"You can get up now, Ben. Male-bonding time is over."

"Male-bonding time is never over. It's just suspended if there happen to be females in the area."

"That's a terrifying thought."

I stole a glance around the room in which we stood. A stack of magazines threatened to slide off the coffee table—*The New Yorker, Cosmo, People.* Beside them were three copies of *The New York Times,* still in their blue plastic bags—where they would stay until the Danziger case was resolved, no doubt. An open can of Diet Coke. A Nintendo game. A Miró poster above the nonworking fireplace. In the corner were Charlie's hockey bag and two sticks. A comfortable, familial clutter.

"I don't usually talk about work here," Caroline informed me. "This is Charlie's time and his place."

"Sorry. I had a thought. I didn't know who else to ask."

She eyed the folder in my hand. "Have you had supper, Ben?" When I hesitated, she said, "Come on," and led me to the kitchen. As I followed, her hand sought out the tail of her shirt and self-consciously adjusted it over her rump.

There was a small round table in the kitchen with places set for two. Caroline called to Charlie to set another place.

"Are you sure there's enough, Caroline? I didn't mean to impose."

She showed me a baking dish lined with eight chicken breasts.

"All for you two?"

Charlie shuffled into the room in stocking feet to explain. "She makes too much so we can keep eating it all week."

Caroline waved the spatula at him in a menacing way and turned back to her cooking.

The kid shared a little smirk with me. He liked Caroline's cooking even if it meant a week's worth of chicken. I smirked back to let him know I understood that.

"Sit down, boys," Caroline ordered.

I sat opposite Charlie while Caroline filled the plates over the stove. "Rice?" she asked, "salad?" There was something oddly moving about the whole exercise. A suggestion of intimacy, of caregiving. "What will you drink? I have milk, apple juice, Cran-apple, orange juice, water, beer—no, sorry, I don't have beer. I have some wine. Do you drink wine?" I told her I did, and Caroline searched around for the bottle. She gave it to me to open.

"I'll have wine," Charlie said.

"You'll have milk."

Dinner passed quickly. I complimented Caroline on the chicken, which gave her an opportunity to needle Charlie. "See? *Some* people like my chicken." For the most part, though, Charlie and I spoke while Caroline listened. An amused smile—a sort of half Elvis—played at the corners of her mouth as her son held forth on a variety of topics. She spoke only to correct his manners. ("The Bruins suck!" "Don't say *suck*, Charlie.") Hockey and movies seemed to be the twin passions of Charlie's life. Without much prodding he would recite the latest comedy film verbatim from start to finish, mimicking all the voices. He was going to spend Thanksgiving with his father, and Christmas and New Year's with his mother. He hated everything about school, and the sum of his knowledge about the Great State of Maine was that it was located somewhere between Greenland and the polar ice cap. Or so he told me, with an Elvis smile of his own. Throughout the conversation, my eyes sneaked over to Caroline. The simple fact of Charlie's presence seemed to soften her. Not her manner so much; she could still be stern with Charlie and prickly with me. No, the change was more physical. It was a relaxation around the eyes and mouth—the slightest, barely perceptible gentling of her features—which transformed a merely attractive woman into one who was very nearly beautiful. No doubt it is a sign of advancing age when a man finds that motherhood flatters a woman, but there it was.

After supper, Charlie dutifully cleared his plate and put it by the sink, then he disappeared to watch TV—tactfully, I thought. Caroline moved to the sink to do the dishes, which I placed in the dishwasher or dried.

"So," she said as she washed, "what was it that was so important?"

"I think Danziger was reopening the Trudell case."

To my disappointment, Caroline did not seem impressed. She did not even look up from the dishes. "Why? Because he had the file? I have files that are older than Charlie. It doesn't mean anything, except maybe that it's a case you don't want to let go."

"Exactly. Maybe Danziger couldn't let it go."

"Too late. That case was dismissed—what, ten years ago?"

"About. But jeopardy never attached. The judge threw the case out before it got to trial. So there was no legal reason why Danziger couldn't reopen it."

"My, my, 'jeopardy never attached.' "

"Isn't that how you say it?"

"That's how you say it. Have you been moonlighting as a lawyer?"

"No, but we can read up in Maine, you know."

"Whole books?"

"Shoor, if they ain't too long."

She smiled carefully and handed me the baking dish to dry.

"I'm right, aren't I? Jeopardy never attached."

"Yes. But even if you're right, even if Danziger did want to reopen the Trudell case, there's still no evidence. There's no proof that Braxton shot Trudell. None. All the evidence got thrown out along with the warrant. Some cop made up an informant, wasn't that it? What was his name, Ragu?"

"Raul."

"Raul. So why would Danziger reopen the case?"

"I don't know. Maybe he'd found some new evidence."

"Doubtful. Look, Ben, cases go wrong all the time. Guilty guys walk. It happens, it's part of the system. Bob Danziger knew that."

"Yeah, but this was different. Trudell was his friend. You can see it in that photo. Artie Trudell wasn't just another victim to Danziger."

"There's still no evidence. It's an unprovable case."

"What if Danziger didn't think so? What if he thought the case could be saved?"

"How?"

"I don't know. What if Danziger thought Raul was real? If he could prove that Raul really did exist—that

Vega hadn't lied on the search warrant—then the warrant would be good and all the evidence would come back in. Braxton would finally get nailed for killing Trudell."

"Ben, if there really was a Raul, the cops would have produced him in the first place. They wouldn't have let a cop killer walk just to protect an informant."

"Julio Vega said he looked for Raul but he couldn't find him because Raul took off."

"Yeah, well, Julio Vega is a liar."

"Maybe Danziger didn't think so."

"Maybe, but with these cases the simplest explanation is usually the right one."

I grunted. "Ockham's razor."

She looked at me as if I'd belched.

"It's the rule in logic that the simplest explanation is the right one."

She turned off the water and stared.

"What? Hey, this isn't a golden retriever you're talking to. I told you, we read books in Versailles. I was even going to be a professor once."

"Yeah? In what?"

"History."

"So what happened?"

"My mother got sick."

"Sorry. Is she okay?"

"No. She passed away. It's a long story."

"I'm sorry."

"No, really, it's okay. She died the right way, if that's possible."

"Alright. If you say so." She laid a wet, sympathetic hand on my arm. "Well, in any event, you're not a history professor now; there's no sense in digging up a ten-year-old case."

"Except that Danziger was digging it up."

She shrugged, reluctant to concede the point. "So what is it you want to do?"

"I want to talk to Julio Vega."

"I wouldn't even know where to find him."

"Boston PD would know. Vega hung on long enough to draw a pension. They must have an address to send the checks to. You could ask them."

"Julio Vega."

"You can find him for me, Caroline. As a favor."

She rolled her eyes a little. "Yeah, sure. What can it hurt?"

After Charlie was in bed, Caroline and I sat on her sofa drinking the rest of the wine. Caroline did not drink much, maybe two glasses, but a boozy flush came over her. She apologized for the mess and made a halfhearted attempt to straighten up.

"Franny told me you're divorced."

"Did he?"

"Of course, he was half in the bag at the time."

"That sounds like Franny."

"And your husband, was that how Charlie . . . ?"

"Yes, Ben, that's where babies come from."

"So what happened?"

She sighed. "We were very young and very stupid. We were in law school together. I got pregnant. We thought that meant we were in love."

"There must have been more to it than that."

"We only lasted eighteen months, so I guess there wasn't much more to it, was there?"

"Do you see him anymore?"

"When he picks up Charlie or drops him off. It's not hostile or anything. It's just, we have nothing in common anymore except Charlie. We're like strangers shackled together."

"What was he like?"

"He's . . . he's very ambitious."

"Do you ever see him in court?"

"No, he gave up on law ages ago. You can only make

so much money charging by the hour. You only have twenty-four to sell every day." She caught herself sliding into cynicism and she shook it away. "I shouldn't—I don't mean to sound like that. He's not a bad guy."

"Maybe you'll do it again someday."

"What, get married? Absolutely not. I did my eighteen months."

"What if Mister Right comes along?"

She snorted.

"I mean it."

"Oh Ben, that's sweet. Look, I hate to burst your bubble here but you might as well know: Mister Right is like the Easter bunny or Santa Claus. It's something you grow out of."

"It'd be a shame if you were wrong, if your Mister Right was still out there somewhere."

"Ben, think about it: if there was a Mister Right for everybody . . . Well, I didn't meet Mister Right, put it that way. Maybe I would have if I'd waited. I guess I'll never know. You can't look back."

"I think that's right. You can't look back."

"I thought you were a historian."

I waved off the remark—waved off my whole former life. I didn't care to think about it. In my mind the thought was germinating, very quietly, that all this retrospection was a waste—an irresistible waste, but a waste just the same. We move through time like a man in a rowboat, looking back even as we move forward.

"Sometimes," I said, "even historians shouldn't look back."

"Agreed."

She raised her glass for a toast, and I had the strongest urge to kiss her then. To put my hand behind her head and lean forward for a *de luxe,* don't-look-back, Cinema-Scope sort of kiss. It was what she seemed to want.

But Caroline said, "It's just a shame we can't have little boys without men."

"Yes, it's unfortunate," I said, emotions in full retreat.

"Anyway . . . I already have my baby, so I guess I'm through with all that."

"Men are good for other things too, Caroline."

She did not seem convinced.

20

The next morning, John Kelly and I were back together. I needled him for skipping out on the tedious chore of sorting Danziger's files, but I did not ask him where he'd been.

The address Caroline provided, the last known residence of Detective Julio Vega, was a bungalow in Dorchester, a misplaced beach house dropped on a tiny lot in a run-down block. The front yard was sand with pimples of crabgrass sprouting here and there.

"You speak to him, Ben Truman. I'll have a look around back." Kelly held the nightstick behind his back and strolled around the side of the house.

I knocked on the door, then stepped down off the stoop to wait. Stiff shafts of crabgrass scratched my ankles. I knocked again, louder.

A man finally opened the door and stood there, behind the screen door. Heavyset Hispanic guy in a T-shirt and sweatpants. Bloated stomach. Pale skin, the color of concrete. This could not be the same guy I'd seen in the photo, the handsome Latino with the mustache. The guy looked me up and down but said nothing.

"I'm looking for Julio Vega."

"What are you? A reporter?"

"No, I'm a cop."

"You're a cop? You don't look like a cop."

I raised my badge holder. The man opened the screen door, took it, and retreated back inside to examine it.

"Are you Julio Vega?"

"Lot of Julio Vegas, man."

He was scrutinizing the badge, holding it close to his nose, his body swaying a little. "What's this?" he said. "Ver-*sales,* Maine?"

It took everything I had to resist congratulating him on the correct pronunciation. Instead, I asked him again whether he was Julio Vega.

"Who sent you here?"

"Nobody sent me. I found your name in Robert Danziger's files."

He glanced around the yard, then opened the door and tossed the badge back to me. "I got nothing to say, Chief."

"Would it help if I came back with a subpoena?" That sounded cool, I thought. A little stagy, maybe, but cool. "There's a grand jury being empaneled. They might like to hear from y—"

He snorted and disappeared into the house. The door closed with a click.

I looked around the scrofulous little yard feeling foolish and self-conscious. It didn't matter that there was no one there to see it—embarrassment is a reflex, evolved, encoded. It no longer requires an audience.

I knocked again.

This time the man opened the door with a clear drink in his hand. He scowled and rattled the ice cubes. "Now what are you gonna do, Joe Friday, break down the door?" It was dawning on me—belatedly—the man was drunk.

"Don't close the door on me again."

"You got that subpoena?"

"I'll get it if I have to."

"Good. Bring it to me. I'll wipe my ass with it."

He closed the door again, leaving me to wonder where exactly this interview had gone off the rails.

Kelly came around the corner, spinning the nightstick. "So?"

"I don't think he wants to talk to us."

"No? Did he say that?"

"Well, those weren't his exact words."

Kelly stepped onto the little concrete stoop and knocked on the door with the truncheon. When the door reopened, Kelly looked down at Vega and said politely, "We need to ask you a few questions, Detective Vega. It won't take a minute."

Vega thought it over, shrugged, and said, "Come on," then he shuffled back into the house.

Kelly gave me a look. *What was so hard about that?*

We followed Vega to a dim room cluttered with trash and yellowed newspapers. There were a few pictures around, all of which seemed to have been sitting undisturbed for years—grinning nieces, old Kodachrome grandparents. Vega gestured toward an ancient armchair, the seat cushion cupped out, the upholstery worn slick and dark. A stained antimacassar hung over the chair back. I was careful not to let my head touch it when I sat. Vega dropped into the chair next to mine, facing the TV. Without the screen door between us, I got my first good look at him. The man was a ruin. He was barefoot, and his toenails had sprouted into angular points. The enamel had a scaly, mineral appearance like yellow mica. I felt myself gawking at those toenails, then at a spongy-looking pink scar on Vega's left wrist, then at his tangled, overgrown hair. The former detective topped off his glass from a fifth of Cossack vodka. There was a heavy glass ashtray on Vega's armrest. He picked up a cigarette from the ashtray's edge, saw it was out, relit it.

"Chief," he said, "let me give you a word. You're a cop, I'm a cop. There's a way you treat people. With respect. You don't treat a cop like he's some shitbird you find in the street. That ragtime about subpoenas and grand juries, you save that for the bad guys. You talk to a cop, that's your brother you're talking to. You give respect. I earned that. Go ask your friend here." He gestured toward Kelly with the cigarette.

I said, "You're right."

"Fourteen years, I earned that. I don't care what you heard."

"You're right. I'm sorry."

"You're a cop, I'm a cop. That's the only reason you're sitting here. Respect."

He shook the ice in his glass, sipped again. Vodka in his right hand, cigarette in his left. He breathed through his nostrils as he drank, working quietly, concentrating. "There's a way you treat people. You ask the old man here."

Kelly ignored him. He was ambling around the room in his long-legged way, looking over the accumulated mess. He held the nightstick behind his back as if it were a rolled-up guidebook to the items on exhibit.

Vega and I watched the TV. Football highlights, a running back skittering away from tacklers.

"You like football, Detective Vega?"

"I like Barry Sanders, man. Look at him."

We watched.

"He's too fast, Barry's just too fast."

"Detective, I need to ask you about Bob Danziger." This brought a glance before Vega returned his attention to the TV and held it there. "What I need to know is, why did Danziger have a file on you in his office? A Probation file."

"There's lots of files on me."

"Lots of files, but Danziger only had one, your Probation file. I figure maybe it's nothing, he was just watching your case for personal reasons, because you know him. Is that it?"

"Don't ask it like that. Good detective doesn't ask yes-or-no questions like that. You keep it open, keep it open. Let 'em talk. Look for inconsis'cies." He was still staring at the TV, or pretending to. He was drunk and yet not drunk—or just drunk enough. "If you're talking, you're not listening, you're not learning shit. You get *him* talking, that's the way. Isn't that right?"

"That's right," Kelly seconded. "Ask again, Ben. Do it the right way."

"Okay. Tell me about Raul."

"I don't know from Raul."

"Tell me what you do know."

"There is no Raul, that's all I know, period."

His attention stayed on the TV, highlights from the previous Sunday's football games. "Look at that. You can't hit him, he's too fast. I always bet the Lions. Give the points, whatever, I just go with Sanders. Fuckin' Lions never cover, but I can't bet against my man Barry, you know?"

"Julio, why was Danziger looking at the Trudell case?"

"How would I know why Danziger was doing anything? You read my file, right? Everything I had to say about it is right there in the file."

Sanders, in silver pants and powder-blue shirt, danced and spun away from tacklers.

"You know why I like football, Chief? I like the field, all those lines. A line every yard, a hundred lines, all nice and straight. It's a grid. Everything happens right out there on that grid. Everybody tries to trick each other, fake each other, beat the shit out of each other, whatever, but it's all out on that grid for everybody to see. Look at Barry, man. He fakes and does all his wiggly shit and everything gets all crazy. But then it's over and they set the whole thing up again, all square and neat. That's why it's exciting when he messes everything up. Because it's only those in-between times, then everything's all put together again, everything's okay again.

It's, like, the tension, you know what I mean, Chief?" He sipped again. "That's why people love football."

"Julio, why did Danziger get killed?"

"He went after a Mission Posse kid, Gerald McNeese. G-Mac took it personal. G-Mac broke the code: He capped a DA. So he's got to pay. That's the rules."

"That's all there is to it? You believe that?"

"Why shouldn't I?"

"Because Danziger was asking you about Raul."

Vega hesitated.

"Julio, Danziger was your friend. Artie Trudell too. You owe them something."

"You leave that alone, junior. Don't tell me what I owe. I know what I owe and what I don't owe. I know what some people owe me too."

"What did Danziger ask you about Raul?"

"You've got it all wrong, Chief. This whole thing with Danziger's got nothing to do with Raul. Artie didn't get killed because of Raul. It's all bullshit. It's always been bullshit."

"All bullshit," I repeated, frustrated, confused. I leaned forward, elbows on knees. "But Raul wasn't bull-shit, was he?"

"The judge said there was no Raul. I made him up. That's how it went in the books. I did my time for it, it's over. That's all I got to say."

"Look, Julio, I'm asking you—as a cop—where did you and Artie get the tip about drug dealing at the red door? If it wasn't Raul who tipped you, then who was it? The information had to come from somewhere."

Vega stubbed out his cigarette and lit another.

"There was a Raul wasn't there? The judge got it wrong."

"You don't understand."

"No, I don't. Help me understand."

"A lot of cops have been using Raul a long time now."

"So he is real?"

"I didn't say that. It doesn't matter, the whole thing doesn't matter."

Vega looked down into his glass. Was he picturing Artie Trudell, dead but still standing, still holding that pipe? How many times did he see it, that endless loop? How many times had he watched Artie Trudell die?

"Artie put himself in front of that door," he said with a crypto-cooperative look. "I did too. We were stupid. The whole thing was unnecessary."

If there was a sign there, I missed it.

"Julio, was Danziger—"

"Ben," Kelly interrupted, "that's enough, it's time to go. Detective Vega, thank you for your time."

Vega kept his eyes on the football highlights, on the grid where everything was refereed and constantly re-ordered.

In the car, Kelly consoled me. "That was fine, Ben Truman. He gave you a little; he's not ready to give you more. Don't worry, we'll come back. Sometimes it takes time."

"He's still lying."

"Yes, he is. But I'm sure he has his reasons."

Vega's lying that day was quickly forgotten. In fact, the whole mess was forgotten—Vega, Trudell, "Raul," the red door, all of it. When Kelly called Caroline to check in, we were informed by SIU that Ray Ratleff was dead, his head blown apart just as Danziger's had been. There was no longer a case against Gerald McNeese; the only witness against him was dead. And it was going to be tough to blame "Raul" for this one.

21

The body was in Franklin Park, sprawled in the wet leaves under a stone-masonry footbridge. It was covered with a vinyl blanket, but Ray Rat was too tall and his lower legs protruded—pant legs pushed up, skinny shins, Nike high-tops.

A crowd had gathered at the edge of the yellow-taped perimeter. News photographers among them circled around for good angles, pointing their long-lensed cameras at the corpse.

A cluster of detectives stood around the body, chatting, oblivious to the thing at their feet. One was explaining that the secret to a true marinara sauce was to make it with a little bit of sugar in addition to all the other things, the tomatoes, the basil, the oregano, the olive oil; and he ought to know because, though he himself was German-Irish and at one point wouldn't have known marinara sauce from Heinz ketchup, his wife was off-the-boat Italian and he'd been watching her make marinara sauce a good fifteen, sixteen years. . . . I half expected the guy to prop his foot on the corpse as if it were a log.

Kelly introduced himself and asked what was going on.

"Somebody juiced this guy," one of the detectives replied. Older guy with an enormous square slab of a face. "It's a jungle out here. Know what I mean?" He made a big vaudeville wink, directed it at me.

Kelly kneeled and flipped back the blanket to see Ratleff's face, or what was left of it. The right eye and eye socket had burst, but the skull and scalp were otherwise intact. Black fluid gleamed in the eye socket and clotted in Ratleff's glorious Afro. Kelly threw the blanket back over the face, but the image lingered there like the shadowy features on the shroud of Turin.

"Monkey business." The slab-faced cop smirked.

Kelly ignored the comment. "When did it happen?" he asked.

"Couple hours ago maybe. Rigor is still just in the face and the eyelids." He corrected himself: "Eyelid."

"Any witnesses? Anything?"

"Nothing. Footprints, but this is a public park, there's thousands of footprints." The cop looked down at Ratleff's body with a wistful expression. "No witnesses. Nobody sees anything around here."

Twenty yards away, Caroline was enmeshed in an animated discussion with Kurth and Gittens. Kurth's severe, pitted face was clenched. He seemed to glow like one of those luminous monks by El Greco.

"How did this happen?" he was asking, agitated and intense, as we approached.

"I'm not sure what you mean, Ed," Gittens replied.

"You find the guy and forty-eight hours later he's dead? How does that happen?"

"I have no idea, Ed."

"How did you find him?"

"I told you, Ed, I got a tip. Ask these guys." Gittens nodded toward Kelly and me. "You're just pissed because you didn't find him. That's your problem, Ed, not mine. What can I tell you? You couldn't find the asshole on an elephant. Is that my fault, Ed?"

Gittens took an insolent delight in tweaking Kurth by

calling him Ed. Nobody seemed to call Kurth by his first name. Either that was Kurth's preference or just the effect of his over-torqued personality. But now Gittens leaned into the word, *Ed,* until it sounded vaguely ridiculous, as any word begins to sound ridiculous when it is repeated over and over.

Caroline intervened. "Alright, Martin, that's enough."

"Look," Gittens insisted, "if Braxton found Ray Rat, it was because Ray fucked up. He came home. Ray knew he shouldn't have done that but he did it anyway. If you're suggesting someone in Area A-3 tipped Braxton off—"

"I'm not talking about anyone else in A-3." Kurth glared.

"What's that supposed to mean?" Gittens affected puzzlement rather than anger, to signal that he did not consider Kurth a threat. "Come on, Ed. If you've got something to say, have the balls to come out and say it."

Ed Kurth began to move forward, but John Kelly stepped between them. He was a head taller than either, and he looked down at them like a disapproving father. "That's enough, both of you. You've said your piece."

But Kurth was unwilling—or unable—to relent. There was a volatile quality to his anger that separated it from Gittens's. He simply could not shut it off. He continued to stare until Kelly laid his nightstick across Kurth's chest and ordered him to "step . . . back."

Caroline said, "Ed, Martin's right, you're out of line. Take a walk, settle down, come back when you're ready to work."

It seemed for a moment that Kurth might lose it then and there, and I'm not sure what would have happened if he had. Just how much coiled, violent strength Kurth possessed, I did not know. But surely if he'd gone after Gittens, Kurth would have broken him in two—in front of a crowd that included newspaper photographers. Fortunately, Kurth did not explode. He turned and stalked off toward the green meadows of Franklin Park. It was, frankly, a relief to have him gone.

"I think he's going to beat up a tree," I said.

"Ben," Caroline warned, shaking her head. *Not now.*

At times Caroline could sound uncannily like my mother. This is a troubling, not to mention de-eroticizing, thought for any man, and usually I swatted it out of my mind the moment it landed. But that one-word warning, *Ben,* could have come directly from Annie Truman's mouth. It stopped me cold.

"It's Braxton," Gittens said matter-of-factly, eyes on Ray Ratleff's corpse.

Caroline nodded yes.

"We have motive, opportunity, a signature crime."

"I agree, there's enough," Caroline said. "Pick him up."

22

Picking up Braxton was easier said than done. He'd found himself a hidey-hole, and no one—not the cops, not the sliders in Echo Park, not even Gittens's Red Army of snitches—had any idea where to find him. There was nothing to do but wait. And wait. Eventually Braxton or one of his crew would make a mistake that would expose him. In all, the waiting would last four days.

The delay grated on everyone's nerves, including mine. Since my arrival in the city, I had been carried along on a current. Events streamed past, stations along the river, and it seemed I would be borne right through to the end. Now the tide slacked and things took on a stanched, dissolute feel. Afternoons, I went with Gittens to the Flats trying to scare up tips. Evenings, I spent at the SIU office or dining with the Kellys or exploring the city, walking the neighborhoods the way my mother used to walk Versailles.

Maybe it was the strange mood of those days, but I decided all at once that I did not like Boston. Something about the place—introverted, parochial, self-doubting— a fit capital for New Englanders, or so I told myself. I could not even appreciate the city's obvious physical beauty. Of course, in hindsight I see the flaw was not in Boston. I'd been happy there once, even considered it a second home. But now everything was different, and I could never see the city the same way. I just could not put my bags down, not there. I was waiting, for what I did not know.

On Thursday night—day one of this idle, interstitial period—I could not sleep, and around midnight I found myself standing in my underwear before the window of my hotel room, thinking of home. Streetlights in the South End winked below. (I was staying at the Back Bay Sheraton, one of those modern concrete cubes dropped into the nineteenth-century Back Bay like spaceships that crash-landed.) Hungry for a familiar voice, I called the station in Versailles on the pretense of checking up on things.

"V'says Peace."

"Maurice, what are you doing there?"

"I'm talking on the phone."

"Well, I see that, but— They have you answering the phone now?"

"Mmm-hmm."

I thought it over for a second. "That's a good idea, Maurice. Whose idea was that?

"Dick."

Dick Ginoux picked up the extension, and he caught me up on the news. Maurice had taken to hanging around the station, and it turned out he was a useful addition, answering phones, sweeping up, and so on. Diane Harned had stopped by that very afternoon to ask how I was doing. "I told her you were going to stay down there," Dick said. "Just about broke her heart." As for Dick himself, he had actually made an arrest on a DWI, which doesn't happen often, since drunk drivers rarely crash into the stationhouse and Dick rarely leaves it.

I missed them all, more than I had expected to.

"Dick, tell everyone I said hi and I'm doing fine, alright?"

"Alrighty, Ben. You keep your head down. I'm sure The Chief is proud of you."

"Dick, I'm the chief."

"I know that, Ben. You know what I mean."

"Any word from the AG?"

"Yessir. They identified Harold Braxton's fingerprints all over the cabin. Eight different places, something like. I guess he's your man. And one other thing. Red Caffrey called. Said he figured he ought to let us know, a couple weeks before the body turned up in that cabin, a black kid with a funny haircut pulled into Red's Gulf station in a white Lexus with Massachusetts plates. The kid bought a map and a tank of gas. Red says he didn't think nothing of it, except the kid didn't seem to go with the car, you know? Black kid pulls up in a fifty-thousand-dollar car and . . . well, the kid didn't even know what side of the car the tank was on. Red says he just got a bad feeling, figured maybe the car was stolen. But the ignition wasn't popped. The kid had a whole key chain in there. Anyway, Red took down the plate: *I dock*."

"I dock?"

"Yes, sir. I-D-O-C."

"Did you run the plate?"

"Well, we can't get Massachusetts registry records, but there's no report that it's stolen."

"That's good, Dick. Do me a favor, go see Red Caffrey again and show him those mug shots. And ask around, see if anyone else saw that kid. And Dick, have you seen my dad?"

"Haven't seen him."

"Well, swing by the house, would you? He's in a state, I think."

It was also during this hiatus that I first met Andrew Lowery, Boston's District Attorney. This was a command performance. Lowery sent word through Caroline that John Kelly and I were to appear at his office on Friday at nine A.M. Such meetings rarely come to any good, and this one was no exception.

We found Lowery at his desk in the Sussex County Courthouse. When we first glimpsed him, the District Attorney was leaning back in his desk chair, feet propped on an open drawer, absorbed in a television news report.

. . . police officers continue to comb the Dorchester, Mattapan, Mission Flats, and Roxbury neighborhoods today in search of the slayer of Assistant District Attorney . . .

Andrew Lowery was a slight but handsome African-American man with round wire-frame spectacles, in which at the moment the TV picture was reflected. He wore a blue candy-striped shirt with contrasting white cuffs and collar.

At the door, Kelly cleared his throat.

Lowery waved us in but continued to watch the screen. We waited two or three minutes more while the District Attorney monitored the New England Cable News channel for updates on his own case. (There were actually three televisions mounted in a console opposite Lowery's desk, but only one of the sets was on.)

When the report was over, Lowery slipped on his suit coat for our meeting. It was, I think, the best-fitting suit I had ever seen, and while I am no expert on such things, I assumed it was custom-made.

"Thank you for coming," he said when we'd sat down at a conference table. "I trust you're getting all the support you need?"

The question was directed at Kelly, but Kelly deferred to me.

"Yes," I replied, "we're fine."

"Do you want coffee? Anything?"

"No, thank you. We're fine."

The office was spare and formal, furnished with an expensive-looking Oriental carpet and Bauhaus furni-

ture. Three Harvard diplomas hung on the wall, from
the college, the law school, and the Kennedy School of
Government. The only hint of the usual Government
Office aesthetic was a framed seal of Sussex County,
which showed the three mounds on which Boston was
originally built by literal-minded pilgrims proclaiming a
city on a hill.

"I know you gentlemen are quite busy." Lowery
steepled his fingers. "So I won't take much of your time.
I have a friend I'm quite concerned about. I think you've
met him: Julio Vega."

Kelly and I exchanged a glance.

"I'm told you've questioned Detective Vega."

"Told by who?" Kelly asked.

"A little bird."

"And what did your little bird tell you about our discussion?"

His expression unchanged, Lowery turned away from
Kelly. Just ignored him. "Chief Truman, I hope you'll
understand. I'm going to ask you two to leave Vega
alone. He's not a well man."

"Not well in what sense?"

"In every sense. His mental state—I don't know what
will happen if you two go out and stir up ghosts. I don't
want Vega to make things worse for himself."

"Forgive me for saying so," I remarked, "but it's hard
to imagine things getting much worse for Julio Vega."

"Not hard for me. I'm concerned Julio might hurt
himself someday. He's unstable. And anyway, I don't
see the point in all this. Do you mind if I ask what your
interest is in the Arthur Trudell case?"

I informed Lowery that Danziger had been looking
into it.

"Bob Danziger must have had a hundred open cases.
The question is, do you have anything to tie the two
cases together? Is there a link?"

"No, sir. Not yet."

"Well look, I'm simply asking you to treat Vega

carefully. If you want to speak with him, we can arrange it. Otherwise, why don't we let sleeping dogs lie."

"That seems to be a popular approach."

"Chief Truman—Benjamin—I have a wider responsibility than you do."

"You do, sir?"

He leaned forward, folded his hands on the table. "Yes. My job is not merely to enforce the law; it's to keep the peace. You understand the distinction."

"Not really."

"The Trudell case is a hot button in this city. With respect to race."

At that, Kelly folded his hands on the table, mimicking Lowery's prayerful posture. "I'm sure the Trudell case is a hot button for Trudell's family too. As the Danziger case must be for his family."

Lowery did not react. He regarded Kelly a moment before responding. "Why don't we see if we can treat both cases with discretion, Lieutenant Kelly? For *both* families."

We shook hands and got up to leave, but as Kelly and I reached the door, Lowery added, "Lieutenant Kelly, I realize you have a long history here, but remember you're a guest in this city now."

Kelly: "A guest?"

"Yes. And we've tried to be good hosts. We've extended every courtesy, including the cooperation of the police department. But it doesn't have to be that way. We don't *have* to be good hosts. I hope you'll continue to be a good guest."

23

The first time Caroline kissed me:

John Kelly had taken Charlie for the day on Sunday. Kelly was on a mission that day, as far as I could tell, to do whatever the hell his grandson wanted, an excess of generosity offered up to Charlie as a sort of atonement for the old man's having moved away to Maine. This left Caroline to entertain me, an arrangement that seemed quite natural by then. I'd spent the last few evenings with the Kellys, and already there had developed a homey routine at Caroline's apartment. After dinner, I would play video hockey on the PlayStation with Charlie and sip Bushmills with the old man, then return to my hotel alone.

That Sunday afternoon, Caroline and I arranged to meet at the Avenue Victor Hugo bookshop on Newbury Street. It was a brilliant autumn day. The sunlight had a focusing, clarifying quality. You seemed to see the Newbury Street scene in high definition—grungers slinking like cats outside Tower Records; couples promenading; expensive European cars inching along in traffic.

The bookshop was a maze of aisles and rooms stuffed tight with dusty, time-faded books. The books lined the staircase and the walls, they were stacked on the creaky floors, they overflowed the shelves in every room. It was heaven. Waiting for Caroline, I drifted through the small rooms upstairs. I was happily skimming a travel book when I was brought up short by a woman's voice: "Ben?" I knew the voice without looking up, and I tried to keep my nose in the book until the speaker went away. But the voice was persistent. It inflected my one-syllable name into a sickening little glissando:

en?
e-
Be-

It was Sandra, my grad-school girlfriend, the flower of Boston University Communism. She was thinner than ever, but at least she had traded the heavy black-frame glasses of those days for a more chic model. She folded her arms and grinned. Then, craning her head forward like some predatory bird, she asked, "Are you here alone?"

"No."

"Me neither." She laid her hand beside her mouth vertically, like a bad actress playing to the back row, and confided, "I'm seeing someone."

I heard myself say "Me too" before I could think it through. It seemed important to match Sandra mate for mate. "She'll be here soon."

"I thought you were in Maine?"

"I am."

"And your mother?"

"She passed away this summer."

"Oh, Ben, I'm so sorry."

"Thank you."

"It's good to see you," she lied. "What are you doing now? Are you back in school somewhere?"

I shook my head no.

"What then?"

"I'm—I'm sort of a policeman."

"A policeman! Still? In your little town? What was it called?"

"Versailles."

"Versailles, yes. How precious."

"I'm the chief there now."

"Oh, my."

I tried to parse the phrase for complimentary intentions, but they were hard to find. That *oh, my* meant I had just become fodder for cafeteria gossip. *Do you remember Ben Truman? You'll never guess what he's doing now. . . .*

"What about your work?"

"That is my work. For the time being, at least."

"Oh."

Her cheeks flushed a little. She seemed to be floundering for a new topic.

"So who's your new boyfriend?" I said.

"His name is Paul. He's downstairs. He's brilliant! He has a chair at this foundation Across The River." She confided, "Everyone says he's up for the MacArthur."

"Do they?"

"And your girlfriend? Is she here?"

I paused, fatally.

"Ben?"

"Well, she's not really—I'm not sure when she's getting here."

"Is this her?"

Caroline appeared beside us. She wore jeans and a black baseball jacket, and at the moment she seemed like a higher life-form than Sandra—strapping and confident, radiant at the prospect of a weekend afternoon all her own, with neither child care nor work to consume her.

"Is this her what?" Caroline asked, curious.

"Ben's girlfriend?"

Caroline gave me a bemused look.

"I was just telling Sandra . . ." My tongue swelled into a grapefruit.

Sandra's face registered a moment's confusion, then I saw her put it all together. Another morsel for the cafeteria crowd: *And then—oh, this is rich—he said this woman was his girlfriend but she clearly had no idea. . . .*

The next moment I felt Caroline's hands on my neck and her lips on mine, and warm breath from her nostrils on my cheek, and she pressed a kiss onto my mouth. "Sorry I'm late," she said. "Traffic."

Sandra looked stricken, as if she'd just walked in on her parents in flagrante delicto. She made an excuse and scurried off.

"Thank you," I told Caroline.

"Don't mention it, Chief Truman."

The way Caroline remembered Bob Danziger:

"Bobby wasn't one of these avenging-angel types. He didn't open every file and see the Boston Strangler. He was always like, 'This kid's not so bad' or 'Look at his record. There's no violence. It's all just drug stuff.' He was always so damn *reasonable*." She squeezed the word like a lemon. "I mean, he used to carry spiders outside rather than kill them! Is that the kind of guy you'd think this would happen to?"

We were at a bar called Small Planet, in Copley Square.

As she remembered Danziger, Caroline plowed little furrows in her napkin with a fork. "Something changed for Bobby, though. At the end, he seemed to lose that courage, that equanimity. I used to watch him sometimes when his verdicts came in. He'd never look at the defendant. It was like he was ashamed. He'd look at the floor, he'd look off into space, anywhere but at the defendant."

"Why would he do that?"

"I don't know. Maybe he was worried. There's always

that kernel of doubt, the possibility you got it wrong. You have to be able to live with that. You have to be a little callous to do this job."

"And Danziger wasn't callous?"

"Not at the end, no. You know, just before he died, Bobby got a conviction on a big gang case. I mean, this was a big hook. So I went in to congratulate him. I thought he'd be elated. But he was really down. He seemed sort of hollow, I don't know how else to put it. I didn't know what to tell him, so I said, 'Bobby, what are you feeling right now?' You know what he said? He said, 'Revulsion.' "

"Revulsion?" I echoed. "At what?"

"At the whole system. At the jury for pretending to know the truth, at the judge for pretending to know what to do about it, at the state for locking up an eighteen-year-old in a place like Walpole. Revulsion at the defendant too, not because he committed the crime, but because he'd set the whole thing in motion, this whole irresistible machine. He'd made Bobby do it. Bobby told me, 'It feels like *I'm* guilty of something.' He was feeling all this revulsion at himself, for participating."

"Sounds like he was just burned out."

"No," she said firmly. "Not burned out—shaken. Burnout is a gradual thing. What happened to Bobby happened fast. Something really rattled him."

"What was it?"

"I honestly have no idea."

"So how about you, Caroline? Do you look away when the verdict comes in?"

"Me? No, I couldn't possibly! I look right at the defendant. I *have* to. I have to see that little flinch when he hears the word *guilty.* I want to see those eyes blink when he understands he didn't get away with it, there's a price to be paid after all. And I want him to know I'm the agent of all that."

A smile played on her lips, a bad-girl smile that made me think of a lepidopterist pinning a rare specimen to

her butterfly board. I wondered what unfortunate defendant she was remembering.

"Does that make me a bad person?" she asked.

"Probably."

For no good reason, Caroline and I decided to stop at
every bar we saw on Newbury Street that Sunday, from
the tastefully honky-tonk corner of Mass. Ave. all the
way to the Ritz with its blue awnings and blue-coated
doormen. At the end of this steeplechase, she tried to
pull me into the Ritz Bar too, but I nixed it. "I don't
think I'd be comfortable at the Ritz," I said.

Instead we went into the Public Garden, where even
at dusk there were a few tourists staring up at the statue
of George Washington on horseback. Washington
looked serenely down at them, clutching the remains of
a sword. (The blade has been wrenched out of the general's sword so many times, the city no longer replaces
it. But General Washington stubbornly clings to the
empty hilt.)

"Dude, take my picture?" a guy said to me.

I asked him, Didn't he think it was too dark for the
picture to come out?

"It's okay," he explained, "I'll be able to see it."

"You better have her take it," I said, handing the task
to Caroline. "I've been drinking."

So he stood beneath Washington's statue and Caroline
took the camera.

Pleasantly drunk, I watched her from behind as she
lined up the shot and directed the tourists on how to
pose. And in my thoughts the actual Caroline was dis-
placed by images of her in court a few days before. Not
the whole of her, just glimpses: the soft briefcase
slouched against her ankle, the gestalt flame formed by
the curves of her calves, the arch of her back as she
pulled her jacket tight around her. I tried to displace

these imaginings with other, less charged ones, but it wasn't much use.

We moved to a dessert restaurant called Finale. It was an oval room with small tables and deco fixtures, dimly lit.

"Caroline, why does Lowery want to keep us away from Julio Vega?"

"I imagine Andrew doesn't want anyone mucking around in the Trudell case. He was the DA when the case went south, and it still haunts him. Voters don't like to see cop killers get off. It leaves a bad impression. And Andrew starts a new campaign soon. Did my dad give him a hard time?"

"He bit his tongue, for the most part."

"That's unlike him."

"What's Lowery running for, anyway?"

"The rumor is he wants to be mayor. First black mayor of Boston, and a Republican to boot. But who knows."

"Well, it still doesn't make sense to me. Election or not, Artie Trudell was a cop."

"It's not that simple, Ben. Cases get closed for lots of reasons." She looked at me for signs of understanding but got none. "Look, some cases stay unsolved because somebody wants them to stay unsolved. Like the DeSalvo case, the Boston Strangler. For thirty-five years around here, the worst-kept secret among cops and DAs has been that Albert DeSalvo was not the Strangler. They stuck him in a lockup with a serial rapist who told DeSalvo all about the murders, and DeSalvo was an unstable guy himself, so he took all these stories and he went out and confessed to things he never did. He got all kinds of details wrong, but nobody cared. It was just easier to let people believe the case was solved. It was what they needed to believe so they could sleep at night. The trouble is, if anybody ever did prove that DeSalvo wasn't the Strangler, then a lot of people would have to account for their actions. See what I mean? It's not always about the truth."

"So who is it that wants the Trudell case buried?"

"Lowery, for one. Julio Vega and Franny, too, I'm sure. None of them covered themselves in glory."

"Franny says you think he's crooked. Is it because of this?"

She shook her head. "Look, I have no idea what Franny really did in the Trudell thing. I have my suspicions. It's hard to believe Vega made up all that crap about 'Raul' by himself. But my issue with Franny isn't that he's crooked. It's that he's a drunk, which would be his business except he's not a very good lawyer anymore."

"So why does Lowery protect him?"

"Because Franny knows more than he's said, and Lowery wants to keep it that way. So Lowery keeps Franny on the payroll, and Franny keeps his mouth shut."

The first time I kissed Caroline:

She stepped back, smiled, and said my name. Then, "Are you sure you want to do this?"

"I'm really, really sure, yeah."

A car drove past and we watched it self-consciously. We were standing outside my hotel. The doorman was watching us. The night air was chilly.

"Ben, you don't have to charm me, you know. It's not necessary."

"What if I want to?"

"Don't waste it."

In the hotel room we kissed, awkwardly, and Caroline suggested we get in bed. I said that was fine, and we undressed and lay side by side, facing each other. She leaned forward to kiss me again. Our knees bumped. There was the predictable prod as we slid close, but Caroline did not acknowledge it. She held my face in her hands and studied it. She said, "Why do I have this feeling I've met you before?" I said, "I don't know. I think I'd remember you."

Later, Caroline gathered her things and went into the bathroom to wash and get dressed. I turned on the TV and, when she came out, I was staring at an old movie.

Caroline asked, "What's that?"

"*Rio Bravo*. You want to watch?"

"Is that a John Wayne thing?"

"Right now it's an Angie Dickinson thing."

"From *Police Woman*?"

"Yeah."

"I liked *Police Woman*."

"I never knew what was going on with her and Earl Holliman on that show."

Caroline shrugged her jacket on. "He liked Angie Dickinson but he couldn't say so because of their jobs."

"Oh."

"Ben, I have to get home to Charlie."

On the TV, Angie Dickinson was telling John Wayne, *That's what I'd do if I were the kind of girl you think I am.*

"That's alright. I know how it ends anyway."

She grimaced. "How does it end?"

"Everybody was wrong about everybody else, basically."

"Doesn't sound like much of an ending."

"Well there's a gunfight too. But it's not really the point."

24

After four days of searching for Harold Braxton—since Caroline had given the go-ahead to pick him up after Ray Rat's murder—the Boston police had nothing to show. Braxton had vanished.

Gittens and I trolled the Flats daily, questioning anyone who had ever passed him a tip. It was fascinating to watch Gittens, a supple man who was able to connect with all sorts of people. This he accomplished with an arsenal of small talents. He spoke passable Spanish. He had a politician's knack for remembering names, not just the names of informants but their relatives and associates too. And most important, Gittens used good judgment. He had no desire to pile up the arrests, and he was perfectly willing to turn a blind eye to petty offenses where other cops might not. It is too much to say that all this skill was appreciated by a grateful populace. Gittens was still a cop and people were leery of him. But he handled his role gracefully, he was respectful, he spotted nuances and complexities that others missed. He was a great cop—and he knew it.

In this case it wasn't enough. Braxton had vanished, and by this point the police were no longer searching for him so much as they were waiting for Braxton to reveal himself. Officers were posted in likely locations and left to wait there like hunters behind duck blinds. Convinced he knew Braxton better than anyone, Gittens positioned a few officers from Area A-3 at various locations in the Flats. Kelly and I drew assignments from Gittens too. I was stationed, alone, outside the apartment building where June Veris's girlfriend lived—an unpromising site, I thought, although Gittens assured otherwise.

I arrived at my post early Monday morning, around seven. Under a dreary gray sky, I leaned in a doorway and sipped from a paper cup of coffee. My assignment was to eyeball the building opposite, on the off chance that Braxton might have stayed there the night before. In movies they call this a "stakeout," though I've never heard a cop use that term. Call it what you will, it is a phenomenally boring task. And to a worrier like me, it is an invitation to trouble. An idle mind and all that.

My thoughts turned to Caroline and our encounter the night before. What had it meant to her? And to me? It is all very well and good to take someone to bed with blithe intentions, but there is always the danger that things will seem more complicated in the morning—particularly when it is unclear who took whom to bed. It was not that I had fallen in love with Caroline. Nothing so dramatic or unambiguous had happened. I am too cautious a person to be struck by those thunderbolts anyway. But something had happened. I could not stop thinking about her—or, more accurately, about my idea of her, for it must be said that Caroline Kelly was a difficult person to know. She could be warm and mettlesome one moment, chilly and remote the next. You got the sense she simply did not want to be known, not until she was good and ready. Not until she'd decided. When she'd said the night before "You don't have to charm me, Ben," her voice seemed to carry a warning: *Don't think you can charm me.* Was that streak of circumspection the result of her divorce? Impossible to know.

In hindsight, I see that Caroline's contradictions were precisely why I could not let go of the subject. The more she puzzled me, the more I thought about her; the more I thought about her, the more puzzled I became. Was she beautiful or just vivid? Was she warm, as she'd been with Charlie (and me), or irascible, as she sometimes delighted in being? I wanted to understand her in my academic way, I wanted to flatten all that wonderful complexity and elusiveness into a few bald adjectives. No, I had not *fallen in love*. After a certain age you do not *fall* in love. Falling, with its implications of delirium and loss of control, is no longer the right metaphor. What you do is study your lover. You consider her. You turn her over in your hand like a coin from a foreign country. But then, that is a kind of love too.

All of this I was considering—Caroline, the taste-memory of her mouth, the feel of her strong back—the complicating factor of Charlie—the possibility of love—all these considerations swarmed in my mind, and I was in the process of sorting them out—categorizing them—because you have to be prudent with these things—emotion, I mean—you have to consider it, not rush in like Annie Wilmot did with Claude Truman—when Bobo showed up.

Bobo looked different than he had a week before, when Gittens rousted him from the Dumpster-cum-shooting gallery at the garbage collection plant. Gone were the Lakers sweatshirt and the stained work pants. Gone too was the druggy stupor. Now Bobo was flashing a definite sense of style. He wore his Greek fisherman's cap down over one eye. And he walked with a rhythmic strut, limping slightly on his left leg so that he moved down the street like a bird with a broken wing.

Bobo was still half a block away when he recognized me, or at least recognized trouble. A white guy in this neighborhood—a white guy with a bad haircut standing around drinking coffee, a white guy looking at him in a familiar way—all things considered, to Bobo it meant trouble. Trouble of the law-enforcement variety. He immediately crossed the street, looking both ways, to put a little distance between us as he passed.

Even law-abiding people often become anxious when cops are around. But Bobo did not seem unnerved in the least. Bobo was cool. As he reached the parked cars on the opposite side of the street, he looked across at me and that was all. No sign of recognition, let alone fear. Then Bobo disappeared around the corner.

I hesitated, then, with a last forlorn look at 442 Hewson Street—the building I was supposed to be watching—I decided instead to follow Bobo. It was an impetuous decision. I did not know whether I would try to talk to him or whether I was just curious to see what he was up to. Mostly, I think I was fed up with staring at June Veris's girlfriend's apartment building—staring, sipping coffee, pissing at the convenience store on the corner, staring some more. Four straight days of that was enough. So I followed Bobo.

There was not much of a crowd on Hosmer Street, a fairly busy road that runs east–west through Mission Flats, so I kept a good block or two behind him. He strutted his way down Hosmer a few blocks, then hooked a left onto a side street with the winsome name Blue Moon Lane. By the time I reached the corner, Bobo was already slipping through the doorless entry to a brownstone.

The brownstone was one of eight or ten that lined the street. All but one were well-kept, Bobo's being the exception. I have seen pictures of Berlin after World War II, and the best way I can think to describe this building is to say that it looked like something out of Berlin in 1945. There was no front door and no glass in any of the windows. Every delicate piece of the structure—glass, window frames, gutters—had been blown away. What remained was the beautiful stone facade, a chain-link fence sliced open with wire cutters, and an ominously worded NO TRESPASSING sign.

I guessed (incorrectly, it turned out) that Bobo had gone inside to score drugs. What other reason was there to hang out in such a building? So I decided to wait until he came out again. Five, ten minutes—how long could it take?

But Bobo did not emerge after fifteen minutes, or thirty, or sixty.

So I decided to go in for the simple, all-explaining reason *That's What Gittens Would Do.* After watching and admiring Gittens's mastery of Mission Flats police-work for the last few days, I had begun to ape him consciously. I drew my gun for the same reason, though in three years as a cop I had never done so before. *That's What Gittens Would Do,* or so I hoped.

Inside, there was a central staircase. The apartment doors were missing, and sunlight poured in from the empty windows to light the empty rooms. The floors were silted over with dirt and rot. But the seaminess was offset by poignant vestiges: scraps of wallpaper adhering to the walls; a fireplace where a family had once warmed themselves; old newspapers; a stained mattress. I worked my way up the staircase to the second floor, where there were more empty rooms, then to the third, where at last I found Bobo.

He was on the floor, alone, in a room at the front of the building. A piece of cardboard was propped in the window, leaving this room gloomier than the rest. Maybe Bobo had blocked the window himself, looking for privacy or a place to sleep. He lay against the wall, apparently sleeping. There was a needle by his side with a little yellowish fluid remaining in the syringe. It was unlikely that Bobo had shot up only half a syringe. He had probably passed out while preparing a second one.

"Bobo!" I knelt beside him and felt his neck for a pulse. I shook him. "Bobo!"

He groaned. His eyes opened, fixed on me with milky pupils, closed again.

"Bobo! Wake up. Are you alright?"

"Mmmm."

"Jesus, Bobo, I'm going to get you an ambulance." I took out my radio, which I'd been given in case I spotted Braxton over on Hewson Street.

"No am-uh-lance, no am-uh-lance." Bobo pushed himself up to a sitting position. Drowsily, he covered his face with his hands, rubbed, then opened his hands like a child playing peekaboo. "I seen you before?"

"I'm a friend of Martin Gittens. We saw you at that garbage place the other day."

"Yeah yeah yeah," he murmured. "You hit me in the balls."

"No."

"Those were my balls, man. You think I forgot?"

"They were your balls but it wasn't me that hit them."

He closed his eyes again. " 'At's alright, 'at's alright. I'm not mad at you. Just balls, right?"

"That's right, Bobo."

I wondered what he'd been shooting. Heroin, presumably.

"Give me my works, man."

"I can't do that. I'm a cop."

"You gonna arrest me?"

"No."

"Then give me my works." He stretched out his hand toward the needle but seemed incapable of moving further to get it.

"Can't help you, Bobo. Sorry."

He closed his eyes and drifted off. After a while he said, "What you come here for?"

"I'm looking for Braxton."

"Thought you were looking for Ray. You heard about Ray?"

"Yeah, I heard. That's why we're looking for Braxton."

"You guys fucked Ray good."

"We did not fuck Ray, Bobo. Braxton did that."

"Whatever you say, boss." His head lolled. "You

come in here looking for Braxton? Ain't going to find him here."

"I came in here to talk to you."

"Yeah? What we going to talk about?"

"Braxton. You know where he is?"

"Maybe I do." The sound of this answer pleased him, and he repeated it with a crooked smirk. "Maybe I do."

"Bobo, I could still take you in if I had to."

"You already said you weren't going to." He opened one eye. "Besides, Gittens won't let you. He helps me out."

"Is that how it works?"

"That's how it works. Come on, boss, you help me out too." He pointed with his chin toward the syringe on the floor.

"Bobo, I can't do that."

"What's your name, anyway?"

"It's Ben Truman."

"Well, Officer Truman, let me tell you how it is. You want to *get*, see, you got to *give*. That's what it's all about. Capitalism."

"Bobo, do you know where Braxton is?"

"See, that's it. You want to get, but you don't want to give."

I took out a twenty and tossed it on his lap. This was no small thing. Twenty dollars was a lot to me. I didn't have Gittens's Robin Hood instinct for robbing the dealers to pay the snitches.

He glanced down at it but did not move. Struggling to lift his eyes from his lap, he mused, "Just give me my works, will you."

"No."

"Go find Braxton yourself then."

"Bobo, I could give you another whack in the balls. That seems to help you open up."

"You could but you won't."

"Yeah? Why not?"

"Because you don't want to."

"You don't know me."

"Yes, I do," Bobo assured me. "Yes, I do."

He made a lethargic grab at the syringe, but I snatched it away. Bobo fell on his side and lay there, laughing. I took the syringe to the window to look at it in the light. It was a cheap plastic thing but surprisingly clean. It weighed almost nothing. I shook the little bit of fluid in the cartridge.

"Just give that here."

"Bobo, I told you, I can't do it. You don't need it now, anyway."

"Suppose you let me decide that."

"Suppose you tell me where Braxton is."

"Suppose I do? Then you help me out?"

I shook my head no.

"Then we'll see who he kills next."

I walked over and handed the needle down to him.

"I need that too." He nodded toward a belt on his own lap.

"Just take it," I said.

"I can't, man, I'm fucked up. You help."

I handed him the belt.

Bobo prepared the syringe with a few flicks of his finger, then he wrapped the belt around his upper arm, pulled it tight into a tourniquet, and clasped the free end in his teeth. He held the needle out to me.

I walked away, refusing it.

Bobo laid the needle down and took the belt out of his mouth. "You want me to tell you about Braxton or not?"

"Yes."

"Well I can't talk with this in my mouth. I only got two hands."

I knelt beside him.

"Hold this."

I held the belt tight.

Bobo searched a long time for a vein. The needle pierced his arm four times. When he'd found one, he sighed and asked, "You want to do it?"

"Bobo, just tell me where Braxton is. I gave you the dope."

"You want to do it?"

"Where is he?"

"You do it."

"No."

He took the thumb of my free hand and placed it on the plunger, then put his own thumb over mine. "We'll do it together. You want to be a cop, you should know how this works."

I did not resist.

"Let's do it together." A lunatic smile.

"Bobo, where's Braxton?"

"There's a church on Mission Ave., Calvary Pentecostal. This priest there, Reverend Walker, he puts Braxton up sometimes when he's in trouble. The Reverend's known Braxton since Harold was in diapers. He helps him out. Maybe you'll find Harold there."

With that, Bobo's thumb pressed down on my thumbnail, and the plunger, after a brief, virginal resistance, slid down the syringe. I allowed the belt to go slack. Bobo's eyes squeezed shut as the heroin orgasm washed over him in a warm rush.

I told myself, *He would have done it anyway, whether I'd helped or not. I didn't really do anything. Nothing Gittens wouldn't have done.*

I did not find Braxton at the Calvary Pentecostal Church that day. But I made it part of my routine to stop by the church when I wasn't staring at the apartment building on Hewson Street. Soon enough, I conceived a hero fantasy in which I would capture Braxton singlehanded at this church, effectively ending the case.

What I did not realize was that the Boston PD had already identified a new suspect—me.

25

Your name was in Danziger's files."

It was a startling moment, though the statement itself was not surprising. I was not shocked to hear that my name was in Danziger's files: Danziger and I had spoken the day he arrived in Versailles. No, the startling thing was how suddenly and irrefutably this fact made me a pariah. How easy it was for Lowery and Gittens, based on this single datum, to imagine me rifle-blasting Bob Danziger's head. You could hear it in their voices. I was out. It was the day before Halloween. Gittens, Andrew Lowery, and I had gathered in a windowless interrogation room inside the Area A-3 station.

Lowery, in a soigné double-breasted suit with peaked lapels, seemed comically out of place here. He stood at the furthest corner from me, looking small and doll-like.

Gittens's fingers worked the skin on that elongated forehead, a gesture of benign puzzlement. "Mr. Truman," he said, "do you want to explain what's going on?"

" 'Mr. Truman'? Explain what exactly?"

"Why you lied to us."

"I didn't lie to you. I just did not think it was relevant."

Lowery burst out, "Oh come on! You didn't think it was relevant?"

"What does it have to do with Danziger's getting killed?"

"Motive!" Lowery said.

"Ben," Gittens soothed, "do you want a lawyer in here with you?"

"No! Jesus, Martin! Where's Kelly? Why didn't you call him in here too?"

"We don't think he belongs here right now. We don't think either of the Kellys should be present for this, frankly. Do you need me to read you your rights?"

"Of course not."

"Then you understand your rights and you waive them?"

"Martin, what are you talking about?"

"Do you understand your rights and waive them?"

"No! Yes! What the hell are you talking about?"

Lowery quick-stepped in from the corner on little dancer's feet. "What are we talking about? Why didn't you tell us your mother killed herself? Why didn't you tell us Danziger was investigating *you*?"

"I didn't tell you my mother killed herself because it's none of your damn business. And I didn't tell you Danziger was investigating me because there's nothing to investigate."

"Nothing to investigate?" Lowery snapped open a file. "August 16, 1997, Anne Wilmot Truman found dead in Room 412 of the Ritz-Carlton Hotel in Boston. Cause of death: suicide by barbiturate overdose."

"My mother committed suicide. So what?"

"Ben," Gittens explained, "assisted suicide is illegal in Massachusetts. It's murder."

"I didn't say it was assisted. I said my mother committed suicide."

"Danziger apparently thought differently."

I leaned back in my chair and stared at the ceiling tiles with an incredulous grin. I said, "Danziger came up to speak to me, to check it out. In his shoes, I'd probably do the same. We talked, he asked what happened, I explained the whole thing to him. He was satisfied. That was the last we ever heard of Robert Danziger until the body turned up."

"*We?*"

"Me."

"What did you explain to him?"

"You must already know."

"Tell me again."

"I told him my mother had an incurable disease. I told him she knew the Alzheimer's was eating her up and she did not want to ride it out to the bitter end. I told him she made a horribly painful decision and I supported her. But *she* made the decision. She did what she had to do and that was all. There was no case, certainly not a murder."

"Then why did you lie about it?" Lowery insisted.

"I told you, I did not lie about it."

"You just didn't volunteer that you had a motive to kill Danziger."

"I did not have a motive to—Jesus! Are you listening to me?"

Lowery cross-examined me for the benefit of an imaginary jury. "Chief Truman, your mother's illness trapped you in Maine. It disrupted your life, all your grand plans for the future. Wasn't it enormously convenient for you when she died?"

"No!"

"Her death set you free, didn't it?"

"That's not how it was."

"Why did she do it in Boston? Why not at home?"

"This was home. She wanted to die here. She was never really at home in Versailles."

"And when Danziger showed up?"

"I told you. We spoke very briefly. I told him it was a suicide. He said he was sorry for my mother's death. I thanked him for his condolences. End of story. My bad luck that Braxton found him while he was still in Maine."

"Your fingerprints are all over the murder scene."

"Of course my fingerprints are all over the murder scene: I discovered it. That's why I submitted my prints—so they could be excluded as evidence, same as any cop's would be. Braxton's prints were all over the murder scene too."

Lowery paced, arms folded. His cuff pulled back to reveal an elegant gold watch the size and thickness of a quarter. "Is this why you insisted on coming here? Because it never quite made sense to me until now. I mean, why come so far to stay informed about a case when you could just as easily keep tabs with a few phone calls? But now I see. Your interest wasn't professional at all, was it? You had a personal reason for coming. What did you hope to accomplish here? Were you going to steer us toward someone else? Braxton maybe? Or was it that you just couldn't stand to be kept in the dark, knowing the trail would inevitably lead back to you?"

"That's ridiculous. Every word of it. Martin, are you going along with this? Do you really believe I could have done this?"

"You should have told us up front, Ben." Gittens seemed at a loss.

I shook my head. "This is surreal."

"Oh, it's very real," Lowery intoned, "I assure you. Let me give you a word of advice. Go back home. Hire a lawyer. There's more evidence against you than you know."

"What does that mean?"

"Ben, did you think Danziger was just guessing when he went all the way to Maine to talk to you? Did you think there was no evidence?"

"You're setting me up."

"Nobody is setting you up," Lowery said.

"I'm being set up."

"Just stay away from this investigation. Better yet, stay away from this city, for your own sake. If it comes out that you're a cop killer—"

"Mr. Lowery, are you threatening me?"

"I'm just telling you, this is how it is."

26

My first instinct was to reject the whole thing as a mistake, a Kafkaesque fantasy of opaque charges, hidden evidence, a false trial. Of course I was no murderer. Martin Gittens at least must have known that. There was also an absurd reaction: It crossed my mind that I was miscast in the role of the homicidal baddie, that I could never make a convincing show of it. Who would believe it? But before long the reality of the situation won out. On the street outside the stationhouse, I looked about with the smeary, frantic paranoia of a fugitive—quickened to the environment yet removed from it somehow.

I tried without success to reach John Kelly, then rushed downtown to the SIU office to see Caroline—to explain. Or, perhaps, to get an explanation.

Caroline at first refused to see me. Franny Boyle made several thick-necked attempts to move me out of the lobby, and when I refused to leave he threatened to call the cops himself. It was not until I began to push my way past Franny with a lineman's swim move that Caroline finally appeared in the waiting area and agreed to hear me out, albeit with the condition that a cop be present too, to witness the conversation.

"Caroline, you need a witness just to talk to me?"

"What do you want me to say?"

"How about that you believe me."

"Ben, I don't even know you."

She called Edmund Kurth, and for the next twenty minutes or so we waited in silence while he rushed over. Caroline was being careful. Kurth's eyes and ears would save her from being called to the stand as an essential witness, lest I blurt out a confession. In theory, his presence would preserve the possibility that Caroline might someday prosecute me personally for Danziger's murder.

When he arrived, Kurth stood scowling at me, his coiled presence more ominous now that I was the object of his attention.

"Alright," Caroline said, "what is it you want to say?"

"Do you know what's going on?"

"Yes, of course I do."

"Then tell me."

"You lied."

"To who?"

"To me, to my father, to everyone."

"No. I don't accept that."

"Did your mother kill herself?"

"Yes."

"And did Danziger question you about it?"

"Yes."

Caroline shrugged. *There it is. QED.*

"Don't you want to hear my side?"

"Not really. If you want to give a statement to Detective Kurth, I'll wait outside."

"No. I want you to hear it. Caroline—just listen for one minute."

She sat down at the conference table, her face blank. She seemed to have receded entirely. I got the sense the real Caroline—her essential self—was observing me from some hidden place, while this other Caroline—the mediate Caroline, the stand-in—sat at the table in this room.

"I can't do it like this."

"Like what?"

"Does he have to be here?"

"Kurth? Yes."

"I don't know where to start."

"Tell me why she did it."

"She had Alzheimer's disease."

"You can't die of that."

"You can! Not directly, but you can—you do. You didn't know my mother. She was not going to let it happen to her. She was a smart, sophisticated woman, and then this thing just came along and—you can't imagine."

She stared.

"It began to chew through her mind bit by bit, like a caterpillar on a leaf. She couldn't just watch herself be erased. She made the decision while she still could."

"The decision to kill herself."

"The decision to die in a way that was acceptable to her."

"And you helped?"

"I listened, I talked to her, yes."

"How did she do it?"

"Seconal. Her doctor prescribed them to help her sleep. She hoarded them until she had ninety of these little red capsules. She'd researched it. She knew precisely how much she needed for a fatal dose."

"Why the Ritz-Carlton?"

"She loved it there. She remembered going there for afternoon tea when she was a kid. Her father used to take her. They had a falling-out later on, when she got married. After that they barely spoke. She could tell you just where they'd sit, she and her dad, always by a window looking over the Public Garden. She could describe the blue drapes, the cobalt-blue glasses, the whole room. It was their special place."

"And where were you when she did it?"

"Where should I be, Caroline?"

"Why didn't you tell anyone Danziger spoke to you about it?"

"Because I was afraid of this. I was afraid of exactly this."

"So you lied and made it worse."

"Yes, I lied. I made it worse. For that I'm sorry."

"I'm sure you are."

A shadow crossed her face, and for a moment I thought I'd glimpsed the true Caroline—the invisible one standing by the window with crossed arms, the Caroline who'd been with me just a few days before, kissing me. But the moment passed. The connection vanished.

"Is that all you want to say?" she said.

"I guess so." It was impossible to hide the hurt in my voice, pathetic as that sounds.

"Alright then. I listened. I did what you asked."

"Where's your father? I tried to call him."

"Ben, I don't want you calling him. Or me."

With a glance at Kurth, I said, "Caroline, can we talk for a minute, alone?"

"No. Absolutely not." She got up to leave but hesitated. "I'm so disappointed in you, Ben. I thought you might actually be someone."

27

The Calvary Pentecostal Church of God in Christ had begun its life as the Temple Beth Adonai. That name was still visible, impressed in the architrave above the main entrance. Other vestiges remained. Six-point stars woven into the wrought-iron fence. Stained-glass windows, now protected by steel grates, depicting Old Testament stories: Adam and Eve leaving the garden; the sacrifice of Isaac; Moses receiving the tablets on Mount Sinai. The overlay of Christian symbols was relatively impermanent. You had the sense that, if the lost Jews of Mission Flats ever decided to return from the suburbs, their temple could be restored in just a few hours.

I came here directly from my meeting with Caroline. The last few days, I had made this church part of my rounds, part of the hunt for Harold Braxton. But now I came here for a different reason. I had nowhere else to go, no place to think. It was hard not to think of the church as a sanctuary in the archaic legal sense, a sacred place where fugitives like me were immune from arrest.

I entered the building through a mammoth wooden door. Inside was a lobby and then the worship space, which soared to an onion-shaped dome—a bit of eastern

European exotica that again recalled the building's original tenants. Water-stained and veined with cracks, the
dome had the power to stop you cold.

My hand touched each of the benches as I moved
down the aisle. I went through the habitual motions of
looking for Braxton. I tried doors—offices, storage
rooms, vestry, anyplace that could serve as a hideout. As
usual, the building appeared deserted. All the rooms had
a stale, dusty smell, suggesting they had not been used,
or even aired out, in quite a while.

I sat down in a pew. There was an urge to let go and
cry, and an equally powerful urge to fight back, to prove
my innocence. I slumped and let my head loll back
against the bench. On Sunday mornings, no doubt,
bored little kids studied the cracks in the dome, traced
them as they threaded upward, only to end abruptly or
merge into other, deeper cracks.

I became aware that I was no longer alone.

At the back of the church, a kid stared at me. He was
thickset and tall, very dark-skinned, with a showy red
bandanna tied around his head like a skullcap. Not
Braxton. This was a kid I'd never seen before. He stood
with arms crossed, watching me.

His eyes flickered up to the dome.

"Who are you?" I said. "What are you doing here?"

No response.

I came out of the pew and down the red-carpeted
aisle. The kid was already gone. I raced out to the
church steps. He had disappeared.

Back inside, I stood in the spot vacated by this visitor
and retraced his glance up into the dome. There was, I
saw, a ring around the base of it, a feature I'd never noticed before. It dawned on me that there must be a way
up there. There must be a way to reach the dome to
clean or paint it or to replace a bulb. It was the only
place I hadn't looked.

In an office off the hallway, I found a secretary stuff-
ing envelopes. She asked, "May I help you?"

I identified myself as a cop, even flipped open my badge holder to make it official. "Is there a way up to that dome?"

"Why would you want to go up there?" she asked, bewildered.

I told her, honestly enough, "I'm not sure." She led me to a staircase behind a locked door.

In better circumstances, I would have called in my position, just in case. That was obviously impossible now. Yet confronting Braxton alone, if indeed he was up there, was foolish. Where was John Kelly? Where was he constantly disappearing to? I wrote down Gittens's name and told the secretary, "If I'm not back in ten minutes, call this number and tell him Ben Truman is here, alright?" It was up to Gittens. He could leave me here or come, as he saw fit. At this point, it was all the precaution I could muster.

Up and up. Up a staircase that switchbacked six times. At the top, a narrow door, so narrow you had to turn your shoulders to avoid the door frame.

Out onto a catwalk that circled the base of the dome.

Very high, with a handrail set at thigh level—too low to be seen from the seats below—and too low to put your hand on when you looked over the edge. The church floor was far below—two, three stories at least. A red carpet ran up the center aisle and spread out over the altar.

Nearby on the catwalk, a pile of bedding—no, just clothes bundled on the floor.

And on the opposite side of the dome was Harold Braxton, wide-eyed, gaping at me.

I pulled my gun. Two times in one week. *Cops on TV always draw their guns.* I racked the slide. The gun felt heavy, foreign. *I'm on TV. My own TV show.*

I looked down at the gun in my hand. Then across at Braxton.

There was a hollow *flump.*

The sound echoed. It was inside my head and outside my head. *Flump.* A sound but no pain. No sensation at all.

I was down on the catwalk. Dusty brown linoleum. My cheek was pressed against it. I had not fallen. The film had skipped a frame somehow—I was standing, then I was on the floor.

I looked up at June Veris—enormous in a red T-shirt—a great leonine head, pale, sleepy-eyed. He was holding some sort of truncheon that reminded me of Kelly's nightstick. "Don't you look at me, motherfucka. Don't you fuckin' look at me!"

I kept looking at him.

"What'd I just tell you? Look the fuck down!"

I looked down. Rolling my head started a dull, pressurized pain. The brain sloshing in its shell like an egg yolk, quivering, threatening to split the delicate membrane. I touched the back of my head. My hair was damp.

Veris said, "What do we do now, cousin?"

I looked up.

Another sound—not pain, but sound—*whoom*—reverberating in and around my skull.

There was a strange calm. Dreamy. I analyzed the sound. It was recognizably the truncheon striking my skull. I wanted to remember that sound.

This time the blow drove my head forward. Drove my chin into my chest.

My body coiled, reflexed—my face burned along the floor until it loomed out over the edge of the catwalk and the red church floor stretched three stories below. I jerked my head back.

Veris again: "I tol' you, look the fuck *down*!"

I looked down at the floor. The egg yolk trembled. Not pain but something more remote—the objective awareness of injury—a rumor of pain.

Veris's hand rifled through my pockets, extracted my wallet and badge holder. "What you want to do now, cousin?"

A voice said: "Leave him. It's okay, you go."

I turned my head to see Veris trundle off, squeeze

through the door and disappear. His footsteps echoed on
the staircase.

Harold Braxton was holding my gun. "Serious piece,"
he mused. It was a nine-millimeter Beretta. He dropped
the magazine out of the handle, then racked the gun to
clear the chamber. The cartridge fell over the edge and
landed on the carpet far below us with a soft sound.

There was a brief gap—like sleep—then I awoke to
Braxton asking, "Why'd you come here?"

"The DA wants you picked up."

"You all there is?"

I nodded. The egg yolk rolled, shivered, but held together, although now the pain was very real. I decided to
keep my head perfectly still. "Yeah, just me."

"You really from Maine?"

"Yeah."

Braxton closed my badge holder and tossed it on the
floor beside me.

"I didn't cap that DA."

"Oh."

"Listen to me! I didn't shoot him."

"It doesn't matter."

"It doesn't matter?"

"The DA just wants to question you. You can tell her—"

He snorted. "Tell her what? That I'm innocent? Gee,
you think she'll believe me? They think I killed cops. I
never killed no cops."

"Actually they think I killed one too." I pushed myself
up on all fours.

"Stay down," he ordered. "What are you talking
about?"

"They think I killed that DA."

"You're a cop, right? And they think *you* killed a DA?"

"That's right."

"Man, that is fucked up. That is ... " His voice trailed
off. He could not think of another way to describe it.
"That's fucked up."

I struggled to my feet. Above me—very close now—

was the navel of the dome, that shadowy little dimple. To my left, only space—air—and below, the carpet spilling red down from the altar and into the aisle.

Braxton stepped away from me. He tossed my empty gun on the floor and pulled one of his own, a little snub-nose thing.

I said, "You can help me."

"Help *you*?"

"They're going to put it on me, the Danziger thing. I can feel it."

"It's Gittens, idn't it?"

"What?"

"Gittens. Up to his old tricks."

"What do you—"

There was a sound at the front of the church.

Standing now, dizzy, I twisted to look over the edge of the catwalk—down—*who was here?*—the fluid in my skull shifted—it pulled me—I reached for the railing but it was too low and I missed it—momentum began to carry me over—the egg yolk, bleeding—and I fell.

My arm hooked the steel railing, jolting my elbow. But the bar slipped down my sleeve and past my fingers. I had time to realize, *I'm falling.*

Braxton punched my back as he grabbed my sweat-shirt—then slapped his other hand down on my arm.

We looked at each other. He was breathing heavily, frightened now, and straining against the weight of my body. "Pull!" he snarled.

I flailed for the railing or the ledge of the catwalk, but I was clumsy, scared, disoriented.

Braxton leaned precariously over the rail, his breath rasping. Before long my weight would carry us both over.

"Don't let go!" I pleaded.

There was a clatter below. Gittens burst in. He looked up at Braxton and me, swore under his breath, and sprinted for the stairs.

"Gittens," I said.

"Fuck!"

Braxton tugged me up high enough that I could grab the railing again, and together we were able to pull my body back over. I fell onto the catwalk like a sailor toppling into a lifeboat.

Gittens's steps on the staircase grew louder.

Braxton hustled over toward his pile of clothes, shuffling, moving as quickly as he dared go on the narrow catwalk.

I staggered up again. The weight of that swirling yolk made me unsteady, threatened to carry me over again. I lurched toward Braxton, around the narrow ring.

Braxton, who had been gathering his clothes, straightened up to watch me. He had an incredulous expression. He shook his head and returned to his clothes, tying off knots in the pile. Teetering toward him, I must have looked like Frankenstein. Why would he give me any thought?

When I reached him, though, I clapped my hand around his upper arm and squeezed. He tried to pull his arm away, but I had decided that nothing—nothing— would force me to open my fingers. Braxton was a strong kid, but it turned out I was pretty strong too. Those were Claude Truman's hands he was pulling against.

"There's nowhere to run, Harold. There's no way out. Don't fight them."

"I didn't do it," he implored. "I didn't do it."

"Harold, what are you going to do? Fly away?"

Gittens appeared at the door. He was panting. He stepped onto the catwalk, holding one hand on the doorpost to steady himself.

"Let me go," Braxton growled. "I didn't do this."

Gittens held a pistol, a blue-black Beretta like mine. "Ben. Get down."

Braxton's eyes were on the gun, then on me.

"Ben, if Braxton did it, then you didn't. Get down."

Gittens racked the Beretta, and at that instant—when I heard the metallic movement of the slide—

I saw Gittens—

Why should I get down?—

and I understood. I knew what was about to happen.

"Ben," Gittens repeated. "Get down."

Gittens meant to kill him. It wasn't in his face or in his voice. But I knew. There was not going to be an arrest. It was an execution, pure and simple. And he was offering a bargain: Braxton instead of me.

I decided that was not going to happen.

"Ben!"

Even if it was all true and Braxton was a murderer and a cop killer—even if he owed an eye for an eye, a life for a life—and even if it would get me off on this absurd charge of killing Bob Danziger, a man I'd met all of one time—I couldn't allow it, much less take part. I'd gone far enough.

I released Braxton's arm. "Go," I said.

He looked at me, not sure whether to trust me. Then he grabbed the clothes and tossed them over the ledge. The bundle unfurled into a crude rope, shirts and towels and whatnot, each item tied to the end of the next one. He'd secured the rope to the railing. It was too short, though. The end dangled ten feet from the church floor.

"Ben, get out of the way!" Gittens ordered.

I looked at him.

Braxton went over the railing.

Dizzy, I slumped to my knees.

Braxton clung to the rope for a moment, swinging, legs scissoring.

Gittens fired at him but missed.

The gunshot boomed through the empty church.

Braxton dropped onto the red rug below. He splayed on his knees but quickly scrambled to his feet and sprinted under the catwalk, where Gittens did not have a shot at him.

Gittens scurried around the platform to find him, but there was no chance. He had no line of fire until Braxton bolted through the door, and at that point he did not even take the shot. Instead Gittens put up his gun and, across the shadowy dome, glared at me.

PART THREE

"Let no one, unwise and un-
learned, presume to ascend
the seat of judgment, which is
like unto the throne of God,
lest for light he bring darkness
and for darkness light, and,
with unskilful hand, even as a
madman, he put the innocent
to the sword and set free the
guilty, and lest he fall from on
high, as from the throne
of God, in attempting to fly
before he has wings."

Bracton, *On the Laws and Customs
of England*   Circa 1250 A.D.

28

Failure is a fixed point, a mooring in the current that keeps hauling you back. Back to *this* place, to *this* time. Back to the moment of error, when all the branchings of the stream radiated out in front of you and the choice was still yours. You return as a spectator, melancholy, reproachful, to say, *This is what I should have done* or *This is what I should have said*.

Twelve hours after my encounter with Braxton, I awoke in a hospital bed, plagued by reproaches. Should I have told the Bostonians about my mother from the start? Was I ridiculous to then go after Braxton alone? Or was I just desperate to prove that Braxton—or anyone other than me—was guilty of Danziger's murder?

Outside, there was quiet bustling in the hall. Smells blended in the air, the distinct hospital potpourri: ammonia, bleach, alcohol, urine. I lay still, pretended to sleep. A bubble of respect surrounds sick people as they sleep, and I was anxious to preserve that privacy while I sorted through the events of the afternoon.

The church with its nippled dome. Teetering toward Braxton, clasping his arm, then letting him go so he could slip down that makeshift rope and dash out of the church. I recalled: *When it was over, cops swarmed the building. Skittish, on high alert. Afraid to move me, they took turns kneeling and looking into my eyes. They parroted doctorly advice, much of it contradictory, "Don't move" then "Can you move?" Two EMTs arrived and, after a bewildering quiz to establish my brain was still essentially intact ("What day is today? Who is the president?"), they helped me to my feet and escorted me out. On the sidewalk, someone handed me a towel. I caught my reflection in a car's side mirror. My ear, neck, and shoulders were smeared with blood. There was no sign of Braxton.*

In my hospital bed, I walked through these events over and over, shuffled and reordered them.

A man cleared his throat to announce his presence. I struggled upright to find John Kelly sitting by the foot of the bed. There was a pen in his long fingers, *The Boston Globe* Sunday crossword on his lap. He wore little half-glasses that made him look rather old and distinguished.

"What are you doing here?"

"Visiting a friend in the hospital."

"Right, but . . . haven't you heard? I killed Danziger. That's what everybody thinks."

"Yes, I did hear that."

"You don't believe it?"

He shrugged. "I don't believe or disbelieve it. I don't have enough information."

"So you think I might have?"

"There's that possibility."

"That I'm a homicidal lunatic."

"I don't think you could be. I don't believe you could do it, Ben Truman. But I may be wrong. We'll see how it goes."

I grunted, *hunh*. Kelly returned to his crossword puzzle.

I slipped in and out of sleep. When I awoke again I asked, "What time is it?"

"Almost two."

"What hospital is this?"

"Boston City. They kept you here overnight for observation. You'll be out in the morning. How do you feel?"

"Like in a cartoon. You know, when someone gets hit with a frying pan and his head vibrates and he gets those shaky lines around him?"

Kelly squinted. *What?* "They gave you something for the pain. It'll make you drowsy."

I sank back into the pillow. "Braxton helped me."

"He decided not to kill you. It's not the same as helping you."

"No. I fell over the rail. I was going to fall. He pulled me back."

"I'm sure he did what he thought he had to do. Let's not go give him any medals."

"Right. Mr. Kelly, why did you . . . ?"

"Why did I what?"

"You keep disappearing. I needed you. Where do you go?"

"To my daughter's grave."

I remembered the pale little girl with the cowl of black hair in the photo in Kelly's living room. "Theresa?"

"Theresa Rose."

"Caroline's . . . ?"

"Caroline's little sister, yes. She was not like Caroline, though. She was more delicate. More gentle." He smiled. "Not that Caroline isn't delicate and gentle."

"She won't talk to me, you know."

"Can you blame her?"

"No. Well, at least you're here. You don't think I did it, do you?"

"I just told you."

"Tell me again."

He slipped off his glasses, wiped his eyes with his thumb and index finger, then put the glasses back on with a soft sigh. "I don't think you could have done it."

"Good. Because I didn't do it."

My eyes closed.

When I woke, I said, "How did Theresa Rose die?"

"Cancer."

"How old was— Do you mind talking about it?"

"No, it's alright. She was eight when she got sick, ten when she died."

"I'm sorry."

"Cancer devours you, did you know that? It's a living thing. It feeds on you so it can grow." For a moment Kelly seemed lost and ineffably sad. "Well, it's not an excuse. You're right. You were my partner, I should have been with you. It's the First Commandment. I'm sorry."

"How often do you go to her grave?"

"I try to stop by every day, if I can."

"What do you do there?"

"Just sit."

"Why?"

"Because it makes me feel she's closer."

Since the funeral, I'd never gone back to my mother's grave. "Doesn't it just make things worse?"

"It gets better with time, Ben Truman. It never quite goes away, but it gets better."

It was not clear what part Theresa Rose Kelly played in her father's decision to come to my bedside that night. But I thought she was part of it. An impotent father's urge to protect. To defend me, his ward, against the latest arbitrary supervening danger.

By this point Kelly and I were both getting uncomfortable with the topic of dead relations, and an awkward moment passed between us. To fill it, I asked how he was doing on the crossword puzzle.

"Oh, this. I found it in the waiting room. I'm awful at these. You know a four-letter word for *kiln*, begins with *O*?"

"Oven."

"Doesn't fit."

"Oast."

"Oast?"

"O-A-S-T."

He gave me a skeptical look uncannily like one of Caroline's. "Go back to sleep, Ben Truman."

"O-A-S-T. Just fill it in, trust me."

I lay back down in a sleepy fugue, and at once doubts began to swarm. Maybe I had dreamed the whole incident in the church, or at least misperceived it. Was Gittens really going to kill Braxton? What proof did I have of his intentions? That's the core problem with history: Events can only be seen through a cracked prism, the faulty perceptions of witnesses. Historical truth, if it exists in the first place, is immediately lost in a fog of bad eyesight, bad memory, bad reporting. Great topic for a dissertation, if I ever do write one.

I shook the doubts away. I'd seen it alright. I knew what Gittens had planned, and I'd released Braxton rather than abandon him to Gittens. I'd saved Harold Braxton.

"Can I tell you something, Mr. Kelly? I thought Gittens was going to . . ." But in that moment I reconsidered it. My head ached. I must have been wrong about Gittens. It was impossible. "I don't know."

"Try to sleep, Ben. I'm going to sit here awhile."

I wanted to thank Kelly for coming. He was the only one. I wanted to tell him how much I appreciated his being there. But the words stuck in my throat and I gaped at him stupidly, like a boated fish gasping for air.

"It's alright, Ben, I know. Just get some sleep."

In the dream, I floated on Lake Mattaquisett. Above me was a cloudy sky. At the periphery of my view, the green hillsides around the lake, all mossed over with pines. At some point I could no longer feel the water under me. It must still be there, I assumed; I was still floating on something. But I couldn't feel it. I rolled onto my stomach. The lake surface pillowed under me as it would under the feet of a water bug—a film of surface tension just strong enough to support my weight. But beneath me, the lake water had disappeared. I could see all the way down to the sunlit lake bed, where crabs and bottom fish scuttled about on dry stones. Fish fluttered past, their tiny fins flapping audibly in air. I knew if I moved, the soap-bubble surface that held me up would burst. So I concentrated on lying still. Hanging there, breathless. My arms and legs began to ache. Soon I would have to move. The floor of the lake became dark and weedy, a treacherous place of sea insects and eely, chomping creatures, and my ability to hold still was sifting away.

Now, let me say right off the top that I don't much believe in reading Freudish significance into dreams. I write them off to biochemistry—enzymes react with brain meat; random images are unintended by-products. So interpreting dreams seems to me an act of faith, like seeing the face of Jesus in your meatloaf. The interpretation reveals more about the perceiver than the thing perceived. But the raw emotions triggered by dreams are no less real. Enzyme hits brain meat, sizzles—and dreamer feels fear or sadness or vertigo or any number of things.

When I woke up, the anxiety of the dream lingered. I felt threatened.

I leaned up on one elbow. My head throbbed. The room was dark.

There was a shape at the door. A man I did not recognize. Short, neither thin nor fat. He moved into the room with arms half extended, like a lobster's claws.

"Who are you?" I said.

He stopped.

I groped for the light. "Who are you?"

It was a cop, in uniform. "My name's Pete Odorico." The name rhymed with *Oh for Rico*.

"What are you doing here?"

"You screamed."

He took another step toward me. The equipment on his belt rattled.

"Just stay where you are."

"I'm a cop."

"Everyone's a cop around here. Do me a favor, stay put. What are you doing in here?"

"Watching you."

"Watching me? Who told you to watch me?"

John Kelly came into the room. "Ah, I see you've met Peter."

"Who the hell is he?"

"He's a friend."

"Of whose?"

"Of mine."

"Well, I don't know him."

"He's alright, Ben. I worked with his dad. I've known Peter since the day he was born. I asked him to stand guard tonight."

Pete Odorico shot me a sour look. "Hey, pal, I've been off duty since midnight. You don't want me here, I'm happy to go home to bed."

Kelly patted his shoulder. "You'll stay till sunup," Kelly informed him.

The officer studied me for a moment, then said, "What was the dream?"

"Never mind the dream."

"Maybe I can help."

With that, Kelly snaked his long arm around the policeman's shoulder and ushered him back to his post in the hall. When he'd shut the door, Kelly said of the forty-year-old cop, "He's a good kid."

"You posted a guard? Why?"

Kelly considered it a moment. "Because something doesn't feel right."

29

Friday morning. At seven-thirty there was a polite, brushy knock at the door, and Caroline came in, carrying a shopping bag. "Good morning," she said. Surprised to see her father, she made a face. "Sorry to wake you."

"No, no," I said.

"How's the *cabeza*?" She made a shampooing motion at the back of her head.

"I'm okay."

I scrunched the blanket in my lap to cover a daybreak hard-on, which threatened to poke its head out of the sheets like a squirrel. The tumescence was less a matter of sexual excitement than simple hydraulics, the usual wind-sock action of sleeping men. But it triggered memories of Caroline's body, which only made things worse. I studied her outfit, tried to see through it. She was wearing another vaguely bohemian skirt suit, this one with a five-button jacket open at the throat. There was nothing provocative or revealing about it. The skirt was hemmed an inch below the knees. The jacket revealed just a narrow V of skin with tiny, lovely freckles.

Caroline started unpacking some new clothes from

the shopping bag. There was a halting quality in her movements, as if she did not want to be here, as if the whole errand was distasteful to her.

"I didn't expect to see you here," I said.

"I didn't expect to be here."

"But you had a change of heart?"

"No," she sniffed. "It seems you have a new friend."

"Oh?"

"Harold Braxton is asking for you."

"What?"

"We picked him up last night. He won't talk. He says he wants you, and if you won't come, he wants Max Beck."

"But Lowery told me I was off the case."

"You are off the case." She crossed her arms, tipped her head forward, and eyed me from beneath her brow, the stern-mother look. "Are you saying you don't want to do it?"

"No, it's just . . . I'm surprised you're asking."

"Look, Ben, this isn't exactly the way we'd want to do it. But we don't have enough to hold him, so we don't have much choice. If bringing you in to do the interrogation gets Braxton to talk, then that's what we have to do."

"Even though I'm a suspect too."

"We'll be listening. To both of you."

"Why should I help you?"

"If you get anything out of him, it could only be to your benefit."

"And if I don't?"

She did not answer.

I asked John Kelly what he thought.

"It has to be your decision, Ben. If you decided to stay out of it, no one could blame you."

"I guess it's already too late for that, isn't it?"

"Good," Caroline said decisively. "Kurth is waiting outside to drive us." She tossed me a shirt from the little pile she'd made. It was a conservative white button-down oxford. "Your shirt was all bloody. I got this for you."

"Thank you. What do I owe you?"

"You get Braxton to talk, we'll call it even."

Her tone was mechanical, unfamiliar, cool.

"Caroline, can we talk for a minute?"

"We have nothing to talk about."

John Kelly began to excuse himself, but his daughter told him to stay put.

"Alright then," I said. "Okay. Thank you for the shirt."

She pinched out a little half smile that was pained and sardonic in equal measure. "Usually," she observed, "it's the defense lawyer who puts the murderer in a clean shirt."

30

In those last few days of its existence, there was a sense of fatigue about the old Boston Police headquarters on Berkeley Street. The building seemed ready to heave a sigh of exhaustion before expiring. (A month or so later, the Boston police moved to a glass box further up Tremont Street, a sleek modern building for a sleek modern department. That was the idea, anyway.)

Kurth and Caroline led John Kelly and me to an interview room down the hall from the Homicide office. It was a gloriously run-down little room with cracked paint and cloudy windows. The only concessions to modernity were a drip coffeepot and a toxic-looking air conditioner that blocked half of one window. Otherwise the flatfoots who'd worked here during Prohibition would have recognized the room straightaway.

We met the remainder of our team, such as it was. District Attorney Lowery was turned out in a maize bow tie and stylish cap-toed shoes. I could see my distorted reflection in the convex lenses of his spectacles. He greeted me with a grim nod. Martin Gittens shook my hand with extra care, a soulful two-hander, and asked about my injuries. His sudden concern for my well-being was a relief

after the high drama of the day before. I took it as a sign
that his suspicions of me had abated for some reason.
Perhaps I'd earned a measure of trust now that I'd been
blooded in combat. That was what I wanted to believe,
anyway. Probably it was what Gittens wanted me to believe too; he used the momentum of my own panic—my
neediness—against me in a kind of emotional judo.

We moved to a cramped room behind a one-way mirror. From this room, Lowery warned, my conversation
with Braxton would be watched and recorded. "You'll
be on that tape too, Chief Truman," he said, "not just
Braxton." I told him, "Well, that should help me relax."
Kelly, looming over the group like a protective daddy,
gave me a reproachful look. It said, *Ben, just shut up.*

Braxton was brought into the interview room, two
uniform cops at his sides. He wore drooping jeans, flannel shirt, and a Brooklyn Dodgers cap embroidered with
Jackie Robinson's number 42. Cuffed at the ankles, he
inched his way to the chair in geisha steps. After Braxton
sat down, one of the cops cuffed his right foot to the
chair leg and left him alone in the room. He stared into
the mirror as if he could see through it, as if he were
watching us.

And for a minute or so we watched him too. I'd seen
Braxton only the day before, but this was my first chance
to look at him for any length of time. I searched for some
manifestation of his famous lethality. From the over-
heated descriptions of Braxton, I half expected him to
glow like a hot coal. But his physical appearance was dis-
appointing, just as his mug shot had been. He was quite
small, maybe five-nine or so, and wiry hard. His manner
was all street-corner badass. He manufactured a sneer;
he folded his arms (or as nearly folded them as the handcuffs would allow). But there was a sense of disingenu-
ousness about all the posing. It was theater. Braxton was
acting out the role of a gangster, but it was someone
else's vision of a gangster, not his. Maybe it was all for
our benefit. We demanded a certain style from him—a

style that may have owed more to Hollywood than to Mission Flats, but we wanted it just the same—so he gave it to us. His eyes moved around the room, and he seemed to calculate and recalculate his position.

"Let's go," Braxton said to the mirror.

Kurth escorted me into the hall. "Give him his rights, make sure he signs the card," he instructed. He handed me an orange Miranda card. His eyes drilled into me: "Remember, we're listening."

And a moment later I was sitting opposite Harold Braxton.

"Hi," I said.

No response.

Braxton's nearness came as a surprise. In the observation room, the one-way glass and tinny speakers had exaggerated the distance between us. He had been a figure on a TV screen, glassed in, mediated, broadcast from a studio who-knew-where. But now, separated by just a few feet of photo-wood tabletop, Harold Braxton was undeniably present.

"I need to inform you of your rights," I said, and I recited the Miranda catechism. When it was done, I slid the card toward him. "You have to sign it."

He flexed the card between his thumb and index finger, then slid it back as if unsatisfied with its tensile strength.

"I can't talk to you without that signature."

"No."

I slid the card back. "Just sign it. Otherwise I'm out of here."

A smile played around his mouth. He signed the card—almost as a favor to me, I thought, to reassure me.

"Do you know a guy named Ray Ratleff?"

"Knew him, yeah."

"What do you mean, 'knew'?"

"He's dead. Didn't you hear?"

"Do you know anything about it?"

"Just what I seen on TV."

"Why would anyone want to kill him?"

"You tell me."

"I'm asking you, Harold."

"Ray was a junkie. Probably had something to do with it."

"Meaning?"

"Meaning, you hang out with pipeheads and sliders and shit, you usually end up dead. I seen lots of guys like Ratleff. You come to my neighborhood sometime, I'll show you some."

"Have you ever been a slider?"

"What's that got to do with Ray Ratleff?"

"You said yourself, sliders might have done it."

He smiled. "You got my bop. You know what I done."

"Your bop?"

"My record, my Board of Probation record. Those guys have it, I'm sure." He nodded toward the mirror. "It's alright, dog, I'll tell you what's on it. There's some juvenile stuff, hot boxing mostly. Then I got two distributions, class B, all powder. Straight probation on both. Some other small shit. Otherwise I'm clean."

"Clean? What about Artie Trudell?"

Braxton's eyebrows crushed downward.

"The cop who got shot through the door, Harold."

"I didn't have nothing to do with that. That case got dismissed."

"Why'd you get charged? Did they just pick your name out of the phone book?"

"Ask your friend Raul."

"Who's Raul?" I said.

He smirked.

"Maybe you're Raul. That's the rumor, isn't it?"

No answer.

This was pointless. "Look, are you gonna answer any questions or not? You haven't told me anything."

Shrug. "Don't know anything."

"Then what are you doing here, Harold?"

"I got arrested."

"You went to the trouble of getting me down here just to tell me you don't know anything?"

"Do they really think you capped that DA?" he asked.

"I don't think they know."

"Did you?"

"No."

"On your mother's grave?"

"On my mother's grave."

"Well I didn't do it neither."

"So that's it? You're innocent?"

"Yes."

"Why tell it to me?"

"This is Boston, dog. B-town. Alabama of the North."

"You're saying it's a race thing?"

"It's always a race thing."

"I don't think so, Harold, not this time. There's plenty of proof."

Another caustic smile. He leaned forward, dragging the handcuffs across the table, and rested on his forearms. "Let me tell you something," he confided. "These cops don't need proof. They always find proof after they solve the case." He stared at me a moment. A dusting of blackheads marred his nose. Otherwise he was handsome, with his brown eyes and monkish ponytail. "Go on, finish asking your questions."

"Have you ever been to Maine?"

"Why would I go to some backward-ass—"

"Is that a no?"

"Fuck no."

"Did you know Robert Danziger?"

"Course I did."

"How did you know him?"

"He prosecuted me like fifty times."

"How did you feel about that?"

"Oh, I was real thrilled about it."

"Answer the question. How did you feel about Danziger prosecuting you over and over?"

"How would you feel?"

"It would depend on the circumstances."

"That's right. The man had a job to do. I had no problem with that. There wasn't nothing between me and him."

The questions were obtuse and Braxton knew it. There was something approaching friendliness in his tone, in the patronizing way he answered. Criminals often show a false bonhomie toward cops, a desire to connect, an appeal to their goodwill. But this was something worse—he was condescending to me.

"Where were you Tuesday night and Wednesday morning, when Ray Ratleff was killed?"

"Party in Grove Park. There were twenty or thirty people there. You want names?"

I got a yellow legal pad from a side table, and Braxton wrote out some names in neat block letters.

"That all you got?" he asked.

"Is there anything else you want to tell me?"

"I want to talk to you, Chief True-Man."

"It's Ben. Why me?"

"Because you and me need each other."

"Yeah? Why do I need you?"

"You need to prove you didn't do it, same as me. They're going to put it on one of us, right? You can see that, can't you? So if you figure it out, that helps us both. Now, do you want to go figure it out, for both of us?"

I hesitated.

Braxton looked over my shoulder at the mirror, then his eyes tripped from one corner of the room to another. At the time I thought he was looking for cameras; in fact what he was looking for was a microphone. He leaned forward, rested his chest on the edge of the table and whispered, "Come here."

"No."

"I ain't gonna hurt you."

I shook my head.

"You think I'm gonna beat down some cop *in a police station*? With these on?" He held up his handcuffed wrists. "You think I'm that stupid?"

"Anything you tell me, Harold, I'm just going to tell them anyway."

"That's on you. I figure you'll do the right thing."

I leaned forward to listen, warily, like a lion tamer putting his head in the lion's mouth.

The speed of what happened next shocked me.

Braxton's hands snapped up over my head. He trapped my neck in the handcuffs and yanked me down against the table. I could not move. The handcuff chain cinched into the back of my neck.

There was shouting behind the mirror, muffled, "Hey hey!"

The plastic-wood tabletop was immediately in front of my eye. It was scratched, oily.

I felt Braxton's mouth inches from my ear. It crossed my mind that he might bite it, gnaw it right off my head.

"You helped me yesterday in the church. Why?"

"I don't know. I didn't want—"

"They're playing you." His breath was warm and humid in my ear.

"What?"

"They're playing you, they're setting you up. And me. Both of us."

"Alright, you're innocent. I get it."

"No!" He thumped me against the tabletop. I felt his frustration. Everybody claims to be innocent; he was telling me something more. "I need to tell you—"

A door slammed and feet clattered in the hallway.

Braxton pressed his face close so I could actually feel his lips brush my ear. "Find Raul."

"What?"

"Find Raul. It's got nothing to do with Ratleff. *Follow Raul.*"

"Okay."

"Follow Raul. From Danziger to Trudell, maybe back further. To Fazulo. Watch—"

He never got to finish.

Kelly crossed the room in two long strides and cracked Braxton in the small of the back with the club. The blow made a hollow sound. Braxton arched back. Kelly lifted him bodily away from the table and suspended him against the wall. The chair, still handcuffed to Braxton's leg, dangled between them.

Once pinned to the wall, Braxton hung there like a doll, offering no resistance. But his face was transformed. He was all sneering badass again. He broadcast disdain—and the pain of the blow to his back—to anyone who cared to register it.

Kelly pulled him away from the wall and slammed him back against it. He pressed the nightstick against Braxton's throat.

"That's enough!" Max Beck shouted. I had not even seen the lawyer enter. His face was red and already, at ten in the morning, his tie was pulled down to his sternum. "Put that man down!"

"Yes," Lowery said, coolly. "Put him down, Lieutenant Kelly."

Kelly complied. He straightened his sport coat and asked me if I was okay.

"Yeah," I said, "I'm fine, it wasn't like that."

"It's an A.B.P.O.," Kurth said. "Good. Now we can hold him."

It would surely have gone that way, of course—a swift arrest, an arraignment that morning at the B.M.C., a prohibitive bail. It would have gone that way but for one thing: The District Attorney was there and he had a broader agenda.

"What do you say, Chief Truman?" Lowery asked. "You're the victim here."

Before I could answer, Gittens blurted, "Harold, if you ever lay a hand on a cop again—"

"Detective Gittens," Lowery soothed. He gestured

with his hands, palms down: *Calm down.* "Chief Truman, what do you want to do about this?"

Braxton was staring at me.

Kelly watched too, with an attentive frown.

Lowery said, "Chief Truman?"

"Let him go."

31

Kelly agreed to reinterview Julio Vega with me. I told Kelly the fact that Danziger had reopened the Trudell investigation still nagged at me. So did Vega's evasiveness when we'd asked him about it earlier. Kelly accepted these explanations, or seemed to.

At Vega's shabby little house in Dorchester, there was no answer when we knocked at the front door.

"We'll wait," the old man announced.

"But we have no idea where he is."

"Precisely why we'll wait, Ben Truman. No sense chasing him all over creation."

In his thirty-odd years as a policeman, John Kelly had probably spent ten just waiting. It was part of the job. Movie cops never wait around much. They dart from clue to clue like hummingbirds because they only have two hours to solve each crime. In reality, policemen wait for radio calls and they wait for speeders and they wait for breaks. In courthouses, on street corners, in parked cruisers. Walking around in circles, driving around in circles. They are bored. They stamp their feet on cold nights.

"How long do we wait?"

"Till he turns up."

"What if he doesn't?"

"Oh, he'll turn up soon," Kelly said. He glanced up at the sky as if Julio Vega might drop from above. "Let's take a walk."

"Good idea. Why don't we play a round of golf while we're at it?"

"There's time, Ben. We'll have a little walk."

We strolled toward Dorchester Avenue, Kelly looking blithe, me anxious. He pulled out his nightstick, which he kept tucked in his belt at the small of his back. Holding it by the leather strap, he twirled the truncheon absently, as he had in Versailles, with that repetitive rhythm of whirring and palm-slapping. Two revolutions clockwise, *slap!* Two counterclockwise, *slap!* The rhythm matched our steps. *Whir, slap! Whir, slap!*

I should say here, again, that I do not pretend to be objective in my description of John Kelly. I tend to form bonds of loyalty quickly or never, and I'd decided long before that Kelly was a man I liked and admired. Maudlin as it sounds, I felt closer to him than the scant few days we'd spent together would seem to justify. So admittedly my view of Kelly that morning was clouded by affection. That said, as we walked along Dorchester Avenue, he seemed to me the distilled essence of a policeman. You could have dressed him in a gray flannel suit or surgical scrubs—hell, you could have dressed him in clown makeup—and still people would say, "There goes a cop." Until I met him, I'd never thought that was a quality to be admired.

Spin, *slap*.

"There's something I don't understand, Ben. This morning Braxton asked for you—you specifically—just so he could proclaim his innocence and then attack you? It doesn't make sense."

I ambled along in silence.

"Then you told Lowery you had no idea what Braxton was up to."

Spin, *slap*.

"I may have told a little white lie there."

"Ah. Lot of that going around."

"When he jumped me, Braxton whispered in my ear. He said, 'Find Raul.' He said this all has something to do with Artie Trudell. And he mentioned another name—Fazulo?"

"Fasulo."

"Fasulo. You know who that is?"

Kelly ignored the question. "Why did you hold that back?"

"Because Braxton told me I was being set up."

"Did you believe him?"

"I don't know. Kind of, yeah. Like you said, he went to a lot of trouble to get the message to me."

Kelly grunted, *hmm*.

"I should have told. I shouldn't be keeping things from other cops."

"Don't be ridiculous. We don't work for the Boston police. We're conducting our own investigation. You tell them just as much as you want to tell them. They have information they're not giving us. That's how it works. Welcome to the brotherhood of law enforcement."

"I meant, I'm sorry I didn't tell you."

"Well. You've told me now."

We walked a little ways in silence.

"Do you know who Fasulo is?"

"Who Fasulo *was*," Kelly corrected. "The only Fasulo I ever heard of died a long time ago, in '77 or '78. He killed a cop. Frank Fasulo and another guy—what was his name? Sikes, something Sikes. The two of them were juiced out of their minds. They tried to stick up a bar in the Flats called the Kilmarnock Pub. It's gone now, the Kilmarnock, and not missed. Bucket of blood, that place was. Fasulo and Sikes went in just after closing, they stuck a gun in the bartender's face, told him to empty the register. Only they took too long and a cop in a patrol car wandered in. They jumped him and—" Kelly took a few steps before continuing. "Well, Fasulo was a hard case. He'd been in and out of Walpole, Bridgewater . . . Rapes, armed robberies. There are guys like that, just . . . vicious, animals, psychopaths. Not many, but they're out there. There's nothing for it except to kill them."

The comment surprised me. I didn't see Kelly as the hang-'em-high type.

"Sounds bad, huh? Well the truth is, our system is built to punish crimes after the fact. We're helpless to prevent a crime before it's committed, even if everyone sees it coming. Everybody who ever ran into Frank Fasulo knew he'd kill someone someday. He was a homicide waiting to happen. But all we could do was wait for it to happen, then go in and clean up the mess. It shouldn't be that way."

"So he killed the cop who interrupted the stickup?"

"He raped him. Then he killed him. Then he danced around the bar and celebrated." Kelly stopped spinning the nightstick. "Well, this is all a long time ago, Ben Truman."

The spinning and walking resumed.

"So what happened?"

"We—the police—tracked down Sikes in a hotel a day or two later. We had this military sort of unit then. 'Tactical Patrol Force,' they were called, TPF. Helmets, black outfits, the whole shebang. It was big in those days. Every city had one. They stormed the hotel room and shot Sikes dead. Fasulo jumped off the Tobin Bridge a few days later, which was probably the only sane thing he ever did."

We were coming into a charmless intersection anchored by a scruffy used-car dealership, which consisted of a portable office, a half dozen compact cars, and hundreds of little triangular vinyl pennants. Beside us was the euphonious Pleasant Spa. (In the old Boston dialect, a convenience store was referred to as a *spa*, and you still see the word in store windows around town.)

Kelly stopped to survey. The nightstick twirled. Spin, *slap!*

"How do you do that?"

"This?" Spin, *slap!*

"Yeah, how do you make it . . . ?"

Kelly regarded the stick as if he hadn't noticed it was spinning until that very moment. "I don't know. You just . . ." Spin, *slap*.

"Show me. Do it slow."

Spin. *Slap*.

"You just kind of let it fall away from your wrist a little, then yank it by the strap here."

"Let me try."

"Do you know how long I've had this thing?"

"Come on, it's not the crown jewels. It's a stick. Let me try."

He passed it to me and I slipped the leather strap over my hand. I tried to imitate him, letting the baton fall forward then snapping it back toward my chest. The free end flashed up in my face. I ducked.

"Nice and easy, Ben Truman. Don't knock yourself out."

"Do me a favor. If I do knock myself out, just in case—shoot me."

"Nice and easy."

The club wobbled through a complete revolution and I grabbed it. The trick seemed to be that it did not turn in an even circle. The weight was unbalanced (the free end was thicker and heavier), and the strap introduced enough play that the axis of rotation shifted constantly. Plus, the thing was barely shorter than your arm, so it threatened to whack you in the head every time it passed.

"Harder than it looks," I said.

"Here, you better give that thing back before you hurt yourself."

32

You again."

Julio Vega leaned his shoulder against the door frame. The ex-cop tried to fix his filmy eyes on me but they were sluggish; he let them wander to a spot on my chest somewhere.

"What is it now, Maine? Gittens send you back for more?"

"No, sir. Gittens doesn't even know I'm here."

"Of course he does." Vega snorted, then padded off barefoot.

Kelly and I followed him to the same room where we'd spoken ten days before. Vega fell into one of the sweat-slicked wing chairs and returned to his television show, ESPN SportsCenter.

There was something disquieting about Vega's appearance. It wasn't simply that he was drunk or exhausted— though he was obviously both drunk and exhausted. Something was missing, something had gone out of him. Whatever it is that hangs behind the curtain, behind the gristle and bone of the face, whatever it is that animates the eyes and nose and mouth, it had simply left. I could imagine Vega removing that pouchy, unhandsome face and laying it down like one of Dali's liquid clock faces.

"Have you been drinking, Julio?" I asked.

"Course I been drinking." He blew a scornful little sniff. Stupid question.

"I need to talk to you about Raul."

No response.

"I said we need to talk." My voice was too loud, as if I could reach him by shouting.

"Hey, Maine, I'm drunk, not deaf."

Kelly and I exchanged glances. What was wrong with this guy?

"Julio, what did Frank Fasulo have to do with the raid on the red-door crackhouse?"

"Frank Fasulo? What the fuck you talking about?"

"That night you raided the apartment with the red door, the tip from Raul had something to do with Frank Fasulo, didn't it?"

"Man, I don't even know who Frank Fasulo is." He watched basketball highlights on the screen.

"Tell me about the night you and Artie Trudell did that raid."

"I told you already, I got nothing to say about that."

"Julio, that isn't gonna fly anymore. We're going to talk about it."

He shook his head. "Nothing to say, homes." The words were defiant, but Vega's tone was not. He was reciting lines he'd rehearsed over and over, an actor walking through a part he'd played for too many performances.

"Julio, I need to know who Raul was."

Vega ignored me.

Kelly said, "Alright, that's enough of this bullshit." He switched off the TV with a slap. "You're going to cut this shit out and answer the man's questions."

"Who the fuck you think you are?"

"Shut up." Kelly turned to me. "Ask him again."

Vega started to rise from his chair, presumably to turn the TV on again.

With the tip of the nightstick, Kelly nudged him back into the chair. "Sit down."

"Who the fuck are you? Turn the TV back on, man."

"You want me to turn it off for good?" He raised the nightstick as if to smash the screen.

"HeyHEYHEY!" Vega appealed to me: "What is this? Like good cop, bad cop?"

"I said shut up. Ben, ask."

"Hey, didn't your boy here tell you?" Vega's voice was soft, aggrieved. "I'm a cop."

"A cop? Is that what you think you are? A cop?" Kelly wagged the nightstick at him. "You're not a cop, you're a disgrace. Don't you ever call yourself a cop."

"What are you talkin' about?"

"You broke the code, Julio."

"What code?"

"You sold out your partner."

"I didn't sell out no one. Artie got shot."

"Yes, he got shot, and *then* you sold him out. You let his killer walk. You sinned."

"What are you talking about, 'sinned'? I *loved* Artie."

"Then why did you let Harold Braxton get off?"

"Me and Artie, we were like brothers, man—"

"Who put Artie in front of that door?"

"I don't know. It was . . ."

"It was what, Julio?"

"We had a tip."

Exasperated, Kelly stepped in front of the chair and leaned over Vega. The old man looked like some Grim Reaper come to collect Vega's mortal soul. "That's right, you keep it to yourself. Protect Raul, whatever you do. I don't know if you're a coward or if you're crooked or just stupid, but I never thought I'd see a cop protect a cop killer."

"I'm not!"

"What is it, Julio? Raul was your snitch, is that it?

Your snitch killed your partner, is that what you're afraid
everybody is going to find out?"

"No, I, I—"

Kelly loomed over him. "Don't ever call yourself a
cop. I'm a cop. This man is a cop." He pointed at me.
"Artie Trudell was a cop. You're nothing. Understand?
You're *nothing.*"

"I loved Artie." Vega's voice was disappearing.

"I can't listen to this bullshit anymore," Kelly sighed.
He went to the window.

For a time nobody spoke. We heard the sounds of kids
nearby, teens maybe, needling each other, laughing.

Vega's soft voice: "I never knew who Raul was."

More young shouts from outside, a radio, a distant
siren.

"I never met him."

I shot Kelly a glance. He was staring out the window,
shaking his head.

Vega again: "It was just a tip."

"I don't understand," I sputtered. "This whole
thing—Braxton skated because you wouldn't give up
Raul. The whole point was to protect Raul from getting
killed. Wasn't it?"

Vega stared at the blank television screen.

"You couldn't find him, you said. You testified— You
said you drove around looking for Raul but you couldn't
find him."

"Maybe there never was a Raul."

"What?"

"I never met him."

I knelt down in front of Vega so I could look into
his eyes.

"Julio, it's real important you tell the truth. No more
lies. Everything that's happened up to this point—none
of it matters now. You can't go back and do anything any
different. You see what I'm saying? But you can do the
right thing now."

Nothing.

"Julio, if Braxton killed Artie Trudell, we'll get him. But we need to know what really went on that night. If the tip about the red-door coke did not come from Raul, where did it come from?"

Nothing. I had the sense the real Julio Vega was retreating like a boat on the horizon.

I prodded, "Listen to me, Julio, it's not too late. You can still make this come out right. You can go back and make it right for Artie."

Then, unexpectedly, Vega's reserve simply collapsed. Maybe he gagged, finally, on the acid he'd been forced to swallow. Remorse and guilt and longing over Artie Trudell's death. The thumbs-down of policemen, the loathing of the city, the finger-pointing—the community wheeling on one of its members, the many encircling the one. Of course all of this is my own supposition. Vega gave no outward signal, no movement in his face, no tears, no melodrama. The only motion he made was an involuntary tremor in his hand. But all at once, the truth poured out and out.

"Everybody knew about it," he said evenly. "It was like, that summer everybody in the Flats was scoring coke from that place. Everybody had this red-door coke. And everybody knew it was MP dealing out of there. We all knew it. We had to close the place. The whole neighborhood was terrified, with all the sliders and the drugs and the gangs. But nobody would say anything. We tried to do a few buys but nobody would help us. They didn't want to get mixed up with it. So we couldn't get a snitch in there, and without a snitch we couldn't get a warrant."

"So you just made up Raul?"

He shook his head no.

"Where did the tip come from?"

"Gittens."

My jaw literally dropped.

"Gittens always had snitches, man. When he was in Narcotics, it was like he knew more than anyone else. He was like the king of Mission Flats. Me and Artie,

when we come along and we got to Narcotics, sometimes he'd help us out, like he'd give us some tip one of
his snitches gave him. He was just helping us out so we
could get a few pinches, right? You got to understand,
nobody talks in the Flats. No-body. It's like the Code of
Silence, like the Mafia or whatever. So we went to
Gittens and asked if he could help us out. We told him,
we got to close down this red-door place but we can't get
a CI—a confidential informant, you know? You need a
snitch for the warrant. So Gittens tells us he'll ask
around. A few days later he comes back and he says this
guy Raul told him all this stuff about the red door and
Braxton. Gave up the whole thing. So we used it. We just
wrote it all down and we used it. It was a good tip. The
warrant was good."

"How do you know he was a good snitch? Maybe
Gittens made him up."

"Gittens didn't have to. He had guys would just talk.
Everybody talks to Gittens. He's just got a way. Besides,
I'd heard about Raul before. Gittens used him in other
cases. I don't think that was his real name, Raul, but I
know Gittens used him in other cases, called him Raul."
Vega's voice was flat, his tone did not waver.

"You waited ten years to say this? Why?" Kelly was
incensed. "Why didn't you just tell the truth and then let
Gittens find Raul? Jesus, you let a cop killer walk!"

Vega shook his head. His pupils moved with his head
like the button-eyes in a stuffed animal. He was not seeing anything. "We had to," he said. "We had to stick with
what we said in the search-warrant application. If it
came out that we lied in the warrant, they'd have thrown
out the whole case. My partner got killed, man. This was
my brother. How could I let them throw out the case?
We had to stick to the story. We needed that warrant to
stand up."

He pleaded, "What did it matter where the tip came
from? What difference did it make? The tip was true.
Every word of it was true! What was I supposed to do?

Admit we cleaned up the warrant a little? Braxton would have walked right then and there!"

But Kelly wasn't mollified. "Why didn't you just ask Gittens to give you Raul? All you had to say was, We need to give up the snitch because this is a cop killing and all promises are off. Gittens would have understood that."

"I told him that. He said he did not know Raul's real name, he only knew his street name."

"OG," I prodded, remembering the file in Danziger's office.

"That's right. Old Gangster, some bullshit like that. Gittens and me, we looked for that guy, Raul, OG, whatever. He took off. He didn't want to get caught between the cops and the Posse. I'd have done the same thing. Raul was dead no matter which side found him. Even if the cops had found him, he knew we couldn't protect him, especially after the trial. So he took off. We were locked in," Vega said.

"We?"

"Me and Gittens. Well just me, really. Gittens didn't have nothing to do with it."

Kelly sighed wearily.

"I don't suppose there's no way we could just keep this between us?" Vega asked.

"No chance," I said.

"No. Didn't think so." One of Vega's hands sought out his forehead and began to knead the slack skin there. He said, "It wasn't like you said, you know. It was all for Artie. I was trying to save the case. I'd do anything . . ."

I nodded. There was nothing to tell him, no comfort to offer.

"I'd do anything."

"Julio," I said finally, "maybe there is something. You can take us back to that night."

33

The triple-decker at 52 Vienna Road in the Flats had been vehemently rehabilitated. What had once been a fortress with a crack dealership on the top floor was now a trig little three-family home with October-colored mums out front.

On the third-floor landing—where crackheads had stood and passed rolled-up bills through a slit in the red door—there was a bristly mat so visitors could wipe their shoes. The red door was not even red. It was beige. The beautiful battered-down, rifle-blasted, wood-pane red door of my imagination had been replaced by a hollow-core steel job. The landing was tiny, about four by four—much smaller than I'd pictured it—and the two of us cha-cha'd around each other as different details caught our attention. When we were through, Kelly and I climbed up the next few steps, vaguely relieved to be out of the killing zone in front of the door.

Vega, who had been obliged to wait below on the staircase, stepped up onto the little stage. "Man, they really cleaned this place up," he said apprehensively, as if we would not believe him. "It didn't look like this."

"It's alright, Julio," I reassured. "Just tell us what happened, start to finish."

Vega recounted the raid in detail. He named the cops on the entry team, where they were positioned, he described the dripping heat of that summer night, even the apparent strength of the door itself. Yet he did it all in the same hollow manner I'd noticed when he'd met me at the door an hour earlier. It was like listening to a dead man.

"When Artie got shot, at first I didn't see nothing. Just the sound. Like *boom*. People always say guns sound like firecrackers, like *pop pop*. This was no firecracker, this was *BOOM*! I was looking at the door, and the top of it just kind of blew out, like from the inside. I remember I'm thinking, *That's weird, the way the top of that door exploded like that*. The things you think about, you know? I was kneeling beside the door, down here like this. I looked up and Artie had kind of turned around, like his back was to me. And then he just dropped, man. There was a lot of blood. I mean a *lot* of blood." Vega rubbed his eyes, which were dull and world-tired. "I figure the guy must have been standing right behind the door, right up close so he could aim at Artie's head. He must have waited to figure out where Artie was hitting the door so he could line him up. Then he just shot through the door where he figured Artie's head was at. Only it doesn't make sense, because if he wanted to kill him and be sure of it, he'd have aimed at Artie's chest, where the target was biggest. It's like he knew Artie was wearing a vest. . . . Sometimes I think, Artie was just such a big dude. I'm talking maybe six-two, six-three, two-sixty, two seventy-five—*big*. And the shooter, he aimed so high, like maybe he did not want to hit him, just scare him. Only he did not know Artie was gonna be so damn big. . . ."

"Just tell us what happened next." My voice was cool, ministering.

"Nothing happened. I, like, tried to reach out to Artie and see if he was okay. At the beginning I didn't realize he was dead. I mean, I knew he was dead but part of me did not know for sure, you know? Then I had my radio and I called in and told them we were in trouble. I did not know what to do. The others were all up those stairs where you are now and down here, on the stairs down to the second floor. None of us knew what to do."

"Did you hear anything inside the apartment? Footsteps? Voices?"

"It was all, like, crazy time in here. People were shouting and the radio was going and my ears were ringing and all this blood was coming toward me on the floor. I didn't hear nothing."

"Did anybody look through the hole in the door to see who was in the apartment?"

"No, man! Nobody was going to get in front of that door."

I remeasured the little square of wood flooring in front of the door. Barely big enough to hold Trudell's oversized body. No wonder Vega could not escape the spreading blood. He'd been paralyzed there, not brave enough to go forward, not cowardly enough to go back. How ordinary was his reaction, how like the way I would have reacted.

Vega stood up, sliding his back up the wall. "You know what I was thinking? I was thinking, 'Artie, you stupid shit, you did this to yourself.' "

"What do you mean?"

"I don't know. I don't know what I mean. I just had this feeling the couple weeks before this all happened, like something was wrong. It doesn't make sense. I know this wasn't Artie's fault, but it felt like it was. I felt like, Why did you do this? Why did you let this happen?"

Kelly, who had not uttered a word since we'd entered the building, said, "Why do you say Trudell did it to himself?"

"Just the way he was acting: real quiet, like he was upset, nervous. I knew something was bothering him. I even asked him about it. Me and him used to talk all the time. But he swore it was nothing. I told him if he was in a beef with someone, did he need any help? Cuz Artie was my boy. I'd'a never let anything happen to him. Only he didn't want any help. Maybe when you're that big like Artie was, you figure you can do it all yourself because you're untouchable. Like elephants, you know? They're so big nothing can kill them, in the jungle. Then they get shot and it's like, they must be surprised because they thought nothing could kill them and then there's this little human with a little stick and, bang, they're dying. They must be surprised. Because they're so strong."

I didn't quite follow the point about elephants, but I did not blink at it. I did not want anything to interrupt the momentum of Vega's narration. He'd held all this in for ten years.

"I figured maybe it was something at home," Vega continued, "like it was none of my business. Artie had a wife and a couple of kids. Now I don't know. Maybe he knew something he shouldn't have known. There are things you don't talk about. Anyway, I figured if he wanted to tell me what was up, he would. Artie always told you everything sooner or later. He wasn't one of these guys that keeps shit secret. So I figured, just let it go. We were both so busy putting together this warrant for the red-door coke and there wasn't time. This was it for us, man. This was *it*. I figured whatever it was, we'd talk about it later."

Kelly shot me a glance to underline the importance of the point. *Remember that!*

"Go on, Julio," I coaxed. "Artie goes down. What happens next?"

"Well, like I said, we were there, just like ten guys, no backup—"

"Why wasn't there any backup?" Kelly interrupted.

"That's how we always did it. We had to get in here quiet. If they seen us coming with cruisers and all that, there'd be nothing left by the time we got inside. We had to surprise them. Plus, in the A-3 you didn't tell anybody anything, not in that station. It was the Hotel No-tell. We had guys there that were tighter with Braxton than with you. Some of them were on the take, some of them just knew a kid from the neighborhood or whatever. If they heard about the warrant, they would have made a phone call. So we didn't tell nobody about that raid till the night we did it, and we picked those guys by hand because we trusted them. *You* know what I mean." This last was directed at Kelly.

"Alright," I prodded, "we get it. No backup. Keep going."

But before Vega could reply, a man's voice behind the apartment door announced, "I don't know who you all are, but I'm getting ready to call the police."

None of us said anything.

The man opened the door partway and spied us. A seventyish African-American man with a formal bearing. A gentleman retiree maybe, the sort who puts on a tie every day to read his newspaper at the kitchen table. "This isn't a place to hang out. What are you fellas doing out here?"

I stepped forward (I was technically the senior officer), flipped my badge, apologized for disturbing the man.

"Nobody called the police to come here." He took up a guard post at the threshold.

"Well it's an old case. It's nothing to worry about."

The man did not react.

"There was an accident here a long time ago," I said. "A policeman was killed."

"I know all about it. They set up that boy for it."

Vega's eyes swelled, a bubble of sadness.

"That's not necessarily what happened," I offered without conviction.

"Mmm-hmm. You mind if I stay here?"

"Yes," Vega blurted.

"No," I overruled him. "No, I think it would be helpful if you stayed, Mr. . . . ?"

"Kenison."

"Mr. Kenison. Ben Truman." We shook hands. "John Kelly, Julio Vega."

The old man hesitated before taking Vega's hand—did he remember the pariah's name?—but he shook it, then returned to his post at the door like a Beefeater.

The presence of this interloper seemed to inhibit Vega. He studied the floor as if he'd dropped a coin there. "Anyway, like I said, I had the radio and there's blood all over and I can hear Gittens calling the turret. I knew Gittens was going to be around because it was kind of his warrant. You know, in the sense it was his snitch"—a glance at Mr. Kenison—"I mean informant. Plus, he was our friend, he watched out for Artie and me. So I hear him call in and he says he's coming up. Next thing I know, here comes Gittens up the stairs. Out of nowhere, he's just *here*. It was like some cartoon, like 'Super Friends' or something. So Gittens comes up behind me and he says, 'What the fuck happened?' And I tell him, 'Artie got shot through the door.' So Gittens is all pissed. He stands up and he grabs the pipe and he starts breaking down the door himself. No vest. He just jumps in front of the door and starts banging away. He kept slipping because of the blood on the floor, and he had Artie lying there around his feet. But he was going in that door no matter what. It took a while, but Gittens got through and we followed him in."

Vega moved to enter the apartment, but Mr. Kenison was blocking the door.

"Excuse me."

The old man stepped aside. His eyes never strayed from Vega's face.

Vega led us into the apartment just as Gittens had led the search-warrant team a decade before.

"We get in and it's empty. Nothing. No shooter, no gun, no coke. Not even furniture. Just some little stuff in the cabinets, cereal, shit like that. Paper and shit all over the floor. It was dark too. The only light was from the street outside."

Vega's description jarred with the bright, well-scrubbed apartment we stood in. The walls were freshly painted in a creamy yellow, there were new appliances in the kitchen, even the windows had been replaced with up-to-date vinyl-sash models.

"Did you do all this?" I asked Mr. Kenison.

"Yes, I did." His tone carried the hint of a challenge.

"It's really nice."

Vega went on: "Like I said, we'd never been inside this place. We didn't know what the fuck it was going to look like in here." To Mr. Kenison: "Excuse me, we didn't know *anything* about what it was going to look like. Sorry. We come in, we secure it, next thing I know Gittens is running down a back staircase and everyone is running after him. We did not even know there was a back staircase. After that I'm kinda unclear. I didn't go with them. I went back to stay with Artie."

"But do you know what happened?"

"Yeah. Gittens found the weapon in the back of the apartment near the door. Big pump-action shotgun. Ballistics made it the murder weapon, fingerprints made it Braxton's. We tore the place up, found all kinds of other evidence Braxton had been here. There was a back stairway and a back door, which was how the shooter got out. Simple case. It was Braxton, no doubt about it."

Mr. Kenison said, "That boy admitted he'd been here other times. So you found his fingerprints or whatever; doesn't mean he was here that night." His tone was neither angry nor deferential. He was simply stating a fact, unabashed by the fact that we were police officers.

"His fingerprints," Vega exclaimed, "were on the gun!"

"They could have taken that gun from the boy anytime and dropped it in the yard."

"Oh come on!" Vega said.

"It happens."

"You really believe that?"

"I believe it happens, yes."

"But do you believe that's what happened here? We

planted the gun? I mean, you *live* here, you see what goes on. Do you really believe that's what happened?"

"I don't know who of you-all to believe. I don't believe that boy and I don't believe the police. That makes him not guilty."

"You think he's innocent."

"I didn't say innocent. I said not guilty. Could be he did it. But you police officers should have done a better job."

Vega's chest and shoulders drooped perceptibly. After all, this was the common wisdom on the Trudell case. Braxton's guilt or innocence was almost beside the point. It had become a case about civil rights and police lying—Vega's lying—not murder. A morality play for the masses, with Braxton the incidental beneficiary.

Vega looked around the apartment, searching for something familiar, a portal back to that night. In the kitchen, he ran his palm over the Formica counters. It was as if the refurbished apartment disoriented him. It mediated between himself and his own history. Vega had replicated the coordinates along the Y-axis of place only to find the X-axis, time, completely blocked, the grid itself inaccessible. The moment of fracture—August 17, 1987, 2:25 A.M.—was lost.

He murmured, "That kid killed Artie."

No one responded.

"That kid killed Artie."

Vega was drenched in remorse, and it occurred to me that he'd reached a terrible decision: He intended to kill Braxton. But it was a fleeting suspicion, crowded out almost immediately by a more pressing concern.

Framed by the apartment windows, the strobe of a cruiser's lights glinted from the street below. I looked down to see Martin Gittens and a backup car, three cops in all. They had come for me.

34

Ben, we need to talk again."

"Am I under arrest?"

Gittens hesitated when he heard the question, and I felt compelled to make an explanatory little wave toward the two uniform cops and the strobe flashes from the cruisers' light bars.

"No."

"Then why the backup?"

"People tend to get emotional," Gittens replied, "when things start to look bad."

"Is it starting to look bad?"

He gave a pained shrug. "I'm sure you can explain."

The Area A-3 station was just a few blocks away. We returned to the same painted–cinder-block interrogation room where Lowery and Gittens had confronted me twenty-four long hours earlier. This time, Lowery was not there. Kurth had taken his place.

"I want Kelly in the room."

"No," Gittens said. "Sorry."

"Then I have nothing to say."

"However you want to play it, Chief Truman. You can just listen, if you want. Or talk. Your call."

"And if I just leave? Invoke my right to remain silent?"

"Then we'll have to wonder. Which is *our* right, Chief Truman."

"And what about—" I was thinking of the fact that I was a cop and was owed a measure of professional courtesy. But something in Gittens's demeanor warned me it was too late for that. Something behind all that elaborate courtesy, all those respectful *Chief Trumans*.

"What if Kelly watches from the glass?" I nodded toward the one-way mirror.

Gittens considered a moment before deciding to allow it.

Kelly urged me not to participate in the questioning at all. There was nothing to be gained by it. But I felt—foolishly—there was nothing to gain by lawyerly dithering. I wanted to show my innocence; I wanted to walk the walk. More important, I had a fatal curiosity about Gittens's continuing suspicion of me. Why me? What did he have? The whole thing was inexplicable. I had to see the evidence against me, even took morbid pleasure in it. Freud once described pleasure as the release of tension; at least now the tension caused by being kept in the dark might be released.

But when Kelly had left the room, it was Kurth, not Gittens, who took over the interrogation. The switch was disconcerting. It moved the case from a local A-3 detective to a Homicide detective. It signaled that the ball had been passed. Kurth exhibited none of Gittens's false friendliness. "We just got this back." Kurth put a heat-sealed plastic bag on the table. It contained a drinking glass, which had been fumed and powdered for prints. The gold-leaf shield of the Ritz-Carlton Hotel was smudged with black powder.

I tried consciously to slow down my body, to master the subsystems—respiration, metabolism, heartbeat. Do not blink, do not blush, do not hyperventilate, do not react in any way.

"It's from the room where your mother's body was found. Those are your prints. The fluid inside tested positive for barbiturate residue."

More staring.

"Do you want to explain how your prints got there?"

"Not at the moment."

"It's a murder weapon."

"No, it's not, and you know it."

"Did she drink it? I thought they were pills."

No answer.

"Danziger had this glass. Come on, you must have known that. Did he ask you about it?" Kurth waited a beat. Then, "There's more too. Video of you in the hotel with your mother, checking in and out. Video, Chief Truman. We haven't done a handwriting analysis on the hotel's paperwork yet, but it doesn't really seem necessary at this point. You were there with her."

I wore a cast-iron poker face, the one valuable thing I inherited as Annie Truman's son.

"You helped her do it, didn't you?" A beat. "You murdered her."

"It's not murder," I said.

"It is in this state. Did Danziger tell you that? He was going to indict you, wasn't he? Of course he was. Why else would he go all the way up to Maine except to talk to you about it? He was going to take it to the grand jury. A cop involved in a murder—excuse me, a suicide. How could Danziger look the other way? Not on this one, not this time."

"I didn't murder anyone," I said.

"Why wasn't Danziger's file on the case with the rest of his things?"

"I don't know what you're talking about."

"His case file on your mother's death, the folder, it's missing. He must have brought the file with him when he went to Maine, since he intended to work on the case there. We had to reconstruct it from duplicates and from files he kept on his computer. So where's the original file?"

"I have no idea."

He laid a piece of paper on the table.

"Is that your signature?"

I glanced at the document with stagy blitheness, the way you might look over a day-old newspaper or a dessert menu.

"*Versailles Police Department,*" Kurth read, "*missing firearm. Nine-millimeter Glock 17 pistol. Firearm reported missing from evidence locker by Officer Dick Ginoux. Dick to follow up. Signed Chief Benjamin W. Truman. September 29, 1997.* Let me guess, Chief Truman: The Glock was never found."

"No."

"Any idea where it might have gone?"

"No."

"Would you be surprised to hear that a nine-millimeter Glock 17 is consistent with the weapon that murdered Bob Danziger?"

"Oh, come on, Kurth, I saw the body. There must be a hundred guns that would be consistent with that scene."

"Strange coincidence, though, wouldn't you say? Big gun like that just disappearing from the evidence locker in a little Podunk police station like yours?"

"Shit happens."

"Shit happens," he repeated. "So what did you do to follow up? Or weren't you concerned about a nine-millimeter semiautomatic lying by the side of the road?"

"Of course I was concerned. We searched, we investigated. We couldn't track it down."

"You had access to that locker, didn't you? You could have taken that gun."

I didn't answer.

"Chief Truman, can you tell me why you went out to the cabin that morning? When you found the body, I mean. What were you doing there?"

"It's routine. We check all the cabins as part of our rounds."

"Even in winter?"

"Especially in winter."

Gittens broke in at this point. He sat down opposite me, rested his hands on the table and interlaced his fingers. It was a thoughtful pose. "Ben, why don't you help yourself out here. Get ahead of this a little, before it goes too far down the track. All these things, you see what it adds up to, don't you? Motive, means, opportunity. Danziger told you he was going to indict the assisted-suicide case, so you shot him, then you ditched the gun somewhere, probably in the lake. Then you took Danziger's file."

"That's your theory?" I said.

"That's our theory, yeah."

"It's not true. Martin, I'm not a murderer. What else can I tell you?"

Gittens shook his head mournfully. He'd wanted to hear more.

"Gittens, are you going forward with this?"

"That's up to the DA."

"Then I'm free to go?"

"You're free to go. Unless there's something else you want to say."

"I didn't do it," I told them. And again, "I did not do it."

And again to myself—to remind myself of the truth: *I did not do it.* Braxton's message played in my head, too, with renewed urgency: *Find Raul.*

35

Danziger's house was a miniature colonial with green shutters, one of four identical homes built side by side on a leafy crescent in West Roxbury. This was no bachelor's flophouse. An apron of flower beds circled the house—finicky arrangements with evergreens in back, mums and marigolds in front. The tiered ranks reminded me of a class picture, bright smiling girls seated in front, awkward blank-faced boys standing in back.

I had come here, frantic, looking for Raul—for any hint that Robert Danziger had located the informant responsible for putting Artie Trudell in front of that red door ten years ago. Solving the riddle of Raul was now a more desperate proposition. I was now the prime suspect. I could feel the weight of the evidence enfolding me. I looked guilty, even to myself. Panic was seeping through me.

Danziger's backyard was an orderly space. A pair of brightly painted Adirondack chairs, a birdhouse crafted to resemble the actual house.

On the upper half of the back door were a dead bolt and four panes of glass, an arrangement that could deter only those few burglars too squeamish to break a window. I punched an elbow through the glass. No alarm, no barking dog, nothing. My first B&E, and nobody cared.

The door opened into a kitchen. Expensive-looking pots hung from a brass rack, cookbooks and cooking magazines lined two shelves. "Oh my God," I mumbled out loud, "it's Martha Stewart's house."

In the living room, framed photos crowded the mantel above a fireplace. Danziger himself was in most of them, smiling behind his tortoiseshell glasses and walrus mustache. Another man appeared in these photos— handsome, younger than Danziger—and it occurred to me that Danziger was gay. The idea brought me up short. It was the first human detail I'd learned about him.

Until now Danziger had been little more than an abstraction. Occasionally in my thoughts I'd dignified him with the title *victim,* but it is a peculiarity of murder cases that the victim is unknowable and therefore unreal. The detective has only the body, and even that must be objectified as *evidence* for professional and psychological reasons, for how else could the detective handle the constant reminder of his own mortality, of the ease with which flesh is ruptured and life ended? Children who are murdered seem to evoke a more visceral, emotional response, but in general the homicide investigator keeps his distance. In his own home, though, for the first time, Bob Danziger was no abstraction. He was a living presence. You felt him. I remembered Danziger as he'd been when he first approached me in Versailles. He seemed about to ask for directions or some other routine business. *Chief Benjamin Truman? I was wondering if I could have a word.*

I studied the family photos. In one snapshot, Danziger and his partner stood side by side at a party of some kind, both wearing tuxedos. Another photo showed them at the beach, standing with arms draped over each other's shoulders like old pals. In this picture, Danziger wore a gold Star of David around his neck; a

Claddagh ring was discernible on his partner's finger. Such pregnant images, so suggestive of the infinite complexity of Danziger's life, of any life.

I wandered through the empty house, opening drawers and cabinets. I looked inside the medicine chest in the master bathroom. (A partial inventory: green plastic toothbrush and a full tube of Crest Extra Whitening toothpaste, a Panasonic beard trimmer, tweezers, Edge shaving cream, a Gillette disposable razor, a stiff brush with red hairs caught in the bristles, a fine-tooth comb for the mustache, moisturizer with SPF 15 sunblock for Danziger's fair skin, two prescription bottles containing codeine pills prescribed in 1995 for back pain.)

In the den, I sat down in the flattened chair facing the TV. A hardcover edition of Updike's *Rabbit at Rest* lay beside the chair where, I presume, Danziger had put it down. He had used the flap of the dust jacket to hold his page, and I opened the book to read a few lines there. The book was signed on the inside cover in blue ink, *Robt. Danziger, 1/17/92*. Practiced, Palmer Method letters.

I imagined him then, on January 17, 1992, inscribing his book for posterity. He couldn't have known, could he? When Bobby Danziger bent over this page and signed his name, when he decided after some hesitation to abbreviate his first name to *Robt.*—an artifice calculated to mask the attention he was lavishing on the signature—he could not have known that the fatal trajectory of his life was already set, the string of coincidences already in motion, bearing him toward that cabin in Maine five and a half years later. In fact, the chain of causation had begun even earlier, in 1977 with the cop killing at the Kilmarnock Pub—an event I'd already linked with the first murderous cells dividing and metastasizing in my mother's brain. Maybe, I imagined, Fasulo fired the death shot into that policeman's head at the precise moment the first malignant cell pinched itself in two. There ought to be a pattern in these things, a system, otherwise it is all just chance and absurdity, isn't it?

Otherwise it is just stupidity—trucks skipping over guardrails, plaque encrusting the arteries of men's hearts, hydraulic systems failing over the North Atlantic. Each of us marching ignorantly toward his own random, pointless finish. And yet on a day like today—rustling with dry leaves and the smell of winter coming on, alive with the sense of degeneration and regeneration; the sort of day that is New England's special gift—who would want to know? Who would reverse the flight of the arrow? Why would Danziger ever want to preview his own perishing, the when, where and how? Why would he want to foresee his own body on that cabin floor, the slurry of blood and bone chips sprayed on the walls? So he could choose a different path? If he had seen the end, would he have left Artie Trudell's murder unsolved? Run off to a monastery somewhere and hidden from his fate? Maybe. But he did not know. He followed the branchings until he reached that cabin, and, stupid or not, that is the way it has to be. None of us knows.

In a small office on the second floor, I sorted through papers and files looking for anything connected to the Trudell case. I searched Danziger's personal papers, through files tabbed *Auto* and *Taxes* and *House*. There was nothing about Raul or Trudell or anything else. The air in the room was warm and close. Dust motes hung in the sunlight.

Behind me a hoarse, grinding voice—a voice out of a gangster movie—said, "What are you doing here?"

I jumped.

Edmund Kurth stood at the office door.

"Jesus, Ed! Do you always sneak up like that?"

"What are you doing here?"

"I'm—I'm doing a search."

"A search? You have a warrant?"

"I don't need a warrant to search a dead guy's house."

"You don't need a warrant if you're a cop. You're not a cop, so it's trespassing. I could arrest you."

"Do you need to see my badge, Ed?"

"Your badge doesn't mean shit here. You've been told to leave."

"So you're going to arrest me for trespassing."

"Maybe."

Kurth lingered in the doorway. He glowered with the flamboyant ferocity of a boxer in the prefight staredown. The evil eye. There was such feral, unaffected menace in it—the sense of energy held just barely in check—that his mere presence implied a threat.

"This won't help you, you know, being found here. You're only making it worse."

I pressed my temples between my two fists, looking, I'm sure, like the very model of a guilty man.

"What is it you're looking for?"

"I don't know exactly."

"We already searched this place." He drifted into the room. "There's nothing left for you to find."

From Danziger's desk, Kurth plucked a crude-looking shiv, a souvenir of an old trial, no doubt. The weapon was little more than a five- or six-inch strip of metal with cloth tape wound around one end as a grip. "Ever seen one of these, Chief Truman?"

"No."

"They make them in the prisons. They take the leg of a bed or a table and sharpen it into a knife like this."

"Interesting, Ed. Thanks for the information."

He ignored the sarcasm. "It's not a very good knife, it's not that sharp. But it gets the job done."

He held the blade about a foot from my nose. He let it rest in his open palm, presumably to demonstrate that he did not actually intend to stab me. Small comfort. He stood pondering the thing a moment longer, then flipped it around and offered it to me handle-first. When I didn't take it, he laid the odd-looking dagger carefully on the desk.

"One more time, Chief Truman. What are you doing here?"

"You wouldn't believe me."

"You'd be surprised."

What was left at this point but to trust him? "I know why Danziger was killed."

"Yeah? Why?"

"He was looking into the Arthur Trudell case, from '87. I think he found Trudell's killer."

"So who did it? Braxton?"

"I don't know. Yet."

"Well, where did your information come from?"

I winced. "Braxton."

Kurth actually smiled. He looked down at me and grinned, and sunlight illuminated the pits in his cheeks where birds seemed to have pecked him with their beaks. "That's just too perfect," he said.

"Kurth, you have to look into this. You *have* to!"

"Why?"

"Because it's the truth." I groped for a more compelling reason. "And because it's your job."

"I'll look into anything. On one condition: You tell me everything you know about it. No Fifth Amendment bullshit, no lawyers. You tell the truth for once, Mr. Country Bumpkin."

"Of course. I'll tell you everything I know. Just please look into it. Please."

"Alright," he said, "so tell."

36

The inflection points in history are rarely apparent to the players, who experience events in real time. The meta-patterns show up only in hindsight. I see now that that day, when Gittens and Kurth presented the case against me, was just such a pivotal moment. After that, the investigation seemed to turn away from me, temporarily at least. It is a common enough pattern in criminal investigations. Detectives swarm after a likely target, then a new suspect emerges and the detectives are pulled toward him, changing direction like schooling fish. For all the talk about "following the trail of evidence," usually there is no such thing; there are many possible trails, and the preconceptions of the investigators influence which they will see and follow. That I was soon to be dropped from the list of suspects in Robert Danziger's murder was not apparent to me at the time, and I spent an agonizing weekend in limbo, smothering my inner hysteria, fantasizing scenarios in which I would be arrested, tried, imprisoned. By Monday morning—November 3—I was hollow-eyed with exhaustion and worry.

That morning John Kelly and I returned to Mission

Flats District Court, where, no longer part of the police team, we would follow the investigation from the cheap seats.

"A-a-a-all rise!"

At 9:01 there was a rustle in the First Session courtroom as the audience stood and stragglers rushed in from the hallway to grab a seat on the crowded benches.

One of the court officers, an enormous potbellied man in a blue polyester uniform, rumbled through a proclamation, which he exhaled in four bored, murmurous breaths. "OyezOyezOyeztheDistrictCourtofthe-CommonwealthofMassachusettsfortheDistrictofMission Flatsisnowinsession—abeat—"theHonorableHiltonZ.Bell-AssociateJusticeoftheDistrictCourtpresiding.AllYehav-ingbusinessbeforethiscourtdrawnearandYeShallBeHeard GodsavetheCommonwealthandthisHonorableCourt."

"Can I get an amen," one of the lawyers sighed. In front of the judge's bench, prosecutors and defense lawyers whispered and smiled. The daily chitchat.

Judge Bell emerged from a side door at stage right and swept up onto the bench, his robe unzipped and billowing behind him.

"Commonwealth versus Gerald McNeese the Third!" the clerk rushed to announce, as if he'd been waiting all weekend to do so. "Number ninety-seven dash seven-seven-eight-eight. Case brought forward on a motion by Mr. Beck."

McNeese appeared in the little glassless window at the side of the courtroom, the prisoners' dock. His shaved head now had a shadow of hair. He smirked. Apparently he knew what was coming.

On the opposite side of the courtroom, Kurth and Gittens watched him.

"I'll hear you, Mr. Beck," the judge said. There was a fatalistic note in his voice. Judge Bell knew what had happened, he knew what Beck was about to say. But there was a protocol to be followed. We had to go through the motions.

Beck marched across the courtroom to the prisoners' dock, to the cymbal-beat of jingling coins in his pockets. "Your Honor, I've brought this case forward on a motion to dismiss based on a tragic change in circumstances. Since the arraignment, a man named Raymond Ratleff was found dead in Franklin Park, apparently murdered."

Kurth shifted visibly.

"Mr. Ratleff was an essential witness in this case," Beck went on, "the only witness—the only evidence of any kind—that placed my client at the scene of this crime. If you recall, my client is alleged to have assaulted Mr. Ratleff by striking his head against the sidewalk, a charge he vehemently denies. It would appear that, without Mr. Ratleff, there is no evidence to support the charge. Therefore, I would inquire of Ms. Kelly whether she has a good-faith expectation—"

"Mr. Beck," the judge snapped, "this is my courtroom. If anyone is going to inquire of Ms. Kelly, it will be me."

"Alright, then I would ask the court to inquire of Ms. Kelly whether there is any real chance this case will ever be indicted. If not, the charge should be dismissed and my client should be released forthwith."

"Forthwith," the judge repeated to himself. "What about it, Ms. Kelly? You still have a case?"

Caroline stood. "There is some blood," she answered halfheartedly. "It was on the defendant's shoes. It's at the crime lab now."

"Just blood? Nothing else? No way to determine when or how the blood got there, even assuming it is the victim's?"

"No."

"Do you want to be heard on the motion?"

Caroline shook her head. "No." It was the only time I ever saw her give up.

Judge Bell massaged his chin in a pantomime of deep thought. In truth, the decision was a no-brainer. With Ray Rat dead, G-Mac was entitled to a free pass. But it

was all so distasteful, such a ham-handed sort of treason.
The judge fancied himself a gentleman jurist, a Holmes
born out of his time. This was all well beneath him. So
he turned his nose up at G-Mac's manipulations and hesitated. But in the end there was nothing to be done about
it. "The motion is allowed," he sniffed.

McNeese whooped loudly. A woman seated near us
in the back of the courtroom did too.

"Mr. Beck!" the judge reprimanded. "Instruct your
client—" He didn't bother to finish. What difference did
it make if G-Mac whooped it up a little? The damage
was done.

A court officer unlocked the handcuffs and leg irons,
and Beck led G-Mac past us out of the courtroom.

The woman, a very beautiful Hispanic woman who
appeared to be in her early twenties, jumped up and
down with girlish excitement then followed G-Mac into
the hall where she whooped again.

At that moment, something in Kurth snapped. He
stalked out after them. At the courtroom door, Kelly put
out a hand to stop him—"Ed, don't"—but Kurth
brushed it aside. He pushed through the two sets of
swinging doors out to the lobby, where McNeese was
standing by the elevators.

Kelly followed behind Kurth. I was right behind
Kelly.

Beck, who had been instructing McNeese on something or other, and McNeese's girlfriend, who had been
stroking his shoulder, both looked up with puzzled expressions. *Who's that? A cop? The scary-looking one with the
bad skin? He's coming toward us. Does he want to tell us something? Did we forget something?*

Kurth kept moving, disregarding Kelly's plea to "slow
down, slow down."

Beck, probably forgetting that he was holding a yellow legal pad, raised his hand to stop Kurth.

Kurth slapped the pad out of the lawyer's hand. He
stood inches from McNeese, who was a good deal taller

but leaned backward anyway, turning his face to the side. Kurth poked McNeese's chest with his finger. "You think this is over? You think this is over?"

Kelly attempted to calm him: "Ed, not here, son, this isn't the time."

I put a hand on Kurth's back, hoping to quiet him the way you would a coughing child. There was an animal hardness to his back, a suggestion of strength that I had no wish to test.

"Answer me. You think this is a fuckin' game?"

"Yo, get this crazy motherfucker away from me."

People began to drift out of the courtroom, following the noise.

Caroline squeezed to the front of the gathering crowd. "Oh, Jesus, Ed."

At this moment, right beside us the elevator door opened. Inside was a lovely old woman in a red overcoat. Kurth glared at her, G-Mac glared at her. The lady's eyes bulged. The elevator door closed again.

John Kelly stepped in front of Kurth, squeezing between the two men, and ordered him to "back off."

Kurth pointed his finger at the old man, then he caught himself and stepped back.

"That's right," McNeese threw in, "back off, crazy motherfucker."

"Shut up," Kelly told him.

McNeese fell silent.

"Ben," Kelly said, "take Mr. Beck and his client out of here."

Kurth hissed, "Hey, shithead, tell Braxton this was a big mistake. Tell him this isn't over."

"You can't touch him." McNeese smirked.

"Ben!" Kelly said. "I said get them out of here."

The elevator door opened again and the silver-haired lady peered out. "Excuse me," she said tentatively, "where would I find the Probate Court Clerk's office?"

Caroline held up four fingers.

"Four," I informed her.

"Thank you, Officer."

On the windswept plaza in front of the courthouse, I pulled Max Beck aside. "I need you to give a message to Braxton." Leaves and candy wrappers eddied around us. "Tell him I want to see him. I need more information."

"Are you joking? I'm not going to tell Harold any such thing. Have you even heard of the Constitution?"

"Counselor, just give him the message." I squeezed his arm at the biceps.

McNeese objected on his lawyer's behalf: "Hey."

"Shut up," I said, as Kelly had just a few minutes earlier. And again McNeese did shut up, which surprised me as much as anyone.

I told Beck, "I need Harold's help."

"You want to tell me what this is all about?"

"I can't. Sorry. If I told you, you'd have to use it."

The lawyer regarded me a moment. "Are you alright, Officer Truman?"

"No, I'm not. Just tell Harold."

"Alright. I'll give him the message. Then I'm going to tell him to ignore it."

37

While Kelly chatted with one of the old-timers in the courthouse, I called Versailles from a pay phone to check in.

Dick Ginoux answered. I could imagine him at the station, feet up on an open drawer, eyeglasses propped on his bald forehead, *USA Today* spread out on the desk. "Hello?"

"Dick? Is that how you answer the phone?"

"Hey, Chief Truman. Yeah."

"What happened to 'Versailles Police Department'?"

"Well, Ben, I expect people know who they just called."

"That's not the point. The point is to sound professional."

"For whom?"

I had to give Dick credit for that *whom,* which he threw in for my benefit as the brainy college boy. But he was as stubborn as he was grammatical.

"Dick, just answer the phone the right way, will you?"

"Righty-o, Chief."

Dick skipped the Versailles gossip this time. He was burning to tell me something more important. "Jimmy

Lownes—you know Jimmy—called just t'other day and he says, 'I heard you been asking around about a white Lexus.' I hadn't got ahold of Jimmy before that. He was off to the lakes or somewhere for the weekend. So when he got back, somebody told him I'd been asking about it. Anyway Jimmy says he seen the kid out on Three Mile Road. Said they both come to those stop signs there, where it crosses over 2A, and they slowed down and kind of looked at each other. He says he saw the kid. He couldn't remember the face too well, but he says the kid had this weirdo haircut, kind of shaved along the sides with a little Japanesey-type ponytail. You know, like a samurai? So I had him come in and showed him the mug shot of that Braxton character. And Jimmy says he thinks that's the kid. He was almost positive. It was your man Braxton, just like those guys said."

I was stunned. Both at the ID and at the fact it was Dick who discovered it. "Dick, you did all that?"

"Yessir."

"That's great."

"I figured you'd be happy to hear it."

We were talking about different things, but it was okay.

"Hold on, Ben, there's someone here wants to say hello."

There was a series of clicks and muffled voices. Dick had his palm over the phone, but I heard him say, "Go on, just say hello."

"Hi, Ben." A big basso boomed out of the tiny speaker in the earpiece.

"Hey, Dad."

"How's everything going down there?"

"Just alright, Dad."

He fell silent.

Another conversation was audible on the line. Women's voices, faint, the words indistinct but the tone cheerful. Two women unaware of Claude and Benjamin Truman and all our history. There must have been millions—billions—of voices out there murmuring in the network.

"What does that mean, 'just alright'? Is something wrong, Ben?"

"Yeah, you could say that."

"What is it?"

What could I tell him? That his son was a murder suspect? What would he have done about it? And what would the news have done to him?

"It's nothing, Dad. Don't worry about it."

"You say it's nothing like maybe it's something."

"No. It's really nothing. I'll tell you all about it when I get home. Just don't worry. And don't drink anything."

"Don't—I'm not—" I could hear his breath huffing in and out in big greedy nostrilfuls as he composed himself. He cleared his throat. "I'm not drinking."

"Good."

"You want me to come down there, Ben?"

"No, Dad. Don't do that."

"I feel like I should be there with you. I feel like I'm letting you—"

"No. You stay put. There's nothing to worry about. It's nothing."

"Everything's nothing with you."

"Dad, you got to do what I tell you, just this one time. Don't come down here. You understand?"

"I can come down just to see you, make sure you're alright."

"No. You can't. I'm alright, I promise."

I could see him in the little stationhouse, holding the base of the phone in one hand and the handset in the other, as was his habit.

"It's not something you can help with, Dad. I've got to do it myself. It's gonna be alright."

I wanted to tell him more. I wanted to tell him everything. And I wanted to hear him say nobody was getting to me without going through Claude Truman—and nobody was getting through Claude Truman. But this was one problem he could not fix. He could not twist its arm or bully it into submission. He couldn't make it come out right. I was on my own.

Now, looking back, I'm glad I did not tell him more. Just a few hours later the case would be broken and I would be cleared of all suspicion. There was no need to worry the old man.

Around two that afternoon, Gittens called me personally to say it was over. "You can breathe again," he told me. I was no longer Danziger's killer.

Turned out, Gerald McNeese was wrong—the cops could touch Braxton after all.

38

Bullshit was John Kelly's favorite word, shorthand for anything he did not respect. The Kennedys, the designated-hitter rule, the U.S. Attorney's Office, National Public Radio—all these were bullshit. There was quite a lot of bullshit in the world, Kelly believed. It wasn't always clear what this Wrong Stuff was, but Kelly could spot it readily enough to divide the world into the bullshit and the not bullshit. It was all pretty simple to him, just ones and zeroes. I did not yet have the knack of distinguishing the bullshit from the non-, especially in the nonbinary world that cops inhabit. So it came as a surprise to me when Kelly pronounced Gittens's behavior that afternoon *bullshit.*

True, when we met him at the Homicide office around two o'clock, there was an exuberant, cocky swagger to the detective. "Ben Truman!" Gittens beamed at me. "Looks like I just saved your sorry ass!" He hugged me, welcoming me back to the fold. No hard feelings. All a big misunderstanding.

And it wasn't just Gittens. In the Homicide office, cops sat on desks and smiled and laughed over their paper coffee cups. The corked-up anxiety of a stalled investigation had finally been released.

Gittens announced to the room, "I'm getting tired of carrying you all on my back!"

"Bullshit," Kelly whispered to me.

I was not so sure. Didn't Gittens have a right to be exuberant? He had plunged into Mission Flats like a pearl diver with a knife clenched in his teeth and emerged with the solution. It was a tour de force. And the fact that—by finding Danziger's killer and maybe Trudell's too—Gittens had cleared my own name only magnified his accomplishment. So I wrote off Kelly's comment to old-fartism and, inside at least, joined in the general celebration.

The cause for all the self-congratulations sat in an interview room, a doughy, caramel-skinned kid squirming with a case of phantom hemorrhoids. Andre James struck me as one of those boys who radiate vulnerability, sensitive boys at the edge of the playground whose victimhood is so inevitable it evokes both pity and its opposite, a desire to distance oneself, to avoid the oncoming crash. How on earth did such a kid get tangled up with a roughhouse crew like Braxton's? The boy's father sat beside him, earnest, slight, a churchgoer in tortoiseshell glasses.

Gittens swept past us and, in the high spirit that pervaded the office, invited us to "come check out this kid's story. It's fuckin' dynamite."

I shook the kid's damp hand, then his father's. Gittens introduced Kelly and me as "the officers leading the investigation" and instructed Andre to tell us the story "just the way you told me."

Andre squirmed until his father chastised him, "Do what the officer told you." The father assured us, "He wants to help."

Clearly the kid wanted anything but. He spoke only after another bout of fidgeting and a sharp look from his father. "It's like I told 'Tective Gittens. I seen Harold like a couple weeks ago. His mother lives in this apartment next to us in Grove Park. That's like the project. Harold doesn't live there no more, but his mother still does. I don't really know him. I know his mother. She's a nice lady. I used to know Harold a little, back in the day, like before he blew up. He still comes around sometimes, he helps out people in the neighborhood, like he gives money to people sometimes if they can't get groceries and stuff, like old people, you know?"

Gittens rolled his finger in a circular motion. *Get on with it.*

"Anyway I'm coming out of the elevator and I see Harold coming out the stairs. So I say like, 'Yo, Brax, wuzzup?' Like, 'Why you taking the stairs?,' cuz we live on the eighth floor, right? So he doesn't really say anything. Or maybe he just says like, 'Hey, Dre' or something like that. And he goes in his mother's apartment and I just figured, like, *whatever,* and I go into my apartment."

"Did you notice anything about his appearance?" I asked.

He glanced nervously at Gittens.

"It's alright, Andre," I reassured him. "I'm just asking. Did you see any marks on him?"

"What kind of marks?"

"Scratches, stains, rips in his clothes, anything."

"No. I don't remember anything like that." He gave Gittens another glance, then continued. "Anyway, I heard Harold like banging stuff around in there, like pots and pans, you know. Because the walls are really, really thin. We hear everything. Sometimes we hear the TV shows playing next door and we can just sit and listen, you know?"

Gittens rolled his eyes and rolled his finger.

"So I'm thinking Harold isn't acting right, and then I hear him go back out into the hall. It made me kind of curious, like maybe something was wrong. So I open the door and I see Harold out there in the hall with this bucket and a bottle of Clorox. It was weird. I knew Harold didn't go running up all them stairs just to do his laundry out in the hallway."

Andre smiled at his own joke and looked around for one of us to reciprocate. His desire to please was as plain as a dog's wagging tail. "So Harold, he had water in the bucket and he pours in this bleach and he sticks his hands in there and he starts washing his hands in it. I figured it must burn but he washes it around, like on his hands and arms. So I stick my head out and I ask him, 'Brax, what are you doing? That stuff isn't for your skin,' and I make some joke like 'The black won't come out' and 'Who are you, Michael Jackson?' Only Harold doesn't answer, he just tells me, 'Shut the door and never mind.' "

I interrupted again: "Did you see anything on his hands? What was he washing off?"

"I didn't see nothing. Whatever it was, I guess he didn't want it to get on the floor in his mother's apartment so he took it out in the hall. Anyway, when he was done with that, he went back inside."

I looked at Gittens and shrugged. *So?*

"Keep going," Gittens instructed.

"Like I said, this was all kind of buggin', so I kept on listening. And the walls are real thin, right? So I could hear everything. And I hear Harold get on the phone and he tells somebody, 'We don't have to worry about that DA no more.' And then he keeps talking and he says like, 'I put a cap in him and then I jelled up.' "

"Jelled up?" I asked.

"Yeah, that's what he said, 'I jelled up.' "

"What does that mean?"

"I don't know. I guess he, like, froze."

"Did he say anything else?"

"No. He just said, 'I capped that DA and then I jelled up and I took off and I drove his car into the lake so nobody would find him for a while.' "

"Just like that?"

"Just like that." The kid looked at Gittens to confirm he had not left anything out.

"What else did he say?" I pressed.

"I don't know. I guess I didn't hear the rest."

"I thought you could hear everything."

"I could. I mean, I guess I just don't remember every word he said."

"But you remember that part?"

"Yeah. I definitely remember that part."

Kelly was listening from a corner of the room. "Did you ever tell this story to anyone before today?" he asked.

"Nah. I didn't want to tell anybody cuz this was MP and everybody knows you don't want to get mixed up with them. But then Officer Gittens came by this morning and he asked, so I just decided to tell the truth."

"You waited all this time and then all of a sudden you decided to tell the truth?"

"Nobody ever asked before."

I studied the kid's full-moon face.

Gittens broke in to explain. "Andre has been doing some work for me. He got caught up in a little drug thing. He got talked into doing something stupid. These sliders recruit the good kids to act as mules because they know the cops won't bother them. Andre got caught with a little coke. I've been letting him work it off."

The kid looked at Gittens with an eager expression.

"He's been doing some undercover stuff for us, some buys outside the Flats where no one knows him. Sometimes if he hears something, he passes it to us. He's doing just fine. In six months if he holds up his end, we'll drop the charge. Andre has a clean record. He's got a three-five at English Academy. He belongs in college, not jail."

The father put his hand on Andre's hand to reassure him, to protect him.

The kid looked down at his father's hand. He seemed to realize there was not much the old man could do for him now.

"Andre," I said, "are you sure about everything you just told us?"

"Yeah."

"And you'd be willing to tell it to the grand jury? And at a trial?"

"If I got to."

In the hallway outside, I asked Gittens, "Will that kid really show up to testify?"

"Let me tell you something about Andre. I have to hold him back. He's always after me to do more, more, more. We can't even use him in the Flats anymore because everyone knows he's cooperating. They call him Five-O. No one will even talk to him, never mind sell to him. So now he's all hot to do more buys in other neighborhoods, Roxbury, Dorchester. He can't get enough. Believe me, Andre will show up."

"I feel bad for him," I said. "Braxton'll kill him."

"Well," Gittens replied philosophically, "he made his own bed. We're just offering him a way out."

"A first-offense simple possession? Wouldn't they just dismiss it anyway?"

"Maybe." Gittens shrugged. "But look, we got to do what we got to do. It's no fun for me either, jamming up a kid like that. Andre's a good kid. But the alternative is to let Braxton walk and then maybe he kills someone else. Besides, I didn't make Andre a witness. He happens to live there. Somebody has to live there."

Kelly folded his arms, apparently satisfied with this explanation. It was a rough game Andre had chosen to play. It would get a lot rougher when Braxton heard about his testimony.

"You mind if I talk with him, alone?" I asked Gittens.

"Be my guest. Caroline Kelly's on her way down, though. She won't like it if we take too many statements. It creates inconsistencies."

In the interview room, Andre and his father both had their hands on the table with fingers laced, as if they were praying.

"Sir," I said to the father, "do you mind if I talk to Andre alone?"

"No, of course not." He stood up slowly, reluctant to leave his son. Mr. James stood there with his spectacles and narrow shoulders, hovering over the boy, impotent, and I projected onto him all the Everyman virtues of the nine-to-fiver: humility, dignity, decency, discipline, generosity. I saw him getting up before dawn to catch a bus. I saw him reading quietly at night. I saw him bragging on his son who was going to go to college. I wanted to tell him, *Take your kid and get out of here. Run. Disappear. Don't be so damn virtuous. For once, don't tell the truth. Stay out of this.*

Instead I told him, "It's okay. I just want to ask him a few more questions."

When the man had left, I said, "Andre, the thing that bothers me is, how come you waited so long to tell anybody this?"

"I was scared."

"But you're not scared now."

"I talked to Detective Gittens. He told me it was the right thing."

"It is the right thing, Andre. I just want to be sure. I know Gittens is letting you work off that drug charge. I just want to be sure this is the truth."

"It is the truth, straight up."

"And if I told you I could have that drug case dismissed myself and you wouldn't have that hanging over your head anymore—you wouldn't owe Gittens or the DA or anyone else—would it still be the truth?"

He smiled to let me know he understood the question, he spotted the trick. "The truth is the truth."

And so it is.

By the time Kurth and Caroline arrived, we were beginning to realize what the Homicide detectives already knew: The case had been broken. The evidence against

Braxton had reached critical mass, and by some mysterious fission a very complex case had suddenly become very simple. Harold Braxton had murdered Danziger. There were loose ends to tie up, of course. We had not recovered a weapon or any other physical evidence. And the motive was still shadowy. (Even there, we were already down to a few likely candidates, though. Choose your favorite motive: (a) to protect a gang lieutenant, Gerald McNeese, whom Danziger was preparing to prosecute, (b) to protect Braxton himself by ensuring that G-Mac would not cut a deal with Danziger to avoid prosecution by squealing, or—the most credible—(c) because Braxton had acted viscerally, lashing out at a tormentor just as he would on the street.) There was still work to be done. But the anxious, baffling initial phase of the investigation was over. We were no longer asking *Who done it?* We'd moved on to the lesser mystery of *How to prove it?* All the *agita* I'd been feeling since the day I found Danziger's body in the cabin—flop sweat and confusion, guilt and mother loss, and the hysteria of being accused myself—all of it was lifted and a tipsy sense of relief set in. I grinned and, looking around the room, saw the same dumb grin on any number of cops.

Even Kurth was swept up in the euphoria, in his reptile way. He tried to apologize for blowing up earlier at the courthouse, which may sound like a perfunctory thing but for Kurth was like gnawing off his own right arm at the shoulder. "I'm sorry about . . . what happened . . . Caroline . . . you know, this morning . . . what I said . . ."

Needless to say, Caroline ran her sword hilt-deep into him. "Well thank you, Boo Radley, that was very articulate."

Our group laughed loudly, Gittens loudest of all. I doubt Gittens knew who Boo Radley was, but he had the sense of it and anyway he was the hero of the moment.

Caroline gave Kurth a blithe hug and even Kurth smiled. At least his mouth twitched a little.

Caroline hugged me too. A tight, unembarrassed hug. She whispered, "I'm very, very happy for you. I'm so sorry you had to go through this." As condolences go, it was a pale thing. But at the time it felt profound.

We made our way to Kurth's office to assemble the evidence for an arrest warrant. Gittens recounted what Andre James had overheard: "I put a cap in that DA, then I jelled up and I took off." Kelly and I then related how Braxton had been seen in Acadia County in a white Lexus. The Lexus was registered not to Braxton, but to an ophthalmologist—I-DOC, the license plate read—in suburban Brookline. I called the car a loaner, which, it turned out, was the wrong term.

"It's a half-G car," Gittens corrected. "Dealers borrow them from these rich junkies from the suburbs. They take the car for a few hours instead of taking cash for the drugs. That way they get a clean ride. For a few hours the cops don't recognize them and don't bother them. And the junkie gets a free score before he goes back to Weston or Wellesley. We'll need a warrant for that car too."

"Nice car," I said. "Lexus coupe."

"Yeah, well Harold had a long ride all the way to Maine. These kids love the Benzes, but Lexus is a nice ride too. Nobody buys American anymore. It's a shame."

Caroline was anxious to bring Gittens down a peg.

"Detective," she said, "if you can fit your head through the door, it would help if we knew where to find Braxton."

"Ben and I will find him," he announced.

I grinned, delighted to be back among them, accepted. "How are we going to do that?" I asked.

"It's garbage day," Gittens said. He checked his watch. It was just after two-thirty. "Come on, Cinderella, while there's still time."

On the way out, Gittens and I passed the interview room where Andre and his father sat waiting stoically. That was the only qualification of our mood at that moment, the only blemish on our sense of triumph—a reminder that somebody was going to pay a price for all this happiness.

39

We don't think about our garbage much. We may have a cloudy notion of it streaming into dumps or landfills or furnaces somewhere, but for all practical purposes it just vanishes. Maybe that is why, come garbage day, we take all our most intimate secrets, mix them in with a few chicken bones and tuna-fish cans, and leave them out on the street corner for anyone to see. Block after block of plump plastic bags in white and olive drab. A policeman—or anyone else, for that matter—who rummages through your trash can obtain your phone records, your credit-card statements, account numbers of all kinds, letters, notes. He can tell what magazines you read, what you eat, what you earn. And, if you are sloppy enough, he can determine whether you are dealing drugs by looking for the telltale by-products: sandwich bags with the corners snipped off, scales, razors, cutting agents, wrapping materials (foil and plastic to wrap a brick, or kilo, of cocaine; Saran wrap or heat-sealed envelopes for smaller amounts, often found with traces of the drugs still on them). And here's the best part: A cop does not need a warrant for any of this because it is no longer yours. By setting your trash out on the street corner, you renounce ownership of it. This is why cops love garbage day—especially cops who have worked narcotics, as Gittens had.

His plan was to determine where Braxton was by sifting through the garbage at the likeliest places. Anything that suggested his location—mail addressed to him, especially—would be enough to direct us. Simple enough. And it went fairly smoothly as we gathered up bags from the curb in front of a couple of chipped-paint houses where Braxton had stayed at various times. At a few places the garbage had already been picked up, but we were able to accumulate a half dozen bags or so, which we labeled with masking tape and Magic Marker.

Unfortunately, according to our eager snitch Andre, Braxton had also been seen at the Grove Park project where his mother lived. And there is no garbage day at a multiunit apartment building. There is just a garbage chute that empties into a Dumpster—and somewhere among all those bags was the one or two Braxton might have tossed in.

Gittens led us to the Dumpster in the basement of the C Building in the project. On the side was a label from the Zip-A-Way Waste Disposal Company on Mission Ave., where Bobo made his home in a Dumpster, albeit a much nicer Dumpster than this one.

"Up you go," Gittens told me cheerfully.

"What is that, 'up you go'?"

"Well, somebody's got to get in there."

"Well, it's not going to be me."

"It's your case," he said. "Happened in Ver-sigh."

"But this was your idea."

"That's why you have to get in there. I can't do everything."

I struggled for a counter-excuse. The only thing that came to mind was *But I'm the guest.*

Gittens offered a pair of rubber gloves from his coat pocket. "Come on, Ben, we don't have time. Upsydaisy."

My eyes bounced around the Dumpster. All around it, sticky fluid was candied to the floor. I checked my shoe bottoms.

"Isn't this what you wanted?" Gittens said. "Bright lights, big city?"

I snapped on the gloves and hoisted myself into the open mouth of the Dumpster. The garbage chute filled it from the back, so the front was relatively empty. I slid down the angled front wall of the Dumpster until my feet hit the steel bottom. The garbage bags pressed around my shins in a comforting way, maternal, bosomy.

"Look out for the rats," Gittens advised.

My eyes bulged.

"Kidding," he said.

The banter was such pleasure. It had the feel of an oblique, manful offer of friendship. A restoration, a re-acceptance.

I rustled through the loose items, newspapers, grease-stained paper bags, scraps. A method quickly developed: grab, glance, toss it out of the Dumpster, grab, glance, toss.

"So," Gittens said, "do you feel a little different about your friend Braxton now?"

"He was never exactly a friend. But yes. I guess you knew the truth about him all along. The last ten years anyway."

"I've known the truth about Harold Braxton longer than ten years."

"Since the Trudell thing, I meant."

"What makes you say that?"

I poked my head out of the Dumpster. "I spoke to Julio Vega."

"Did you?"

"I did."

"When was that?"

"Few days ago."

The information can't have come as news to Gittens;

it had reached all the way to District Attorney Lowery long before. But Gittens made a surprised face—eyebrows raised, mask-of-tragedy frown—as if he'd never heard about it.

I explained, "I was looking through Danziger's files. Turns out he was looking at the Trudell thing. I figured I'd better find out what he was so interested in."

"So what did Julio have to say?"

"He said Raul was your snitch."

Gittens smiled a cryptic smile.

"Is it true?"

"Off the record? Yeah, of course it's true."

"How come you and Julio never told anybody?"

"Who were we going to tell?"

"The judge, the DA."

"We told everyone who needed to know."

"Including the DA?"

"Put it this way, Ben: Julio and I did what we thought was best for the case and for Artie. We made a judgment call. We did our job, we protected the case."

"Does that mean you told the DA or not?"

"It means we did what we thought was right."

I pulled out a crumpled copy of *Newsweek* and made a show of reading the address label, holding it over the lip of the Dumpster to see it in the light. A moment to think. At length, I tossed the magazine on the floor with all the other trash.

"Why didn't you just give up Raul?" I asked.

"What is this? What are you trying to say, Ben?"

"Nothing. I'm just saying. If you'd given up the snitch, maybe the case wouldn't have gone south."

Gittens eyed me. "I tried to give him up. I turned this neighborhood over and shook it. I couldn't find him. Julio told the judge that."

"What about his name?"

"I didn't have his name. Jesus, Ben, it's not like getting a tip from your stockbroker. These are vagrants. They appear, they disappear. They change their names like you change your socks. Raul didn't have a name, he didn't have an address, he didn't have a phone number. How could we produce him? What were we supposed to do? What would you do?"

I did not have an answer.

"We did what was right," Gittens insisted. "The judge fucked up. He didn't understand the situation."

"Maybe. Then again, you didn't tell the truth."

"Oh, Ben, come on, this isn't kindergarten."

"I'm just trying to figure it out, is all."

"Alright, well let me help you figure it out. A cop was dead, a good cop who happened to be a friend of mine. Harold Braxton blew Artie Trudell's head right off his shoulders. What was I supposed to do? Go to the judge and say, 'Your Honor, Julio Vega might have left out a detail on the search warrant. Raul was really my snitch, not Vega's. So go ahead and dismiss the case, Your Honor, let Braxton walk.' Would that have been the right thing to do, Ben? Would it?"

At Gittens's feet, the concrete floor was crumbling. He picked up a chunk of concrete the size of an apple and flung it against the wall, where it burst.

He shook his head. "Who are you to lecture about the truth? You of all people. Did you tell the truth when you came down here? Did you tell us everything about your mother's case? About why Danziger went to Maine in the first place? No, you did what you thought was right. You tried to make things come out the right way."

"You're right. I'm sorry."

"You should appreciate what I've done for you, Ben. It was one of my snitches that gave up the truth in this case. Otherwise you might be looking at life in Walpole."

"You're right. I'm sorry, I spoke out of turn."

Gittens stood with hands on hips, unsure whether to stay or go. With his sport coat pulled back, I could see the nylon holster on his belt. It crossed my mind that if he shot me here in this Dumpster and closed the lid, I would probably never be found. I would be trucked to a landfill and buried among the plastic bags. I shook away the image. It was crazy.

"Hey, Gittens, it's ancient history. I'm just trying to get it all straight."

"You want to know what happened? I'll tell you what happened. Julio wanted credit for the pinch because he wanted to make sergeant and maybe get out of Narcotics someday, maybe get out of the Flats altogether. Simple as that. Same as everybody else wanted. All I did was pass him a tip from this rat I had. Happens all the time—you hear something, you pass it along. Cops help each other. That's how we survive."

"I'm sorry I brought it up. I wasn't accusing you of anything, Martin."

Gittens shrugged to signal all was forgiven. No offense taken. But then he picked up another chunk of concrete and fired it at the wall. "I need to get some air. Just finish this, Ben."

We left the Grove Park complex—empty-handed, alas—and returned to Area A-3 to sort through the garbage bags we'd collected. At the station-house we tore open the plastic bags one by one, spilled the contents out on a conference table covered with newspaper, and searched for bits of paper that could be linked to Braxton. We stood on opposite sides of the table, barely speaking.

"Is police work always this glamorous?" I ventured finally. An invitation to conversation.

Gittens acknowledged the comment with a smirk but said nothing.

He and I had never been friends exactly, and for a while—when he'd suspected me in the Danziger case—we'd even been adversaries in a professional way. But this little frisson of tension between us felt like something new. This felt more personal. I had broken trust by questioning his role in the Trudell case, and now a cool cordiality descended between us. My own mood suffered too, and when we finally did uncover a trove of Braxton's trash—including a credit-card slip bearing his signature—there was a sense of anticlimax.

"Looks like you did it again," I congratulated him.

"Ten years too late, right?"

We were on different terms now.

40

One hour later, in an unmarked cruiser, John Kelly and I sat staring at a small apartment building—surveilling it, in Kurth's word. At some point, according to the garbage evidence, Braxton had stayed here. Now our assignment was to ascertain whether he came or left in the hours before the police stormed the building. A few miles away, Caroline was at Mission Flats District Court getting the warrant. The moment she got it, under the paranoid rules of engagement that governed in Mission Flats, we would rush to carry out the search before anyone in the Area A-3 stationhouse could warn Braxton we were coming. In the meantime there was nothing to do but wait, surveil, and hope the fluttery feeling in my stomach did not worm its way south to my bowels.

"You nervous, Ben Truman?"

"Yup."

"Good. If you're not nervous, you're stupid."

"You nervous?"

"I'm too old to be nervous."

Across the street was number 111 St. Albans Road in Mission Flats, a mold-green clapboard structure with two entrances, each apparently leading to several apartments. The building sat atop a mortar-and-puddingstone foundation, which leaned precariously to the left so that one imagined the building sliding right off it like a fried egg slipping off a plate.

We sat there awhile. And then awhile longer.

Kelly produced an apple from his coat pocket and began munching. He gazed out the windshield, blithely unconcerned with 111 St. Albans Road or, apparently, anything else. It was hard to focus with all that apple-crunching. I pulled my gun and fussed with it. I checked the clip, pressed it back into place, racked the slide once. One round up. Better safe than sorry. I sighted along the spine of the gun to a mailbox.

"Put the gun away," Kelly said to the windshield. He popped the apple in his teeth to free his hands, then he took the pistol, removed the clip and the chambered round, and handed it back unloaded. "The gun's fine. Leave it alone." He returned to munching and gazing out the windshield. "You'll do fine, Ben Truman."

"How long do you think she'll be?" I meant Caroline. "How long does it take to get a warrant?"

"It takes what it takes."

I nodded. "You ever shot anyone, Mr. Kelly?"

"Sure."

"How many?"

"I don't know. A lot."

"A lot?"

"In Korea. We didn't keep count."

"I mean when you were a cop."

"Only one."

"Did you kill him?"

"God, no. Shot him in the ass."

"I've never shot anyone, you know."

"I figured."

"I can't even shoot a deer. You ever seen a deer get shot?"

"No."

"Well I did, once. It's bloody. I figured the thing would maybe stagger around and grab his chest and fall over. You know, 'Good night, sweet prince' and that's it. Forget it. I shot this big buck and we came up and he was lying there, still alive. He kept kicking his feet, trying to get up. His eyes kept blinking. He was scared, you could tell. I was supposed to shoot him again. I couldn't do it. One of my buddies had to finish him off."

"It's not like shooting a deer, Ben."

"I don't even like to fish—"

"Ben!"

I slid the clip back into the Beretta and Velcro'd the gun into the holster on my belt.

After a time I said, "I talked with Gittens today. He fessed up, told me Raul was his snitch, just like Vega said. I keep thinking: Maybe it doesn't matter. So ten years ago Gittens passed along a tip—so what? And then I think: Danziger never knew Gittens was involved."

Kelly gave me a blank look.

"Remember you said good cops do bad things for good reasons, and bad cops do bad things for bad reasons? Well, arresting Braxton is a bad thing."

"Why do you say that?"

"It just doesn't feel right."

He stared out the windshield. "Look, Gittens is a good cop. Let's wait and see what happens. For now, just make sure you get home tonight in one piece. That's all you should be worried about." He opened his door to drop the apple core on the curb. He tried to drop this comment out the door too: "Caroline will kill me if anything happens to you."

"What? What does that mean?"

He gave me a look. "Ben Truman, you may be too dense to make it as a detective."

"What? Tell me!"

"It means she's thirty-seven years old, she has a son at home. A lot of guys don't want that. It's not easy for her. Where's she going to meet a man?"

"You know, Mr. Kelly, don't take this the wrong way, but maybe she doesn't want to meet a man."

"You think she's gay?"

"No. It's just, maybe she doesn't want to get married. Maybe she likes her life the way it is."

"Jesus, you think she's gay."

"Trust me, she is not gay." Then: "I mean, I don't catch a gay vibe off her. I have a pretty good sense of these things."

"So you're just not interested in her."

"I'm just saying, I think she wants to be out on her own right now. She's like a man that way."

" 'She's like a man'?"

"With the independence, not . . . the other thing."

"I look at her and she's beautiful. Don't you think she's beautiful?"

"Oh she's—" I puffed my cheeks and exhaled heavily, the way a mechanic does when you ask him how much it will cost to rebuild the engine in your Saab. "She's very, very attractive, yes," I said carefully.

"I just don't want to see her wind up alone, that's all."

"Well, you don't have to worry about Caroline. I think she can take care of herself."

"Everybody tries to look that way, Ben Truman, but nobody can really take care of themself. Not even Caroline."

"Maybe." I shrugged, uneasy with the topic. "Anyway, if she knew you were talking like this, she'd kill you. Besides, I don't think she's especially interested in me."

He shook his head, disappointed in me. "Ben, I bet you could tell me what color Martha Washington's eyes were, but if there was a real live woman in front of you, you wouldn't know which end was the front and which was the back."

"Martha Washington's eyes were green."

"You're joking."

"No. It's in the correspondence."

He grunted and shook his head some more.

We returned to surveilling number 111 St. Albans Road. And waiting.

And waiting.

An hour later, the ninjas arrived.

41

They emerged from the back of a modified panel truck, ten guys in commando-chic outfits, black from their *Wehrmacht*-style helmets to their combat boots. They even wore gloves so their pink hands would not draw attention. The ninjas jogged along the sidewalk then crouched behind a low wall, out of sight of the house.

Their appearance caused a ripple of excitement on the street. Kids gaped at the men before running off with high-pitched screams and laughter. Maybe the cops seemed funny to them—grown-ups in soldier outfits playing war games—or maybe it was just nervous laughter. The adults did not laugh or run off. There were mostly women on the street, a dozen or so gathered in twos and threes. They were old and young, mothers and girls. Most of them stood and stared, mesmerized by the sight or just rubbernecking. But at the time I had the sense there was something more distinctive and sinister going on. The awareness of race hung in the air like fog. Not racism or racial tension, nothing as grand as that. Just racial awareness, or maybe it is better to say racial wariness—the quickening attentiveness to race that lives under the thin membrane of civility.

Kelly and I jumped out of the car and ran across the street to join the ninjas. We waved our badges above our heads all the way across, just in case.

The commando leader grimaced at me. Under all that equipment, it took me a moment to place the El Greco face of Ed Kurth. "He show up?" Kurth asked.

"No," I told him in a distracted way. Then: "Is all this really necessary?"

"Tactical Operations Unit. They're trained for dangerous situations. Hostages, riots."

"But we don't have any hostages or riots."

"We do have a dangerous situation, Chief Truman."

I looked the cops over. Metallic rattles emitted from their equipment. "All this for one kid?"

"The kid's killed a cop and a DA. You think we're going to fool around with him?"

"No, but— These guys look like they're ready to invade Poland."

Kurth blinked twice and reassured me, "We're not going to invade Poland."

Our conversation might have stalled there, but Gittens and his own crew pulled up in three unmarked sedans, four men to a car. No lights, no sirens, no uniforms. No particular urgency. They wore jeans, sneakers, and vests, and carried rifles. Most had paunchy bellies and receding hairlines. But they had a scruffy, jock confidence, and I guessed they'd done this hundreds of times.

One of them, a burly fifty-something with a drinker's flush and a cigarette dangling from the corner of his mouth, greeted the commandos with an archetypal high-school taunt: "Afternoon, ladies."

With all the old swagger returned, Gittens said to Kurth, "Are you guys here to back us up?" Then to me, "How about you, Ben? You in?" If he was still upset about my comments earlier in the day, he wasn't showing it.

I said I would come along, imagining a complete rehabilitation from suspect to arresting officer in the space of one day.

Gittens directed that somebody issue equipment to Kelly and me. The red-faced guy with the cigarette escorted us to one of the cruisers and produced rifles and vests from the trunk. Up close, the man's face was fascinating, distorted as it was by a bulb-tipped nose and a web of burst capillaries. I doubted this guy could chase Harold Braxton across a room, never mind across the neighborhood.

"You know how to use one of these?" he asked as he handed a rifle to me.

"Yeah, you pull this thingy here, right?"

The guy smirked, pleased to have found a fellow smartass.

But Kelly saw through my bravado. "Pay attention," he said.

Suitably fitted out, we rejoined Gittens and Kurth at the head of what was now a sizable contingent.

"We'll go first," Gittens said.

"No," Kurth told him. "It's my scene. I'm the senior Homicide officer here. We'll go first."

"Bull*shit*," Gittens retorted. "These guys know the neighborhood, they know Braxton. We'll go."

Kurth removed his helmet. "Gittens—"

"I guarantee we get in without a problem."

Kurth shook his head no.

"Ed, how do you think he's going to react when you burst in with the fucking Eighty-second Airborne? Don't be stupid."

Though Kurth was the ranking officer, the fact is the police are not the military—politics matters as much as chain of command. Kurth was not going to ram anything down the throat of the precinct detectives, with whom he had to work every time there was a homicide in the Flats. He put his helmet back on, resigned. "Fine. We'll both go."

It was a bad decision. There was bound to be confusion. Looking back on it, though, it probably didn't matter which team went in, Gittens's Rough Riders or Kurth's ninjas. Emotions were running too high. We were looking for trouble.

The lobby of 111 St. Albans Road was fairly noisy considering there was no one in it. Sounds drifted down the stairs: babies crying, TVs blaring. Somewhere a couple was arguing. (A man's voice: *Right now. What'd I just say? Right now!*) The canned laughter of TV laugh tracks mixed with my adrenaline to create a druggy, funhouse atmosphere. *Ha ha ha ha . . .*

Up the staircase, Gittens and Kurth in the lead.

On the third floor, a short hallway stretched out before us, lined with four dented metal doors. One of the doors was cluttered with Halloween decorations.

Gittens pointed to the door at the rear left corner, number 3C. "That's the one," he told me. "Braxton's in there. Come on, buddy. Bright lights, big city." Was it possible he was enjoying this? "You want to knock and announce, Ben?"

"Me?"

"Braxton seems to trust you. He sure as hell doesn't trust us."

"He doesn't trust me that much."

"Hey, you don't have to."

For some reason, I did want to do it. I wanted to stand where Artie Trudell had, I wanted to feel it. It's a stupid reason, of course, but there it is. Young men do stupid things, there's no more to it than that.

Kurth objected, but Gittens overrode him. "He wants to do it," Gittens said, "let him."

Kelly said, "Absolutely not. What's wrong with you, Gittens?"

"Ben wants to do it."

"It's alright," I told them, "I'll do it."

I pressed up against the wall to the right of the door. Because 3C was a corner unit, it was impossible to stay away from the front of the door on this side. The others spread out along the walls. A few fanned out in the hall-way so they could see the door.

Only Kelly came with me to the exposed right side of the doorway. He laid his arm across my chest as if he were going to hold me back, prevent me from stepping in front of the door. "Don't do anything stupid," he said.

The wall was cool against the back of my head.

A sweet smell from one of these apartments. What? Peanuts. No, peanut sauce.

Gittens reached across the door to hand me the war-rant, six sheets stapled and folded in thirds. He pointed at his watch: *Time.*

Deep breath. I stepped in front of the door.

There was a surreal, suspended moment, a fermata during which I heard a line of sitcom patter on a TV somewhere—*Don't worry, sir, we'll have you doing the Lam-beth Walk in no time*—followed by that funhouse laughter, *ha ha ha ha ha ha.*

The fermata ended and things began to move very fast.

I pounded on the door. "Police. Open up. We have a warrant."

The rasp of my own breathing.

Don't worry, sir, we'll have you doing the Lambeth Walk in no time.

Kelly pulled me back against the wall.

"Harold, it's Ben Truman! Please open the door please."

There was shuffling inside the apartment but no ac-knowledgment.

A beat. Two beats.

Inside, a man's voice said, "Okay, hold on a second, one second."

Gittens made a face. Crouching beside the door, he snapped, "Go!"

Two guys came forward with a battering ram. It had a square steel plate welded on the front.

"Wait. Gittens, he just said—"

"No time, Ben, it's taking too long. Can't take the chance. Let's go, let's go!"

And I thought, *They mean to kill him.*

The door flew open, cracked at the doorknob.

Gittens rolled around the edge of the doorway into the apartment, staying low, leading with his rifle.

I stepped forward but was shoved aside by the surge of rushing cops.

"Police!Police!Police!"

I floated in after them with the rifle at my shoulder.

Inside was chaos. Motion. Screaming. Cops rushing around—"Police! Police! Police! Don't move! Get down! Get down on the ground!"—running from one room to another.

A blur of a little girl scurried across the room, shrieking. One of the ninjas scooped her up with one black-gloved hand and carried her out. Her shrieking echoed in the stairway, softer and softer.

"Do *not* move! Do *NOT* move!"

The cops were flooding the apartment room by room.

"Show me your hands! I said show me your hands!"

The shouting was in a back bedroom. I began to move that way when a gunshot banged through the apartment.

Don't worry, sir, we'll have you doing the Lambeth Walk in no time.

Kurth and two ninjas rushed out of one room and disappeared into another. I followed them.

The single bed was neatly made, with a nubbly chenille bedspread. A cross and an image of Jesus Christ on the wall. Cops squeezed shoulder to shoulder at the foot of the bed. Kurth pushed them apart, then fell to his knees over a body. I pushed in behind him.

The man on the floor was African-American, around seventy years old. He wore a crimson shirt with a priest's collar. His face was gray.

Kurth yelled, "Get an ambulance!"

The priest rolled onto his side. He was struggling to

breathe. Kurth fumbled with the collar until he found the clip in back and opened it. It made no difference. The priest continued to writhe and suffocate.

"Get back! Damn it, get back!"

We stepped back.

In the hallway behind me, one of the commandos moaned, "I didn't shoot him, I didn't shoot him."

I looked for blood on the priest. There was none.

"I didn't kill him! Why didn't the fuckin' guy just show me his hands? I told him to show me his hands!"

The priest was no longer struggling.

Kurth felt his neck for a pulse. He rolled the man onto his back, pulled up the shirt and an undershirt, and put his ear to the old man's chest. "Damn it," Kurth said. He began mouth-to-mouth.

Gittens rubbed his eyes as if he were very tired. "Jesus."

A woman came to the bedroom door and screamed. No one reacted to her. She threw herself across the priest's body, which forced Kurth to turn away from the priest's open mouth long enough to spit out the command "Get her out." Two of the ninjas took her by the arms and pulled her away.

Kurth continued the CPR for several minutes. Long minutes, an hour in each minute. He meant to keep it up until the EMTs came, I suppose. He kept on puffing air into the man's windpipe while, one by one, we realized it was too late. No one said anything, though, and for a while the only sounds in the room were Kurth's huffing and the woman's sobbing prayers. It was Kelly who finally stepped forward to tell Kurth the man was dead.

The priest, I later learned, was the Reverend Avril Walker, retired pastor of the Calvary Pentecostal Church of God in Christ, on Mission Ave. Braxton's one-time protector, dead without a scratch on him. Cause of death: heart attack.

42

For a time after the priest's death, the dozen or so cops in that room stared at their feet, abashed, like kids who have smashed a vase and know it can't be put back together and there'll be hell to pay. Gittens radioed the news to the A-3 stationhouse. After that, the word spread faster than I'd have thought possible. By the time we got downstairs, there was a small crowd gathering on the sidewalk. Twenty minutes later, it had swelled to a hundred people. As the streetlights buzzed overhead, the ritual crime-scene tape was strung between the light posts. The crowd grew, which required more police, which in turn drew news vans with klieg lights, which in turn drew more crowds. The raid team milled around for a time in the lobby, away from the stares and the cameras.

Then the questions began. Eventually they would all distill down to one: Did the Boston police kill Reverend Walker? But in those first hours after his death, there were a hundred different questions, from DAs and detectives and CPAC troopers. *Had we confirmed that Braxton was staying here? Had we felt pressured to make an arrest in this case? Would the warrant hold up? Was it a no-knock warrant? Had we knocked and announced, or just barged right in? Who fired the shot?* I answered as patiently as possible, even when the questions became more accusatory. *What were you doing there in the first place? Did you feel pressure from any Boston cops to do anything you felt was inappropriate? Or were you trying to prove something?*

I measured my words carefully, I told as much of the truth as seemed necessary. "No, we did not feel pressured to make an arrest." "Yes, we knocked and announced" (but then the damn cowboys from the A-3 decided to smash the door anyway). "Yes, I think proper procedures were followed." I repeated these near-truths because they were as true as anything else I might have said, and as I recycled my answers they became the truth, or at least one version of it. Eventually my voice took on a whingy, impatient tone. "I think I've answered that," I told them, and "My statement already covered that." Someone from BPD reassured me I would not be hung out to dry on this, which made me feel all the more vulnerable—it had not occurred to me that anyone would be hung out to dry. And if it came down to it, no doubt, they would sacrifice the hick from Versailles, Maine, rather than one of their own.

One question caught me flat-footed. *In hindsight, would you do anything differently?* It was another way of asking who was at fault, and I was beginning to think I knew the answer. Danziger's killer was to blame. For all this—for the raid, for the priest's death, for these questions. It was just as Bobby Danziger had confided to Caroline—*I felt revulsion at the defendant, not because he'd committed a crime, but because he'd set the whole irresistible machine in motion, he'd made us do it. And revulsion at myself too, for participating.*

An hour later, I made my way to the hotel downtown, utterly exhausted, where I promptly fell into a deep, black sleep.

▪ ▪ ▪

At some point during the night I felt a presence in the room, very faint, like a pinpoint of light that unfolded and unfolded until the presence could not be ignored and I was startled awake. I had no idea what time it was or how long I'd been sleeping. The only thing I knew for sure was that, at precisely the moment my eyes opened, there was a ripping sound which I recognized as the Velcro closure of my holster. I lifted my head off the pillow an inch, no more, before it was pressed back down by the barrel-end of a gun. The steel ring slid around in my hair. To this day I can feel it nuzzling my scalp as if it were snuffling for a familiar scent.

"I trusted you, motherfucker," a voice said. Braxton's voice, coming from the other side of the room, near the window.

I whispered, "Don't, don't—"

"I thought we were friends, you and me."

"Friends. We are friends."

"This is how you do your friends? You kill Reverend Walker? Motherfucking cop motherfuckers, you killed him. Why?"

"We didn't. He had a heart attack or something. He just died. We didn't touch him, we didn't do anything."

"You broke into his— There was a little kid there. You see her?"

"Yes."

"Where is she?"

"She was running. Somebody picked her up. I didn't see her after that."

"That was my daughter."

The gun sniffed at my scalp again. I pressed down into the mattress to move away from it. The only sound was the whisper of my own breathing. "I can try and find her," I offered. "I'll try and get her back."

He made a scornful sound.

"What's your daughter's name?"

"Tamarrah."

"Okay, where should they bring her?"

"To her grandmother. I'll write down the address here."

"Okay, good. I'll try."

There was a delay, then Braxton said, "Let him up, cousin."

The gun lifted, and slowly I sat up on the edge of the bed.

Braxton was standing by the window, gray and featureless in the phosphorous city light. His wiry silhouette was unmistakable, though, with its little tufted ponytail. His arms were folded and he was holding a gun—my gun, presumably. The other man, Braxton's muscle, stood in the gloom by the door. About all I could make out was the enormous shadow of his outline, a nylon jacket, and the white band of a skullcap he wore low around his brow.

I began to get up, and the shadow by the door pointed a howitzer at me. I protested, "I'm just getting my pants. Do you mind?" The man picked my jeans up off the floor, frisked them, and threw them at me. "Thank you," I said.

Braxton turned to look out the window. The lights of the South End winked below. "This is a fine view."

"Haven't had time to look at it."

"You should make time. I want my little girl back tonight. Hear me? Tonight. I don't want her in no foster homes or shit. You can make that happen."

"She's probably back already. The cops aren't interested in baby-sitting a four-year-old girl."

"She's six. And she's not back yet."

"Alright, I'll see what I can do."

"What about Fasulo and Raul and all that? You check it out?"

"Did I check it out? No, I didn't *check it out.*"

"Why not? What you been doing all day?"

I was stepping into my pants at the time, but I stopped so I could straighten and face him. "What have I—Harold, I've been looking for you. The whole city's looking for you. They have an arrest warrant."

"For what? I didn't do nothing."

"For killing Danziger. They have a witness who says you confessed."

"Who's saying that?"

"I can't tell you."

"Oh, it's like that? You're one of them now? You listen to me, dog, I don't know what's going on there, but I did not shoot that man and I did not confess to no such thing. Somebody's feeding you shit. Where's the evidence?"

"There's evidence, Harold! The witness!"

"Here we go again with that shit. Who's the witness? 'Raul'? Did you see him?"

"I saw him, yeah."

"For real?"

"For real. And there's other evidence too. The warrant is good, Harold."

Braxton shook his head and turned back to the window. "So why don't you go on and arrest me?"

"Okay, you're under arrest. You too," I told the giant at the door. "If you could throw down your weapons, I'd appreciate it." The giant didn't smile. "No," I said, "I didn't think so."

"You got to get ahead of this, man."

"Harold, how can I get ahead of it if you won't give me anything?"

"I already gave you the whole thing. I told you, it's something about Fasulo."

"What about Fasulo? What does Fasulo have to do with this?"

"I don't know exactly."

"You don't know? All this and you *don't know*? Then how the fuck do you know Fasulo is connected at all?"

"Can't tell you."

"Oh, come on, Harold. You're giving me nothing. Just more of the same bullshit."

The lummox at the door emitted a groan as a sort of inarticulate warning, but I knew by now they did not intend to hurt me. I could not help Braxton's daughter if I was dead. This was an empowering thought, like realizing the pit bull that's been growling at you is actually on a chain. I sneered back at the guy, "Would you just shut up."

Braxton gazed out the window, still pondering. "Danziger had it all figured out. This whole thing with Fasulo and Raul and Trudell. He figured it out."

"Jesus, why don't you just tell me what's going on—"

"Because I don't know!" He snapped his head at me in a curt little nod: *So there.* "I don't know."

"How do you know what Danziger was looking at?"

"I can't tell you that."

Now I groaned, frustrated.

"I have sources, that's all," Braxton told me. "I need to find things out."

"So you knew what Bobby Danziger was working on when he got killed."

"That's right."

"I don't believe you."

"I don't give a shit what you believe."

"Harold, what were you doing in Maine? A witness saw you there right before Danziger got killed."

"I can't talk about that."

"But you were there? You admit that?"

"You want to read me my rights?"

"Jesus," I sighed. "I need a glass of water."

Braxton instructed, "Get it, cuz."

"Yo, what do I look like, room service? I'm not getting water for no popos. Why should I?"

I said, "Because I'm dry!"

"So be dry, motherfucker."

"Just—!" Braxton held up his hand and calmed himself. "Just get him the water."

The giant lumbered into the bathroom and returned with the water in one hand, a pistol in the other. "The air in these hotels," I said, "it's very dry." The guy grimaced at me and returned to his post at the door.

"You should leave a glass by the bed," Braxton suggested.

"Harold, even if I believed you about Fasulo being connected somehow, there isn't much I can do about it without evidence. These guys aren't exactly going to take your word for it. They've got you down for two cop killings."

"I never killed no cops."

"Come on, Harold."

"I said, I never killed no cops. Ever."

"You didn't shoot Artie Trudell?"

"Why would I? I didn't even know who he was."

"Because you were trapped in the apartment. The cops showed up and started breaking down the door. You had to shoot your way out."

"How could I be trapped in there? I'd have to be crazy."

"It was your apartment. You'd have to be crazy, why?"

"Because I knew they were coming."

"What?"

"I knew the motherfuckers was coming." He shrugged. There was a little boastfulness in his voice, but more than anything it was just a matter-of-fact assertion. "I told you, I hear shit. I make it my business to hear shit."

"You hear shit from who? From cops?"

"That's all I got to say."

"Are you saying someone tipped you off?"

"I'm just saying I hear shit."

"Harold, who tipped you off?"

"Hey, Chief True-Man, I just told you—I can't say. I'll tell you what, though: There was a lot of people that didn't want to have a trial on that case, believe me, a lot of people."

"So who killed Trudell then, Harold?"

"How should I know? Some crackhead, someone stupid enough to be in there when the cops came."

"But that crackhead wasn't you."

"Wasn't me."

We stared awhile, each gauging the credibility of the other. There was no reason for me to believe Braxton, and no reason for him to expect he would be believed.

"If I leave here, you going to try and arrest me, Chief True-Man?"

"Yup. There's a warrant on you."

"Even though you know that warrant is shit."

"I don't know that."

"But you'll look for my daughter?"

"I said I would."

Braxton sighed again. "Alright, tie him up," he ordered. "Sorry, dog. Just to slow you down a little, till we get out."

The giant tucked the .45 inside his coat and stepped toward me with a smirk, and it was that smirk more than anything else that grazed a raw nerve—the brazen disrespect of it—the presumption that I would submit, that I could be overpowered—that people and things and time could be taken away from me, and my own wishes weren't worth a two-penny fart—all that I'd thought was lost when it seemed I would be accused of Danziger's murder, and all that I'd lost before then—the pressure, the frustration, the worry—all of it, at this unlikely moment, brimmed over. With the belated resolve of the unassertive, I decided, *I am not going to let this happen.* I surged from the bed, took two steps, and threw the most glorious roundhouse into the giant's eye. Under my fist I felt the boiled-egg softness of the eyeball and the delicate bones of the socket. The man lolled back against the door then slid to the floor.

Pain like electric current jumped from my knuckles up the back of my hand. I yelped and shook my fist.

Braxton racked a pistol—my own—to get my attention. "Motherfucker," he drawled. *Motherfucker* apparently could carry any number of meanings. In this context, spoken with innocent wonderment, it meant something like *Jeez, would you look at that.* Braxton held the gun on me while he prodded his man with little kicks. "Yo, TC, you alright, cuz?"

"I can't see," the guy groaned, both hands pressed to his eye.

"Alright, just hold the gun."

"I just told you, I can't see."

"Use your damn other eye." Braxton was exasperated. You can't get good help anymore.

The guy got to his feet and took the gun, but it dangled at his side. Braxton handcuffed my arms behind my back, wrapping the chain through the slatted back of a chair.

"You didn't need to do that," he told me.

"I've had a long day, Harold."

They left me cuffed to the chair, my hand throbbing. Braxton made an ambiguous little gesture before he left. He pointed at me with both index fingers like six-shooters, which I took to mean *I'm counting on you* but could as easily have meant *Watch out or I'll shoot you,* and with that he closed the door behind him.

43

I lingered over the evidence in the room, burned the details into memory—a smear of blood on the door, body odor, the ache in my fist—as if to convince myself of what had just happened. This blood, this odor, this pain was real and actual. This was the proof. Yet there was no fear, no thrumming nerves or pounding heart, no *emotional* evidence. Just this sense of unreality and draining mood. Plane-crash survivors seem to know this emotion. They do not celebrate their survival. They wander out of cornfields looking shocked and hung over and vaguely remorseful.

But I had given Braxton my word. So, after a period of staring into space, I rolled onto the bed with the chair clinging to me like a jealous child. My keys were in a coat pocket and at length I was able to extract them and uncuff my hands. It was only quarter past midnight, to my great surprise.

I called Caroline at home to ask about the little girl. Only a day earlier, she'd had no trouble believing I could be Bob Danziger's killer. Her words were fresh in memory, an audio loop of her voice that I could still hear:

Ben, what do you want me to say?

That you believe me.

I don't even know you.

It was hard to fault her for being cautious. She was a prosecutor, and I a suspect. Truly she didn't know me; she'd had no reason to trust me. In her shoes, I might have done the same thing. All of which may not have mattered anyway. It may have been too late for me to simply erase Caroline Kelly from memory. The heart recalls what the head would rather forget. But now where did we stand?

So I called, woke her, and sketched in the incident, omitting the detail of the gun against my scalp.

Caroline was instantly awake. Throughout the tale, she repeated, "Braxton *what*? He *what*?"

"Look, can we not make a big deal of it? I'm beat. I'll file a report tomorrow."

"Not make a big deal? Are you insane?"

I didn't answer.

"Ben, are you okay? You sound kind of spacey."

"I'm fine. Something's going on and I don't know what it is. You'll check on the kid?"

"Ben, I'm coming over."

"No, don't do that."

"You'll let Harold Braxton come but not me?"

"Caroline, please. I'm tired. I just don't want to play that whole scene. I don't want to write a report, I don't want twenty cops in my room. We'll talk tomorrow."

"I won't tell anyone. I'll come, just me."

As much as I wanted to see Caroline, I did not want to do it right then. I needed a chance to compose my thoughts, to sort things out first. "Caroline— Look, you and I have to talk. I mean, really talk. I just don't have the energy to do it right now."

"I just want to see if you're alright."

"I know. But—don't take this the wrong way—you're hard work."

At the other end, the mouthpiece rustled against her

chin. "That's not true." A pause. "I'm just going to come and see if you're okay, then I'll leave."

"Caroline, I just got through saying—"

"I know, Ben, but see, I'm not asking you for permission. I'm telling you, I'm coming. You can think I'm a bitch if you want to."

"I didn't say that."

"Is there anything you need?"

"A restraining order."

"Ha ha."

"Caroline, you know, we're not gonna . . . you know."

"Oh, Jesus, Chief Truman! Don't worry, I won't take advantage of you."

"That's what I mean about hard work. Stuff like that."

"What? I'm sorry. I was just teasing."

"Well I don't want to be teased, alright? I've had a rough few days here, in case you haven't noticed." I caught the note of whining in my voice. "Can you just turn it off for one night?"

"I'm coming."

It was like telling the cat to stay off the sofa. "Alright, fine, come. Bring some booze, as long as you're making the trip."

Thirty minutes later, Caroline was at the door with a bottle of Jim Beam.

She poured a glass, thrust it at me, then retreated to a corner chair, where she made a gesture of surrender, hands up, fingers splayed, as if to say *I'm keeping my distance.*

I stood at the window, at the spot where Braxton had looked out. There was an atavistic simplicity to this view of the city. Under a full moon, the South End stretched for long, low blocks of eighteenth-century brownstones, and the steeple of Holy Cross Cathedral was still the highest structure in sight. Somewhere off to the northwest was Mission Flats. And superimposed over all of it was my own face reflected in the glass.

"Are you bleeding?" Caroline asked. She pointed to a streak of blood on the door.

"That's not mine. It was some monster Braxton had with him."

"What happened?"

"You're not going to believe this, but I hit him."

"I'm impressed."

"Don't be. I think I broke my hand."

The whiskey scraped a little going down but it warmed my stomach. "Did you take care of that thing with the little girl?"

"It's all set. They're bringing her to her grandmother's now. She wouldn't talk to anyone at the station. They didn't know what to do with her."

"Good, I'm glad. Thank you for doing that."

I peered out the window a moment longer.

"Ben, is something bothering you?"

"No, I'm fine. They didn't touch me."

"I meant, are you upset about something?" But she thought better of pursuing me. Leaning forward, she said, "Maybe you don't want to talk about it. I'll go if you want. I see you're not hurt."

"No, stay. I mean, if you want, you can stay."

Caroline leaned back again, pulled her knees up, and sat curled in the chair. She was wearing jeans and a baseball jacket, and even this simple outfit she invested with stylishness. There was always something about the way this not-quite-beautiful woman wore her clothes that compelled me. I have no doubt that if she were wearing the PROPERTY OF BUFFALO SABRES T-shirt that I had on at the time—a relic as dingy and thin as a moth's wing—she would have looked elegant in it, too.

"What are you thinking about?" she asked.

"I'm just feeling a little lost, that's all."

"Why lost?" I didn't respond and she prodded, "Say it."

"My mother's dead."

She tilted her head in a sympathetic way, and I hurried to cut her off before she could offer the usual sticky condolence. "I'm just still getting used to the idea. My mother's really dead."

Caroline waited for more, but how could I explain it? How could I convey the three-dimensional reality—the skin, the warm breath, the voice—of the person who'd vanished? What would the obscure, lost history of Annie Truman mean to someone who'd never met her?

"There's a lake in Versailles," I said to the window, "called Lake Mattaquisett, very beautiful, very cold in springtime. We have a home movie of my mother floating on a tire tube in that lake. She's wearing a yellow bathing suit and she's pregnant with me. We used to pull out the movie projector on rainy days and we'd watch it. In the movie she's young, maybe thirty or so, a little older than I am now. She's laughing, happy. I have that image in my memory. I'm not sure why."

"Because you miss her."

I nodded.

"I'm sure she was proud of you, of how you turned out."

"I guess."

"Ben, I'm a mother too. Trust me, she'd be proud of you."

"I think she'd be happy I came back here, to this city. She'd get a kick out of this, too, what we're doing."

"What are we doing?"

"Flirting. Or not flirting, whatever it is. She'd love this."

"Are we flirting, Ben?"

"I don't know. Aren't we?"

She pretended to fiddle with a thread.

"Do you know your dad goes to your sister's grave every day?"

"Yes."

"Every day. Still."

"It gets better, Ben. It takes time."

"That's just what your father told me."

I sipped some more, the warmth of the bourbon streaming through me now.

"Ben . . . I don't feel like I owe you an apology for last week. But I hope you understand. I had to be careful. At the time it seemed like Gittens was right about you and Danziger. You had motive, means, opportunity."

"Sometimes you have to forget all that Agatha Christie crap, Caroline. You have to look at the person too."

"Okay. I guess that's right."

"The other thing is, about when my mother killed herself—"

"Ben, I don't want you to tell me anything about that. You'll put me in a terrible position."

"We have to get past it sometime."

"Ben, please, don't. I mean it."

"Okay." I tapped a knuckle against the window. "You know, last winter my mother got in a car accident. She wasn't supposed to be driving at all. We weren't supposed to let her. I used to unhook the battery cables so the car wouldn't start. But somehow she got it started. Either I forgot or she figured it out. Maybe someone helped her reconnect the battery, someone who didn't know what was going on. My mother could be . . . insistent. Anyway, she got all the way out to I-95. Who knows how. I guess she just kept driving and driving. Maybe she was lost. Or maybe she was trying to drive all the way down here, to Boston, to come home. She was born here, did I ever tell you that? She loved this place."

My eyes began to seep.

Caroline was silent.

"Somehow she wound up on the wrong side of the highway. She was going north in the southbound lanes. She must have gone on the wrong ramp or got confused by the signs or something. It must have been terrifying, all those cars coming at her. She drove into a concrete bridge support."

Caroline made a soft, startled sound.

"She was okay. Bumps and bruises. She had a black eye. It took forever to heal. The car was totaled. My dad had a fit.

"That was when she decided. She said, 'I don't want to be a vegetable, Ben. I'd be mortified.' That's the word she used, *mortified*. She said she did not want to go through it alone and my father was not someone she could turn to, not for that kind of help. She was—"

"Ben, please. Don't do this."

"She got a book. That was Anne Truman: She researched the whole thing. The Seconal, she had a doctor friend. I won't tell you his name. He gave her an anti-nausea drug too, so she could keep it all down."

"Ben, I don't want to hear this. I can't."

"There were ninety pills. We had to empty them all into a glass of water. Ninety red gel-capsules, one by one. They didn't want to dissolve. We had to keep stirring and stirring."

"Ben—"

"It was supposed to taste bitter. She said you were supposed to chase it with something to dull the taste. Jell-O or applesauce or something. She used bourbon."

Caroline walked over to the window where I was standing. She stood in front of me, close, and said, "Ben, stop. I *can't* hear this."

"I need you to understand."

"I do understand."

"Mum said, 'Ben, hold my hand.' So I held her hand. And she said, 'My Ben, my Ben.' And she went to sleep."

"Ben, no more. For your own sake, please. Please. I understand."

I brushed my eyes. "Do you?"

"I understand," she whispered.

We kissed, leaning against the window. It was a different—better—sort of kiss, because this time Caroline gave herself to it completely.

44

I woke up early the next morning, just after dawn, and stood by the window. The city was gray, the sky above it a dark slate that was reluctant to brighten. I drew a circle on the glass with my finger, a little greasy circle around the area I took to be Mission Flats.

"What are you doing up?" Caroline said.

"I need to find out more about the Trudell case."

"Why?"

"Because Braxton said— Where can I find more information?"

She groaned. "You've already seen the files."

"There has to be more."

"Ben, it's too early—"

"I can't sleep. I keep thinking there has to be more. What else is there?"

"Do we have to talk about it now?"

"No. Sorry, go back to sleep."

"Try the detectives' notebooks."

"Good." I thought a moment. "Wait—what detectives' notebooks?"

"Homicide detectives keep notebooks on every investigation. It's routine. Sometimes there's information in the notebooks that doesn't make it into the reports. You might find something there."

"Where are they?"

"Archives, I imagine."

"Okay, then I need to see those notebooks. Can you get me into the archives?"

"Not right this minute."

"Alright, when it opens, then."

Without lifting her head or even opening her eyes, she said, "Ben, all the Trudell files are privileged. They're not circulated. Lowery saw to that. You'll need to file a request with Archives, and it probably won't be granted. You could file a Freedom of Information request with the AG, but it would take a while."

"How long is a while?"

"Six months. Maybe a year."

"A year! We don't have a year."

"What can I tell you."

"You can tell me how I get in to see those notebooks today."

One of Caroline's eyes popped open. She propped herself on one elbow. "Chief Truman," she said carefully, "if this case ever comes to trial, it will be important that the prosecutor not be aware of any improprieties in the way evidence is obtained. And it would be unethical for me to tell you how to evade the public-records laws."

"Right. Sorry. I shouldn't—"

"What I will say is this: If—I said *if hypothetically*—you needed to get those records without the proper clearance, the best way would be to take my dad with you and see a man named Jimmy Doolittle over at Berkeley Street. And you would never ever tell the prosecutor that you got those notebooks illegally, because then she would have an ethical obligation to report it to the court."

"Um, what might I tell the prosecutor?"

"What you might tell the prosecutor is that an anonymous person provided the notebooks to you, or better yet a dead person like, say, Bob Danziger. And you would have to be prepared to say that under oath. Is that all clear?"

"Crystal. Thank you, Counselor."

Her head dropped back down on the pillow. "My dad was a good detective. He'll get you in. If you wanted to get in to the Pope's underwear drawer, he could get you in."

"I'll keep that in mind. You never know."

"Ben, maybe you should come back to bed. The archives won't open till nine."

"I'm not feeling very tired."

Eyes closed, she grinned and said, "Me neither."

45

Jimmy Doolittle was the archivist of the Boston Police Department, overseeing a musty basement room blocked in with cardboard boxes and steel shelving. In these last few days of the Berkeley Street headquarters, the Records Room was even more chaotic than usual. Files had been boxed up and boxes stacked up, ready for the moving vans. These same boxes would soon be re-interred at the new headquarters or at a state archive facility, but for now there was an appealing sort of clutter here. It was like an old antiques shop—you wanted to open some of these musty boxes just to see what was inside. Someday very soon, of course, boxes like these will disappear altogether as police reports are increasingly maintained on computers, but most Boston cops still scratch out their reports longhand or whack them out with IBM Selectrics, which seems to me a very good thing.

John Kelly tapped on a desktop bell, the type you might see in an old hotel, and a voice deep in the warren of boxes growled, "I hear ya, I hear ya." When he emerged, Doolittle pointedly removed the bell from the counter.

"You're Jimmy Doolittle?" I asked.

"I am."

For some reason—probably the heroic (or anti-heroic) name borrowed from the bomber pilot—I had assumed Jimmy Doolittle would project a little glamour. Instead, he turned out to be a pug, short and slight, with two badly bowed legs. His face was handsome but spoiled by a crushed nose that looked like a dollop of plumber's putty. He was older than I'd expected, too. Probably sixty or so, far too old, I thought, to be using the diminutive form of his name. Even in the testosterone-rich environment of a police station, where forty- and fifty-year-old Bobbys and Billys and Johnnys are relatively common, it was surprising to meet a sixty-year-old man who still called himself Jimmy.

"We need to look at a file," I told him.

Doolittle slapped a powder-blue *Document Request Form* down in front of me. I filled out the form with the scant information I had. *Case/File number:* UNKNOWN. *Defendant/suspect:* HAROLD BRAXTON. *Victim:* ARTHUR TRUDELL. *Charge:* MURDER (1ST). *Date of Offense:* AUGUST 17, 1987.

Doolittle scanned the sheet with a critical eye. "It's a black file. Sorry." He slid the form back across the counter at me.

"A black file? What does that mean? I need to see it."

"A black file means it can't be released without the Commissioner's say-so. I need something written."

"From who?"

"I just told you from who, from the Police Commissioner. Soon as you get that, I'll get you the file."

"Caroline Kelly sent me."

"What'd I just say? I haven't seen the paper today. Did somebody die and make Caroline Kelly Police Commissioner? I don't think so."

I shook my head, incredulous. I'd been threatened by cops and by gangsters, I'd had a gun put to my head—

after all that, it was inconceivable that I could be stopped cold by an intransigent file clerk.

"Mr. Doolittle, I didn't say she was the Commissioner, did I?"

"Hey, I'm not going to argue with you. It's a black file. Nothing I can do."

"That's not good enough. I need to see it."

"Can't help you."

"This is a homicide investigation."

"I'm sure it is, sir."

"But I can't see the file?"

"Rules, sir."

There it was, the elaborate formality of the bureaucrat, armed with his inch-wide, mile-deep expertise and a single pointless regulation.

"This is bullshit," I informed the clerk. "Complete and total bullshit."

Doolittle glared, then turned to retreat into the stacks.

"Jimmy," Kelly interceded, "could I borrow your phone a moment?"

Doolittle gave him a suspicious look, as if the phone too was restricted. "You can't dial out. It's just an intercom."

"That's alright, Jimmy. I'm just calling upstairs." Doolittle slid the phone toward him, and Kelly punched in a two-digit number. "Commissioner Evans, please," he said into the mouthpiece, "this is Detective John Kelly. That's right. . . . Oh, Margaret, I'm fine, dear, how-uh-you? . . . Haw haw, that's right, still above ground, ye-e-e-es. . . . Oh, Caroline's just fine. . . . No. No babies yet. We're working on it. . . . Yes, I'll hold." Kelly tapped the counter with his fingernail, looking exquisitely bored. He directed a reassuring smile at Doolittle. After a time, he jerked the phone back up to his ear. "Paul? Yes. . . . Grand, and you? . . . Yes, I hate to impose on you, my friend. I'm in a little bit of a jam. I'm downstairs in the Records Room and I need to see a black file, but I'm told I need a clearance from you. You have a very efficient clerk here named Jimmy Doolittle. . . ." Kelly chatted with the Commissioner awhile, then held the phone out to Doolittle. "He wants to talk to you, Jimmy."

Doolittle took the phone reluctantly, as if it might explode in his hand. "Hello?" His face flushed as he recognized the Police Commissioner's voice. A moment later, he hung up, shell-shocked. "He says it's okay," Doolittle mumbled. "I have a job to do, is all. I didn't mean . . ."

"Well," Kelly comforted, "no harm done. Not to worry, Jimmy. Simple misunderstanding."

Doolittle retrieved the file—all eight boxes of it—and spread them out in a little office off the hallway.

"Excuse me," I said, still pissed off, "what exactly is a black file?"

"It's just a file that can't be released, like if it's sensitive."

"How does a file get to be a black file?"

"The Commissioner makes it one. You know, like if a judge orders that something not get released—what's that word?—impounded. Sometimes it's just that people want them for the wrong reasons, like if a case has a celebrity for a defendant, a movie star or an athlete or whatevah, that'd be a black file for sure. You know, a Chappaquiddick kind of thing. Internal Affairs files are all black. So's child abuse."

"And if a file is not a black file?"

"Then anyone can walk in and get it. Any cop or DA, I mean. Not many of 'em do, though. These are all closed cases. Nobody gives a rat's ass."

"So if anybody ever tried to look at this file?"

"Then they'd have to have permission from the Commissioner's office. Usually a deputy Commissioner signs it."

"Would there be a record of that somewhere?"

"Right here, on the front of the first box. Here." Doolittle pointed out a single sheet on one of the cardboard boxes. It was a perfunctory one-sentence letter from the Commissioner on Boston PD letterhead:

> *Per the request of the District Attorney, ADA Robert M. Danziger and/or his designee(s) may review, photocopy, and/or photograph any document(s), evidence, or other materials in the above-referenced file at any time within one year of this date.*

"So nobody else has opened this box besides Danziger?"

"Not since they closed the case. Could have been hundreds of people pawing through it before it got sent down here. I can't control that, you know."

"Is there any way to tell who requested this file be black?"

"A 'course." He lifted the form to reveal another. "Lowery. The DA." Doolittle turned to leave, then paused to ask, "Hey, you guys want coffee or something?"

Amazing what a call from the Commissioner can do.

"No, thank you, Jimmy." Kelly smiled. He waited until the clerk left the room, then asked, "Alright, now, what are we looking for?"

"The Homicide detectives' notebooks. Anything that didn't make it into the reports, anything that connects Trudell to Frank Fasulo."

"And we're doing this because Braxton says so?"

"You got any better ideas?"

We scavenged through the boxes, which contained mostly papers. The physical evidence—bloody clothing, slugs extracted from the walls, drug paraphernalia—had all been buried in some other archive, presumably. A few items remained, including a thick file of gory photographs. As for the papers, most of them I had already seen photocopied in Danziger's own file on the case. He had apparently created a duplicate file of his own containing

copies of every scrap in these boxes. Only one thing had
been missing from Danziger's file: the detectives' original
notebooks. The absence of these notebooks sent up a red
flag. Obviously if Danziger's theory was that the detectives had missed something the first time around, their
contemporaneous notes would be a crucial bit of evidence. "Danziger copied the notebooks," I told Kelly.
"Somebody took them out of his office. I'm sure of it.
Danziger wouldn't have left them out."

The notebooks themselves were not fancy. Most were
the spiral-bound type that students use. A few were
breast-pocket–sized. Only one of the detectives had assembled his notes into a three-ring binder. Kelly and I
read through the notebooks for the better part of the
morning. Each was a diary of mundane tasks, the metic-
ulous combing-out of good leads from bad (interviews
with neighbors, friends, suspects, snitches), and daily
interactions with others in law enforcement (telephone
calls with prosecutors, forensics labs, other cops). It was
grunt work and it yielded nothing. In the late summer of
1987, Mission Flats had been struck by a plague of am-
nesia and lockjaw. What evidence the investigators had
obtained, including the murder weapon, had been recovered within minutes of the shooting.

The needle in the haystack was this note, scribbled by
a Detective John Rivers the day after the Trudell shooting:

> *Per JV [Julio Vega?] V [victim, i.e. Trudell] upset,
> "not right," consulted FB [Franny Boyle]. JV
> unsure re. Nature of problem?*

Time to talk to Franny Boyle again.

As Kelly and I drove to Government Center, where
the SIU office—Boyle's office—was located, it occurred
to me that I had nearly forgotten the morning's other
revelation. "I didn't know you were friends with the
Commissioner," I said.

He gave me a skeptical glance.

"No, really. I'm impressed."

"Ben Truman, don't be daft. I wouldn't know the Commissioner if he stood up in my soup. That was Zach Boyages from Admin."

I cleared my throat. "Oh."

46

Franny Boyle saw me at the door of his office and tried to manufacture a little of his old muscular presence. He pressed his head down into that thick, bullfrog neck and tightened his pecs. "What's going on, Opie? You look real serious." But Franny's act was not convincing anymore. For all his puffing, he seemed to be shrinking before my eyes. He was seated behind an enormous oak desk, an aircraft carrier of a desk, and its size diminished him further.

"Franny, we need to talk."

"Oh man, this *is* serious. Nothing good ever comes after 'we have to talk.' Last time someone told me 'we have to talk,' I wound up divorced." Franny gave me a wiseguy smirk. It was an invitation to smirk along with him, which I declined.

I closed the door behind me.

"Where's the old man? Kelly?"

"He's outside. I thought we'd just talk, you and me."

"You gonna read me my rights?"

"You need to hear them, Franny?"

He pursed his lips, disappointed he could not jolly me out of my solemn tone. "Well, sit down at least." He pointed to a chair that was covered with files. "Just throw that shit on the floor."

"That's alright, Franny. I'm good here."

Seated in his desk chair, he laced his hands on top of his bald head, flaunting two crescent moons in his armpits.

"Franny, I'm not going to bullshit you. Kelly and I just came from the Records Room at Berkeley Street. We were looking through the Trudell file. We know Artie Trudell came to you with some kind of problem."

"Lots of cops used to come to me with problems. I was the only lawyer a lot of them knew—personally knew, I mean. People give lawyers too much credit. They figure we can answer questions about any kind of problem. I've had cops come to me with questions about divorces, real-estate closings—"

"Franny, this wasn't about a real-estate closing."

"No? How do you know?"

"Wild guess."

"So what do you think it was about, hotshot?"

"Frank Fasulo."

Franny smiled. "Frank Fasulo?"

"That's right."

A poker player who reveals the value of his hand with a gesture has what is called a *tell*. Franny Boyle, I could see, had a tell: to mask his concern, he smiled too quickly and too much.

"Where'd you come up with Frank Fasulo?" Franny said.

"I got a tip."

"*You* got a tip? From who?"

I thought about naming Braxton. I had promised Franny I would not bullshit him. But then, I'd made other promises too.

"Let's say I got it from Raul."

"No, really. Who?"

"I can't tell you that, Franny."

"Jesus, you certainly learn fast. Who the hell are you getting tips from? Not Gittens, I know that."

"Why do you say that?"

"Gittens usually plays it close, and he doesn't know you well enough. No, my guess is it must be Ms. Kelly. I hear you and Princess Caroline are getting . . . close."

He studied me, looking for a tell of my own.

"Franny, before he died, Artie Trudell came to you with a problem. We know he did because he told Julio Vega. Vega said he was upset, he 'wasn't right.' I'm asking you: What was Trudell so worried about?"

"I don't know."

"You don't know meaning you don't remember? Or you don't know meaning it didn't happen?"

"I don't know meaning I don't know what you're talking about."

"Franny, do you want a lawyer?"

"I *am* a lawyer."

"Then cut the shit and answer me! What was Artie Trudell so afraid of?"

"I told you, I don't know what you're talking about." He pushed back his chair and stood up. "I don't know what you're talking about and maybe I don't like what you're suggesting—"

"Sit down, Franny."

"This is my office."

I knocked him once in the shoulder then again, hard, in the chest. He fell into the desk chair with a clatter. He pushed himself back up, and I knocked him down again.

Kelly opened the door. He glanced at me standing over Boyle, who was sprawled awkwardly in his chair. "Sorry," he said, "I thought there might be a problem." He disappeared again.

"You don't like what I'm suggesting, Franny? Let me fill in the blanks so you know exactly what I'm suggesting. I don't think Artie Trudell came to you for a real-estate closing because I don't think you know shit from pound cake about real-estate closings. I think he came to you because you're a DA, and the only reason to go to a DA is to report a crime."

"What crime?"

"I don't know yet, but I'm going to find out."

"Yeah? How are you going to do that?"

"For starters, I'm going to talk to Julio Vega. Whatever Trudell knew, Vega knew. They were partners, remember?"

"Vega's a wing nut. The whole town knows it."

"At least he's not crooked."

This brought a glare. "Kid, you don't know what you're talking about."

"Maybe. But I know Trudell had information about Frank Fasulo and that cop who got killed at the Kilmarnock, and about the red-door cocaine and Raul. Trudell had all this information and he brought it to you because he thought you'd do something about it. He trusted you; he thought you'd do your job. But you didn't do your job, at least not fast enough, and Trudell got killed. And I think Danziger figured it all out."

Boyle smiled. "Is that what you think?"

"Yeah, that's what I think. And I think when it all comes out, everybody's going to know the whole thing wasn't Vega's fault."

He smiled and smiled.

The door opened again. This time it was Gittens. He took in the scene—which at the moment had me jabbing my index finger toward Boyle's nose—and his eyebrows rose as if it were all a mild but not unpleasant surprise.

"Everything alright in here?"

"Yeah. Franny and I were just talking."

Gittens studied us, then said, "Lowery wants to see you, Ben."

47

"You probably think there's some grave injustice going on here."

"I don't know exactly what to think, Mr. Lowery."

"That's a politic answer. Are you being politic with me, Chief Truman?" Lowery was standing at the window with his back to Kelly and me. But with this question he twisted to face me, coiling at the waist as if his handmade shoes were nailed to the floor. "Or are you being honest?"

"Honest, sir."

"I'm not sure I believe you. I have a sneaking suspicion you know more than you're saying."

Lowery returned his attention to the window. Before him was the downtown skyline with City Hall in the foreground and a wall of office towers behind it. The view from the District Attorney's office was fine, with three TVs to keep an eye on things. It occurred to me that Lyndon Johnson famously watched three TVs at once. Maybe Lowery was aware of that.

"The rube is running a con on the city slickers," Lowery ruminated. "Well, it serves us right, I suppose, after what we put you through." He sighed. "Chief Truman, I want you to understand my position."

"You don't owe me any explanations, Mr. Lowery."

"You're right—I don't owe you anything. It's not about owing. It's about responsibility, Chief Truman. You were in the archives this morning fishing around in the Trudell file."

"Yes, sir."

"I presume you think there's some connection to Danziger's murder."

"There might be."

"There might be. I see. You don't think Braxton did it?"

"I'm not 100-percent certain, no."

"Did you expect to be 100-percent certain?"

"Ideally."

He thought it over. "Ben, I'm an old trial lawyer, and at the end of every trial, do you know what the judge tells the jury? He tells them they must find the defendant guilty 'beyond a reasonable doubt.' Think about that, 'beyond a reasonable doubt.' Not beyond *all* doubt; beyond a *reasonable* doubt. See, there is never 100-percent certainty. Doubt is built into the system. It is a wonderful system but it is administered by humans, so there will always be doubt and error. We have to accept that. We have no choice. None of us has a monopoly on the truth, none of us has a window to the past. We look at the evidence, we make our best guess, and we pray we've done the right thing. It's an awesome responsibility, Ben."

"It is, sir."

"We pick the man we're going to accuse, and then it doesn't matter if we're 100-percent sure or only 51-percent sure. Once we choose our man, once we choose our version of the case, that becomes our gospel, that becomes the one true faith."

"Yes, sir."

I glanced at Kelly, who was seated in the leather chair beside my own. He stared up at the ceiling as if balancing an object on his nose. A little wisenheimer smirk played around his mouth. The District Attorney might have been droning on about the Treaty of Ghent or the reproductive habits of Galápagos tortoises, for all Kelly cared.

"You have some doubts that Harold Braxton is guilty, Chief Truman?"

"I do."

"Let them go."

"Excuse me?"

"Let them go. Braxton is the one."

"How do you know?"

"I know because I've been doing this a long time. There's enough evidence here to convict Braxton three times over for killing Bobby Danziger. Hell, I've won cases that weren't half as strong. You don't need the Trudell case. Just let it go. Believe me, it's a cleaner case without going back and dredging up a ten-year-old case that has nothing to do with this. It's cleaner for the jury and it's better for this city." The District Attorney turned to face me, to gauge my reaction. "What we do here has a political dimension, Ben. Surely you understand that. Right now the races in this city get along beautifully. Crime is down across the board, the police are respected, African-American communities are doing better than they ever have. Meanwhile in other cities, New York, L.A., the police are distrusted—no, they're hated. It's a political decision, Ben, and I mean that in the best, noblest sense.

"Now, when I present my findings—and even if the case is prosecuted in Maine, I'm going to have to tell the people of this city *something*—I'm going to tell the public just what the evidence shows: that this was Braxton and no one else. I'm not going to drag up the past."

"The past is always getting dragged up, sir."

"Ben, I'm asking you to forget the Trudell case. Leave it alone. Ten years ago, that case split the city in two. It hit every button: black defendant, white police victim. Now it's just sitting there like a big vat of gasoline, Ben. For the sake of this city, don't throw a match in the gasoline."

John Kelly said, "I think we understand." He managed somehow to inject the faintest undertone of *fuck you*. He'd seen Andrew Lowerys come and go; this one would pass too. Kelly stood and said, "Let's go, Ben."

Lowery turned his back on us again to look out over the city. He shook his head. "It's always just below the surface."

Outside the courthouse an African-American kid played a makeshift set of drums. He sat on a milk crate with an array of plastic buckets in front of him plus a few metal objects (an ice tray, a cookie sheet) for cymbals. The beat was insistent, joyous. I could not help thinking it was more eloquent and more honest than anything Lowery had just told us—closer to the true heartbeat of the city.

Kelly and I found ourselves, inevitably, pacing to that beat.

"What did you make of all that, Ben Truman?"

"It was bullshit."

"Precisely. You are my prize pupil. That was one-hundred-proof, high-octane bullshit. Now, why would Lowery not want us poking around the Trudell case?"

"Because there's something he wants kept quiet."

"I'd say that's a very good theory. Perhaps it's time we paid another visit to Julio Vega. He knows more than he's given us."

We did not know it, but it was already too late. Julio Vega was dead.

48

Vega was hanging in the kitchen of his tiny house. He had used an electrical extension cord which he'd looped around a ceiling light fixture. A slipknot behind the ear forced the head to slump forward. In front, the cord disappeared into the fatty folds of his neck. The chair he had stepped off lay on its side.

Kelly touched the back of his own hand to Vega's hand. That slight contact caused the body to twist a bit before resettling under the noose. "Cold," he said.

Kelly called it in. The machinery had to be started. BPD Homicide and a State Police team would be here soon. Even suicides are considered "unnatural deaths" and must be examined.

Julio Vega's death could not have been more natural, though. It was the logical conclusion to a decade of shame and recrimination and exile. It was the only way for Vega to repay his debt. It was the only way, too, for Vega to escape a second go-round with the Trudell case. A new round of questions to account for the fresh victim: *How might the raid on the red-door crackhouse have led to Bob Danziger's death ten years later?* Even Vega's body suggested the naturalness of his suicide. Unlike the rifle-blasted, gas-swollen remains of Danziger and Ratleff, Vega's body might plausibly have been sleeping. His bowed head, the chin on his collarbone, eyelids slightly ajar, fingers curled at his sides, even the belly button that winked out from under his sweatshirt—every detail suggested the humanity of Vega's corpse. Whatever the police may have called it, this was anything but an "unnatural death." Death naturalized Julio Vega.

But dead bodies must be inspected like so many sausages, and so the processors came: uniform cops, then detectives, photographers, forensics people. A black van from the Medical Examiner's office waited to take the corpse. Cops who had known Vega showed up too, including Martin Gittens. "I figured it would come to this someday," Gittens sighed. "It was cruel, what they did to Julio."

Gittens was obviously in pain. In the mid 1980s, Vega and Trudell had been his protégés. He'd fed them information, lent them his street-corner credibility, helped them get established. For a long time Gittens stood apart from everyone, silent. I thought about approaching him but decided against it. My relationship with Gittens was tenuous enough already.

Kelly pulled one of the detectives aside and asked what they were finding out.

"It's a suicide," the guy said. "We're just dotting the *i*'s."

In the middle of all this hung the body. It could not be cut down until it had been photographed, a job that was delayed by the fact that Crime Scene Services was needed in several places that morning.

When the activity around the body had ebbed, Kelly and I stood under it and stared up. I tried to follow Kelly's eyes, to see what so fascinated him. Up close, Vega reminded me of a paratrooper caught in tree branches.

"Look at the ligature marks, Ben Truman."

Two stripes scored the neck where the cord had dug into the soft skin. The larger of the two ran from ear to ear across the crease of the throat, above the Adam's apple. The cord was embedded in this mark, and above the cord was a smudge of lividity, the rosy blush of settling blood trapped by the cord's pressure. Above this mark was a second, smaller line. Here the cord had actually cut the skin in places and blood had beaded and dried along its track. There was lividity around this mark too, though it was not as distinct.

I made an uncertain grunt, *hm.*

Kelly looked down at me with a disapproving expression. "Do you notice anything unusual about that?" He sounded annoyed at having to point out something so obvious, as if he were talking to an obtuse child.

"I don't know. I've never seen anyone who hung himself."

"Well I've seen people who hung themselves. But I've never seen anyone who did it twice."

We waited around in the anemic atmosphere of that house to see Vega cut down and laid on a gurney. They zipped him up with the electrical cord still wound around his neck like a scarf. Entrenched as it was, the cord could not be removed without damaging the skin.

Caroline arrived. She handed me a pink phone-message slip with a number but no name.

"Why didn't you write down the name? I don't know this number."

"Because," Caroline informed me, "it's Max Beck."

49

The mallards in the Public Garden were agitated. From the little island in the middle of the lagoon where they were gathered came a cacophony of honking. The males in particular, with their shimmery green necks, were on edge. They ran at one another, braying and slapping the water.

Max Beck was watching them. He sat on a bench under a sagging willow, absently munching on a sandwich. The paper wrapper from the sandwich was tucked under his thigh to prevent it from blowing away. Beck seemed to have shucked his Defender of the Despised persona, with its strutting righteousness and combativeness, just laid it down on the bench beside him like a coat. Here by the duck pond, he became ordinary—an office worker creeping toward middle age, overweight, curly salt-and-pepper hair riffling in the wind.

"Mr. Beck?"

He startled. "Yes? Oh, Chief Truman, thank you for coming." He jumped up and cleared a space on the bench facing the lagoon. "Have a seat. You want a sandwich? I got you tuna-fish."

I took the sandwich and turned it over in my hand.

"It's okay," he said, "it won't turn you into a defense lawyer."

I sat down. "Do you take your lunch here a lot?"

"Nah. I don't usually eat lunch. There never seems to be time. I'm either in court or on the way to court. I have to watch it anyway." He patted his belly. "I picked this place because I thought we could be alone here."

The ducks kicked up another round of honking. *Rhonk rhonk.*

"They're upset about something," Beck said.

"It's getting cold. They're anxious to leave."

I opened my sandwich and the two of us ate in silence. An awkward etiquette pertains at lunchtime meetings. It requires occasional conversational pauses for chewing, and it disfavors asking questions of someone who has just inserted a bolus of tuna-fish sandwich in his mouth. So Max Beck and I—strange bedfellows, unsure how to speak to each other—sat for a while eating our lunches.

"Does anyone know you're here, Chief Truman?"

"No. On the phone, you said it was confidential. Besides, it's not exactly something I'd brag about to my cop friends."

"Your cop friends think I'm one of the bad guys."

"They think you're a devil worshiper."

Beck grinned. Being thought a devil worshiper did not seem to trouble him. "Well then, thank you for coming. We'll make this quick, before anyone sees you. Usually I'd call a prosecutor to arrange this. My client wants to surrender."

"So let him surrender."

"Well, that's the unusual part. He wants to surrender to you."

"Me? Why me?"

"He trusts you."

"He shouldn't. Did your client tell you he broke into my hotel room last night with one of his goons and put a gun to my head?"

Beck shook his head.

"Maybe I'm not the best cop for Harold today."

"I see. But you haven't taken out a charge against him, have you?"

I did not answer.

"Harold said you helped get his daughter back."

"It wasn't a big deal."

"It was a big deal to him. Chief Truman, Boston PD is on a rampage looking for my client. It's important they not find him. Do you understand that?"

"I think it's important they *do* find him. There's a warrant out for him."

"Yes, there is that. What I meant was, it's important that Harold not be in their custody, that he not disappear into a holding cell somewhere or find himself being chased down some dark alley by a bunch of white cops with guns. This isn't about the legalities."

I bristled at the generalization. I was a white cop with a gun too. "Is this you talking or your client?"

"My client and I speak with one voice."

"Ah. That's the devil-worshiping part."

Beck frowned. He broke off a piece of bread and tossed it on the ground, where the ducks pulled it apart. "My client asked me to deliver a proposal to you. He says he is willing to surrender on the warrant but only on two conditions: He'll only surrender to you and only on the condition that he be taken immediately to Maine for trial. He is not afraid of a trial. But he doesn't want Boston to have custody, even for one day, even one hour. He feels strongly about that, so that's the way it would have to be."

"Otherwise?"

"Otherwise Boston PD can keep looking for him, and when they find him Harold won't surrender. Someone will get hurt."

"Probably Harold."

"Yes. Probably Harold. Do you take comfort in that, Chief Truman?"

"Of course not. Are you that cynical about cops?"

"Some cops, yes."

"Well you don't know me. I haven't earned that from you."

"No, you're right. I apologize. My client feels he is in danger from certain Boston cops, that's all I meant. Here, let me show you something."

Beck put his sandwich down and wiped his hands on his thighs. He rummaged around in his briefcase until he found a letter on the District Attorney's letterhead, three or four pages long, single-spaced. The word CONFIDENTIAL was typed across the top. The subject line read, *Re: Agreement By and Between the Commonwealth and Harold Ellison Braxton*. "Skip to the back," Beck suggested. Three prosecutors had signed the letter: the state Attorney General, District Attorney Andrew Lowery, and Assistant DA Robert M. Danziger.

"Harold asked me to show that to you. Do you know what it is, Chief Truman? It's a cooperation letter. Signed by Bob Danziger. Did you know Harold was working with Danziger?"

"No."

"Don't you find it strange that Harold would go off and murder a prosecutor who's just given him immunity? Look here." He reached over and opened the letter to the second page. *"Use immunity* for Harold's testimony regarding the events of August 16–17, 1987, the night Artie Trudell was killed. Do you know what *use immunity* means?"

"Yeah, it means anything he gives them can't be used against him, unless the state can show they had an independent source for the information. They can still charge him with the murder, but they can't use his own words to convict him."

I scanned the letter, which did not explicitly identify the crime Bobby Danziger was investigating. But it was obvious. "Jesus, Danziger actually flipped Braxton. He was using Braxton to reopen the Trudell case."

"Yes. And I'll tell you what else that letter means. It means Bob Danziger didn't think Harold killed Artie Trudell. You don't give immunity to a cop killer, even limited immunity like this."

"I don't understand. If Harold didn't kill Artie Trudell, what would he know about the case?"

"Chief Truman, Harold's relationships with the police are complex. He's not the monster they make him out to be. He's helped out a number of detectives, including your friend Martin Gittens."

"Braxton was a snitch for Gittens?"

"Is. Braxton *is* a snitch for Gittens."

"I don't believe it."

"Ask Gittens. They've both been in the Flats a long time, coexisting quite happily. I'm not saying they're friends. It's a business relationship: an exchange of values. Gittens gets information, Harold gets"—he searched for the discreet word—"room to maneuver."

"'Room to maneuver.' You mean Gittens has been protecting him. I don't believe it."

"Not protecting him. He just helps Harold stay out of trouble. If there's going to be a raid, Gittens may give him a heads-up, that's all. It's not so uncommon. Spies and counterspies."

Beck must have seen I was flummoxed by all this because he fell silent while I took it in. To pass the time, he tore off a piece of bread and tossed it on the ground. He took care to leave it where a little finch could peck at it for a moment before the enormous honking mallards chased the bird off.

"Understand what I'm telling you, Chief Truman, Martin Gittens is a good cop. He does what he has to do. He takes his information where he finds it. Gittens works narcotics cases, and the only people with information *about* the drug trade, unfortunately, are *in* the drug trade. What are you gonna do?" He shrugged. "Actually, I kind of like him, as cops go."

"Did Gittens protect Braxton in the Trudell case?"

"He warned Harold about the raid, yes. That's why Harold wasn't there. But after that, Gittens played it straight. When he thought Harold was the shooter, Gittens went after him harder than anyone else. It was Gittens who found the murder weapon, remember."

"With Braxton's prints on it."

"Those prints were planted."

"Oh, come on."

"Look, prints can be lifted. All it takes is a piece of Scotch tape and a little know-how. We had a forensics guy ready to testify those prints were put there, probably by some cop trying to shore up a weak case."

"So Braxton was Raul?"

Another theatrical shrug. "Who knows."

"Well what did Danziger want Braxton for? What was he going to testify to?"

"Just that Gittens had tipped him off to the raid. That's really all he knows about it." Beck fixed me with a look that approximated sincerity. "Chief Truman, Harold did not kill Bob Danziger. I don't say he's an angel, but he didn't do this."

"How do I know that for sure?"

"Because Danziger knew it. Danziger knew Harold didn't kill Artie Trudell. That's why he gave him immunity. Figure out what Danziger had, figure out how he knew."

"Well unfortunately I can't ask Danziger, can I?"

"He must've had something—evidence, a witness, something. My client trusts you. Harold asked me to show you this document for a reason: He wants you to trust him too. Not be his friend, not approve of everything he does, just trust him. Let him surrender."

I tossed the rest of my sandwich to the ducks, who surged around it frantically. "Alright, how does this work?"

"We pick a place outside the city limits, where Boston

PD doesn't have jurisdiction. Harold will surrender himself voluntarily to your custody. From there you would take him straight to Maine for trial."

"If I were him, I wouldn't be so anxious for a trial."

"Chief Truman, if you were him, right now the trial would be the least of your worries."

50

Battery Point is a bulge of land that extends into Boston Harbor at the southeastern edge of Mission Flats. There is a little park, not much more than a turn-around for cars. A plaque explains that English cannons once were stationed here to guard the southern approach to the city. A knee-high stone wall surrounds the lookout point; beyond it the land quickly melts into a soggy marsh. If you stepped off that wall, you'd find yourself standing in water up to your waist. A few more steps and you'd be under water completely. The land is unbuildable and too far from the city center to tempt developers to fill it in, as they did the Back Bay. So it has been preserved in something like its pristine condition. In fact, if you ignore the modern intrusions—the planes banking away from Logan Airport, a field of oil tanks, trash snarled in the grass—with no great leap of imagination, you can catch a glimpse of this place as it must have appeared when the first Englishmen arrived here. Lush and fecund; rocky and wintry and terrifying too. A new England suited to the rapturous Puritan vision of a community without sin, a fundamentalist Christian theocracy, an anti-America. A New World. They must have sailed right past these marshes. If you'd been standing on this spot four hundred years ago, you would have seen them, proto-Americans searching for a better landfall.

Gittens kept me waiting here for some time. When he finally arrived, we stood on the concrete parapet looking north toward the city skyline. The wind off the harbor fluttered our jackets. I crossed my arms to keep the chill off.

"Some spot," he said.

"I thought we'd better talk privately."

"Oh?"

"I have some information about the Trudell case."

"Jesus, are you still on that?"

"Martin, doesn't it bother you that everybody involved in the case is dead? First Trudell, then Danziger, now Vega."

"Vega? He killed himself."

"No. There were two sets of ligature marks, and you can't hang yourself twice. Vega was murdered. Somebody staged it to look like a suicide. Vega must have struggled, he must have escaped the first time, so the murderer had to do it again."

"Who are you, Nancy Drew?" Gittens was annoyed. "You're making this much harder than it is. Forget Vega, forget Trudell. Braxton shot Danziger because Danziger was a DA. Don't you get that?"

"What about Trudell?"

"What *about* Trudell?"

"Who killed him?"

"Gee, maybe it was the second shooter on the grassy knoll."

"I'm serious, Martin."

"Alright. Braxton killed him. Is that what you need to hear?"

"Impossible."

"Impossible? Why? Because Braxton's such a swell guy?"

"No. Because he wasn't there. Braxton knew the raid was coming. You warned him."

For a moment the only sound was the sough of the wind in my ears.

"That's a crock of shit, and don't you ever repeat it to anyone. Somebody's playing you, Ben. I didn't warn Braxton. Who told you that?"

"Danziger. It was in his file, and it gets worse. Danziger had given immunity to Braxton. He was going to have him testify to all this; he was taking it to a grand jury."

"Untrue."

"It is true. Here's the cooperation letter. At a minimum, it explains why Braxton was in Maine. He wasn't there to kill Danziger; he was there to meet with him. He was going to be Danziger's star witness."

Gittens studied the letter without comment, his face expressionless.

"Martin, Danziger knew."

"Knew what?"

"He knew Braxton was your snitch. He knew you protected him."

"That is just false. Look, have I gotten information from Braxton? You bet I have. Have I given something back to him in exchange? Absolutely. That's how it works. It's my job. That doesn't make Braxton 'my snitch.' "

"Did you tip him off about that raid when Artie died?"

"Of course not!"

"Did you ever protect him?"

"No. Not the way you mean."

"Was Braxton 'Raul'?"

"No. And don't you ever fuckin' put in a report that you even asked that question."

I shifted, suddenly unsure of myself.

"Ben, listen carefully: Braxton. Killed. Trudell. Case closed."

"It doesn't make sense. If Harold was tipped off about

the raid, why would he still be in the apartment when Trudell got there?"

" 'Harold'? What is this? Are you getting all this from Braxton?"

"Why did he leave the gun, Martin? Braxton's way too smart to drop the murder weapon with his fingerprints all over it. Why would he do that?"

"Why? Because in real life things get fucked up, that's why. Why was he in the apartment? How the hell should I know? Maybe he had to go back to get something. Maybe he meant to get out sooner but he got held up. If he was warned—and in the Flats, who knows, maybe he was—maybe the raid team just got there sooner than Braxton figured they would. He fucked up. And once he was trapped inside, he had to shoot his way out because that's all he knows how to do. What else would he do? Negotiate? He isn't Henry fuckin' Kissinger."

"And the gun? Why did he drop the gun?"

"Because he's human. Because he was under stress and he made a mistake. Yes, he's smart, but smart people commit crimes imperfectly. It happens all the time. That's how they get caught. Jesus, Ben, that's what murder is. It's not cool calculation; it's hysteria."

"What about Raul?"

"Would you forget about Raul! It never mattered about Raul. I told you, there was no Raul and there were a thousand Rauls. It doesn't make any difference."

He rested one foot on the stone wall and looked out over the harbor toward the airport on the opposite bank. "There aren't neat solutions to every mystery. The world is messier than that. People get involved and they"—he waved his hand in exasperation—"they *complicate* everything. They do things for reasons even they don't understand. They do things for no damn reason at all. I know this is your first murder and you want to figure everything out. But sometimes you can't figure everything out because you can't ever really understand other people. You can't understand why they do what they do. You just have to accept a little mystery, Ben. People are mysterious, the world is mysterious. You can't know everything. You're not supposed to. This isn't a history book. It's just the world. It's a messy place."

It struck me then that Gittens was the perfect cop for Mission Flats. He was a natural broken-field runner, with just the supple temperament for that chaotic, unbounded place. When the rules did not work, he bent them. When the facts did not fit, he bent them too. And in general that was a necessary—even a good—thing. Without people like Gittens, the system would jam. But all that sophistication made Gittens tougher to decipher than Franny Boyle had been. He was certainly a better poker player than Franny. I'd been bluffing when I said all this information had come from Danziger's files. In fact it had come from Vega, Braxton, and Beck. I'd bluffed, but Gittens had not revealed his cards. Unlike Franny, Martin Gittens did not have a tell. He was indignant at the suggestion he'd done anything wrong—and guilty or not, who wouldn't be?

He said, "What do you intend to do with all these . . . theories about the Trudell thing?"

"I'm not sure. I still don't know who the shooter was. For all I know, maybe it was Braxton after all. All the rest is just—I guess it's just the way the game is played around here."

Gittens tore up the cooperation letter and dropped the shreds into the water. They caught in the reeds. Some landed in open water, where after a time they sunk. I was offended at the gesture, but when Gittens spoke again, his voice was so reassuring that I knew he'd torn up the document for my own good. Some secrets should remain just that.

"Well," he said, "be careful out there. There are people who don't want the case reopened. Important people."

"So I've been told. But what can I do? I can't just stop."

"Knowing when to stop is part of the job, Ben. We're not supposed to answer every question, we're not supposed to follow every lead to infinity. There isn't time. Our job is just to solve the case in front of us then move on to the next one. At some point you have to just stop."

Gittens was right, of course. Mysteries always remain.
In any murder, a hundred tiny enigmas—what was
the victim doing there?, why did he cry out (or not cry
out)?, why did the killer drop the weapon?, why did he
linger at the scene? You can swat at these gnats all day, to
no real purpose. Homicides, with their randomizing violence and missing eyewitness, simply breed mysteries.
Most are insignificant, and investigators learn to live
with them. A case is "solved" when the essential fact—
the killer's identity—is established. There are no
drawing-room scenes in which the suspects are gathered
and the sleuth delivers an immaculate, all-explaining solution. Gittens was right: The world is a messier place
than that.

So I was prepared, after my conversation with
Gittens, to accept a little uncertainty. If Artie Trudell was
worried about something in the weeks before he died,
we'd probably never know what it was, and there was no
reason to think it mattered. Frank Fasulo and the Kilmarnock case; and "Raul" and the red door and the
Trudell murder; the killer who'd moved Danziger's dead
body looking for something—in all likelihood no one

would ever know the truth about any of them, and maybe none of it mattered. The Danziger murder was solved. The hard evidence pointed to Harold Braxton, all of it. The rest was just background noise—rumor and gossip and tips. I had to accept that.

There was one mystery, though, one of those gnats I could not resist swatting. Alone among the witnesses, Franny Boyle still had not come clean. I left Gittens and went straight downtown to find him.

I parked on Union Street and began to make my way on foot, past Faneuil Hall and the statue of Samuel Adams, past City Hall with its looming concrete geometries, and out into the open space of City Hall Plaza.

This is a plaza in name only. It is too big and featureless, too empty to be a plaza. Rather, City Hall Plaza is a void. A barren, windy clearing the size of four or five football fields completely tiled over with red bricks. It is not a place where you linger. It is a place where you quicken your step to get across to the other side.

And that is precisely what I was doing, quick-stepping my way across the red bricks toward Cambridge Street. My thoughts were on Gittens—had I judged him unfairly?—and on the history of this real estate—on the loopy urban planner who decided fifty years ago to bulldoze Boston's honky-tonk old Scollay Square and replace it with this monochromatic pinball table—specifically I was thinking that Bomber Harris was not half as thorough in leveling Dresden, and congratulating myself on the cleverness of that remark, thinking perhaps I would find a way to repeat it to Caroline, to impress her—all of which is to say, the usual slurry of thoughts was burbling through my mind, I was thinking of many things and of nothing—

when a little burst of brick exploded at my feet like a land mine.

My first thought was that someone had thrown a stone or that a rock had fallen from a building. But there was no one nearby, and the nearest building was fifty yards away.

I heard a hiss, then a ghost slammed my left arm in the triceps with a hammer. The arm jumped across my chest. My jacket sleeve was torn and the arm was bleeding. There was a dull, swollen pain in the muscle—*my* muscle!—a pain that blossomed only after a delay, after that first unbelieving moment.

It was not until the third bullet raised another plume of brick dust that I accepted the obvious: Someone was shooting at me.

My brain whited out. There was no thought at all, only the primal urge—run.

I ran. At first toward Cambridge Street, away from the shots. But the only shelter on this fucking tabletop was the subway entrance, a bricked-over bunker behind me. So I doubled back and ran for that, even though this path took me back toward the shooter.

People bustled around the subway entrance. Lawyers and secretaries, office workers finishing a long day. They turned to see me running. They had not noticed the gunshots. There had been no *bang!* to alert them. The small crowd regarded me—a man sprinting toward them, his arm bleeding—an odd sight but as yet no cause for alarm. A yuppie in a suit smiled tentatively as if there might be some kind of joke, a punch line.

In a dead run, I pulled my pistol and racked it. This was a bit of action-movie flapdoodle I ought to have skipped. I had no idea where the shots were coming from and, in any event, how could I shoot back with so many people around?

Now, ironically, it was my gun that triggered a panic.

There was a scream. The commuters pushed back into the mouth of the subway entrance, then, when the lobby filled and they could not get past the turnstiles, they burst back out of the doors and scattered, screaming.

I did not bother to show my badge or announce I was a cop. I ran.

I reached the subway entrance and crouched against

the wall. My arm was throbbing now, my shirtsleeve heavy with wet blood.

In the token booth, the clerk pressed himself against the back wall. His eyes were locked on the gun in my hand, his mouth hung open in a perfect O.

"It's okay," I told him. "I'm a cop."

"You want me to call the cops?"

"No!" I snarled. "No cops."

I pressed my arm to stanch the bleeding and riffled through the possibilities. Who would take a shot at me? Braxton? Another gangbanger? Gittens? After all, I'd offended him just minutes earlier with questions about the Trudell case. But none of them made sense. Braxton had made me his confidant. And as far as I knew, Gittens was still in the Flats. With no ready explanation, paranoia set in.

I stepped up to the token window and tried to engineer an ordinary transaction, as if the events of the previous sixty seconds had never occurred. "One please." I fished in my pocket for a dollar to buy a token but I came up empty. "Jesus, I don't have any cash. Sorry."

The clerk gaped. He had not budged from the back wall. "It's okay, buddy," he assured me, "you can go around."

52

By the time I made it to the Special Investigations Unit, the pain in my arm had subsided, but my sleeve and left hand were wet with blood. When I appeared in her doorway, Caroline jerked back in her chair.

"Ben! Oh my God, what happened to you?"

"I think I got shot."

"You *think*?"

"I guess. It's never happened before."

She rushed off to get a first-aid kit, then we sat on her couch so she could clean the wound with alcohol and a gauze pad. She ordered me to strip off my jacket and the bloody shirt. I was still wearing the same PROPERTY OF BUFFALO SABRES T-shirt I'd worn the night before, when Caroline had come to my hotel room. If she noticed this, she didn't mention it.

"It just grazed you," she said, presumably to calm me down.

"It *grazed* me? I got *shot*."

"Well, you didn't really get *shot* shot. It's a scrape."

"Excuse me, I was under the impression that when a bullet hits you, that means you've been shot."

"Okay, Ben," she said, "you got shot. I meant, you're okay."

"Caroline, don't do that."

"Do what?"

"That thing you do, with getting your way."

"I just said you got shot. I'm agreeing with you."

"I know, but it was the way you said it."

She frowned at me. "Sorry. Just trying to help. You're right, you got shot." She dropped the gauze into the first-aid kit, then said, "I'm on your side, Ben. You know that." She gave me a look to reinforce the point, aiming her eyes at mine until I acknowledged that I did know it—she was without a doubt on my side. "Don't forget it," she said.

"Sorry, I'm a little freaked out here."

We kissed, for no particular reason except something told us to, and I understood—in a way I had not quite until that moment—that as difficult as it was to get close to Caroline Kelly, she was one of those selective, ferociously loyal people who, once they have taken you in, will stand by you through the most desperate times. Such people have few acquaintances and many friends. They withhold their affection because it costs them so much to give it so completely, and because they never—ever—revoke it. If you are lucky, you may meet one or two of them in your life.

From a desk drawer, Caroline produced a sweatshirt and tossed it to me. Long strands of her dark hair clung to the sweatshirt, which had the Boston PD logo and the slogan AMERICA'S FIRST POLICE DEPARTMENT.

"Thanks."

"It's okay. I give one to everyone who shows up here with a gunshot wound."

As I was putting on the sweatshirt, Caroline picked up the phone.

"What are you doing?"

"Calling the police."

"No."

"Oh, Chief Truman, don't be ridiculous. We have to report this."

"Absolutely not."

I gave her a look and she hung up the phone. "You're being paranoid. Why would anyone want to shoot you?"

"Maybe they don't like hicks."

"You're no hick." This she said in a dismissive voice, lest I mistake it for a compliment.

"It's the Trudell thing. Somebody doesn't want me sniffing around that case. Is Franny here? I need to talk to Franny. He's the only one left, and he's been lying from the start."

"He's in his office."

I got to my feet.

"Wait," Caroline said. She reached for the phone again.

"I said no cops."

"I'm calling my father."

"Good. Okay, good. Get him in here."

"Ben, can I suggest one other thing? Call Kurth. Franny won't try anything with Kurth there. He wouldn't dare."

"Jesus, Caroline. Don't you think that guy's a little . . . ?"

"I know, he's a little odd. But, Ben, if there's one cop you can trust, it's Kurth."

53

Franny seemed to be waiting for us. He was horribly transformed in the few hours since I'd seen him. He slumped behind his desk looking exhausted and ill and desperately sad. I thought he might even have been crying—his face was glazed with damp sweat like tears—but tenderness was so far from Franny Boyle's character that I presumed instead that he was simply drunk, which no doubt he was.

Franny did not stir when we appeared in the door. He gazed at each of us in turn: me, Caroline, John Kelly, and Kurth. "Looks like the gang's all here," he said. A beer bottle was pinched between his thighs. He lifted it to take a swig. "You guys want one? Just don't tell the boss—I don't want to lose my raise." Then a shadow passed over his face and the kidding stopped. The bravado was just too much effort to keep up and, at this point, why bother? "I been wondering how long it was gonna take you."

"Franny," I said, "you want a lawyer here?"

"Again with the lawyer. No, Opie, I don't need a lawyer."

His eyes drifted to the wall behind me. "I ever tell you

about my first homicide, Opie? It was when we had real gangsters, the old North End types, not these Asian kids. The real goombahs. My victim, they found him chained to a pile under this pier down near the Red Falcon Terminal, on the waterfront there. They took him down under the pier at low tide and they tied him to the pole and left him there while the tide come up. That's old school, baby. We never solved it. Nobody would talk. What the hell—I wouldn't have talked either." He slumped further in his chair. "I think about that guy all the time: chained there, watching the water come up. Nothing he could do. Just sit there and watch it." He wiped an invisible tear from his cheek and looked at me as if I were very far away.

I turned away from his face.

On the desk was the picture that had been hanging in Danziger's office, the Special Investigations Unit as it was composed in the mid-eighties—Assistant DAs Bob Danziger and Franny Boyle, Detectives Artie Trudell, Julio Vega, Martin Gittens, about a dozen others—hanging on each other, brimful of confidence. The bomber crew assembled on the airstrip for a snapshot before their last, doomed run.

I said, "Franny, Bob Danziger asked for your help, didn't he? You were one of the only witnesses still out there, you and Julio Vega. Danziger wanted to go after Artie Trudell's killer."

Silence.

"Did he ask you to help, Franny? Or was he going to subpoena you?"

"He didn't need a subpoena," Franny mumbled. "He told me I owed it to Artie. That was enough, after all that time. The thing was, Danziger didn't know what he was getting into until we started talking. Now he knows." His eyes were drifting left and right as if he were watching a badminton match taking place somewhere behind me. "Maybe I'll end up the same way. Got to be better than this."

I should point out that, according to Caroline, in his

day Franny Boyle was the most feared, most eloquent, most charismatic prosecutor in Boston. He was never much on the legal fine points, and by order of the DA he was not permitted to try a serious felony without an appellate attorney in the second chair, ready to hedge him in when he began to push the limits of courtroom oratory. But the true measure of a trial lawyer's talent is winning, and Francis X. Boyle won over and over again, so much so that it became a perverse point of pride with him when it could later be proven that he'd actually convicted innocent people. The defendant's innocence, he believed, merely raised the bar a little.

That evening—by this point the sun had set, leaving Franny's office in a dim half-light until someone finally turned on the fluorescent overheads—we caught a glimpse of Franny's gift when he pulled himself together sufficiently to tell the tale of Bob Danziger's murder, a tale that stretched back twenty years. What few legal rules I am aware of, Franny broke in telling the story. He dipped in and out of characters' heads, he threw in hearsay and rumor, he added facts he could not possibly have known, he may even have misstated a little evidence. He was as he had always been, in Caroline's words, "an appeal waiting to happen." But the man could tell a story. He must have been a hell of a lawyer, because drunk and broken down as he was, he could still spin a yarn for you. He made you see it. Franny Boyle put you right there.

Frankie Fasulo has to hold on. He has to wrap his left elbow around the I-beam beside him and hug it against his ribs or else the wind blowing across the Tobin Bridge is going to lift him right off the guardrail where he is standing, it will carry him up and over the side and it won't matter, it won't make one fuckin' bit of difference whether he has the balls to jump or not. Fuckin' wind! There is something behind it, Fasulo thinks, a presence. The wind is alive, like in some Bible story—like God appearing

to the Jews as a little sand-tornado or a sandstorm or whatever.
I mean, this fuckin' wind is pushing him in the back, in the ass,
the backs of his legs. It is trying to push him over the side. It
wants him to go over the side. So Fasulo hugs that I-beam. It
hurts to hold the thing on account of he has no gloves and the
steel is fuckin' cold, so cold it stings his hands like electric current, and he can feel the cold right through his jacket, which is
just a piece-of-shit olive-green Army jacket with a peace-sign
patch on the shoulder. He grabbed it off a bench in the Trail-
ways station on St. James Ave. when this hippyfreak wasn't
looking. Somewhere there was one shivering-cold hippy cocksucker wondering where's his piece-of-shit Army jacket with the
pussy peace-sign patch, and even up here Frankie Fasulo doesn't
forget that. Ha! No wonder the fuckin' gooks kicked our ass in
Vietnam: These fuckin' Army jackets don't do shit in the cold!
Fasulo tries to look straight ahead, straight out to—what the
fuck is that?—Chelsea, Charlestown, some fuckin' place, all lit
up, and the whole Boston skyline spread out beyond that. It's
beautiful. He's aware of that: it's fuckin' beautiful, man. He
tries to take in the view but he can't keep his eyes from looking
down into the darkness under his feet where the water surface is
reflecting little lightpoints from the city all around, and how far
down is that? It's like a mile, maybe, he figures, or—how
fuckin' much is a mile anyway? Can a bridge be a mile up? It's
too far. He can't do it. He can't let go of that I-beam and step
off and just fall and fall. But then, he can't step back either.

It is March 20, 1977, 4:06 A.M.

"I can't do it!" Fasulo screams but the crosswind up here is
so strong he figures maybe nobody can hear so he shouts again,
"I can't fuckin' do it!"

"Your choice, Frankie," comes the voice behind him, all
strutty and cool cuz it's not his fuckin' ass standing up here on
the guardrail a mile-or-whatever above the Mystic fuckin'
River.

Jesus, Fasulo's legs are shaking so bad, they're gonna shake
him right the fuck off the little rail he's standing on. He'll shake
all the way down to that black water. But it's so goddamn cold

*he can't hold his muscles still. Or maybe they're afraid. Maybe
his muscles are scared shitless just like the rest of him.*

"I'm getting down!"

"Your call, Frankie."

"What happens if I get down!"

No answer.

"I said, what happens if I get down?"

"Just like I said, Frankie, you get a little of what you gave.
Only I tell you what, Frankie, I'll make you a deal. Just to show
I'm not a bad guy. I won't make you suck my dick, how's that? I
won't give you back everything you did to that cop, Frankie, see?"

"I didn't—"

"You didn't what, Frankie? Come on, what didn't you do?"

"I didn't!"

"Now don't you fuckin' lie, Frankie! Don't you fuckin' do that!"

"Alrightalrightalright, I did! I did! He wasn't supposed to be
there! We just wanted the money! He shouldn't have come in
like that! What were we supposed to do?"

"I can't listen to this shit anymore, Frankie. You can get off
either side of that thing, I don't give a shit which. Just don't talk
anymore, alright? I'm giving you a choice, Frankie. That's more
than you gave that cop. That cop was my friend, Frankie, did
you know that? You don't even know his name, do you? Did
you know he was my friend?"

"I didn't know."

"Well you should have known before you stuck your dick in
his mouth, Frankie."

"I didn't! know!"

*Fasulo looks down again. Maybe it won't be so bad. Not so
fuckin' bad. Lot of guys died making the Tobin Bridge, that's
what everybody says. They fell off, maybe, and that's all there
was to it. Some of them even fell into the wet concrete and they
got built right into the bridge, isn't that what people say about
this bridge? Isn't that right? Or do they say that about every
fuckin' bridge? So how bad can it be just falling? Who is this
fuckin' pig? How did he fuckin' find me? Somebody fuckin' rat-
ted me out, some fuckin' cocksucker, and I'll fuckin' kill that*

cocksucker, whoever it was, only I won't kill that cocksucker cuz I'm never gonna get off this FUCKIN' BRIDGE—

"Come on, Frankie, we don't have all night. What's it gonna be?"

"I can't!"

"You can. Don't tell me you can't."

"I can't!"

"Then don't. Climb down off of there."

"What? You mean it's off?"

"Yeah, come on, Frankie. Just climb down."

But the cop punctuates his offer by racking his gun and that sound—metallic, precise, machined—carries right into Frank Fasulo's eardrum like the gun is right next to him.

"Come on, Frankie. Your choice. You want me to do it, or you want to do it yourself?"

"It's not right!"

"Don't tell me about right, Frankie. This is right, believe me."

A deep breath—the smell of cold, the taste of it on the tongue like mercury—and Fasulo leans forward slightly, just enough that he begins to lose his balance, begins to spin forward around the pole in his left elbow—begins to turn around the pole like it's a streetlamp and he's just going to spin around it—and a step forward and there is nothing under him and the wind is holding him up, he is floating, hanging for just a moment——

flying——

and then he is not flying but he is falling——

and falling and falling——

and it's not so bad after all, not unpleasant at all——he has time to think, to feel the sensation——the wind is loud and it sticks his ears and his cheeks like needles——and it's blowing his pant legs up over his shins and he can feel the cold on his calves——and his hair whipping in his eyes——and his body begins to cartwheel——and the wind begins to pull off his coat——

and on top of the bridge Martin Gittens——in plain clothes——his face unworried and handsome——carefully clips on the safety and puts his Beretta back in its holster because it's all over now and it had to end this way——nobody needed to tell him what to do——

only his partner, the big redhead with the full-moon face——a face like a big ball of dough, Gittens likes to say——a face they could use for the first-base bag at Fenway, he likes to say——only Artie Trudell is staring with that big face at the spot where Frank Fasulo the cop-raper and cop-killer went over the edge——staring as if some miraculous wind were going to catch Frank Fasulo and sweep him back up onto the bridge.

"Kurth, you gettin' all this?"

Kurth nodded. He was scratching furiously at a legal pad, trying to catch up to Franny. I assume he was not trying to copy it all down verbatim. Even so . . .

"You need me to go back and tell it again, you just say so."

"Don't worry about me, Franny," Kurth said. "You just keep talking."

"I don't want you to miss anything. Everybody who hears this story, they tend not to be around when that grand-jury day comes." He gave us all a little leer to be sure we got the point: The price for watching this danse macabre was that sooner or later any of us could be pulled from the audience and made to join in.

Ten years. That's how long it has taken before Artie Trudell can no longer bear the thought of Frank Fasulo going over the side of the Tobin Bridge. Ten years of returning to that bridge over and over in his thoughts. Ten years of seeing Fasulo up on the parapet, hugging that beam and screaming to make himself heard above the wind, "I can't!"—then stepping—no, he did not step, not at first—he leaned, Artie Trudell distinctly remembers that—he leaned the way a diver does at the beginning of a dive when he tips his chest forward ever so slightly, listing, tipping, extending the moment of counterbalance, feeling the accelerating pull of gravity as the diver surrenders—Artie Trudell can feel that fatal instant of imbalance, when the body's weight begins to move not forward but downward—he can feel it, the irreversible loss of balance. Then Fasulo spun—oh, that awful rotation of his body, that half-turn to his left caused by his hand still gripping the I-beam—the twirl, again so like a diver's, that suggested Fasulo could not let go, that he had not decided to jump but was falling or being pushed—pushed by Gittens—not Artie, Gittens—and then the hand slipping off the beam and Fasulo disappearing over the edge. Artie Trudell had not been able to move, of course. He could not even pull his eyes away from the spot on the guardrail where Fasulo went over. So Trudell did not actually see the man in free-fall, but that has not spared him the visions of it. No, it has only unleashed his imagination to conjure up endless vertiginous falls—tumbling and spinning in the black emptiness of cold and stars—speed and terror of such purity—and impact . . . Trudell never quite reaches the moment of impact. He wakes up or he simply stops replaying the scene before Frank Fasulo slams into the water.

Ten years of this.

It was not so bad at the beginning. At first, there was a period of shock when the whole thing seemed unreal. The memory was too sharp, too big, like a movie. Trudell stuffed it down into the same dark hole where he kept the other ghoulies. He "repressed" it, as observers would later say.

And when it began to claw its way out of that hole, Trudell went to Gittens, because who else could he take his murderer's guilty conscience to? And Gittens would soothe him. Gittens saw the big picture. Gittens reminded him what Fasulo had done. Rape, murder. And not just the cop in the Kilmarnock, bad as that was. Frank Fasulo was evil, Gittens said. Fasulo got what he had coming to him, and who knows how many other lives were saved because of it. Martin Gittens slept like a newborn babe, he claimed, he slept the sleep of the just. Those little counseling sessions would take for a while too. They would calm Trudell and allow him to go about his business of patrolling, first as a beat cop, then as a Narcotics detective in the Flats, the hot zone, where everyone wanted to be. That's where Artie Trudell is now. Area A-3 Narcotics—Mission Flats. "Little Beirut," the cops call it, and who's to say it isn't worse than *the actual Beirut in this hot summer of '87? And didn't Martin Gittens stick by him? Didn't Gittens smooth the way for him? Even Julio Vega—who seems to know more about department politics than the Commissioner himself—Vega, who always keeps a jealous eye on the guy above him in the rankings—even Vega knows Gittens is a man to trust. So if Gittens says it was the right thing, then it must be the right thing. Period.*

But in this summer of 1987 Frank Fasulo has begun to crawl back into Artie Trudell's consciousness in a new and surprising way. Trudell stopped using the Tobin Bridge long ago. Now, on those rare occasions when he has to get to the North Shore, he makes the long sweep around Route 128, the ring road around Boston. A few extra minutes of driving time is a small price to pay for avoiding the nightmares that crossing the Tobin dredges up. But there is another bridge Trudell has to cross, one he can't avoid. It is the Sagamore Bridge, one of two bridges that separate Massachusetts from Cape Cod. The Sagamore is a high bridge, much more graceful than the Tobin, a 1930s WPA project that spans the Cape Cod Canal. And isn't it Artie Trudell's dumb luck that his in-laws have a place in Dennis? That his wife insists on going to the Cape, for the kids, she says? Trudell is able to wiggle out of most of these trips. He can pile on the details and the double-shifts and jam up his schedule so tight in the summertime that there isn't time for trips to Cape Cod. Sorry, honey. But there are too many weekends to avoid it altogether, and eventually she starts in with "do you mean to tell me you never even get a day off, Artie? Not one day? Are you the only cop in Boston?" So Artie Trudell—who never liked to fight, giant though he is—has to face the Sagamore Bridge. Twice each trip, once on the way down, once on the way back. These crossings are causing a kind of anxiety that Trudell can't quite explain. He even looked it up in the DSM, the dictionary of neuroses, the bible for crazies like Artie Trudell feels himself becoming. The proper name for it is gephyrophobia, the fear of crossing bridges, and Trudell's anxiety is nothing compared to some of the case histories in the book. There are people—wack jobs—who get it so bad they can't even be near a bridge, never mind on one. Trudell's anxiety is nothing like

*that. But it is real enough. He becomes irritable, distracted, he
sweats, especially when the Cape traffic leaves him up on that
bridge for fifteen, twenty minutes at a time. He dreads the ride
home and can't sleep the night before. Now, in the summer of
'87, it has gotten worse, much worse, because each crossing triggers memories of Frank Fasulo. Every trip to the Cape to see his
goddamn in-laws, every trip across the goddamn Sagamore
Bridge triggers another round of dreams and night-sweats and
worries. And visions: Frank Fasulo tipping forward like a
chopped-down tree. Fasulo spinning around the bridge support
like Gene Kelly on that lamppost in* Singin' in the Rain.
*Fasulo diving downward at such speeds . . . By July, Trudell is
barely sleeping, and the guilt and exhaustion have begun to feed
each other. Artie Trudell feels himself draining away.*

*And at some point he realizes the truth: He has committed a
murder. The revelation does not come all at once like a bolt of
lightning. No, one day it is simply there and Trudell can't be
quite certain when it arrived. Maybe it has always been there
and he chose not to see it. But there it is, the undeniable truth—
Artie Trudell is a murderer. Or an accomplice or a coconspira-
tor or a joint venturer or whatever the lawyers will choose to
call it. The technical term does not really matter. Whatever
name the lawyers assign, Trudell knows the truest description is
the simplest:* MURDERER. *He knows, at any rate, that he
can't live with the secret any longer.*

*So now it's Monday, August 3, 1987, two weeks before the
raid on the red-door apartment.*

"I'm going to see Franny," *Trudell announces.*

*Gittens does not react. He can see Artie Trudell's big face in
front of him and he knows Artie is just about at the end of his
rope. He looks like shit. His eyes are rimmed with red, his complexion is chalky. Gittens does not want to spook him.*

"I don't know what else to do, Martin. We killed that guy."

"Shh. Keep your voice down, big man."

*They are in the locker room of the Area A-3 stationhouse, a
cinder-block basement that looks and smells precisely like a
school gym locker. The floor is painted concrete. Fluorescent
lights hum overhead. It is eleven P.M. and the room is empty.*

Still, Gittens and Trudell act as if they are in a crowd. Seated on opposite benches, they lean close to each other and whisper. This is the A-3, the Hotel No-tell. We take care of our own problems here—and anyone who looks at Artie Trudell will realize there is a very big problem.

"Martin, I don't know what to do." *Trudell squeezes his head with the heels of his hands as if he could squeeze the thoughts of the* MURDERED *man back down.* "I don't know what to do."

Gittens takes Trudell by the wrists and pulls his hands off his head. "Come on, Artie, stop that."

"Jesus, Martin."

"Come on, Artie, what?"

"I was a fuckin' altar boy!"

"Well, you probably won't get that job back."

"I'm a murderer. We murdered him."

"No. We've been all through this. It wasn't murder, Artie. You know what was going to happen to that guy? He was going to get caught and he was going to Walpole for life. End of story. He was already dead. You can't kill someone who's already dead."

"I don't believe that."

"Artie, if we didn't do it, the guy would still be alive today. Would that be right, after what he did? He might even get parole, Artie, think about that. His lawyer would say he was all coked up and they'd knock it down to second-degree and that's only fifteen years to parole. Would you want to see that, Artie? Would you want to see Fasulo back on the street while that cop he killed is still dead as dirt? That wouldn't be right, now, would it? That cop is dead and he's going to stay dead."

"I feel like I'm dead too."

It looks to Gittens like Trudell is about to cry, so he stops explaining and simply soothes. "Shh, shh. Come on, cut that shit out. Come on. Artie, you've got to pull it together."

"I'm going to ask Franny what to do."

"That's a mistake."

"I don't care."

"You will care, Artie. What do you think Franny's going to say? You think you can walk up to a DA and confess to murder *and then just walk away? Think of the position you're putting him in. Don't do that to Franny. He'll have to report it. They'll put away the both of us. They'll have to."*

"I don't care anymore."

"No? You want to be a murderer?"

"We'll tell them it was, whattayacallit, 'heat of passion.' "

"Artie, Andrew Lowery won't give two shits about heat of passion. Neither will the jury. They'll string us up. Anyway, it wasn't heat of passion; we waited more than a week. Guess what? That's called first-degree murder, my friend. That's life without parole. You want to go to Walpole for life? Is that what you want? You got a wife, you got two kids. How you gonna go to Walpole for life?"

Trudell doesn't answer.

"You've got to pull yourself together, big man, you hear me? Pull your shit together. We didn't murder anyone."

"I didn't murder anyone," Trudell corrects him.

Gittens glares.

"I was just standing there. You were the one with the gun."

Gittens glares.

"I'm just saying, Martin. I didn't do anything."

Gittens glares.

Trudell retreats again. "I'm just saying."

"Look, Artie, don't talk like that. That's the wrong way to think. We've got to stick together on this."

No response.

"Artie, just promise me you won't do anything until you talk to me, alright? Can you give me your word on that? Can you promise me you won't say anything to Franny or anyone else until we talk again? That's all I ask. Can you give me your word on that?"

Trudell shakes his head no then shakes his head yes. "Yeah. I guess. But not forever, Martin, you hear me? This can't go on forever. I can't do it. I'm coming apart here."

Gittens studies Trudell's great elephantine head, then nods in sympathy. "Alright, big man. You just hang in there, alright?

*We'll figure something out. Just don't do anything stupid, okay?
Give me some time to figure something out."*

"Did he come to you, Franny?"

"Yeah, he came to me."

"And?"

"He told me the whole thing, just like I'm telling you.
Told me he was a murderer, and what should he do?
I—" Franny's pudgy fingers worked his cheeks. "I wasn't
sure. I needed time to think about it. You don't just roll
out of bed and indict a cop for murder. I told Artie he
did the right thing coming to me and all. But deep down
I wasn't sure he did the right thing. I wasn't sure I
wanted to know any of it. See, Artie was right: He was a
murderer. We could have prosecuted him, sure. So here
was this friend coming to me for help, and what was I
gonna do? I didn't know. I said I'd figure out the best
way to handle it and get back to him but he should get
himself a lawyer too. In the end, it was going to be up to
the DA, Lowery, whether to indict the both of them or
just Gittens. It was Lowery's call. You could cut Artie a
deal maybe, but they were both up there on that bridge.
I didn't know what to do."

His eyes fell back to that picture on the desk.

"I hesitated."

*Artie Trudell has a sense something is wrong. A mounting un-
easiness about this raid. He can't point to anything specific.
There's nothing obviously out of place. The investigation, the
warrant, the adrenaline rush as the team waits outside the red
door—he and Julio Vega have gone through fifty doors like this
one, maybe a hundred, maybe more. By now—August 17,
1987, 2:26 A.M.—the crack wars have been raging through the
Flats for so long, raids like this have become a fact of life. Even
the shadowy presence of Harold Braxton and his violent crew is
not the source of Trudell's unease. Trudell has hit the Mission*

Posse before, after all. In the Flats, everyone hits the Mission Posse. Besides, Braxton is a businessman. He won't fight to protect this place. He won't leave any of his prized goons in the apartment to defend it. Braxton will sacrifice it and move on. That's how it works with these Posse stashpads: The cops cut off an arm, another grows; they cut off a leg, another grows. On and on, forever and ever, amen. No, it is not the usual dangers that have Artie Trudell on edge tonight. It is something inchoate and inarticulable. The sort of nameless foreboding that causes people to refuse to board airplanes or to listen for footsteps. Something in the air.

Maybe it is everything else. Maybe it is the same static that is in Trudell's head every day now, the background noise that has come to obscure every other thought: Frank Fasulo, gephyrophobia, the Sagamore Bridge. MURDERER. Of course Gittens will find a way out of all that. Gittens is still helping him out, helping him keep up appearances. It was Gittens, after all, who set up this raid by feeding Trudell and Vega the tip from Raul. Hasn't it always been Gittens who nurtured Trudell's career ever since he and Vega came to Narcotics? Hasn't Gittens always been able to find a way out? . . .

Stop! Trudell has to silence the torrent of thoughts. For the next ten minutes, he has to block all that out. After the raid he can go back to dwelling on Frank Fasulo, but right now there is only room for one thought—get through that door and get home alive. This is the moment of supreme danger for any cop, and Artie Trudell knows it. Static could get him killed. Or is that what Artie wants?

It is probably just the heat that is troubling the big policeman. The air is viscous. It is hard to breathe this stuff. Even the walls are damp. Trudell wasn't built for this kind of heat. His clothes are soggy with sweat. His face is sweaty. His balls are sweaty. The palms of his hands. Sweat is running down the crack of his ass. Let's just get this over, he thinks. Let's just get it over and get back to the station where there's air conditioning.

He and Vega are standing on opposite sides of the door frame, backs to the wall. Vega nods toward the red door and gives Trudell a look: Bad door, Artie man. Bad juju.

Trudell musters a smile. He used to be the carefree one, Trudell was. The big kid. The big kidder. Now he summons up a little of the old playfulness to smile and flex his biceps at his partner. No problem, JV. They haven't built a door strong enough.

The cops on the raid team are getting restless. It is dangerous sitting around out here. They need to go or call it off. They can't just sit here with their dicks in their hands. Trudell can sense their itchiness. Everyone there knows he and Vega have never led a raid before. Everyone is watching to see what sort of leaders these two will be.

Vega gives the nod.

Trudell steps in front of the door, hoists the black battering ram off his forearm and grasps the two handles. The concrete-filled waterpipe is unbelievably heavy, even for Trudell. It looks like a torpedo that he is about to load into the back of a cannon.

Vega counts down: five fingers, four fingers, three fingers, two fingers—on one, he points at Trudell.

Boom!

The battering ram shakes the door. The hallway reverberates.

"Come on, big man," *Vega mutters.*

Boom!

There is sweat dripping off Trudell's face but he does not have a free hand to wipe it. It runs into his eyes. It stings a little. He breathes deep. Work on one spot! Keep hitting the same spot till it gives way! He finds a point on the red door, about shoulder level. Trudell focuses on that spot——

where a crack has begun to open——

one more blow right there——

a crack——

and on the opposite side of the door, the same crack——

inside the apartment, the same little fissure in the wood——

and that is precisely where Martin Gittens stands with a rifle—a pump-action Mossberg 500 shotgun—the barrel just inches from the red door.

Gittens is wearing dainty white cotton gloves, jeweler's gloves, to avoid marring the fingerprints that are already on the gun. These are Braxton's fingerprints, of course; the gun was

seized nine months before. Gittens will have to pump the gun
between rounds. That means he will have one shot, maybe two.
Then he'll have to bug out.

    He sights along the barrel to that weak point, the fissure in
the door. That is where the battering ram is being held—and six
inches higher—no, higher still, because Artie Trudell is so god-
damn big—eight inches above the point of impact. Boom! The
door rocks again, and the whole building shudders. The floor
beneath Gittens's feet quivers with the impact.

    Gittens raises the rifle to take dead aim at Artie Trudell's
head—deep breath—slow, cool breath—and squeeze.

"I suspected it even then," Franny told us. "I didn't
know for sure, but I had my suspicions. Artie'd told me
what Gittens did to Fasulo. Then the way Gittens got to
the red door so fast that night and jumped in front of the
door without a second thought . . . I had my doubts. But
I kept my mouth shut because it still looked like Braxton
was the guy. Now I'm certain. Vega's dead, and I'm certain. Gittens shot Artie. I just know it."

    "And Raul? Who was Raul?"

    Franny shrugged. "Maybe there was a Raul, maybe
not. Maybe Gittens did get a tip from some rat and he
used it to set up Artie. I figure there was no Raul—
Gittens was Raul. But what's the difference? Gittens was
the shooter, that's all that matters. Who knows, maybe
Braxton was Raul. All those years Gittens had this know-
it-all snitch in the Flats, and all those years Braxton managed to skate on just about everything. That sure sounds
like someone was protecting him. But I don't know.
We'll never get the truth about Raul."

    "But you stood up in court, you vouched for it. You
said the whole story about Raul was the truth."

    "Chief Truman, I'm a lawyer. I wasn't there. I only
know what my witnesses tell me."

    "Bullshit." John Kelly, who'd been listening to the en-
tire tale in silence, practically spat the word in Franny's

face. "Gittens lied, and you played along. You knew something wasn't right, but it was easier to prosecute Braxton with lies than to figure out what Gittens was really up to."

John Kelly glared at Franny with obvious contempt, as if Kelly, not Braxton, had been the victim of Franny's cowardice and lying.

"I—" Franny fell silent. The little burst of composure and vitality that had carried him through the story was extinguished. You could almost see the light go out. For all his brio and talent, Franny Boyle's life since 1987 had been a relentless ebbing. He must have felt himself receding from that time, carried off by the current.

"If you need me to testify," Franny said to no one in particular, "I'll do it. I said the same thing to Danziger."

Kurth asked Caroline, "You want Gittens picked up?"

She shook her head no. "We have three murders and no proof of any of them. There's no one left who was on that bridge the night Fasulo was killed. With Vega dead, there's no one who can tell us firsthand about the night Trudell died. And there's no one who was in that cabin when Danziger was shot. Three murders, zero witnesses. I'd say Detective Gittens covered his tracks perfectly."

"We do have one witness," I said. "Harold Braxton."

54

Chelsea, Massachusetts, just outside the Boston city limit. 6:34 A.M.

We waited for them in a desolate parking lot. At our backs the Tobin Bridge soared a hundred feet in the air, its exoskeleton of I-beams topped by a vertebral elevated road. Dick Ginoux stood with us, having driven the department's Bronco down from Versailles the night before. He stamped his feet in the cold, looking slightly bewildered in his uniform and Smokey the Bear hat. Kelly wore his usual flannel coat, but this morning he had pinned his little six-point star on the breast pocket: OFFICER, VERSAILLES POLICE DEPARTMENT. He spun his nightstick contentedly and whistled under his breath "I'm Looking Over a Four-Leaf Clover." It was hard to tell if the nonchalance was a deliberate attempt to keep me cool or if Kelly truly felt blasé about being here. For my part, I struggled to suppress an adrenaline smile. The scene reminded me of an exchange of spies in a Cold War novel. In the Bronco I found my Versailles Police Department jacket, with its little embroidered *Chief Truman*.

We did not speak much. The sky was ash gray, the air

intensely cold for November. For a long time the only
sound was the traffic noise on the bridge high above us,
Kelly's whistling, and the spin-*slap* of his nightstick.

Inevitably, Dick picked up the tune and began to sing
softly, *"I'm looking over, a four-leaf clover, that I've overlooked
befo-o-ore. The first is for sunshine, the sec-und for rain—"*

"Dick."

"The third's for my ba-by that lives down the lane."

"Dick!"

"Oh, let him sing, Chief," Kelly advised. "There's
nothing better to do."

"Come on, Ben," Dick prodded. *"I'm lookin' oh-ver, a
four-leaf cloh-ver, that I oh-ver-looked be-fo-o-ore."*

Incredibly, Kelly sang too—and horribly. *"The first is
for sunshine, the sec-und for ra-a-ain. The third's for my
baby . . ."* It was like watching a beloved uncle fast-dance
at a wedding. You didn't know whether to laugh or avert
your eyes. *"There's no use explainin', the one ree-main-in', is
sum-one that I a-do-o-o-ore! Come on, Ben Truman."*

I gave in and moaned along with them for the finale.
*"I'm lookin' over a four-leaf clover that I overlooked—*bum-
bum—*that I overlooked—*bum-bum—*that I overlooked bee-
fo-o-ore."*

Kelly looked down and indulged me with an approv-
ing nod. "Attsaboy," he said.

It was nearly seven when Beck's black Mercedes
sedan slid into the parking lot. The car came to a stop in
front of us, and Beck and Braxton stepped out. Braxton
wore an oversize, hooded sweatshirt under a leather
Avirex jacket. He scowled at us.

I stepped forward, but Kelly caught my wrist. "You're
the senior officer here," he reminded me. "Let me do this."

Kelly frisked Braxton while reciting the familiar
litany: "Harold Braxton, you are under arrest for the
murder of Robert Danziger. You have the right to remain silent. You have the right to have an attorney present at all questioning. You have the right . . ."

Braxton stood with his arms extended, glaring at me,

resenting this whole procedure and resenting me for failing to exonerate him. By his furious stare, he seemed to be proclaiming that he was not submitting, not really, not in his heart. He did not recognize our authority or his own impotence.

Kelly pulled Braxton's arms down to cuff him behind his back.

"Chief Truman," said Beck, "is it necessary for him to ride all the way to Maine with his arms behind his back? Why don't you put the handcuffs in front? It's a long ride."

Braxton looked down. He wanted no part of a plea for leniency.

I nodded. Kelly uncuffed and recuffed Braxton so his hands were in front, then led him to the backseat of the Bronco. This was the trophy arrest every cop in the city was stalking, yet there was little pleasure in it.

"Arraignment will be tomorrow morning," I said in a muted voice.

Beck nodded and turned to leave.

I glanced up at the bridge for one last look—the same bridge Frank Fasulo had jumped off twenty years before. All that exposed framework, miles of girders. It was one of those ugly places where a city's substructure is revealed. We see them—train yards, power plants, manholes—and we are reminded of the hidden complexities. It is as if the skin has been pulled back and the skeleton of the city is exposed, the pumping veins, the secret systems. I'd had enough of all that.

"It's done," I told Kelly and Dick, and myself. "Let's go home."

55

I had been away from Versailles only seventeen days, but I had the sense I'd been away longer and traveled farther. I came back with the peculiar feeling that accompanies the end of a long trip: the pleasant tension between at-homeness and alienness, the sense of being an outsider in your own home. You notice details. You find beauty in a street or park or building where somehow you'd never discerned it before. It is the shock of the familiar, the same jolt you sometimes feel when you see your wife or your lover standing on a street corner, and for a split second you see her as a stranger would. You realize, *She's lovely. I forgot how lovely my wife really is.* Versailles seemed profoundly beautiful, even the parts that I know are not beautiful at all.

Behind the hills, thunderheads were drifting in from the west. From the looks of it, we were in for a cold, wintry rain. Leaf-peeping season was over, the tourists gone. Time for winter, time for the "hard cold" to make its first appearance.

A group of kids played touch football on the green, unconcerned by the storm clouds.

On Central Street, Jimmy Lownes and Phil Lamphier

were loafing outside the Owl, smoking cigarettes and glancing up at the sky. Jimmy gave us a little two-fingered wave, a Marlboro pinched between his fingers. Before long, he'd be spreading the word that I had returned with a black kid under arrest, and the whole town would be aware of it before supper. That was fine too. It would save me the trouble of announcing the news.

At the station, we moved Braxton into the holding cell. Whatever misgivings I might have had about his guilt, Braxton was still under arrest for murder. Procedures had to be followed.

Then Kelly, Dick Ginoux, and I lingered a moment at the front door of the station.

"Gorry," Dick said, "it's gonna be a gullywasher."

"Why don't you go home, Dick, get some rest. I'll sit with him."

"No, Chief—"

"It's alright, Dick. I'll be alright."

He gave me an appraising look. "Alrighty, Ben. If you say so."

"Thank you," I said, "for keeping an eye on things while I was away."

Dick looked away. "I'll stop by to check on you later." Before ambling off, he gave Kelly a little wave that resembled a salute. "Officer Kelly."

"Officer Ginoux."

Kelly emitted a tired sigh. "Well, looks like you made it back home, Ben Truman."

"Looks like."

"You want me to take the first watch?"

"No, Mr. Kelly, I think it's time for you to go home too."

"Home?"

"You're retired, remember?"

"Oh, that. Well."

"There's nothing left to do here. It's Boston's case now. They'll pick up Gittens, if they haven't already. This here is just guard duty. We'll arraign Braxton in the morning, then the staties will take him away until the trial. Really, go home. It's alright."

"You'll be alright with him?"

"Yeah. I've seen worse."

Kelly snorted. He produced the nightstick from inside his coat. "Well, take this. In case he acts up."

"I can't take that."

"Of course you can. What am I supposed to do with it? I'm retired."

"You're sure?"

"Take it, Ben Truman."

I took it.

"Alright then," Kelly said, as if relieved to be unburdened at last of that little baton. "Alright then." He stood there a moment, apparently unsure what to do next.

I told him, "I'll stop by soon, let you know how it all worked out."

"I'd like that."

Kelly went to his car and folded himself into it like a daddy longlegs receding into a crack in the wall. He rolled down the window. "It's a shame, you know. You might have made a good professor someday."

"Who says I still won't?"

He made a knowing little smile then said, with a nod toward the nightstick in my hand, "Don't hurt yourself with that thing."

Back in the station I pulled a chair in front of the entrance to the back room and stretched my legs across the doorway. The nightstick weighed heavy in my lap.

Braxton said, "Just you and me now, huh, Chief Truman?"

By late afternoon the thunderstorms began rolling through. Rain gusted against the stationhouse windows with a snare-drum sound.

Around four I asked Braxton what he wanted for

supper. He had barely spoken during the five-hour ride from Boston or in the four hours since we'd arrived.

"I'll have a lobster," he said.

"You're thinking of a different Maine. Try again."

"Steak."

"Steak? How about like a burger or a sandwich?"

"I told you: steak."

"Okay. Steak."

When the food was delivered from the Owl, I brought it back and unlocked the cell. There was no place to sit in the little hallway, so I sat on the chair inside the cell while Braxton sat on the cot. His steak was gray and cupped in the middle like a recently vacated pillow. He took a bite and grimaced. "What is this, moose or some shit?"

"Yeah, I probably should have warned you about the steak."

He worked his steak awhile in silence. My supper was better, a turkey sandwich. I offered to trade but he waved me off.

"Aren't you afraid I'm going to get out?" He nodded toward the open cell door.

"Nah. Where would you go? You're a hundred miles away from the middle of nowhere. Besides, right now the safest place for you is probably right here in this cell."

"Might be the safest place for you too."

There was a shadow conversation going on here. Braxton had not murdered Bob Danziger. He knew it, of course, and by sitting down to supper with him I signaled that I knew it too. My every polite comment carried the same coded message. *What do you want for supper?* and *How's the steak?* and all the rest were understood to mean *I know you didn't kill Danziger.*

Braxton said, "Gittens is coming, you know."

"I figured."

"What you gonna do?"

"Not sure."

"Well, you better think of something, Chief True-Man, 'cause Gittens is already rolling, I promise you."

"What would you do, Harold, if you were me?"

"I'm not you, dog."

"But if you were, and Gittens was coming?"

"Call my niggers." He used the word easily. It held no political charge for him.

"I can't do that."

"You've got cops. Call them."

"It's not that simple."

"Why not?"

"Because." My eyes sought out a dusty spot on the floor. "It just doesn't work that way."

"What about the tall guy? Call him."

"Kelly? No. I can't."

Braxton nodded—not because he understood, I think, but because he didn't want to waste his breath on a dumb cop who wouldn't listen.

"You want me to call mine, get 'em up here? We'll get your back, if you want."

"No, Harold. No, thanks."

The phone rang. It was nearly five, daylight faltering. The stationhouse groaned in the wind and rain. I knew before I picked up that it was Martin Gittens.

"Ben? We have to talk, Ben."

"Martin. Talk about what? There's a warrant out on you. Where are you?"

"I've been investigating. I have something to show you. New evidence."

"What is it?"

"Oh, I think you should see it for yourself."

I did not respond. For a time, there was silence on the line.

Then, speaking slowly and patiently, Gittens said, "Ben, everything's going to be alright. But we have to stay cool. Stay cool and *think*. Can you do that, Ben?"

"Yeah." My voice failed. I cleared my throat and said, "Yeah, Martin, I can do that."

"I know you can. I've been watching you, Ben. You've been staying cool for a while, haven't you? Now think. It's your decision: Do you want to meet me and see what I've got, or would you rather I just left?"

"I'll meet you."

In the cell behind me, Braxton said, "Don't do it, dog. Don't go."

"Good decision," Gittens said. "Why don't we meet at the lake? We can talk there."

"The lake?"

"Yes, Ben. At Danziger's cabin. Is that alright with you? Or does it upset you?"

"No, it doesn't upset me."

"Good. We have to work together now, you and me. We're a lot alike, you know."

"No," I said, "we're not."

Gittens paused, then told me, "Come alone."

By the time I got to the lake, the air glowed with a numinous phosphorescent light. The rain had stopped, and surfaces glistened. In hindsight I suppose the glow was just moonlight slipping between the clouds, which had already begun to scatter. But at the time the night-light seemed faintly miraculous. It seemed to emanate from the lake itself, shining up from the water to illuminate the sky.

Through the windshield, I saw Gittens standing on the hard-packed sand by the water. He looked out over the lake, wearing neatly pressed khakis and a yellow rain slicker with a designer's name stenciled across the back.

Beside him was my father.

Braxton, in the passenger seat, asked, "Sure you want to do this?"

"I don't have a choice. That's my father with Gittens."

"Alright then. I got your back." When I hesitated, he shrugged. "This is what it is." His meaning was opaque—

this is what it is—but he seemed to feel the aphorism explained this entire situation.

Braxton and I climbed down from the Bronco, and Braxton remained by the truck while I walked down to join Gittens and my father at the water's edge.

Gittens glanced up the access road at Braxton, then returned his attention to the lake, with its weird phosphorescence. "I told you to come alone."

"You also told me to think."

He smirked at me. "Like I'm looking in the mirror."

Dad's appearance was shocking. He wavered as if he might tip forward in a dead faint. Dark circles sagged under his eyes, and his hair, soaked, fell out in sparse curls. His hands were crossed over his belly.

I said to Gittens, "Take the cuffs off him."

Gittens did so without hesitation, and my father massaged his beefy wrists.

"Dad, are you drunk?"

His eyes fell, embarrassed.

I said to Gittens, ridiculously, "You did this to him."

"No, Ben. He did it to himself. I found him this way."

"Dad, what did you tell him?"

My father searched the sand for an answer.

"Claude? Did you say anything to him?"

Gittens said in a soothing tone, "Of course he did."

"I didn't ask you!" I grabbed my father's arms at the biceps and shook him. "Dad?"

Gittens intervened, "It's alright, Ben, calm down. I already knew."

"What do you mean, you already knew?"

"Ben, come on, *think*! I had an advantage: I knew I didn't kill Danziger. I was the only one who could have known it for sure."

I began to feel dizzy. My eyes scanned Gittens. Granules of sand adhered to his loafers and the cuffs of his pants. Rainwater beaded on his coat. As he moved, the beads skittered down his sleeves.

Gittens said, "It's okay, Ben. Stay cool." He opened

his raincoat and produced a gun, working it out of his belt with a seesaw motion.

As he turned to me, however, we were interrupted by a shout: "Hey!" Braxton paced toward us pointing a gun at Gittens.

Gittens let the pistol dangle from his finger in the trigger guard, and he held it out for me to take. "It's alright, Ben. You and I don't need guns."

I took the heavy gun, the same big black .38 my father carried for years as chief of police.

"Murder weapon," Gittens said simply.

"That's crazy."

"If you say so, Ben. We'll let ballistics confirm it."

It crossed my mind that I could heave the gun out into the lake. I imagined it twirling in the air, against the luminous sky, splashing, disappearing.

Gittens turned and said to Braxton, "It's alright, Harold. We're just talking."

Braxton lowered his gun—my Beretta—and took a step back.

Gittens said, "The longest time, I could not figure out why you went to such lengths to follow this case, why you took such risks. You seemed too smart to take those kinds of chances. At first I thought you really must have killed Danziger. It was the only explanation. But it didn't quite fit. You're no killer. Even if you were, you'd never be so sloppy about it. It took a long time before it occurred to me: You were protecting someone."

"Braxton—"

"No. Harold's too smart. Besides, he didn't need to do it. Harold and Danziger already had their deal."

In my hand, the .38 was heavy and still warm from Gittens's belt. I wrapped my fingers idly around the plastic grip for the sensuous pleasure of its shape and its raised crosshatch texturing.

I said, "Dad, I think you better go. Martin and I need to talk."

He said, "I'm sorry, Ben." He looked at me, then

grabbed me in a bear hug. His nose beside my ear, I could hear deep breaths whiffle in and out of his nostrils. He squeezed my arms hard against my sides. I said, "Okay, Dad," and tapped him to signal the hug was over. But he did not let go. Maybe he could not let go. "Okay," I said again. Still he held tight.

Over his shoulder I saw Braxton standing by the Bronco, watching us.

That night in September—could it have been only six weeks before? it felt like another lifetime—my father had appeared at the stationhouse with a spray of red blood on his shirt and face. He seemed to be in shock. Rambling, incoherent. He could not explain the blood and, mistaking it for Dad's own, I searched his body for an injury. It was Danziger's blood. Dad had killed him with a single shot from the .38.

Facing me in the stationhouse, he repeated the same question and answer: "What have I done? I did it. What have I done?" And then, "Ben, what are we gonna do?"

I hesitated. What were we going to do?

Danziger. In our one brief conversation, hours before he was killed, I'd sensed Bob Danziger's gentleness. I'd even liked him—his obvious decency—even as he said he would indict me for the assisted suicide of Anne Truman.

Wasn't there something I could tell him? he wanted to know. *Wasn't there anything he could hang his hat on, anything to mitigate the facts in his file—a cop participating in a mercy killing. A cop! Help me out, Chief Truman, help me understand. I came up here myself hoping you could tell me something, hoping you could change my mind. If you weren't a cop, then maybe, maybe . . .*

I told him I had nothing to say, he'd wasted a trip. It was a family matter anyway.

You know, Bob Danziger told me, *it's first-degree murder, you understand that? The intent is there, the whole thing was planned. I've tried to worry it down to second-degree or manslaughter, but I can't see a way. The facts just don't fit.* With one hand, he worked the skin around his eyes. There were red freckles on the backs of his fingers. *Sometimes,* he said, *this job is just too much.*

A few hours later Danziger was gone.

And here was my father, a thread of Danziger's blood caught in his hair. He said, "I couldn't let them take you, Ben. Not you and Annie both. I just couldn't let him do it. When I heard, I just—"

He said, "What do we do?"

I hesitated.

What was I going to do? What was a son and policeman supposed to do?

I hesitated—then, in a moment, it was decided. "Where's the gun, Dad?"

"I dropped it."

"Where?"

"The cabin."

"Dad, we have to go get it. Right now, you hear me?"

I do not excuse my actions, and I certainly do not excuse my father's. I simply did not have the strength—of will, of emotion, of character—to erase my family completely. My mother was dead, now a man named Danziger was dead too. I tried to stop the chain of suffering there.

We went to the cabin, retrieved Dad's gun, and locked the place up.

And we waited.

An hour became a day became a week.

I went back to the cabin again and again. I pored over the body. I read Danziger's files and discovered the pattern of kill shots used by the Mission Posse: a gunshot to the eye, just as my father had shot Danziger. It was a fateful convergence. I tweaked the scene, made it look like a gang murder. I burned the file on my mother's death. To delay the discovery of the body and destroy

the papers that now bore my fingerprints, I ran
Danziger's Honda into the lake one night after dark.

Then I closed the cabin and waited. It took only a
week before Dad started sneaking a drink here and
there. Still I waited, unsure, needing someone else to
find the body so I would have no link to its discovery; at
the same time hoping the body would never be found,
hoping its decay would inexorably destroy Dad's connection to it—and mine. When it seemed I could wait no
longer—when my own paranoia and Dad's unraveling
seemed to limit the time we had available—I "discovered" the corpse.

As a student of history, I should have known better.
Any historian will tell you: There is no end to any chain
of events, ever. There is no cause without an effect, no
incident without its sequel. I tried to break this chain of
suffering, but I couldn't. I couldn't prevent my father's
pain. I could only deflect it onto others.

The hillsides across the lake, mossed over with pines,
were darkly illuminated.

Gittens said, "We went to a place like this once, in
New Hampshire, when I was a kid. Cabin by a lake, my
whole family. I remember there was this girl in one of
the other cabins. She was about my age, pretty little
blond girl in a blue bathing suit. She used to do gymnas-
tics on the beach. She had this springy way of walking,
like any moment she was going to jump into one of those
tumbling runs." He looked out at the water. "You know,
I never said a word to that girl."

I could barely listen. I had a sense of myself crum-
pling—of some interior structure finally buckling and
collapsing. It was not fear; fear already seemed irrelevant, the time for it long past. The feeling was more like
exhaustion. Acceptance. Surrender.

It must have registered on my face, or maybe Gittens,

with his instinct for weakness, just sensed it. He said, "Stay cool, Ben. Think."

"What do you want, Gittens?"

He regarded me, then reached into my coat and patted my chest, sides, and back for a wire.

The rain, until now a mist suspended in the air, began to fall again. It ticked in the bare trees.

"What's your next move here, Ben?"

I did not respond.

"Did you leave yourself a way out? An exit strategy?"

"I don't know what you're talking ab—"

"Oh come on, Ben, stop! We're too smart for that!"

"What's *your* way out? What's your exit strategy?"

"Don't need one."

"No? Franny Boyle is going to testify you killed Fasulo and Trudell."

"Franny's credibility is nonexistent. Lowery won't indict anything with Franny as the only witness. Besides, all Franny has is hearsay—rumors whispered in his ear by dead people. None of it's admissible. There's no case against me, no proof. You're a smart guy, Ben. Come on now, you've got to *think*."

But there were no thoughts. There was no exit, no future. Only the past.

"I can help you, Ben, if you just let me. Cops help each other. Let me help you."

"Help me how?"

"Ben, without me, there's no proof. *I'm* the one your old man confessed to, *I'm* the only one who knows that gun in your hand is the murder weapon. If I keep my mouth shut, there's no case against your old man. Or you."

"What happens to the Danziger case? They'll need someone for it."

"Braxton," Gittens said.

"They'll never buy it. Danziger had given him a deal."

"They'll buy what I sell them. Especially if you back me up, if we work together."

"But . . ." My voice trailed off.

"Let Braxton take the hit, Ben, for all of it. He's got it coming to him. He's hurt enough people in his time. This just evens the score. Braxton's not with the good guys, Ben. We're the good guys. Remember that. Let me talk with him. He'll confess to both—"

"Confess? He didn't do anyth—"

"He'll confess! He'll confess, then he'll attack me just the way he attacked you last week. He'll grab my gun and it'll go off."

"It's murder."

"No, it's the right thing. We've got to do what's necessary, Ben."

I shook my head. "I can't."

"You don't have to do anything. Just let me do the heavy lifting."

I couldn't answer.

"Ben, there's no other way. If I walk out of here, your old man does life without parole. They'll whack you, too, for obstruction. Let me help you. You're not thinking straight right now."

I heard myself say, "What do you get out of it, Gittens?"

He shrugged.

"You get rid of Braxton," I said. "He's the only one left who can hurt you. That's why Danziger wanted him so badly. You tipped Braxton off that night. He's the witness who can put you behind that red door."

With a nod, Gittens asked for the .38 in my hand. I gave it to him, my thoughts dreamy and slow.

"Ben, what I'm offering you here is the only way out. Take it."

I stared out over the lake, with its lunar phosphorescence and dark rim of hills.

"Take it," Gittens urged.

I shook my head no.

Gittens let out a frustrated sigh. "Don't do this, Ben. It's what you do after checkmate that matters. We have to trust each other."

"Is that what you told Artie Trudell?"

There was a silence. The rain plinked the surface of the lake.

He weighed the .38 in his hand, then replaced it in his belt. "It's a hell of a choice you're making, Ben. This is your father we're talking about."

I looked back at my father, who was standing with Braxton by the truck. The Chief. So withered, rain-soaked, and small.

What happened next I do not recall clearly. There are glinting memories of that instant: my arm whipping down, a chuff of breath rushing out of my mouth, the stinging vibration in my palm. What remains vivid are the sounds: the *clop* of John Kelly's nightstick on Gittens's skull, a hollow sound like a horse's foot on pavement; then Gittens's body flumping on the sand.

The nightstick bounced up off Gittens's head with such force I lost my grip on it. It twirled over my shoulder and landed in the sand.

There was no blood at first. The body lay facedown, motionless.

I looked up to see Braxton and my father rushing down the access road, then I looked back toward the lake and was struck again by the water's glow.

The body stirred. Its legs bicycled slowly in the sand.

Braxton and my father stared down at it.

"It's the only way out," I told them.

My father looked up at me. His features were fallen, his lips parted slightly.

I said, "It's the only way."

I heard my voice—so self-possessed, so calm—and was surprised by it. I was anything but calm. Something was loose inside me, some wild energy I could not control and did not wish to. I glanced around for the nightstick. Where was it? I'd heard it hit the sand—I'd *heard* it!

Gittens groaned and struggled to his knees.

I looked again for the nightstick. Where the fuck was it? I needed it now!

Gittens dragged himself toward the lake with an indistinct grunt. In his hair, there was blood salted with grains of sand.

I said to my father, "What now?"

He did not answer. Just blinked at me, frowning. Creases sunk into the skin near his mouth, and sad little blankets gathered around his eyes, and rain fell on his face.

I couldn't look at him. I turned to Braxton: "What now?"

Braxton gestured with his chin toward Gittens, who was attempting to raise himself on all fours. He said, "You want me to do it?"

I told him no.

Gittens sprawled forward. His forearms were in the water now.

Braxton said, "It's the right thing."

I stood over Gittens, hooked my arms under his chest, and heaved him forward into the shallow water. The cold revived him. He pushed up with his arms to lift his head and shoulders out of the water. It was only a foot or so deep. With my right hand on the crown of his head, I pressed him down into the water. He shook his head free and came up with a gasp, thrashing wildly. His yellow raincoat glimmered. My hands gripped his skull, fingers over his ears, thumbs squeezing down on the occipital bone, the little bony horn at the back of the skull. I pressed his face all the way down into the sand. A thin screech bubbled from the water. It cut through the sound of his thrashing. High-pitched, like a baby's cry. It was the worst sound I've ever heard.

Epilogue

It is nearly a year now since that night by the lake. A year since I decided to set down these events on paper, to work out for myself the how and why of it. To make my confession.

No doubt you want to know how the story ends. The details. The truth, the whole truth and nothing but the truth, as the lawyers say. You want the answers. Okay, then.

They found Martin Gittens's body in Boston Harbor, submerged in the muck off Battery Point in the Flats. The coroner's report noted that his lungs were filled with freshwater, not the brackish stuff of the harbor. But nobody seemed too troubled by this inconsistency, not after the rumors began to float up—rumors of Gittens's own history, of Fasulo and Trudell and, yes, Bob Danziger. Once everyone—prosecutors and editorial writers and good citizens alike—reached an unspoken agreement that Gittens had committed these murders, the detective's own drowning seemed a less urgent matter. Rough justice and all that. Best not to look too close. It is, technically, still an open investigation. A cold case.

Suspicion for Gittens's murder fell briefly on Harold

Braxton, until it was revealed that Braxton was in custody in Versailles, Maine, at the time. Had anyone bothered to check the lockup in Versailles that night, they would have found the cell empty, Braxton and Chief Truman both gone, unaccounted for until nearly sunup. But nobody did check. And nobody did notice the soaked carpet in the back of the Bronco, where we laid Gittens's body under a blanket for his last ride to Boston. As for Danziger's murder, all charges against Braxton were dropped within a couple of weeks, and, so far as I know, Braxton vanished, with Ed Kurth in pursuit like The Furies.

Andrew Lowery is still the District Attorney for Sussex County and will, no doubt, be mayor of Boston someday. He'll be a damn good one, too.

As for John Kelly, his ancient nightstick sits on my desk as I write this. But Kelly is gone. Hit from behind by a drunk driver as he waited in line at a toll booth on the New Hampshire Turnpike. The driver was seventeen and blew a .20 on the Breathalyzer. He walked away from the accident unharmed. Kelly was buried next to his wife and daughter, Theresa Rose, forever ten years old.

I escorted Caroline to the funeral on a raw, drizzly morning. There was a perceptible change in her face that day, a naked bewilderment. It was unnerving to see her so shaken, but I understood it. She had not expected her father to die, had not thought he was capable of it. I recognized the emotion—the selfish terror that infuses mourning—because I'd been feeling it myself for the better part of a year.

I have seen Caroline many times since then. I don't know what will come of it except an exorbitant phone bill and a few more miles on my crappy old Saab. For now, it's enough just to go down there and be with her. Caroline cooks, I take Charlie to Red Sox games. It is the closest thing I have to a home.

On one of these visits, Caroline gave me a present: a heat-sealed plastic bag containing the drinking glass from the Ritz-Carlton. The glass was smudged with my ninhydrin-stained fingerprints. "Smash it," she said. I told her I couldn't. It was the last thing my mother ever touched. "Smash it," she said again. I never did.

There are, of course, secrets I have not shared with Caroline—family secrets about the Trumans' own wild streak, about the deaths of Bob Danziger and Martin Gittens at our hands. I have not told her that I can still feel Gittens's scalp twisting in my fingers, still hear that water-muffled yawp he emitted. I know I can't have Caroline while I keep my secret; at the same time I can't tell her the truth and expect her to stay. But I'm not ready to see her go yet, so I say nothing.

In August, Caroline and Charlie finally came up to Versailles and we rented a cabin on the lake. Caroline took to the lake just as my mother had. When she swam, I had a notion the lake was embracing her, welcoming her. And in my mind's eye I saw that flickering movie of my pregnant Mum as she floated on an inner tube and waved to the camera, *Hi, Ben!* At the end of that week, I remember, Caroline stood knee-deep in the lake, hands on hips, and took in the view. Concentric rings of water, hills, and clouds. She said, "It's pretty to be here. Everything is so clean, so clear."

I said, "We need DAs here, too, you know."

She laughed. "Yeah, okay, Ben. It'd be like living on Mars."

"Well," I told her, "that's a start."

My father? The stain of Danziger's murder has stayed with him. He's managed to climb back on the wagon and stay there, but his heart has given him trouble. In the spring, he asked me for a job as a volunteer in the department so he could have something to do. He said, "I'll be a crossing guard, a file clerk, anything." I told him no. Sanctimoniously, I told him the murder was not the end of his life, but it did unfit him for police work. It was a moment of high hypocrisy, and eventually I relented and allowed him to hang around the station. After a few days he stopped coming, though. In June, he moved to a neighboring town. The Chief's exile was a source of puzzlement around Versailles. People assume he'd died a little when his wife passed, as spouses often do. It was a misperception I did nothing to correct. I do not know if it is possible for Dad to find forgiveness for what he did. But I expect he will outmuscle his troubles, eventually, and get on with his life. It's the Truman way.

And me. I am still the chief in Versailles, though I don't know how much longer I will stay. The town deserves better. In the meantime, I have made it a habit to walk a beat, as John Kelly would insist I do, though the only beat in this town is Central Street, all two blocks of it. I've taken that stroll twice a day, every day, stopping to chat at the Owl and McCarron's and the General. For a while I carried Kelly's nightstick on these rambles. I even spun the thing, or tried to. *If you carry it right,* Kelly said—*if you carry yourself right—you'll never have to use it.* It was a bit of police wisdom I wanted to hang on to, but I couldn't believe it anymore. Not with the touch-memory of Gittens's head in my hands, not with him thrashing between my legs in one foot of water. No. I don't carry the nightstick anymore. It sits on my desk or in a drawer. Maybe I'll give it to Caroline. Or Charlie. I don't want to have it around.

So those are the details, the "facts." That is how the story ends.

But the story never ends, does it? History—the rolling wave of incident after incident, propelled by currents of chance and luck and coincidence—streams right along with no regard for beginnings or endings. The only true end is the present moment, the seething forward edge of the wave.

So let me bring you right up to the present. As I write this, it is September. The summer temporaries have all returned to their winter jobs, and the department is back down to Dick and me. Disgorged of the summer people, Versailles is back to its population of several hundred. It is foliage season again, but that's no real bother. The leaf stalkers are an older crowd than the summer tourists, and they're generally nice people, even the flatlanders from Taxachusetts. It is a quiet time.

I am at the station, alone at my desk. It is dusk but I haven't turned on the lights yet. It feels comfortable in the gloom.

As soon as I am finished here, I'm going down to the lake for a swim. This is the best time of year for it, my mother always claimed. In the evening the air is chilly, but the water is still warm after a summer under the sun. In fact, the air and water temperatures are close enough to create an illusion: while you are night-swimming, at certain moments you can't tell air from water, and in the darkness there is a sense of zero gravity, of weightlessness. On my way to the lake, I will pass right by the spot where Bob Danziger's cabin stood. (The cabin itself has been razed, not for health reasons but because it was considered unrentable. I sometimes use the spot for a parking place.) I will leave my clothes in the Bronco and walk right into that water, let it take me in and envelop me, and swim out to the center, stroke by stroke, to the deepest part.

AUTHOR'S NOTE

As any Bostonian will tell you, there is no place called Mission Flats. Nor, to my knowledge, is there a Versailles, Maine. Where actual places are mentioned, I have cheerfully altered details whenever necessary, according to the needs of fiction. For the rest, the usual warning applies: The incidents and characters depicted here are purely products of the author's imagination.

ABOUT THE AUTHOR

William Landay was born and raised in Boston, where he now lives with his wife and son. A graduate of Yale University and Boston College Law School, he served for six years as an assistant district attorney before turning to writing. *Mission Flats* is his first novel.

If you enjoyed William Landay's award-winning debut, MISSION FLATS, you won't want to miss his next crime novel, THE STRANGLER, coming soon in hardcover from Delacorte. Look for it at your favorite bookseller's.

Read on for a tantalizing preview of THE STRANGLER.

THE STRANGLER

by

William Landay

Coming soon from Delacorte

THE STRANGLER

coming soon from Delacorte

Welcome to Boston. The year is 1963. The president has been assassinated. The Boston Strangler is on the loose. And that's just the start.

Ricky Flatley

On the subway car no one spoke. Every face wore the same grief-stunned expression, and as the steel wheels shrieked around the curve at Boylston Street people closed their eyes.

Outside Park Street station people stood on the sidewalk or shuffled into the Common. Offices had closed early. Should they go home? Or stay here, among the crowd? Something held them, the possibility of news.

Cars slid by without honking.

On Tremont Street, strangers clustered against a car to hear the news on the radio. They shushed one another as the driver turned up the sound to drown out the shrilling of newsboys, "President Kennedy shot!" "Kennedy a-*sass*-inated!" "Latest photos ex-*clu*-sive in the Herald!"

Ricky Flatley crossed the Common in a gray overcoat and hundred-and-twenty-five-dollar suit. His shoes, new black brogans bought for the occasion, were stiff. He had tried to soften them by wearing them around his apartment, but they still pinched across the top of his feet. He had succeeded, at least, in dulling the gloss of the leather by rubbing the shoes with saliva. They should look polished but not new. New shoes drew attention.

By the Frog Pond, a woman on a slatted park bench held a handkerchief to her mouth, balled up in her fist. Her eyes were watery. Did she love Kennedy that much? What was she crying for, really?

The day was very cold. The sky was gray and unfocused. All wrong, Ricky thought. The weather should be crisp and clear, the sky should be cloudless blue, that was the mood, that was what all these people were feeling: their own overwhelming sense of the present, the *now*ness of this day. How strange the sensation was. We talk about the present but we cannot define or describe it, we cannot even perceive it. We live only in the future and past. Only they exist for us. The future scrapes against the past, and between them the present occupies no space. But today was different. The frictional moment between past and future had unfolded and unfolded into a boundless now. These people, that woman on the bench, were trapped in now, now, now. No future or past. Only today, November 22.

Friday afternoon. Gray sky. And Kennedy dead. Who could deny that there was a little secret pleasure in it, a hard little nut of pleasure in awakening to the present moment? Maybe that was what held them here, Ricky thought: They enjoyed it, they were excited by it. They were alive.

Ricky stopped in front of the woman on the bench, asked if she was okay.

"Yes," she sniffled, "I'm fine, thank you."

He walked on toward the Public Garden. His heels *clop-clop*ped on the pavement. His breath made little clouds in the cold. It was a fortunate thing, an opportunity, this Kennedy thing. It had shattered people. It would work to his advantage. He was almost sure of it.

The doors to Arlington Street Church were open. He could see the lighted interior, warm and eggshell white. He went in and stood by the wall, watching the door. People drifted in and out. They sat in the pews and prayed or just stared. He waited for someone to eye him up. No one did.

Ricky worked his way west through the Back Bay carefully. On the residential side streets, he turned each corner, stopped, and looked back for a good long while. Any cop who saw him dressed this way would know he was working. But he did not see any tails. Everything was clear.

Still, still, the job did not feel right.

He was breaking all his own rules by going ahead with it. Ricky Flatley believed in preparation. He believed in pressing out every last bubble of risk. And he believed in taking no chances, walking away at the first whiff of risk or surprise. Now it seemed to him, on second thought, that the news about Kennedy added too much risk, too much unpredictability. He ought to walk away from this job. Greed was clouding his judgment. He did not need to work today. His various safe deposit boxes held cash enough to last a couple of years. This decision had the feeling of a classic blunder, the tragic mistake that everyone in the audience can see a mile away but the hero somehow misses, or underestimates, or ignores. What was the danger, exactly? How did the news about Kennedy make this job more dangerous rather than less? How did it make people more alert, more confrontational? If he could have named the danger, he would have listened to his instinct and walked away. But he could not. And now he could not walk away, either. The score was too big, he'd poured too many hours into clocking the job. *Fuck it,* he decided. *I'm doing it.*

He walked straight across to Copley Square now, abandoning the mazy route he'd used before.

At the Copley Plaza Hotel, a doorman in a long overcoat with gold braiding and epaulettes held the door for him. "Good afternoon, sir."

"Afternoon," Ricky said, taking care to glance at the man for only an instant.

He moved quickly but not too quickly, purposeful, proprietary. He calibrated his movements to the room.

In the lobby he used the house phone to dial room 404. No answer.

Up the elevator to 404. Two firm, unembarrassed knocks on the door. No answer.

Back down, to the Oak Room bar to wait fifteen minutes, to be sure. He ordered a highball and declined the bartender's offer of a menu. "Just waiting for someone," Ricky said. "Crazy day. We'll see if she shows." He checked his coat. At the bar, he watched the door rather than gawk at the luxurious room, with its carved plaster ceiling and heavy furniture. He folded his arms across his chest, straining his suit jacket, because he'd noticed that rich people were comfortable in their expensive clothes. They wore a good suit as if it were an old sweater. They didn't care.

After fifteen minutes of this stage business, he called room 404 again on the house phone. Still no answer.

So, back to the fourth floor. He knocked, softer this time, and when he got no answer, he took a key from his pocket and let himself in.

He checked the room quickly. Empty.

Back to the door. He checked the hallway, then took a paper clip from his pocket, broke a quarter inch of wire from it, and carefully slid the wire into the lock. If the occupant of this room—the man's name was Yanofsky, a jeweler from New York—returned and tried to insert his key into the lock, the wire plug would block it. The man would have to go down to the front desk for help, allowing Ricky time to escape.

Ricky's key was a master key to the entire hotel. He had figured out how to reverse-engineer a master key using just an ordinary key and the lock it opens. The technique took less than thirty minutes and a few extra key blanks, and did not require risky behavior like stealing a master key or dismantling a lock. You just had to know how pin tumbler locks work, and you had to ponder the question awhile. It was a simple matter of isolating each pin and . . . well, Ricky really did not think it was all that difficult. In fact, he thought the whole ubiquitous business of using such ancient technology to secure people's doors was a little ludicrous. The design of mechanical locks dated from ancient Egypt, and essentially door locks had not changed in a hundred years. Maybe they were perceived to be reasonably secure, and no doubt they did deter less skilled burglars. But they posed little problem to a reasonably competent burglar, let alone a pro like Ricky. Of course, Ricky could have picked this lock, too. When he was younger, he would have. He was—still—a great pick man, maybe the best in the city. But you could be discovered picking a lock, even if you did it quickly and expertly. And if you did it too quickly, you left scratches and metal dust on the pins and in the keyway. Ricky did not like that. He preferred to leave no trace. Better to leave lock picking to the movies. The prosaic truth was that most burglars used other methods: celluloiding the latch ("loiding"), getting a key, or simply entering through an open door or window.

In the room, Ricky hurried to the dresser. Then the closets. The bed. He worked quickly but without leaving a mess. He found what he was looking for duct-taped to the inside of the toilet tank: a small jewelry bag wrapped in cellophane. He thought he had time to look inside. He had clocked Yanofsky on a dozen prior trips to Boston, where the man bought and sold diamonds from the brokers on Washington Street. The whole thing had begun when one of Ricky's "fingers" had tipped him off that the man came to town every two weeks or so with cash and stones—lots of cash and stones. Yanofsky did not use the hotel safe because he did not want to call attention to his cargo. *Why ask for trouble? If it's not the ganef in the hotel that gets you, it's his friend, the shtarker in the alleyway when you leave. The safest way is to keep your mouth shut.*

He emptied the bag on the bed. Diamonds. Some small jewelry pieces. Packets of hundred-dollar bills, banded. He separated out some of the jewelry, the gold plate, the pieces too bulky to conceal. That left a glinting glassy pile.

The idea now was to keep moving, put back everything you weren't taking, and get the hell out before you "showed face." Be a pro. Count it later. But Ricky could not help pausing to admire the little cone of diamonds. There might be a half million dollars mounded up there. He smirked.

Michael Flatley

Gentlemen, it may be hard to remember now, but only a few years ago this city lay dying. Decaying, shrinking. Young people leaving. Blight spreading like cancer in an old man. And the only hope for this dying man was surgery—radical surgery." Farley Sonnenshein laid his manicured fingers on a white cloth on the table, as if what lay beneath was the cancer patient himself and Sonnenshein meant to heal him by divine touch. Sonnenshein was unseasonably tanned. His head was mostly bald, and he had shaved the remaining ring of hair nearly to the skin. "So we began to operate, to cut that cancer out and save our city. It was our only chance. And so"—a little smile—"we did."

A murmur of satisfaction ran through the crowd

like a wave. You could see it ripple outward—nodding heads, smiles, *hear hears*—until it lost momentum at the back of the room and died at the feet of a young man in a Brooks Brothers bag suit, holding a glass of soda water, watching with a blank expression. This was Michael Flatley, who could not help thinking that he should not have come, he should not be the guest of a developer like Farley Sonnenshein, it was clearly a conflict of interest for an Assistant Attorney General, and in any event he'd rather be home with his wife—

Then Michael's boss, an Assistant AG named Wamsley, was at his side. Jug-eared, grinning that toothy grin. "Ever hear the old joke about 'the surgery was a complete success, but the patient's dead'?" Wamsley said, too loudly. "That's what this guy's talking about."

Michael smiled coolly.

They were at the Museum of Fine Arts, in an ornate room with French Impressionist paintings on the wall: Monet, Renoir, Gauguin. You had to hand it to Sonnenshein. He knew how to put on a show.

"The West End," Sonnenshein continued, "that crowded ghetto, all fifty-some-odd acres of it, has already been swept away, soon to be replaced with a new streamlined complex of shops and apartments. A new Central Artery laid right through downtown to relieve our crowded streets and speed local commerce. A modern turnpike to link the city with the national system. Even Scollay Square—"

A mock plea went up, "No! Not Scollay Square!"

"Yes, gentlemen, even Scollay Square will go! Go it must, all fifty-plus acres, to make way for a modern Government Center. This is the New

Boston. It is the Boston your children will know. And the old Boston, my friends, *our* Boston, will seem as vanished and quaint to them as Pompeii.

"You know, it's only been a week now since the tragedy in Dallas. Just seven days." He shook his head, seemed to lose his train of thought for a moment. "Let us remember what Jack Kennedy stood for: Look forward to the future, do not fear it. Respect your history, but do not be a slave to it. Have the courage to *build*"—he leaned on the word—"because to build is to embrace the future.

"President Kennedy told that wonderful story about the great French marshal, Lyautey. One day Marshal Lyautey asked his gardener to plant a tree. The gardener objected that the tree was slow-growing and would not bloom for a hundred years. The Marshal replied, 'In that case, there is no time to lose. Plant it this afternoon.' Gentlemen, we have trees to plant. Let's plant them this afternoon. That—*that*—is how we honor Jack Kennedy's memory. I give you the next piece of the New Boston: JFK Park."

He slipped the cloth off to reveal an architect's model, a Corbusian apartment complex, four soaring towers set in a pedestrian park. The model was white, immaculate, futuristic, fantastic. There was an audible contented *hmm*. Applause. Mayor Collins, in his wheelchair, peered between the little clay buildings at eye level, beaming. The Cardinal craned his neck.

"To the future!" someone toasted.

"The future!" came the answer, and a little cheer went up.

Michael Flatley looked over the bobbing heads at

Sonnenshein's grinning bald head as it swiveled back and forth, back and forth, gauging the reaction to his model. That was the sort of man who bent the world to his wishes. Visionary, charismatic dynamo. It was the Farley Sonnensheins of the world who would shape the future while men like Michael would stand back and watch. Michael was always, always the smartest guy in the room. What would it matter? A little sour-mouthed pucker twisted his lips.

"What is it, Michael?" Wamsley asked. "You don't like the future?"

"Do I have a choice?"

"No."

"Then I'm all for it."

Jim Flatley

Jim Flatley filled the door of the Chantilly Lounge, pausing while his eyes adjusted to the gloom inside. He had an enormous block of a head, like a slightly oversized statue, and all that squinting and blinking caused his mouth to turn up in a bully-boy smile, quite unintentionally.

The bar was nearly empty. It was three o'clock on a Wednesday afternoon. In a booth a dingy man sat with a few newspapers and a little notebook in front of him. Jim greeted this man as he passed the booth on his way to the bar. "Hey, Fish. How's business?" The man ignored him.

The bartender ignored Jim, too. He busied himself with stocking a beer cooler from a case of Narragansett.

"Hey, I'll have one of those," Jim said.

The bartender opened a bottle from the case, not the cooler, and put it in front of Jim. He slid an envelope onto the bar beside it.

The envelope disappeared into Jim's black leather jacket. "Thanks, neighbor," he said with a tip of his bottle, echoing a line from the Narragansett ads.

The bartender did not acknowledge the little joke, but went right back to filling the beer cooler.

Jim gave up on him. He tossed a quarter on the bar as a tip then moved over to the booth. "What's going on, Fish?"

No one knew why this man was called Fish. His real name was not Fish or anything like it, nor had he ever been involved with fishes or fishing, at least not that anyone knew of. But Fish he was, a small-time bookie who, after paying out the rent he owed to the North End mobsters and to the Chantilly and to the cops, barely had anything to show for his bookmaking efforts. It had been easier before Angiulo took over, before the dagos decided to consolidate all the bookmaking in the city. Then you paid the cops and that was that. Now you paid everybody. You couldn't live off the crumbs they left you. Not like the old days.

Jim slid onto the bench opposite Fish. "Let me see the Army," he said. This was Armstrong's, a daily racing form that covered the East Coast tracks. "What looks good today, anything?"

"I don't get involved, officer."

"Hey, I'm not working, not till five."

"I don't get involved anyways. After five, before five, I don't give a shit. I don't get involved. You make your own picks."

Jim opened the paper and studied the handicapping information closely. He muttered as he read, "Feeling good today, Fish, fee-lin' good. . . ."

Fish shared a glance with the bartender.

"Now, this one's interesting," Jim said. "Sixth race at Suffolk, Lord Jim. Can I get one down for 3:05? What time is it? See, here it is, here it is: Lord Jim."

Fish took the Army with a little frown and found the listing. "Lord Jim," he mumbled. "That horse is at thirty to one."

"No guts, no glory."

"What do you know about him?"

"I know I like him. He's got a good name. Lord Jim, see? Like me. What, are you gonna talk me out of it now?"

"How much?"

"Make it a fin. Make it interesting."

"To win, you mean?"

"Yeah, to win. Of course to win. What do I look like?"

"Let me see the cash."

Jim fished in his pocket but came up with just two crumpled singles. He felt the envelope, hesitated. The bartender was watching. Ah, what the fuck, right? It was Jim's money. He opened the envelope. Nothing smaller than a ten. He growled at the bartender, "I'll put it back."

"That ain't all for you."

"I said I'll put it back."

"Ten," Fish said. He shook his head.

The bartender pulled an old black Bakelite phone from under the bar and put it down with a clatter. Fish called in to get the bet down. It was a dumb bet, but hey, you never knew. Sometimes lightning struck, even at thirty to one. A bookie would only pay twenty to one, max, regardless of what they were giving at the track. Still, it was more than Fish wanted to pay out. Let the North End lay it off. That was what he paid rent for, wasn't it?

Fish shuffled back to his post in the booth. He noted the bet in his book, encoding Jim's name in a cipher of his own invention. He folded the Armstrong's and put it aside, went back to reading the Herald.

The bartender was avoiding Jim's eyes. His movements were sulky, miffed.

"I told you, I'm good for it."

"Yeah, alright, Jim, you're good for it. Whatever you say. I just don't want to hear from some sergeant that the envelope was light."

"I'm good for it, I said."

In the sixth race at Suffolk Downs, Lord Jim finished sixth in a field of six.

Joanne Feeney's apartment on Joy Street, near BPD Station Three, had a kitchen window overlooking the West End, where she'd spent all her sixty-three years. Outside the window now, the West End had been leveled. The old neighborhood was rubble, acres and acres of nothing. Only a few buildings had been spared, including Massachusetts General Hospital. Construction had already begun on a modern luxury apartment complex in the northwest corner of the old West End site. Mrs. Feeney had formed a habit of studying that wasteland from her window, overlaying it with her memories of the narrow streets, the buildings. Now the window was open. Cold air blew in.

Classical music played on the hi-fi set her son had bought for her. Sibelius, the Fifth Symphony. The record ticked and crackled, but the music! The music pulsed in B flat, unstable, prolonged, gasping, building toward a final release.

A long smear of blood on the floor.

A red handprint.

Joanne Feeney lay on the floor. Her pink robe had been ripped open, her legs wrenched apart, ankles pinned in the slats of two chairs to hold them apart, a pillow tucked under her rear end to prop it so that her pudendum was aimed at the front door. A pillowcase and stockings were wrapped around her neck, tied off with a big bow. Bluish bruises and the pink lividity of pooling blood mottled her skin around the garrote. Her mouth was still moist. In her eyes were tiny red spiders where capillaries had burst beneath the cornea.

The Sibelius dropped, finally, into its natural key of E flat—a door opening into boundless space—and then it was over. The needle caught in the gutter and scratched there.